START

Boomsday

A NOVEL

FINISH

R.I.P

BOOMSDAY BOOM

also by CHRISTOPHER BUCKLEY

Florence of Arabia

No Way to Treat a First Lady

Washington Schlepped Here: Walking in
    the Nation's Capital

Little Green Men

God Is My Broker

Wry Martinis

Thank You for Smoking

Wet Work

Campion

The White House Mess

Steaming to Bamboola: The World of
    a Tramp Freighter

BOOMSDAY

CHRISTOPHER BUCKLEY

a Novel

TWELVE

Twelve
Hachette Book Group USA
237 Park Avenue
New York, NY 10169

Visit our Web site at www.HachetteBookGroupUSA.com.

Twelve is an imprint of Warner Books, Inc.
The Twelve name and logo are trademarks of Hachette Book Group USA.

Printed in the United States of America

First Edition: April 2007
10 9 8 7 6 5 4 3 2 1

Library of Congress Cataloging-in-Publication Data

Buckley, Christopher
   Boomsday / Christopher Buckley. — 1st ed.
      p. cm.
   ISBN: 978-0-446-57981-0
   1. Baby boom generation—Fiction. I. Title.
PS3552.U3394B66   2007
813'.54—dc22

2006026661

For Monie Begley

When you are old and gray and full of sleep,
And nodding by the fire, take down this book.

Blessed are the young, for they shall inherit the national debt.

—Herbert Hoover

BOOMSDAY   BOOMSDAY   BOO

"**T**hank you, Wendy Wong in Washington, for that report on the deteriorating economic situation.

"In Florida today, another attack on a gated community by youths protesting the recent hike in the Social Security payroll tax.

"Several hundred people in their twenties stormed the gates of a retirement community in the early hours this morning. Residents were assaulted as they played golf. Demonstrators seized carts and drove them into water hazards and bunkers. Others used spray paint and garden implements to write slogans on the greens.

"One such message, gouged into the eighteenth green, read: 'Boomsday Now!' The word refers to the term economists use for the date this year when the first of the nation's seventy-seven million so-called Baby Boomers began to retire with full Social Security benefits. The development has put a tremendous strain on the system that in turn has sent shock waves through the entire U.S. economy.

"A maintenance worker at the golf course said it might be, quote, weeks before residents were able to play golf.

"In other news today, the vice president has shot yet another lawyer, this time, he says, in self-defense. . . ."

Chapter 1

Cassandra Devine was not yet thirty, but she was already tired.

"Media training," they called it. She'd been doing it for years, but it still had the ring of "potty training."

Today's media trainee was the chief executive officer of a company that administered hospitals, twenty-eight of them throughout the southeastern United States. In the previous year, it had lost $285 million and one-third of its stock market value. During that same period, the client had been paid $3.8 million in salary, plus a $1.4 million "performance bonus."

Corporate Crime Scene, the prime-time investigative television program, was doing an exposé and had requested an interview. In her negotiations with the show's producers, Cass had learned that they had footage of him boarding the company jet ($35 mil) wearing a spectacularly loud Hawaiian shirt and clenching a torpedo-shaped—indeed, torpedo-size—cigar in his teeth while hefting a bag of expensively gleaming golf clubs. Unfortunate as it was, this footage was only the appetizer. The main cinematic course was video of the company's recent annual "executive retreat" at a Bahamas resort of dubious taste. It showed the client, today's trainee, along with his fellow executive retreatants—doubtless exhausted after a hard day of budget cutting and crunching numbers—drinking rum punch dispensed from the breasts of anatomically correct female ice sculptures, to the accompaniment of a steel drum band, a limbo bar, and scantily clad waitresses dressed as—oh dear—*mermaids.* It would all make for a spirited discussion on the upcoming episode of *CCS*, especially when juxtaposed against the footage they were also running of patients parked like cars in an L.A. traffic jam in litter-strewn corridors, moaning for attention, some of them duct-taped to the wheelchairs.

"So they don't fall out," the client explained.

Cass took a sip from her seventh or eighth Red Bull of the day and suppressed a sigh, along with the urge to plunge her ballpoint pen into the client's heart. Assuming he had one.

"That last one was a lot better," she said. They'd done four practice interviews so far, with Cass pretending to be the interviewer from the television program. "If you have the energy, I'd like to do just one more. This time, I'd like you to concentrate on smiling and looking straight into the camera. Also, could you please not do that sideways thing with your eyes? It makes you look . . ." *Like a sleazebag.* "It works against the overall tone of you know . . . transparency." The man was as transparent as a bucket of tar.

"I really don't know why we're even agreeing to the interview." He sounded peeved, as though he'd been frivolously talked into attending a performance of *The Marriage of Figaro* when he'd much rather be at the office, helping humanity, devising new and more cost-effective methods of duct-taping terminal patients to their wheelchairs so they could be parked in corridors all day.

"Terry feels that this is the way to go. In cases like this . . ." The client shot her an "I dare you to call me a criminal" glance of defiance. "That is, where the other side has a strong, uh, visual presentation, that it's best to meet them in the center of the ring, so to speak. We're looking to project an image of total . . . up-frontness."

The client snorted.

"That *no one* is more upset at the"—she glanced at her notes to see what artful term of mendacity they were using at the moment— " 'revenue downtick.' And that you and management are"—she looked down at her notes again, this time just to avoid eye contact—"working around the clock to make the, uh, difficult decisions." Like where to hold next year's "executive retreat." Vegas? Macao? Sodom?

The client generously consented to one final practice interview.

He left muttering about persecution and complaining of the indignity of having to fly back to Memphis via commercial aircraft. Terry had sternly forbade him the company jet. Tomorrow, the client would spend an hour in a soup kitchen ladling out faux humanity to Memphis's wretched, an act of conspicuous compassion that would be inconspicuously video-recorded by one of his aides. If *Corporate Crime Scene* declined to air it, perhaps it might come in handy down the line—say, during sentencing deliberation. Cass sent him off with a DVD of his practice interviews. With any luck, they'd cause him to jump out his corner office window.

Cass wanted to go home to her apartment off Dupont Circle, nuke a frozen macaroni-and-cheese, pour herself a goldfish bowl–size glass of red wine, put on her comfy jammies, get under the covers, and watch reruns of *Law & Order* or *Desperate Housewives* or even the new reality show, *Green Card,* in which illegal (but good-looking) Mexicans had to make it across the U.S. border, past the Border Patrol and minutemen and fifty miles of broiling desert, to the finish line. The winner got sponsorship for a green card and the privilege of digging ditches in some other broiling—or, if he was lucky, frigid—part of the country.

Yes, that would be lovely, she thought, then realized with a pang that she hadn't posted anything on her blog since before work that morning. There was an important Senate vote on Social Security scheduled for that day. She hadn't even had time to glance at CNN or Google News to see how it had turned out.

The light was on in Terry's office. She entered and collapsed like a suddenly deflated pool toy into a chair facing his desk.

Without turning from his computer screen, Terry said, "Let me guess. You had a wonderful, fulfilling day." He continued to type as he spoke.

Terry Tucker had built a successful PR firm, Tucker Strategic Communications, on the premise that those with a debatable claim to humanity will pay through the snout to appear even a little less deplorable. Terry had represented them all, from mink ranchers to toxic waste dumpers, dolphin netters, unzipped politicians, makers of obesity-inducing soft drinks, the odd mobster, and pension fund skimmers. Terry had apprenticed under the legendary Nick Naylor, at the now defunct Tobacco Institute. Cass had been with the firm for eight years. Terry had promoted her quickly, given her regular raises, and promoted her to partner. He'd never once made a pass at her. He treated her like a kid sister or niece.

"Jesus, Terry. Where do you find these clients? In Dante's *Inferno*?"

He kept typing. "Huh?"

"The man's . . . I've seen more sympathetic people on the E! Channel's *True Hollywood Stories*."

Terry's fingers went on clickety-clicking. "This 'war criminal,' as you put it, is a client of Tucker Strategic Communications. Someday, if all the crap we learned in Sunday school is correct, he will answer to a higher authority. Higher even than a morally superior twenty-nine-year-old PR chick. In the meantime, our job as strategic communicators is to—"

"Yeah, yeah, yeah. I just—couldn't we find like maybe just one client who wasn't . . . I don't know . . ."

"Evil?"

"Well . . . yeah. Basically."

Terry stopped typing, leaned back in his leather chair, massaged the bridge of his nose with thumb and forefinger, exhaled pensively. Theatrically, the gesture was just shy of a sigh.

"Do you know what I'm working on right now? What I *was* working on, before you came in to do an existential download?"

"Let me guess. Raising money, pro bono, for juvenile diabetes?"

"The only time, young lady, you'll hear the phrase *pro bono* around this office is if someone is expressing a favorable opinion of an Irish rock star. No, I was doing talking points. For our Brazilian client."

"The one who wants to relocate the Indian tribe to make room for the gold mine?"

"Uh-hum. Were you aware that in 1913, this same tribe—I can't pronounce the name—killed two Mormon missionaries?"

"Well, in that case, obviously they deserve whatever they get."

Terry frowned at the screen. "I know, needs work. Maybe if they fed them to piranhas or something. I'll massage it. Want to get a pop? Defaming indigenous people always makes me thirsty."

Ordinarily, Cass loved going out for a drink with Terry. Listening to his war stories about defending the tobacco industry with Nick Naylor.

"Can't tonight. Gotta go back and blog."

"'Gotta go back and blog.'" Terry shook his head. "I'm offering martinis and mentoring. But if you want to go home and blog . . ." He looked at Cass with his "kind uncle" expression. "Excuse me for asking, but do you by any chance have a life?"

"It's important, what I do."

"I didn't say it wasn't." He reached out and typed. Onto the screen came the blog's home page.

> **C**oncerned
> **A**mericans for
> **S**ocial
> **S**ecurity
> **A**mendment
> **N**ow,
> **D**ebt
> **R**eduction and
> **A**ccountability

"How many hours did it take to come up with that acronym?"

"I know, bit of a mouthful."

"She was a goddess of something."

"Daughter of the king of Troy. She warned that the city would fall to the Greeks. They ignored her."

"And? What happened?"

"You're kidding, right?"

"Just educate me."

"Troy fell. It was on the news last night. Cassandra was raped. By Ajax the lesser."

"Is that why they called the other one Ajax the major? He *wasn't* a rapist."

"Whatever. She was taken back to Greece by Agamemnon—you

remember him, right?—as a concubine. They were both killed by his wife, Clytemnestra. In revenge for his sacrificing her daughter, Electra."

"A heartwarming story. No wonder Greeks look unhappy."

"Cassandra is sort of a metaphor for catastrophe prediction. This is me. It's what I do. During my downtime. When I'm not media-training our wonderful clients."

"It's none of my business—"

"Whenever you say, 'It's none of my business,' I know I'm in for a five-minute lecture."

"Just listen. Your generation, you're incapable of listening. It's from growing up with iPods in your ears. I was going to say, Kid, you're young, you're attractive—you're *very* attractive. You should be out, you know, getting . . . you know . . ."

"Laid? Thank you. That's *so* nurturing."

"You look so, I don't know, oppressed. You work your butt off here—by the way, I'm giving you a bonus for the Japanese whaler account, good work, sales of whale meat in Tokyo are up six percent—and then you go home and stay up all night blogging with people who look like the Unabomber. It's not healthy."

"Finished?"

"No. Instead of staring at a computer screen all night and railing against the government and shrieking that the sky is falling, you should be out exchanging bodily fluids and viruses with the rest of your generation."

"Earth to Terry. The sky *is* falling. You saw about the Bank of Tokyo?"

"No. I've been working on the Brazilian thing."

"It led the news this morning. For the first time in history, the Bank of Tokyo declined to buy new-issue U.S. Treasury bills. Do you realize what that means?"

"They already have enough of our debt?"

"Precisely. Do you get the significance of that? The largest single purchaser of U.S. government debt just declined to finance any more of it. As in our debt. Meanwhile, and not coincidentally, the first of *your* generation have started to retire. You know what they're calling it?"

"Happy Hour?"

"Boomsday."

"Good word."

"Mountainous debt, a deflating economy, and seventy-seven million people retiring. The perfect economic storm." *Not bad,* Cass thought, making a mental note to file it away for the blog. "And what is the Congress doing? Raising taxes—on *my* generation—to pay for, among other things, a monorail system in Alaska."

Cass realized suddenly that she was standing, leaning forward over his desk, and shouting at him. Terry, meanwhile, was looking up at her with something like alarm.

"Sorry," she said. "I didn't mean to . . . Long day."

"Listen, kiddo," Terry said, "that resort in the Bahamas where our client Albert Schweitzer threw the party with the ice sculptures . . . why don't you go down there and check it out? We'll call it research, make Albert pay. Least he could do. Take your time. Stay for a few days. Bring a bathing suit and a tube of tanning oil and a trashy paperback. Take a load off. Get . . . you know . . ." He waved his hands in the air.

"Laid?"

"Whatever."

"You use that word more than I do. It's my generation's word, not yours."

"It's useful. It may actually be your generation's major semantic contribution so far. It's pure Teflon."

"What's Teflon?"

"They coat frying pans with it so stuff doesn't stick. Spin-off of the space program. Like Tang."

"Tang?"

"Never mind. Look, go home. Go to the Bahamas. Hang an 'Out to Lunch' on the blog or something."

He was already back to typing by the time she reached the door. On her way out, he shouted, "If you get any brainstorms on how to make my Brazilian Indian tribe look like bloodthirsty savages, e-mail me."

*   *   *

The computer screen was glowing at her in the dark of her apartment. A prior generation would have called it psychedelic; to hers it was just screen saving.

She showered, changed into comfy jammies, ate a peanut-butter PowerBar, and washed it down with Red Bull. She unscrewed the safety cap of her bottle of NoDoz, hesitated. If she took one, she wouldn't get to sleep until at least four. Unless she popped a Tylenol PM at three. She wondered about the long-term effects of this pharmaceutical roller-coaster ride. Early Alzheimer's, probably. Or one of those drop-dead-on-the-sidewalk heart attacks like Japanese salarymen have. She popped the NoDoz. She could sleep in tomorrow. Terry wasn't expecting her in the office. She wanted a cigarette but had given them up (this morning). She chomped down on a piece of Nicorette gum and felt her capillaries surge and tingle. Shock and awe. She flexed her fingers. Showtime.

She logged on. There were 573 messages waiting for her. Her Google profile had searched for reports on the Senate vote and auto-sent them to her inbox. She read. They'd voted in favor of Social Security payroll tax "augmentation." Jerks. Couldn't bring themselves to call it a "tax increase." She felt her blood heating up. (Either that or the effects of the pill.) Soon energy was surging in her veins in equal proportion to outrage. Her fingers were playing across the keyboard like Alicia de Larrocha conjuring a Bach partita.

She typed: *"The buck has been passed to a new generation— ours!"*

She stared at it on the screen, fiddled with the font color and point size. It occurred to her that as most of her readers were in their twenties and thirties, they would have no idea it was a steal from John F. Kennedy's 1961 inaugural speech, "The torch has been passed to a new generation." Even fewer would know that she'd grafted it onto Harry Truman's famous slogan "The buck stops here." Whatever. CASSANDRA was starting to get hits from older readers. And the mainstream media were also starting to take notice. *The Washington Post* had called CASSANDRA "*the* bulletin board for angry, intelligent Gen-W's." Gen-W being short for "generation whatever." Even one or two advertisers were starting to come in, feign-ing interest.

In a moment of weakness, she'd posted a photograph of herself on the home page, thinking it might bring in a few male viewers. It did. A third of the 573 messages were from men who wanted to have sex with her. She was, as Terry had put it, an attractive girl or, to use the word of her generation, "hot"—naturally blond, with liquid, playful eyes and lips that seemed always poised to bestow a kiss, giving her a look of intelligence in contention with sensuality. She had a figure that, when displayed in a bikini or thong at the resort in the Bahamas, would draw sighs from any passing male. All in all, it was not the package you'd expect to find sitting in front of a computer screen at three a.m., wired on over-the-counter speed and railing at the govern-ment for—fiscal irresponsibility? *Girl,* she thought, *get a life.*

Chapter **2**

Twelve Years Before . . .

"**1** got in! I got in!"

Cassandra Cohane, age seventeen, was exuberant, and why not? The thick envelope she was waving over her head like a winning lottery ticket bore the dark blue "Lux Et Veritas" stamp of Yale University, New Haven, Connecticut. All that work, SAT preparation, studying until her eyeballs burned, signing up for AP courses, all those summers spent tutoring inner-city kids, one working on the archaeological site from hell: helping to excavate a 1980s-era mass grave in Guatemala ("It will look *very* strong on your application," her guidance counselor had said). The endless rewriting of the college essay, gearing up for the sweaty interview. The waiting. And now she was in. She said it one more time. "I got in!" She hardly believed it herself.

Her father wouldn't be home until late. She waited for him in the kitchen. He arrived after ten. She sprang up to show him the letter.

"Honey, I'm so proud of you I could bust." Frank Cohane had gone to an engineering college in California, one that needed to make no apology, but it was—he'd be the first to admit—no Yale University, New Haven, Connecticut.

"Yale!" he said. "Damn. Yale. How about that."

Two days later via FedEx, a box arrived. It was full of Yale car decals, coffee mugs, T-shirts, sweatpants, cap, a bulldog-theme pencil sharpener, pens, pads, paperweights, a mouse pad, and a sweatshirt that read, YALE DAD. The card read, "So proud. Love, Dad." He put so many YALE decals on the car windows, her mother complained she couldn't see out the back. Neighbors stopped and congratulated her.

A few months later, she came home from school and saw an envelope with the familiar blue emblem lying open on the dining room table. It was from the registrar's office, addressed to her parents:

"We still have not received the first installment for Cassandra's tuition. Please contact us at your earliest convenience."

Her mother wasn't home yet. She called her father. He greeted her with his normal paternal exuberance, which, once she introduced the subject, changed to an awkward silence.

"Sug" (pronounced "Shug"), he said—an ominous start: It was a word he generally used, perhaps without realizing it, when sugarcoating was called for—"I really want to talk to you about that. But I can't right now, sweetheart. I've got four people in my office. We'll talk when I get home. Love you."

She confronted her mother when she got home. Her mother read the letter with a puzzled look. "Dad said he'd take care of it." She called him at the office. Cass listened in the doorway, mind racing.

They weren't poor, the Cohanes. They lived in a comfortable subdivision in a respectable but hardly fancy neighborhood. Her mother taught economics at the public high school Cass attended. There were four children in the family. Her father was reasonably prosperous, as far as Cass knew. He'd been a systems engineer at Electric Boat, the company that built America's fleet of cold war–era submarines. He never talked much about his job, since much of it was technically classified and all of it, he assured them, was boring and dry. One day, Cass's younger brother picked the lock on their father's briefcase and examined the contents. He revealed to his siblings that as far as he could figure out, it had something to do with the launch and guidance systems for the subs' ballistic missiles. Not boring, but definitely dry.

Frank and several of his colleagues had presciently quit Electric Boat the year before, assuming correctly that the end of the cold war would sooner or later reduce the demand for submarines that could simultaneously annihilate fifty cities, despite the Connecticut congressional delegation's best efforts to perpetuate a felt need for them. They had a brainstorm for an Internet/software program. In the 1990s, Wall Street was dispensing money faster than an ATM to any start-up ending in ".com." Frank's idea had to do with tracking—not ballistic missiles, but shipping packages. If everything went according to plan, they'd take their company public within the year. They were already trying to figure out what kind of corporate jet to buy. He and his partners were working brutal hours, sometimes sleeping on cots at the old mill they'd rented for their office. He would arrive home looking wiped out, but with sparkly eyes. Once they did the IPO, he predicted, "we'll be richer than King Tut."

Cass listened to her mother on the phone.

"You what? You said you put that in her 529! Oh, Frank—how *could* you?"

Cass did not know what a "529" was, but the other words issuing from her mother were acquiring an unpleasant critical mass: "can't believe" . . . "disgusted" . . . "unforgivable" . . . ending with, "No, *you* can tell her. You get in your forty-thousand-dollar Beemer right now—I don't *care* how many people you have in your office—and come home and tell her yourself." She hung up.

Cass waited for him in the kitchen, as she had the night she got the acceptance letter. When he finally got home, he wore a smile of the kind generally described as "brave."

"What's a 529?" Cass asked.

"Did Mom . . . explain?"

"No. She said you would. She just burst out crying and closed the door to her bedroom."

"Oh. Uh, well, it's an instrument, a college savings plan. You put money in it, and, uh, it's tax-exempt."

"So I have one?"

"Sug, I . . . had to put it into the company. These start-ups take seed capital, honey. But when we do the IPO, I'm telling you . . . Do you know what IPO is?"

" 'I'm pissed off'?"

"Clever girl. Initial public offering. We're going to be rolling in it. Rolling."

"So, basically, Dad, what you're trying to say is that you spent my college tuition money on your dot.com."

"*Our* dot.com. Don't worry, Sug, we'll come up with the money. If I have to . . . I'll come up with the dough. You'll see."

Her father spent most of the following nights at his office. Meanwhile, Cass's mother drove to New Haven to try to sort things out. She returned looking defeated, with the news that the Cohanes did not qualify for tuition assistance, as they called it. They were above the thin red line dividing the truly needy from the truly well-enough-off. There was, her mother said, face darkening, her father's BMW. It might not be a particularly recent model, but you would not find it being used in a remake of *The Grapes of Wrath,* driven by Tom Joad. Then there was—her face now vermilion—his part ownership in the twin-engine Cessna.

On the night her father finally reappeared for a family supper, Cass's mother said, as she passed the mashed potatoes, "Frank, there was a question on the financial aid application: 'How many aircraft do you own? If needed, list on separate sheet.' How many do you have at this point?" That was the end of Mom and Dad's conversation at that happy supper. Her father stormed off into the night, muttering on about how he was killing himself for the family and what thanks did he get? A few hours later, Cass got an e-mail from him, manfully explaining that he used the Cessna "exclusively" to fly to business meetings. In fact, it was deductible as a business expense. Indeed, he managed to make it sound as though selling his share in the plane would be tantamount to economic suicide. The family would be out on the street, eating potatoes that fell off trucks. Irish ancestry is a reliable provider of poverty metaphors.

A few days later, Frank Cohane was waiting for Cass outside her high school. In his Beemer. That, too, he explained sheepishly, was a "deductible business expense." He took her to Starbucks, where, according to a recent survey, 92 percent of Americans now hold their significant conversations.

"Sug," he said, "have you ever given any thought to, uh . . ."

"Religious orders? No, Dad."

"The military."

She stared. She had, as it happened, not given any thought to the military. She supposed that she was as patriotic as any seventeen-year-old American girl. She'd grown up in the backyard of one of the country's biggest defense contractors. Everyone here was patriotic. But her adolescence had been focused intensely on AP French, AP English, AP history, 1585 SATs, and a 3.95 GPA so that she might actually get into—you know—Yale. Hello? Perhaps he'd noticed?

"Hear me out," he said, suddenly animated, as if he had just had a category 5 brain hurricane. "I did some calling around. Turns out if you go into the officers training program—and hell, you'd be a cinch with your scores—and give 'em a few years, heck, *they'll* pay for college." He made it sound like the bargain of the century.

What was his deal? He'd done "some calling around"? On his fancy new cell phone? In the BMW? Or had he jumped into the "deductible" Cessna and flown down to the Pentagon in Washington to talk it over personally with the Deputy Undersecretary for Recruiting Kids Whose Dads Have Blown the Tuition Money? He couldn't actually be serious.

"How many years?"

"Three. And get this—if you give 'em six years, they basically pay for everything. You get all kinds of bennies." He leaned forward. "I called Yale. They said they were expecting you in the incoming class and started to give me some hoo-hah about it, until I said, 'Whoa, whoa—you're telling me you're gonna renege on accepting a patriotic American woman who wants to serve her country?'" He grinned. He did have a winning grin, her father. "Did they ever back down fast. So you see, I fixed it. They'll defer admission until you're discharged from the army. Or navy. Whatever you—"

"You told them—as in Yale—that I wasn't entering this fall? As in the place I have been working my butt off to get into the last four years? You told them that?"

"Well, seeing as how we don't have the money . . . Geez, Sug, do you know it's over thirty grand, and that's without a dining plan."

"I could always, like, not eat for four years." Her head was spinning. "Did you . . . have you discussed this with—Mom?"

"No. No. I wanted to bounce it off you first. Naturally. Sug, when this IPO goes through, I'll buy Yale University a whole new football stadium."

Frank Cohane went on talking, but Cass had stopped listening. She was trying to calculate how many people she'd told about getting into Yale. Fifty? A hundred? Let's see, everyone in her Yahoo! address book . . . plus everyone on her Hotmail address book . . . everyone in the senior class knew . . . relatives . . . plus she'd stopped by the Martin Luther King Jr. Center where she spent that broiling summer as a tutor. They'd all hugged her, said how proud they were of her. Say, two hundred people?

Cass became aware that her father was still talking.

". . . I never went into the military myself. And to be honest, I always kind of wished I had. Not that I wanted to go to Vietnam. Jesus, no one in my generation wanted to go to Vietnam. That was completely screwed up. Anyway, we're not at war now. So really if you think about it, it could be kind of a good experience."

Chapter 3

And so, the following January, when Cass would have been heeling the *Yale Daily News* or attending a master's tea with some visiting eminence, she instead found herself at Camp Bravo (an ironic name, given the enthusiasm level of its occupants) at a place called Turdje—the "d" was silent, though acutely felt—in Bosnia, formerly Yugoslavia, formerly Austro-Hungary, formerly the Ottoman Empire, in the company of several hundred troops, part of America's apparently endless (and certainly thankless) commitment to keeping Europeans from slaughtering one another.

"Sir," she asked one of her superior officers after one especially depressing day, "why are we here?"

A naive question, perhaps, but legitimate enough, inasmuch as she was asking it five years into America's "temporary" deployment in the region. Without looking up from his papers, the officer replied, "To keep World War One from breaking out again." It was said without irony.

Cass had gone through combat basic training at Fort Jackson, South Carolina. She had always been an outdoors girl. She didn't find the training particularly grueling. Her drill instructors were impressed by the zest with which she bayoneted dummies and subdued men twenty pounds heavier than her in hand-to-hand training. Having spent some time in the Connecticut woods with her brother shooting squirrels with a .22 rifle, she took to the shooting part and obliterated the heads and vital organs of targets with her M-16. One of her shooting instructors even suggested that she apply to sniper school. She contemplated it, then decided against it on the grounds that being able to kill at one thousand yards was—thankfully—not a skill in huge demand in the civilian afterlife. She did, however, having passed basic with flying colors, apply to Ranger school with every expectation of acceptance.

So in due course she found herself assigned, by the army's invisible hand—more powerful, even, than Adam Smith's—to Public Affairs. Some functionary deep within the bowels of the Department of the Army in Washington, D.C., while processing her application, saw that she had been accepted to Yale University. Be a total waste to have this one rappelling out of helicopters. No, she was needed—desperately, immediately—in the slushy gray snows of Bosnia, escorting VIPs, issuing press releases, and putting on goodwill coffee-and-doughnut grip-'n'-grins with indigenous locals.

Cass was in one of the trailers that served as the headquarters for the 4087th Public Affairs Battalion ("Spinning Eagles"), 12th Regiment, 7th Division, 4th United States Army, putting the finishing touches on another homeric press release with a stop-the-presses headline—674TH ENGINEER BATTALION COMPLETES PAVING AT GRZYLUK FORWARD AIR BASE—when Captain Drimpilski summoned her.

Captain Drimpilski was in his late thirties, with thinning hair and thickening waist. He, too, had entered the army with dreams of rappelling from Blackhawks into fields of fire, only to find himself plucked by the invisible hand and dropped into fields of paper.

His single triumph over this adversity was that he had not (yet, anyway) become so embittered as to make life intolerable for those under him. He liked Corporal Cohane. She was efficient, good-natured, and easy—very easy—on the eyes. He was, of course, physically attracted. Any male of standard-issue testosterone level would be. But Captain Drimpilski had thirteen years in and seven to go until pension time, and he was determined—repeat, determined—not to end up dishonorably discharged on a sexual harassment charge. A two-star general with a chest full of fruit salad had just ended his career because of an "indiscretion" with someone under him (in both senses). Captain

Drimpilski sublimated his ardor for Corporal Cohane by means of an exaggerated emphasis on protocol and the grammatical expedient of the third-person pronoun.

"At ease, Corporal."

"Sir," Cass said.

"How is the corporal's morale today?"

Cass sensed that the captain's strange locutions and formality had something to do with keeping her at a distance and was content to play along. She liked Captain Drimpilski and sensed his frustration.

"The corporal's morale is excellent verging on sublime, sir."

"Very well. Here's something that will send the corporal's morale rocketing through the stratosphere and out into the far reaches of the galaxy."

"The corporal can barely contain her enthusiasm, sir."

"Try. It appears we have another codel inbound."

"The corporal has no words to express her glee."

Inwardly, Cass sighed. In her eight months here at Camp Bravo, she had escorted numerous congressional delegations ("codels"), consisting of a total of seven congressmen and two United States senators. The male congresspersons had all been quite taken with their attractive young army escort. (Cass looked very smart in her uniform and black beret.) One senator could barely take his eyes off her. He stared at her throughout a long simultaneous translation with grieving Bosnian war widows until finally one of his aides, evidently adept at the procedure, stepped in to obstruct his view and refocus his attention.

"Fact-finding," Captain Drimpilski mused aloud, staring at the VIPVIS printout on his desk. "The fact is we don't have any more facts left. We ran out about a year ago. Still they come in search of them."

"Perhaps the congresspersons will marvel at the completion of the pouring of the concrete at the forward air base paving at Grzyluk," Cass said. "I have the press release here. The corporal's fingers are still warm from typing it. Pure Shakespeare, if the corporal is permitted to indulge in professional self-satisfaction. Sir."

"The captain passed out several times from excitement in the course of reading it. He's recommending the corporal for the Congressional Medal of Honor."

"Eagles spin the way. Hooah, hooah."

Captain Drimpilski blew his nose into a paper napkin. He had a head cold. Everyone at Camp Bravo had a head cold. The country had a head cold and was capable, historically speaking, of passing it on to the entire continent.

"This one's a biggie," he said. "Sits on the Imperial Overstretch Committee. He is not a supporter of our mission here. That's a matter of record, not a personal criticism."

"Understood, sir."

"Jepperson, Democrat of Massachusetts. Good-looking type. More family money than God. Old family. He's related to Uncle John Sedgwick."

"Who, sir?"

"Look it up, Corporal. Civil War. A good Public Affairs officer knows his—her—military history."

"General Sedgwick, sir? The one killed at Spotsylvania by the—"

"*Yes,* Corporal," Captain Drimpilski said with a thwarted air.

"The corporal reads books, sir," Cass said with a mildly apologetic air. "When off-duty."

Captain Drimpilski went back to his VIPVIS form. "He's related to someone else. Revolutionary era. It would appear, Corporal, that a veritable river of blue blood runs through the congressman." He read: "'Harvard.' Where else? Didn't the corporal go to Yale?"

"Negative, sir. Complicated story."

Drimpilski continued with the briefing. "The congressman dates movie stars. Went out with what's-'er-name, the rock star's ex-wife, the one who is continually expressing her conviction that the United States should dispatch troops to every starving country in the world, while simultaneously denouncing U.S. military presence in every part of the world. Venezuelan—"

"Honduran, sir. Nickname of 'the Tegucigalpa Tamale,' if the corporal is not mistaken."

Drimpilski stared.

"The corporal also reads glossy magazines," Cass said. "When not composing Shakespearean-quality media advisories pertaining to our mission here. Sir."

Drimpilski said in a paternal sort of way, "Watch out for
rporal. Just . . . watch out."

The corporal will conduct herself in a manner befitting the United
States Army, sir. Failing that, the corporal will engage the congressman in close-quarter combat."

Most codels flew directly from the States into Turdje. On the way back,
however, they typically stopped "to refuel" at Humphausen AFB, Germany, for the reason that there was a PX there that would make Wal-
Mart look like a mom-and-pop corner store. There the codel could
shop tax-free, with forklifts that would deliver their year's supply
of liquor and electronics onto C-5 Galaxy stratolifter cargo planes.
They would fly on to their home districts with pictures taken with
the troops. These they would post on their websites and send out in
newsletters, accompanied by truly moving descriptions of what they
had seen: "I have just returned from visiting with our brave men and
women overseas, who are doing the hard work of spreading democracy
and American ideals. And as I look back on this truly moving experience, I can only ask myself, *Where* do we get such men and women?"
The last line was from the James Michener Korean War movie *The
Bridges at Toko-Ri,* a favorite insert among Capitol Hill speechwriters, updated to include, "and women."

"Congressman? Sir, we'll be landing at Turdje momentarily."

"Thank you, Sergeant."

Congressman? Randolph K. Jepperson was tapping on his laptop.
One of the nice things about being a United States congressman and
flying about on military transports was that no bossy flight attendant
told you to fasten your seat belt and put away your electronic devices.
One time, on his way into the DMZ in Korea, the landing was hard
and two officious senators got hurled against the bulkhead, to the quiet
satisfaction of the warrant officer whose suggestion to them that they
strap themselves in had been waved off.

Congressman Jepperson pecked away: "It is the general rule among
policy makers to insist that America must never leave a mission unac-

complished, no matter how wrongheaded or ill thought through. Indeed, the more wrongheaded and ill thought through, the more imperative it is to remain and see it through to its dismal and inevitable end."

He reread the paragraph, smiled, and thought, *Not bad, old bean.* It was an op-ed piece that he would send to *The New York Times* on his return from Bosnia. He knew that, really, he should wait to write it *after* his fact-finding mission to Bosnia. He hushed his offended conscience by making a deal with himself that he'd take out the sentences if he saw anything that changed his mind. (Not likely.) He closed the lid of the laptop as the wheels of the large cargo plane announced with a squeak and puff of vaporized rubber that he was now in the Balkans. Randy liked these jaunts. They were his foreign policy credentials, all part of the Grand Plan.

Randolph Kumberling Jepperson IV was a blue blood in a red meat business. His great-great-great-great-great-great-great-granduncle had signed the Declaration of Independence. The family referred privately to their ancestor as "G-7" and to the sacred document as "the Dec."

G-7's great-great-nephew was the aforementioned General John Sedgwick, distinguished veteran of many Civil War battles, esteemed and beloved comrade of General Ulysses S. Grant, and now a Trivial Pursuit subject, owing to the peculiar circumstances of his demise. The family referred to him as "Elephant Man" or "Poor John."

Randy's great-grandfather (on the maternal Kumberling side) had been governor of Massachusetts in the 1880s. His paternal grandfather, Josephus Agrippa Jepperson, enlarged the already considerable family fortune by cornering the world supply of feldspar just as demand for aluminosilicate was peaking. President Franklin Delano Roosevelt appointed him U.S. ambassador to Belgium at an especially tense time in U.S.-Belgian relations. His intervention in the Fleming-Walloon crisis of 1938 proved critical. He donated the opulent Palais Feldspar outside Genk, with the stipulation that the Flemings and Walloons must stop their feuding, which he termed "surely the most pointless squabble in all Europe." He was knighted by King Leopold III and received the title of Chevalier des Pantalons Blancs (Knight of the White Pants), one of the most sought-after honorifics in Belgium.

The mantle of family greatness rested uneasily on the shoulders of Randy's father, Minturn Jepperson. He experienced his first nervous breakdown halfway through a lackluster academic career at Harvard and one night set fire to the history section of the Widener Library. The episode was covered up, and a new history section was donated by the Jepperson Foundation.

Minturn was sent off to a Swiss sanatorium for a cure consisting of aggressive colonic irrigation and primal screaming. (The two therapies rather complemented each other.) It was on his return by ship to the United States that he met and fell in love with Adelaide Pankhurst Pitts, only daughter of Henry Hootz Pitts, chairman of Great Lakes Everything, which, true to its name, controlled more or less all commerce on the lakes. Minturn's parents tried to discourage their son's affection for "Addie" on the grounds that Hootz "sounded Jewish."

When Minturn refused to break it off, the Jeppersons quietly hired a team of genealogists to find out if their potential in-laws were in fact of the tribe of Abraham. When the genealogists reported that the aboriginal Hootz (Gotmunder Von Hutz, 1436–1491) was not only not Jewish, but a direct lineal descendant of the Holy Roman Emperor Odobard II, they breathed a quiet sigh of relief and allowed nature to take its course. It didn't hurt that Addie stood to inherit her father's fortune, estimated at over $800 million, no small sum in the late 1940s.

Minturn and Addie married and spawned three children, the first of whom they named Randolph IV. (Randy's siblings called him "Intra-Venous." The Jeppersons, like many aristocratic families, were keen on nicknames.) Minturn had more "episodes" (eventually diagnosed as atypical psychosis or bipolar disorder). He developed a morbid horror of rushing water and loud noises, thought to trace to his stay in Switzerland. He also took to making strange birdlike sounds, often at inappropriate moments—in the middle of dinner with important guests, in church, at board meetings. But it provided his wife with a cue by which to explain his increasing absences owing to more stays at various psychological institutions. "Daddy's gone bird-watching again, darling."

Despite all this, Addie provided her children with a normal-for-that-era New England WASP upbringing, nourishing them on bland, overcooked food, hiring German nannies who spanked them at every opportunity, and packing them off to grim, Episcopalian boarding schools at the age of eleven. With the children gone, Addie settled down to a life of bridge, committee meetings, and gin and tonics. She became a pillar of Boston society, dowager and standard-bearer of the long Jepperson line.

Such were the strands of Randolph K. Jepperson IV's DNA.

Whatever skeletons rattled about in the family closet—or foyer, for that matter—Randy had a sunny disposition, though in times of stress he sometimes made a low humming noise that sounded like *Mmmmmmm*.

"Randolph," his mother would command, "stop making that preposterous noise!"

Randy went to Harvard. He studied hard, got good grades, and was popular, especially with women, owing to his good looks and easy laughter. The Porsche convertible and cigarette boat he kept at a marina on the Charles River didn't hurt, either, along with the picnic hampers packed with Champagne, foie gras, and the very best Moroccan hashish. He never dropped the family name; he comped the *Crimson*, became editorial page editor, and wrote well-regarded denunciations of President Ronald Reagan's tax cuts. In a development that caused a huge fracas in the family, he turned down the prestigious AD club on the grounds that it was a "marble shithouse."

After graduating, Randy spent a year in the Peace Corps trying to interest Peruvians in water purification and crop rotation, but for the most part snorting an Andean-size mountain of high-quality and inexpensive cocaine. He stayed up until dawn in his rented villa writing letters home to half a dozen girlfriends, hinting that he was actually in the CIA and tracking Abimael Guzmán of the Shining Path.

When he came home at the end of that snowy Wanderjahr morose, he was unrecognizable. He had long, not very clean hair and a beard. A year of stimulants had left him with an involuntary humming that was now incessant. His conversation, once bubbly and witty, was now less than scintillating. He talked of returning to Peru to "finish the job," which didn't really convince anyone. His girlfriends made excuses not to see him. His mother threatened to cut off his allowance.

Appearing downstairs one afternoon after sleeping until five p.m., he was confronted by his mother, who said to him, "You're too young to have a midlife crisis. Pull yourself together. If you continue at this rate, you'll end up in the loony bin like your father. Or being born-again. I don't know which is more boring. And will you *stop making that appalling sound*!"

One day, on the way into Boston to see a psychiatrist that his mother had insisted on—it was either that or leave the house and no more allowance—Randy dropped three hits of windowpane.

It was a peculiar way of striking back at his mother—seeing her shrink while tripping on a monster dose of LSD—but it had a kind of logic to it. Navigating on the highway into Boston became, well, complicated. At one point he looked up, and there, among the strange giant birds that were circling and trying to eat him, he saw, off Exit 15, the John F. Kennedy Library, its I. M. Pei design doing . . . whoa . . . *amazing* things. It occurred to him, through the tsunami of hallucinations, that he had never actually been inside. Carpe diem! It was much more alluring than the prospect of freaking out in front of Dr. Goldberg, so he turned off onto the exit—a breathtaking and very nearly life-ending maneuver. His parking was irregular and attracted the interest of several security guards, but he managed to ditch the car and make it inside without being arrested.

He stood in the cathedral-high glassed-in pavilion lobby looking at the sea and the sky and had himself a life-changing epiphany. It dawned on him that he too had a Boston accent, was good-looking, smart, Harvard educated, filthy rich, and—at least before he began vacuuming cocaine up his nose—a world-quality cocksman, a bantam rooster in any henhouse. He heard a voice—JFK's voice. It said, *Go for it.*

Four years later, after a rocky start or two, Randolph K. Jepperson had been elected to a seat in Congress. Some might say he had bought himself a seat. The sniggers of his colleagues soon began, and he found himself saddled with a new nickname: Randolph "He's No Jefferson" Jepperson IV. But he was determined that they would not be laughing for long.

Corporal Cohane stood at semiattention as the Air Force C-21A taxied to a stop. She'd done some more reading up on Rep. R. K. Jepperson. *The Almanac of American Politics* noted his distinguished DNA, his focus on foreign policy—domestic policy being pretty dull stuff. He'd used his connections to finagle a seat on the House Armed Forces Overseas Projection Oversight Committee, dubbed the "Committee on Imperial Overstretch." This would be the reason for his visit to the Beautiful Balkans.

She doubted he'd come for the PX goodies on the return flight. According to *Forbes,* he was one of the richest men in Congress, with a personal fortune "in excess of $100 million." (Addie had relented in the matter of the allowance after what the family called Randy's "Great Awakening.") This and his striking good looks made him the most eligible bachelor in Washington. More than one glossy magazine had run a profile of him with the title "The Next JFK?" He had a huge house in Georgetown and, indeed, as Captain Drimpilski had noted, "dated movie stars." He'd had a two-year-long "thing" with the Tegucigalpa Tamale. His mother was quoted in *Vanity Fair* calling her a "Honduran tramp." *That must have made for a lively Thanksgiving dinner,* Cass thought.

She studied the photos of him. He looked like the sort of person whose great-great-whatever had signed the Declaration of Independence. He was six feet two, trim, broad in the shoulders, a bit storklike, which gave him a needed touch of vulnerability, as if he might blow over in a strong wind. He had pale blue eyes, a nose that had been handed down since the *Mayflower,* and creased cheeks. He looked like a flesh-and-blood bust done by a distinguished sculptor. It could have a cruel face, but the eyes twinkled and suggested self-awareness and bemusement at his abundant good fortune. And now here he was, approaching her. She had to shout above the high-pitched whine of the jet turbines even as they spiraled slowly to a stop.

"*Congressman Jepperson? Corporal Cohane, sir. Army Public Affairs. Welcome to—*"

"*Well named, isn't it?*"

"*Sir?*"

"*Turd-je!*"

"*Yes, sir. If you'll follow me . . . our vehicle is this way.*"

Cass climbed into the driver's seat of the Humvee, the congressman the passenger seat. His elegant frame and aristocratic bearing seemed somewhat out of context in such a spare, utilitarian space.

He smiled and took her in.

"Cohane, is it?"

"Yes, sir."

"Lovely name. Irish? Surely."

"So I'm told, sir."

"Do you know, I have one of these at home in Washington," he said. "Civilian version, of course. Hummer. Sounds almost indecent, doesn't it? Hummer. I'll pick you up in my . . . *Hummer.*" He chuckled to himself.

Strange duck, Cass thought. This information that he drove a car that got about fifty yards to the gallon hardly squared with the *Almanac*'s description of him as a "staunch environmentalist."

As if reading Cass's mind, he added, "I don't drive it. Just keep it at home. You know. In the event."

"Event, sir?"

"I'm sorry. What's your first name?"

"Cassandra?"

He smiled. "You don't sound very sure. Do you have your baptismal certificate on you? We could check."

"Cass. Sir." She smiled back.

"Tell you what, Cass, sir . . . if you'll stop calling me 'sir,' which makes me feel a hundred years old, I'll start calling you Cass. Deal?"

"Okay."

"Pleased to meet you, Cass." He looked out the window. "I'd forgotten how dreary it is here."

Cass said, "I'm sorry it's just me, but the VIPVIS—the Pentagon—indicated that you didn't want a large escort. The captain would gladly have—"

"No, no, no, this is fine. *Hate* entourages." He pronounced it in a French way, *en-tour-ahhh-ges*. "It's gotten *so* out of hand. My God, did you see about the president's motorcade in Beijing last week? Fifty-four cars long? Imperial overstretch *limousine*, I call that. I mean, *please*. What is it coming to?"

He looked over, saw Cass's uncertain expression, and said, "I'm sorry, Cass. I really wasn't trying to trick you into criticizing the commander in chief. There's often no filter between what passes from my brain to my mouth. I suppose it's not his fault. Security being what it is and all. Still, what kind of message does it send to the world when the American president goes about that way? Couldn't they make do with—*fifty* cars? Jimmy Carter overdid it—he was president before you were born—but I must say I like the *idea* of an American president carrying his own garment bag. Humility! Quite my favorite virtue. Not that I possess it in overabundance. No one in Washington seems to, these days. Dear, dear. Harry Truman used to take walks, practically by himself. Those were the days. Can you imagine an American president popping out for a stroll in the park? *Où sont les neiges d'antan?*"

"Villon?"

"Very good, Corporal." He said it without condescension. "I'll have to stop quoting French, you know, if I run for president. In America these days, a knowledge of the most beautiful, civilized language on earth is considered a disqualification for high office. Much better to say, *¡Buenos días!* and be photographed biting into some revolting burrito. Well, Corporal Cass, shall we commence fact-finding?"

"Where would the congressman like to fact-find?"

"I thought we might just poke about. I hate the planned itineraries. *Oh, gosh, Congressman, we had no* idea *you were coming.* Then you step into the tent and there's a banner saying WELCOME, CONGRESS-

MAN JEPPERSON, and you practically gag on the smell of boot and brass polish. The poor people have been up since dawn getting ready for you. It's tough enough out here without a bunch of Washington assholes sticking their faces in. There's a Special Forces camp near here, isn't there? Camp December . . ."

"November."

"The very one. Let's see what's cooking in Camp November. I like the special ops people. They give it to you with the bark off."

Cass drove. The congressman observed the landscape in silence. After a while he said, "What are you doing here, anyway?"

"Preventing World War One from breaking out again."

"Good answer."

"Not original. I heard a colonel say it."

"Well, we don't have quite as much to worry about this time from Austro-Hungary. But Russia's always a question mark. You know, I got drunk with Boris Yeltsin once. Remember him? God, that man could put it away. We sang 'Home on the Range' in the Kremlin. Took me a week to recover. Can't stand even the smell of vodka now. And vodka doesn't even smell."

Cass kept her eyes on the muddy road, feeling his eyes on her, not in a lecherous way.

"So?" he said.

"So?" she said.

"What are you doing here? Aside from keeping World War One from breaking out again."

"Boring story." Cass smiled.

"You've got me trapped inside a Humvee in Bosnia," Randy said. "Go on. Bore me to death. Give it your best shot."

She boiled it down, nervous to find herself confiding a family saga to a United States congressman. She left out her mother's sarcastic comments at the dinner table about the Cessna but included the detail that her father had secretly taken out a second mortgage on their home to finance his start-up, which continued to founder. After that, her mother took the kids and walked out. That part Cass had learned in a letter received halfway through basic training.

Congressman Randy listened without comment, arms folded over his chest. Cass thought she heard some kind of humming coming from him. Maybe he was bored, singing to himself. They passed the remains of a bombed-out Serb convoy.

"Well," he said at length. "What do you get a dad like that for Father's Day? A hand grenade?"

They drove on. Cass said, "Why do you have a Humvee? Aren't you a big environmentalist?"

"Boring story."

"Your turn to bore me."

"All right. Now don't quote me, because I'll get in a lot of trouble for even talking about it. But there's this *list*. You know how the military and Capitol Police and Secret Service love to scare the shit—pardon my French—out of Congress with disaster scenarios? Drives up their budgets. Well, Tom Clancy, you know, the novelist?"

"I've heard of Tom Clancy."

"Not as good a writer as Villon. He wrote this *preposterous* book that ends with a plane flying into the Capitol building. Can you imagine? Like people are going to start flying planes into buildings? Please. But everyone in official Washington reads Clancy—you don't think they're reading Proust, do you? *Au contraire*—and it scared the *merde* out of them. So they decided, we *must* have a plan. We must have a—*list*. So they drew this grotesque list of who gets evacuated in the event Japanese jingoists or deranged Swiss yodelers or whoever start flying jumbo jets into our buildings. It's called 'List Echo.' What Washington drudge came up with that designation? But wouldn't you know—*I'm not on it*. It's all *senators*. Can you imagine a world repopulated by senators? The living would envy the dead. So I thought, All right, fine, I'll arrange for my own evacuation when the great dome comes down around us. So I bought this appalling vehicle, the station wagon from hell, and parked it permanently in my space in the Capitol garage with a full tank of gas and all sorts of survival goodies packed in." He added, "I really *do* care about the environment. Most of the time I ride a bicycle. Of course, it's not just being green. It kind of helps with the image thing. The Bicycling Congressman."

"So you spin literally."

"Very good, Corporal. Yes. I spin. That's it. An occasion of spin." He yawned. "Do you mind if I doze off for a bit? Didn't get much shut-eye on the way over. I don't want to nod off in front of Special Forces. They'll probably think I'm a big enough wimp as it is. Wake me if we come under attack or anything really thrilling happens, would you?"

Chapter 4

"**F**unny," Congressman Randy said as they drove down the muddy road from the Special Forces camp.

"What?"

"World War One. It finally ended in November. We were just at Camp November. And the war began right here in Bosnia. So in a way, we did a full historical circle in just a few hours." He was quiet for a while and then said, "They were very gung ho, weren't they."

"Special Forces tends to be."

"Did you do all the normal things in basic training? Or do Public Affairs people get a break from the foxhole stuff?"

Cass gave him a sidelong glance. "I didn't join the army to issue press releases and . . ."

"Escort jerks from Congress."

"I didn't say that."

"Ah, but you thought it. Well, Corporal, believe me, I may not be a fan of our mission here, but I've never had less than full respect for the military. Do you know what *I* was doing when I was your age? Snorting cocaine in Peru with the Peace Corps and pretending to be with the CIA."

"Why are you telling me all this?" Cass said.

"Guilt." He winked at her. "With liberals it's a sacrament. I do admire the military. Though thank God I never had to be in it. Wouldn't have lasted two minutes. Do you think they were, you know, laying it on thick for me back there? Spinning? What with me being on the record against our being here and all?"

"To be honest," Cass said, "I think they have better things to do. Like keeping warm. And not getting blown up."

"Touché, Corporal. Theirs not to reason why, theirs but to do or die. Onward rode the six hundred. Had to memorize that at Groton. Suppose these days they have you memorize Maya Angelou. *Such* drivel."

"You don't sound very liberal. You drive a Humvee, admire the military, prefer Tennyson to politically correct poetry."

"On paper I'm pretty pink. My ADA rating is through the roof. But I know what you mean. You know what the French say: 'Think left, live right.' Would you like me to recite the whole of 'Charge of the Light Brigade'?"

"No, thank you. It's a good thing you didn't do that back there. They might have opened fire on us."

"Recited it once during a late night filibuster to block a school lunch cutback. I can do 'The Cremation of Sam McGee,' too. Don't worry. I'll spare you."

"What was she like?" It just came out. Cass regretted it instantly.

"Who?"

"Nothing. I—"

"*Ah*—the Tegucigalpa Tamale."

"It was out of line. I'm sorry."

"Well . . ." Randy cleared his throat. "She *can* be very nice. I think she just thinks it's more interesting not to be. We were actually engaged at one point. Mother . . . God, *that* was a night never to repeat. I tremble at the memory."

Cass heard the humming sound again.

"Is that a—"

"It's called Tourette's. Just a mild case. Came with the genes. My father had a not mild case. He chirped like a South American cockatoo. Rather awkward in the middle of a Chopin nocturne at the Philharmonic. As children, we would *cringe*."

"I don't mean to laugh."

"I've heard worse, believe me. Say, I'm famished."

Cass reached behind the seat and handed him a Meal Ready To Eat.

The wrapper indicated "ITALIAN STYLE. Spaghetti with M/Ball. 1200 calories."

Congressman Randy stared at it on his lap, glumly. "Oh, *yum*." He threw the MRE back. "Mind if I drive?" he said.

It was against all regulations.

"Uh—"

"Oh, come on. Please? I never get to, back home. You're always being driven. Driven—in so many ways. Please?"

Cass used to let her younger brother take the wheel when he was fifteen. Congressman Randy, nearly forty, suddenly sounded like a teenager.

"I could get in serious trouble," she said.

"If you don't let me drive," Randy said in a serious tone of voice, "I'll recite the whole of 'The Cremation of Sam McGee.' And you'll go mad. And run off the road, and we'll both die."

She pulled over. They exchanged places and drove off, smoothly enough.

"Handles a bit heavier than mine," he said.

"It's armored," Cass said.

"Of course. Brilliant. Are there any buttons I shouldn't touch? Missile launchers, ejection seats, smoke machines? There's a village."

They were in a valley. There was smoke rising from a small town a few miles in the distance.

"They'll have something to eat," Randy said.

"Negative that," Cass said. "This road we're on is the perimeter of our area of operations. That town is outside of it. We can get something back at Turdje."

"I bet you that village is the very epicenter of gastronomy in the region. Indeed, the Lyon of Turdje."

"I don't believe there is an 'epicenter of gastronomy' anywhere around here," Cass said.

"See here, Corporal, I'm here to find facts. And the facts I'm most interested in right now include a bit of roast chicken, some fresh cheese, crusty bread, and a bottle of the local plonk. How's the wine here, by the way? Pretty grim? Um . . . probably better off ordering beer."

Against Cass's protest, Randy turned the vehicle off the main road onto a smaller one that led to the village. Cass had visions of Serb snipers popping up from behind hedgerows. She reached for the radio.

"What are you doing?" he said.

"Informing them back at base that I'm being kidnapped by a U.S. congressman."

"Good idea. You never know."

Cass alerted the duty officer of their position. He expressed concern, but Randy was as focused as a pig intent on truffle. A few moments later, they pulled into the village.

There was something resembling a small town square and a few locals. Cass saw a sign that seemed to indicate it might have something to do with food. They went inside. It was steamy and warm inside and smelled of stale pickles. Cass exchanged a few rudimentary words with the apparent proprietor, a large elderly woman with a mole.

"What did you order?" Congressman Randy said.

"*Kulen pita.*"

"Enlighten me."

"Tripe pie."

"Oh," Randy said. "Yum, scrum."

It wasn't bad. Congressman Randy drank a bottle of the local beer, which he pronounced "a bit hoppy."

As they ate, three rough-looking men entered and sat at a table. They stared at Cass in her uniform and her congressman. Randy gave them a friendly look and wave. They returned cold scowls.

"Must be Republicans." He shrugged. He ordered another beer.

"My great-great-et-cetera ancestor," Randy said, suppressing a hoppy belch, "knew Thomas Jefferson. Knew him quite well. They— awkward point—used to buy their slaves from the same dealer. You won't hear me speechifying about *that* on C-SPAN. There are letters between them about it. 'I think I overpaid for Hezekiah. Didn't much like the look of those gums.' Wait till I run for president. How the media will feast. Sorry, I'm rambling. Tripe pie does that to me. Anyhow, to the point. In 1815, Jefferson wrote a letter to someone. I've had it entered it into the *Congressional Record* so many times

I know it by heart. Don't worry, it's shorter than 'Sam McGee.' He wrote, 'The less we have to do with the amities or enmities of Europe, the better.' This from someone who'd been our minister to France. He wrote, 'Not in our day, but at no distant one, we may shake a rod over the heads of all, which may make the stoutest tremble. But I hope our wisdom will grow with our power, and teach us that the less we use our power the greater it will be.' Damn good stuff." He leaned back, gave the brutish-looking men a glance, and said, "And here we are once again—here *you* are, Corporal—smack dab in the center of Europe's enmities."

"Speaking of enmities," Cass said in a low voice, "I think we ought to leave. Those men over there—they're making me kind of uncomfortable."

Randolph gave them an appraising look. "Not nature's most gorgeous specimens, are they, the Bozzies? Why linger? Will you ask Madame Mole what we owe?"

He pulled out a thick wad of hundred-dollar bills. The cash did not go unnoticed by the three men. Cass winced. The men got up and left.

When they were outside, Randy said, "Care for a stroll on the Rialto? Walk off our three-star meal?"

"Get in the vehicle."

Randy walked over to the driver's side.

"I need to drive," she said.

But there was no arguing. He had the key. She climbed in her side. They drove off. Cass watched nervously in her rear mirror. The three men emerged from the café, got into a car, and followed them.

"Shit," she said.

"Yeah," Randy said, "it *was* pretty awful."

"Not the food. Those men. They're following us."

Randy glanced in the rearview mirror. "They're probably going home. Home to their poor wives. The prospect of sex with those three . . . the mind boggles. . . ."

"They're following," Cass said with a trace of anger. "That wad of cash you flashed back there."

"Sorry. Didn't look like they took American Express."

Cass got on the radio and reported the situation.

"Did you just call in an air strike?" Randy said. "Not very sporting."

"They don't screw around here. They're tough."

"Well, I'm tough, too," Randy said with jutted jaw.

Wonderful, Cass thought. *Bertie Wooster Goes to War.*

The car was now close behind them. Suddenly Randy jammed on the brakes. The car almost slammed into them.

"What are you doing?" Cass shouted.

"Seeing if they pass."

They didn't. Two men got out of the car and approached the Humvee on either side. The one approaching Cass's had something long in his hand.

In the next instant, her door window spiderwebbed from the blow of the iron pipe.

"Hang on!" Randy shouted.

Cass felt herself thrown forward against her seat restraint as Randy slammed the Humvee into reverse and floored the accelerator. The Humvee smashed into the Serb car with a loud crunch. He shifted back into forward and drove off.

"Sorry," he said. "Bit sudden. You all right?"

Cass was already on the radio, reporting that they were now officially under attack. In her rearview, she saw the two men rushing back to get in the car. It took off, following.

"I'd have thought that would have put them out of action," Randy said. "So, do we have any guns on board?"

"No."

"A military vehicle with no *guns*?"

"We weren't supposed to be operating in hostile territory," Cass snapped.

"Well, I wish we had some all the same. I'm rather good at skeet."

"That's so reassuring."

Randy turned the vehicle sharply off the road and onto a field.

"What are you doing?" Cass screamed.

"Let's see them follow us through this muck!"

"Randy, there are *mines*! Mines all over this country!"

Congressman Randy took his foot off the accelerator.

"Aha. You may be on to something there, Corp—"

Chapter 5

U.S. CONGRESSMAN WOUNDED IN BOSNIA
Military Escort Also Hospitalized in Mine Incident

Cass stared groggily at the headline. An obliging nurse had brought her *USA Today*'s foreign edition. She'd been in and out of consciousness for the last two days, so the paper was indeed bringing her news. At some point—was it this morning?—she had opened her eyes to find her bed surrounded by uniforms, uniforms of impressive rank. She dealt with the unwelcome discovery by closing her eyes and feigning a coma.

She read:

> Representative Randolph K. Jepperson and his military escort were injured yesterday when their Humvee went off a main road near the Bosnian village of Krkyl and hit a land mine. They were evacuated by helicopter to the NATO base in Turdje and then flown to the U.S. Army medical center in Landstuhl, Germany.
>
> A NATO spokesman said both are in "serious but stable" condition.
>
> Massachusetts Congressman Jepperson is a ranking member of the House Armed Forces Overseas Projection Oversight Committee. He was on a fact-finding mission at the time of the incident. An ancestor was a signer of the Declaration of Independence.

His escort, Corporal Cassandra Cohane, is with Army Public Affairs, based at Turdje as part of the NATO peacekeeping deployment.

It was unclear what their Humvee was doing in the middle of a posted minefield.

Sometime later—was it that same day?—Cass heard a grave, urgent voice.

"Corporal. Corporal Cohane."

She opened her eyes. The uniforms of impressive rank had returned. She saw a colonel, a major, a captain—no, two captains. None bore flowers, magazines, or "get well soon" cards. Cass closed her eyes again, but the voice, blistering with authority, summoned her back from her hiding place behind lids. She was momentarily grateful that her head was bandaged and her left arm encased in plaster. It might make them just the teensiest bit sympathetic. *Okay,* she thought, *here goes.*

"Corporal"—it was the colonel talking—"why was the congressman driving your vehicle?"

"He asked."

This brought a wave of frowns around Cass's bed.

"You understand that was in violation of regulations."

"I'm aware of the fact." Painfully aware.

"And you nonetheless let him commandeer the vehicle?"

"Sir, he's a U.S. congressman."

The uniforms exchanged glances. "What were you doing in the village?"

"Fact-finding, sir." Lovely, morphine. Takes the edge off anything, even the prospect of a court-martial.

"Corporal, you're in a deep hole. Don't keep digging."

"The congressman was hungry. He insisted. I attempted to persuade him to eat an MRE instead. It was apparently not up to his gastronomic standards."

" 'Insisted'? He was *your* responsibility, Corporal."

"Yes, sir. I seem to have screwed up big-time, sir. Might I inquire how the congressman is?"

Deeper frowns.

"They're still working on him. Trying to save his leg."

The uniforms left. Cass had a cry. The obliging nurse gave her a shot, and she tumbled gratefully back into the outstretched arms of Mother Morphine.

When she awoke—was it the next day?—there was a uniform sitting by her bed. It was Captain Drimpilski. He had flowers. When she realized it was he, she began to blubber.

"All right, Corporal. It's all right. Come on now, soldier, enough of that. Eagles spin. They don't cry. Suck it up."

"Yes, sir." She blew her nose. "What is the captain doing here?"

"They flew me in. I talked to the doctors. You're going to be all right, Cohane. You're damn lucky."

Cass stared. "Lucky? In what way, exactly, sir?"

"Could have been a lot worse."

"How's Randy?"

"Randy?"

"The congressman. Whatever. Is he . . . all right?"

"They're flying him stateside for further surgery. They"—Drimpilski sighed—"removed a portion of his left leg."

"Portion?"

"Below the knee."

Cass groaned.

"He's got a dozen broken bones, a collapsed lung, internal bleeding, his left arm got pretty shredded, but they think that'll be all right eventually. He'll be setting off metal detectors for the rest of his life. But he'll live. So it *could* have been worse."

Captain Drimpilski handed her another tissue and helped her blow her nose.

"Cass," he said. It was the only time he'd ever used her first name. It made her start blubbering again. Realizing what he'd done, he self-corrected and spoke gruffly.

"You represent the 4087, Cohane."

"Yes, sir," Cass said miserably. "Eagles spin the way. Hooah."

"All the way. That's more like it. All right, then, let's review the apparent facts. You went beyond the perimeter of operations, broke regs by permitting a civilian to drive a military vehicle, did something to provoke the locals—hold on, let me finish—and in the process nearly lost a United States congressman. A congressman known for being outspokenly critical of our presence here. And who is known to have a certain reputation with the . . . female of the species." Captain Drimpilski pondered a moment. "As you can see, there are a few layers to this onion."

"Is the captain implying," Cass said, suddenly dry-eyed, "that the corporal was having sex with the congressman? In a minefield?"

"No, I personally do not believe that."

"Do *they*?" she said incredulously.

Captain Drimpilski cleared his throat noncommittally. "What I know is that discussions are being held even as we speak. In Washington, D.C., at the Pentagon. And at the White House. I am given to understand that the secretary of defense himself is taking part in these discussions. While I am not privy to these discussions, it is my general understanding that they are not arguing over whether to award you the Distinguished Service Medal or the Medal of Honor. By the way, there are approximately fifty members of the media outside this facility, all of them extremely eager to interview you."

Cass was not one for self-pity, but she couldn't help reflecting that eighteen months ago she was at home in Connecticut opening a letter saying she'd been admitted to Yale and she was now lying wounded in an army hospital in Germany, responsible for the mutilation of a member of the United States Congress and listening to what sounded like a preamble to her court-martial. She began to laugh. She couldn't help it.

"You all right?" Captain Drimpilski said.

"Fine. Fine. So when's the firing squad?"

Captain Drimpilski stood. "I'll stick around, see what can be done." He patted her on the knee. "You get some rest now, Corporal."

"Captain," she said as he was leaving.

"Yes?"

"The corporal was not having sex with the congressman in a minefield."

"Noted."

*   *   *

The next day, off morphine and wishing she weren't, Cass watched CNN and saw Congressman Randy being wheeled off a military air transport at Andrews Air Force Base outside Washington. A large crowd awaited him. His mother was there, along with the entire Massachusetts congressional delegation. Randy gave a thumbs-up gesture—which would be replayed a thousand times—as he was bathed in the flashlight from dozens of cameras. People waved American flags. A welcome banner read, WELCOME HOME, HERO! Cass noted the presence of the secretary of defense and various Joint Chiefs, including the chairman. The secretary's demeanor, not normally jocund, resembled that of a man chewing aluminum foil. She became aware of the reporter saying, "Congressman Jepperson was wounded when the vehicle he was being driven in went off the road and onto a mine. From here he will be transferred to . . ."

Was being driven in? Had she heard correctly?

Cass was not left to speculate for long. That afternoon, the colonel returned, this time alone. He closed the door and sat beside Cass's bed. He handed her a clipboard. There was a sheet of paper on it, with a line at the bottom.

"It's your request for discharge."

"From the hospital?"

"No, Corporal. From the army."

Cass tried to sit up. "Sir, though my mind is kind of clouded up with morphine, I do not specifically recall requesting a discharge."

The colonel gave her a meaningful look. "Does the corporal recall being offered a choice between court-martial for negligent endangerment of a civilian, punishable by up to twenty-five years in military prison—and an honorable discharge for personal reasons?"

So there it was. "Now that the colonel mentions it, I do recall something of that nature. Perhaps the morphine caused amnesia."

"It does that. Sign here, here, and here."

"Shouldn't I first consult with an army lawyer?"

"Cohane," the colonel said with just a fleck of sympathy, "there were those who wanted your flayed hide nailed to the front door of a certain five-sided building in Washington, D.C. Were it not for Captain Drimpilski and Congressman Jepperson, the crows would by now be feasting on your remains. I'm putting it explicitly, but I want to make everything clear for you. Do I?"

"As designer water, sir." Cass sighed.

As the colonel walked away, she said, "Do I get a Purple Heart?"

Chapter **6**

There were no crowds or WELCOME HOME, HERO! banners for ex-corporal Cassandra Cohane.

People seemed unsure how to respond to her, whether to wink (*Banging a congressman in a* mine*field? Party down, girl!*) or disapprove (*you slut*) or evince sympathy (*Well, thank heavens you're alive, but no more minefields for you!*). By the end of the first week home, Cass had dyed her lovely blond hair a shade called "Mississippi Mud," bought clear prescription-type glasses, and spent hours in front of the mirror attempting to make herself unrecognizable even to her mother. She went to the library and looked up articles on cosmetic surgery.

Her mother's eyes widened as Cass emerged from the bathroom after one session of home makeover.

"Well?" Cass said.

"You look . . . Gosh, it's good to have you back."

"Mother. I did basic combat training. I can kill a man with my hands. Tell me. I can take it."

"You look lovely, darling. Just like that movie actress."

"Which movie actress?"

"The one who was arrested for shoplifting. Her mug shot . . . I mean, she's very pretty. . . ."

In due course, a letter arrived from the Department of the Army saying that under the terms of her discharge, no, Cass was not eligible for tuition assistance. Indeed, the Yale admissions office did not sound in any great hurry to have her matriculate. Cass reentombed herself in her room for a week, watching the ceiling and television in equal proportion.

One day her father telephoned. Her mother knocked and entered, bearing the cordless phone as though it were something that had been retrieved from deep within a septic tank.

"Sug? Hey! How's my girl?" He sounded California hearty, as though his veins coursed with pomegranate juice. They had not spoken in a year and a half.

"I'm great," she said.

"Hear you had a little accident over there."

"Yeah."

"What were you doing driving in a minefield?"

"Long story, Dad."

"Well, you sure had us worried."

"Us?"

"Yeah. That's what I'm calling about. Primarily I was calling to see how you are. But secondarily"—this was how engineers talked; by the end of the conversation, he'd be up to "duodecimally"—"I've got news. I'm getting married . . . You there? . . . Sug?"

"I'm here."

"Her name's Lisa. She's fantastic. She can't wait to meet you. I've told her all about you."

"Dad . . ."

"Yeah, Sug?"

"Hang up."

"No prob. I'll call you in a few days. It's going great out here. I'm going to be sending you some money. Soon as I can. This time it's gonna happen. We're on target. Love ya."

No prob? . . . Love ya? This wasn't how he used to talk in Connecticut.

She went back to staring at the ceiling. Ceilings can actually be interesting, if you stare at them long enough. With the right drugs, they'll outperform the Sistine Chapel.

One afternoon three weeks into her self-immurement, she turned on the television and saw Congressman Randy arriving at the Capitol building for his first day back at work. Another huge crowd awaited him. A large banner proclaimed the return of an AMERICAN PATRIOT. He emerged from his car on two crutches, gave his now signature thumbs-up gesture, and caused a roar of applause from the perhaps five hundred people waiting for him on the steps of the Capitol. She had to admit, it made for pretty good TV. It's not every day that a politician is hailed as a living hero.

Both the House majority and minority leaders were there. They welcomed him in terms that would have made Douglas MacArthur blush. When finally Randy was allowed to speak, they both crowded in on him to get in the camera shot, a practice called among Capitol Hill aides "parasiting."

"Thank you," Congressman Randy said. "Thank you, colleagues, dear friends, Americans, for that tremendous welcome. And let me say from the bottom of my heart, it's great to be back at work!"

Thunderous applause and cheering. Cass watched in numb amazement. It reminded her of a documentary she'd seen on TV about a place in India where they paraded the mummy of a five-century-old saint through the streets and people in the throes of religious ecstasy would bite off its toes. If he wasn't careful, he'd lose the other leg. Any minute now they'd be talking about renaming Reagan National Airport "Jepperson Field."

"I want to say," he continued once the din had subsided, "I want to say, to the brave men and women serving in the armed forces overseas, we honor your sacrifice!"

Roars.

"We will not forget you!"

Louder roars.

"And we will fight for you here just as you fight for us there!"

Was that a flight of *doves* she saw in the background? My God. Doves. They were releasing doves, from a cage, on the Capitol steps. *Why bother running for Senate?* she thought. *Why not just announce for emperor?* It was the photo op from heaven. It would be studied in PR academies centuries from now. Now he was limping away from the podium. Women nearby were dabbing tears from their eyes. Was that—music? Yes, music. They were playing Bruce Springsteen, "Born in the USA." To hell with running—just carry him down Pennsylvania Avenue and install him in the Oval Office. Cass turned off the television and went back to watching the ceiling.

She stayed in her room for a week, leaving only to go to the bathroom and forage for food in the kitchen. She subsisted mainly on rice cakes and soda. Her complexion was sallow and waxy, her hair a mélange of about eight different dyes. Finally her mother came into her room and said, "Are you planning to assassinate someone?"

"What?" Cass said, still staring at the ceiling.

"Because the way you're acting, I won't be surprised if the phone rings someday and it's some reporter saying, 'Mrs. Cohane, your daughter has just shot the president. Do you have a comment?'"

"Interesting idea. Thanks for the input."

"Cassandra, don't talk like that."

"Mother. I don't have the energy to shoot anyone."

"You look like something out of an Anne Rice novel. Unhealthy. You haven't been outside in a week. And this room. It *smells*."

"Not if you stay in it all the time."

"Honey, you're going through post-traumatic stress disorder. It's understandable after what you've been through. I want you to see a psychiatrist."

"No."

"A psychologist, then."

"No."

"Licensed clinic social worker. They're almost as—"

"No. Go *away*, Mother."

"What are you reading?"

"*The Fountainhead.*"

Her mother frowned. "Ayn Rand? Is *that* a good idea?"

"It's about someone who refuses to compromise," Cass said, conscious that she sounded a bit robotic. "Someone who stands up against mediocrity and compromise and weakness and bullshit."

"QED," her mother snorted.

"What's that? A British cruise ship?"

"You know perfectly well what it means. You got into Yale, didn't you? I'm sorry, honey, I didn't . . . I just don't see that reading Ayn Rand is helpful at this stage. I had a boyfriend in high school who read *Atlas Shrugged*. He ended up handing out leaflets on street corners about how we all have to watch out for number one. It's an unpleasant philosophy."

"No," Cass said. "We can't have me looking out for myself, can we? I mean, how selfish would *that* be?"

"I was never any good at arguing. It's why I went into economics. Numbers don't argue. How long are you planning to inhabit this cave?"

"Until stalactites form. Could I have some more rice cakes?"

"You can get your own rice cakes."

The next day, her mother came into her room bearing the cordless phone, this time as if it were a trophy. "For *you*." She was beaming.

"Who is it?"

"Bertie Wooster Goes to Bosnia." Cass had confided in her mother the full details of what had happened over there.

"Hello?" Cass said suspiciously.

"Well, *there* you are," said Congressman Randy. "You don't call, you don't write. I didn't know how to find you. Are you all right?"

"Depends on your definition of 'all right.' I'm alive. I see from TV you are."

"Cass," he said, "I don't know where to begin."

"Shit happens. Especially in the Balkans."

"How's your arm?"

"Itches."

"The high point of my day is scratching my stump when I take off the prosthesis. As you get older, it's the little things in life. Look, I'm . . . I . . . I was just trying to . . ."

"Drive across a minefield. It was an accident. We're alive."

"Well, I'm *sorry*. I'll do anything I can."

"I saw you on television. At the Capitol. *Doves?*"

"Don't tell anyone, but they're actually pigeons. They dip them in Wite-Out. Cheaper. I have a new PR man. *Genius* at the photo op. Name's Tucker. Now look here, I'm sending a plane for you. I want you to come down here. I want to talk to you."

"Talk? What about?"

"Your future."

"Do I have one?"

"Those idiots in the army. I told them it was all my fault. Want me to denounce them?"

"No. Leave it. But I could live without the media stuff about how we were having sex in the minefield."

"That didn't come from me."

"Collateral damage, from your reputation."

"Guilty as charged. All right, I feel guilty. I'm wealthy, and a congressman with political ambitions. You're in a spectacular position to make me pay through the nose. And I want to."

"I don't want your money."

"I'm offering you a job. And money if you want it. Your mother hates me. She made *that* perfectly clear on the phone. Put in a good word for me, would you? Can't stand it when the mothers hate me. Guess it goes back to childhood."

Cass heard a humming over the phone.

Randy said, "She told me you're clinically depressed and that you're going to shoot someone. Please don't. It would completely ruin my political career. Are you in much pain?"

"The physical kind or the kind where you spend week after week looking at the ceiling?"

"If it's any consolation, I'm still in pain. I can't get out of bed in the morning without a couple of Percocets. I sit in hearings and drool, like something out of *One Flew over the Cuckoo's Nest.* My aides have to wipe off my chin so I won't glisten on C-SPAN. I'll probably end up at Betty Ford. I could always announce my Senate run from there. Lock up the rehab vote early."

Do not laugh, she told herself. *This man ruined your life.*

"Cass?"

"What?"

"I'm sending a plane. Tomorrow. Will you come?"

"I don't know. I'm a little agoraphobic right now."

"I'll share my Percocets with you. Fifty-fifty."

"Fine."

Chapter 7

Congressman Randolph K. Jepperson's office overlooked a not very impressive slice of Capitol Hill vista. There were the usual unimportant but large trophies, flags, maps, and awards from organizations no one had heard of and the obligatory photographs of him taken during reception line photo opportunities: the standard Washington wallpaper of self-importance. Cass looked for a photo of him with the troops of Camp November. Sure enough, there it was, front and center, signed, "Get well soon." There was also a photo of him with the Central American ex-wife of the rock star, taken on a beach. He was smiling; she looked upset. Perhaps room service that morning hadn't been quick enough. Looming behind Randy's desk chair was a large oil portrait by Rembrandt Peale of the ancestor who'd signed "the Dec."

He greeted her warmly. She sat. He slid a piece of paper across the desk toward her. A check, made out to "Yale University" in the amount of a year's full tuition ($33,000). He said that he'd write a new one every fall. "But I want good report cards," he said, smiling widely.

There it was, in her lap, a rectangle of light blue, her ticket to a bright future.

"Well?" he said. "No oohs or ahs?"

"I'm all out of those. Look, I can't accept this," Cass said.

"Why on earth not? It's not going to bankrupt me, I assure you."

"To be honest, it feels kinda like a bribe."

Randy looked at her. "Why would I be bribing you? What secret am I trying to protect?"

She put the check on the desk. "I haven't talked to the media. And I'm not going to talk to the media. So," she said, nudging the check toward him, "you don't need to do this."

"What do you take me for, Cass? Aside from an upper-class imbecile?" He looked hurt.

"Someone who wants to be president?" she said.

Randy smiled. "Well, you have me there. *Uch* . . ." He rolled up his pant leg, pulled off his plastic limb, and scratched. "Itches. Itches like sin."

"Try not to scratch."

"Thank you, Nurse Ratched. The pills only make it worse when they wear off."

He'd lost weight. The doctors had him drinking eight-hundred-calorie chocolate milkshakes four times a day. His face was still red in places from bits of Humvee shrapnel. He looked like—someone who'd been blown up.

"I appreciate the gesture, but I can't take your money," Cass said. "But I will take a job."

He looked up from his scratching. "Don't you want to go to college? Rub it in Dad's face?"

"I don't care about him."

"Wouldn't blame you if you did."

She glanced around the wood-paneled office, at the bookshelves. "This looks enough like college. Pay me thirty-three thousand in salary."

"You'll have to work your way up, you know. . . . What's so damn funny?" he said, scratching furiously.

"You telling me I'll have to work my way up. Excuse me, but it's just totally hilarious."

"Yes," Congressman Randy said, scratching, "I suppose it is."

So several weeks later, Cass arrived in Washington, D.C., to start a new life with a new name: Cassandra Devine. When she went before the judge in Connecticut, she told him about her parents' divorce and about the episode in Bosnia and said that she just needed to "reboot my hard drive." He was sympathetic and granted the name change.

Once installed on Capitol Hill, she began where many a brilliant Washington career has been launched—answering constituent mail: "My Social Security check didn't come . . . We need a stoplight . . . The highway people say they can put the new interstate ramp through my pig farm. Raising pigs is hard enough without the federal government sticking its nose in. . . . I be writting with regards to my cusin who been in prison for allejedelly runing over the game wardin in his pickup. . . . Don't you see the Jews are taking over the country, and you're just going to *let* that happen? . . . I am asking your support for a projected 500 megavolt wind farm in the Connecitcut River Valley. . . . I read where they are thinking of closing the submarine base in Groton. Why can't we put it here? The water is plenty deep enough. . . ." The warp and woof of American representative democracy. About twenty-five pounds of it, every day, in sacks, dumped on Cass's desk.

Cass's supervisor was a fifty-something woman named Lillian with lips that never unpursed. Her response to any levity was, "I don't see what's funny about that," which had earned her the office nickname "Giggles." She required that every letter from a constituent, no matter how unhinged or idiotic, be answered within three days, ensuring that Cass's workday never ended until after eight o'clock. When Randy formally announced his Senate campaign, the volume of mail increased by two sacks, to fifty pounds per day. Cass now rarely got home until ten-thirty. At least it solved the problem of what to do about a social life. She had just enough energy left to microwave a Lean Cuisine bean burrito and read three pages of Ayn Rand before falling asleep.

One day, Cass had to take some papers over to the Senate campaign office, situated in the worst part of town, not so much to save money as to enhance Randy's image as Champion of the Downtrodden.

She saw Randy and another man in the glassed-in corner conference office. She was putting the delivery package on the desk when Randy saw her and waved her in.

"Meet Terry Tucker," he said. "Our communications evil genius. Highly overpaid evil genius."

"Hello," Cass said. Of course, she knew all about Terry Tucker. His title was communications director, but everyone seemed to take orders from him, including the chief of staff.

Terry smiled. "Ms. Cohane."

"Devine," Cass corrected him.

"In every way."

"You must be in PR."

"In every way." Terry smiled. "Pleasure. I've heard all about you. We owe you."

"What for?" Cass said.

"Our war hero here. You were present at the big bang that expanded our universe."

"You oughtn't to be *quite* so cynical," Randy said. "She's new in town, and young. She might actually have a few ideals left."

Terry said to Cass, "We were just talking about the video I'm assembling for the 'Salute to American Heroes' dinner. The congressman is being honored for his heroism." He turned to Randy. "Sorry, what was that you were saying about cynicism?"

"Wasn't *my* idea," Randy said.

"No, it was mine. That's why you overpay me."

"Good to meet you, sir," Cass said.

Five minutes later, she was waiting for the elevator when she found Terry Tucker standing beside her.

"Got lunch plans?" he said.

"I have to get back to the office."

"No, you don't."

"There's this dragon lady I report to."

"Giggles? Come on." He smiled. "You look underpaid, underfed, and overworked. I can fix the middle part."

It occurred to her, riding down in the elevator, that the last time a man had insisted that she share a meal, she'd ended up in a minefield.

Terry Tucker was in his late forties, more than twice her age. He was lean with dark hair and suspicious but not unfriendly eyes. He looked like someone who would tell you without hesitation something you didn't want to hear but couldn't disagree with. Cass had the radar of a pretty woman and could tell if someone was making a pass at her. He seemed oblivious to this aspect of her. His manner was that of an impatient older brother. *Come on.* She went.

He took her to a place on Pennsylvania Avenue named Carnivore, owned by a lawyer who had made $15 million from a class-action suit against the Salvation Army for dispensing sugar doughnuts to half a dozen diabetic disaster victims. It's a great country.

"Have the four-pound lobster," Terry said from behind a menu thick as Sheetrock and the size of an open newspaper. "It's scary."

"Four pounds? That's not a lobster, it's an ecosystem."

"The People for the Ethical Treatment of Crustaceans used to demonstrate outside the restaurant. I know the owner. He hired me to deal with it."

"What did you do?"

"Buttered them up. Literally. Announced we were feeding the leftovers to the homeless. You get a lot of leftovers from a four-pound lobster. The *Post* did a story on it. Headline was HOMELESS BUT STUFFED. With a photo. We set up a table and everything outside in the back." Terry smiled. "The lobster huggers didn't know what hit 'em. Fucking idiots."

"That's *awful*," Cass said.

"Who gets up in the morning thinking, *What can I do to help the lobsters?* Get a life." Terry shrugged. "You do what you have to. This town is an asshole-rich environment. The crab cakes are good if you don't want the lobster."

Cass ordered a salad. Terry tucked into a sirloin with zest befitting the restaurant's name.

"So here's the deal with me," he said without any prompting, and launched into an admirably condensed story of his life. When he finished, he said, "So what's your deal? Hero Boy told me your dad bailed on the Yale tuition. What a prick."

Cass put down her fork. "Excuse me. But what right do you have to call my father a prick?"

"You're right. I apologize. Let me rephrase it. What a truly wonderful human being your father is for taking your college money—*and* the mortgage on the family house—and putting it into his failing business. Give that man a Father of the Year award."

Cass shrugged. "I suppose he *is* a prick."

"Does he still have the Cessna?"

"I see Randy told you everything. I don't know. He's in California becoming someone else."

"He'll fit right in. You can be anyone you want to there, as long as you don't mind being stuck in traffic. Listen, when this campaign gets going—once it really starts, if he gets the party nomination—you know the media's going to come after you."

"For what?"

"You got into Yale. Do you need me to spell it out for you?"

"This is totally unfair."

"I'm not saying it was your fault. He told me what happened. He's a lot of things, but he's not a complete asshole. He said it was all his fault. He said, 'I feel guilty.' I said, 'You should. You totally fucked up this poor kid's life.'"

"I'm not a 'poor kid,'" Cass said.

"All right. He fucked up a wonderful young woman's life. I told him, 'Way to go. We certainly need more people like you in the Senate. People with judgment.' What is it with Massachusetts politicians, anyway? They don't do so good with women in cars."

"Do you talk to *all* your clients like that?"

Terry smiled. "Not the corporate ones. Only the personally rich ones. They can handle it. They're so used to having their asses kissed, it's almost refreshing when someone tells them the truth. But enough about me. You look like a nice kid. *Woman.* Whatever. I don't want you to get hurt."

"Is the point of this expensive lunch to get rid of me?" Cass asked.

"No," Terry said. "This was my idea. He didn't put me up to anything."

"I don't understand."

"I want you to come work for me."

"In *PR*?"

"Public relations is beneath you?"

"I didn't mean it that way."

"Yeah, you did. For starters, we don't call it PR here. 'Strategic communications.' But before you tell me to go fuck off, let me tell you how it's going to play out. The moment our hero nails the nomination and becomes a serious player—and I think he will—some media dickhead is going to do a story about how you're on his payroll. Never mind that nothing happened over there between you two—other than you both got blown up. He's got a rep as a skirt chaser, and you're a looker. I can even tell you what the line will be: 'Chappaquiddick Two—this time on dry land, and the chick lived to go on the payroll.'"

"That's ridiculous! And it's not true!"

"It's a ridiculous town." Terry shrugged. "How long do you really think you'd last once you become the story? Maybe he's basically a nice guy now. Think he'd risk his entire campaign on you? He doesn't feel *that* guilty. No politician does. They're born with Original Spin. And then what? You're on your butt on the street. You think everyone in town is going to be lining up to hire you?"

Cass stared glumly at her food.

"How was the salad?"

"Not very good, actually."

Terry smiled. "Told you to order the lobster. Think of the homeless we could have fed. Consider my offer. I've got a feeling about you."

"You don't know me."

"I know you're smart, young, and angry. Give me smart, young, and angry and I'll move the world. I was all that, too, but I'll save that story for another time. You should be angry. You've been fucked over pretty good for someone who's still a kid."

"I don't want your pity."

"Good. I'm not offering pity. You think I'm doing this because I'm a nice guy? That's a laugh. Nah. I sense you've got talent. And I'm smart about that. I can spot a protégée a mile off. I'm into the molding thing. Résumés like yours don't come along every week." He added, "And I don't hit on the help, so don't worry on that score."

"I'll think about it," Cass said, her mind reeling.

* * *

Terry drove off in his Mercedes to his world of spin. Cass caught a taxi back to Capitol Hill. On the ride up, she looked at Terry's business card. She reflected that it was the third ticket of admission she'd received in two years: the letter from Yale, the check from Randy, and now this. It was the smallest of the three, in more ways than one. From the ivory tower to Hill rat to PR chick. *There* was a death spiral for you. But then she got back to a sit-down lecture from Lillian over being late. As Lillian went on, and on, about Cass's irresponsibility, Cass found herself daydreaming about the scenario Terry had limned for her and thought that the nightmare would, in all likelihood, begin with a call from Lillian to the media dickhead: *You didn't get this from me, but she's on the payroll.* So after Lillian was finished, Cass went back to her desk, where instead of answering a letter she wrote one, to Randy, thanking him for everything and resigning. She started at Tucker Strategic Communications the next day.

Terry had been right. She had talent. Less than ten years later, she was a partner in TSC. She had a nice apartment, a German-made car in the garage, and a beach condo in Rehobeth that she never used. Terry had been right, too, about her motivation, and now she had the means to pursue her real passion: instilling in members of her generation outrage against the members of the previous one and toward a government that still, in the language of her generation, didn't "get it."

Chapter **8**

Cass sat at the long polished bird's-eye maple conference table in the conference room of Tucker Strategic Communications, trying to stay awake, a fact not lost on her boss. The third time she dozed off, she almost slumped face first into her grande latte, risking third-degree burns.

"Cass," Terry said, "why don't you bring us all up to speed on the mink ranchers?"

"Um? Hm?"

"The mink ranchers? Our new client?"

"Oh. They're . . . it's going . . . aces."

The Canadian Mink Ranchers Association had hired TSC after an antifur group smuggled a live mink into the private office bathroom of the editor of *Glam* magazine in New York. They did it over a weekend. By Monday morning, the mink was very hungry and very angry. After sinking its fangs into the editor, it went on a sanguinary rampage through the offices of *Glam*, causing an episode that still makes fashionistas shudder and twitch at the memory. The editor had to undergo a series of painful rabies shots—some mischievously suggested that it was the mink that should have been given the shots—causing her to miss Fashion Week, a disruption the effects of which were still being felt on Seventh Avenue and the world beyond months later. The first thing Terry did was to have the ranchers rename themselves the Royal Canadian Association for Humane Mink Cultivation and Conservation.

It was Cass's account. And things were, yes, more or less "on track." Normally, she'd have been up to speed, but because of yesterday's

Senate vote on raising the Social Security payroll tax, she'd been up until dawn, blogging away on CASSANDRA.

"When do we hear back from the Pleasure World people?" Terry said. Cass shot him a look that said, *You know that I have absolutely no idea, so why are you asking me in front of the entire staff?*

Pleasure World was the country's largest chain of adult (which is to say sex) accessories outlets and thus the single largest purchaser of mink used not for coats, hats, or wraps. Terry's notion was to get Pleasure World to join in a common-cause, pro-mink public service announcement.

Cass improvised. "They're kind of busy right now getting ready for their annual trade show. It's called 'Expo-sure 2011.' In Las Vegas, where else. Don't worry. I'm efforting it."

"Keep up the good efforting," Terry said.

Several of the younger male staffers unselfishly volunteered to attend Expo-sure 2011.

The meeting broke up. After the others had left, Terry said, "You were certainly at the top of your game this morning. Next time we'll videoconference you in from your bed."

Cass sighed. "I'm *on* the minks, okay?"

"No big deal. I was just under the impression that since you're a senior partner in the firm, you might be involved—even interested—in the profit-making aspect."

"I was up late. The Senate vote on Social Security. I had a zillion e-mails and postings. I think we're reaching a critical point here. I'm feeling a lot of anger out there."

"Happy to be part of your infrastructure," Terry sniffed.

"Why are you so bent out of shape? I'm the one who's being asked to pay for your retirement. The Senate voted yesterday to raise my pay-roll taxes *thirty percent*. And because they didn't want to offend the Wrinklies lobby—God forbid Boomers should have to pay their fair share—they only raised it on everyone under thirty-five years of age. So *you* can retire at sixty-two."

"Fuck the minks. Vicious little bastards. Look, I was just yanking your chain back there. I know you've been working hard. You've been working too hard. Come on. I want you to go home right now, throw a few things in a bag, and go to that resort in the Bahamas. It's an order."

"Can't. Too much going on. I'm calling for demonstrations."

"What do you mean?"

"Demonstrations. Come on, gramps, you remember the sixties. A protest. The time has come. Yesterday's vote in the Senate proved that. I'm calling for an economic Bastille Day."

A look of incomprehension and alarm played across Terry's face, like that of a ship captain upon being informed that a giant squid had just engaged in battle with the propeller—and was winning.

"Cass," he said calmly, "let me explain. This is a *public relations* firm. We're in the business of . . . we apply fig leaves. We spread calm where there is uncalm. If there is noise, we apply silence. We make things *better*. At the very least, we seek to make things *seem* better. See where I'm taking this? Do you think that our clients come to us for help because on the side we urge people to—rise up against the United States government? Let me answer that. No. That is not what we do at Tucker Strategic Communications."

"Cassandra has nothing to do with TSC."

Terry said, "You've been reading Ann Rand again. I can tell."

"*Ayn* Rand. And what's wrong with that?"

"Nothing. Except every time I see one of that nutty broad's books open on your desk, you start acting like some fruitcake messiah."

"Who was it who told me, a long time ago, 'Anger is the best motivator'? Wasn't it your generation that started the whole youth movement thing? Come on, Terry. Forgotten what it's like to be young and angry?"

Terry shrugged. "I'm middle-aged and angry. With good Scotch, I can deal with the anger."

"So we've gone from 'Don't trust anyone over thirty' to 'Don't drink any Scotch under thirty'? Is this what's become of your revolution?"

"The anthems from my revolution are now background music in TV commercials for cholesterol pills, onboard navigation systems for gas-guzzling SUVs, and hedge funds. Everyone sells out. Boomers just figured out how to make it an industry."

"Well, *there's* something to make you feel good in the autumn of your life. In your gated community golf courses. While my generation, in the spring of our lives, are forking over half our paychecks to pay for your meds and martinis."

"I don't even play golf. All right. Fine. You save the world. I'll deal with the fucking minks."

Terry stormed off. He pushed an Aeron chair out of his way; it slid across the conference room and slammed fecklessly into the credenza where he kept his "Spinnies," the Oscar statuettes given by the American Academy of Public Relations.

Cass thought, *Uh-oh. Dad's mad.* But there was work to do.

It was at 4:02 a.m. the following morning that the idea came to her.

She'd had little sleep, a lot of NoDoz, and way too many Red Bulls. In a calmer, sunlit hour of the day, she might not have written what she did. But the day had been a trying one. A few hours after her head butting with Terry, she read on the Internet that her father, now hugely wealthy from yet another California high-tech start-up, had just donated $10 million to Yale University.

She was no longer on speaking terms with him, and she didn't want to upset her mother, who was not all that well. She called her brother, who was in some sort of touch with their father. His report did not improve Cass's mood. Lisa, the current Mrs. Frank Cohane, had a son by a previous marriage. He was now seventeen and applying, as it happened, to Yale. As her brother relayed all this, Cass remembered her father telling her years ago, "I'll buy Yale University a whole new football stadium!"

Cass hung up the phone in a daze. No doubt this unhappy episode contributed to the 4:02 a.m. posting on CASSANDRA calling for "actions against gated communities known to harbor early-retiring Boomers."

"Turn on CNN," Terry said when she arrived at work just before noon, tired, but a good tired.

"Why? What's up?"

"Oh, nothing. Riots on golf courses in Florida. You know, the usual youth movement thing."

Suddenly awake, Cass went to her office, flicked on the TV, and watched. She slumped in her chair. There's a difference between typing on a computer all alone at four in the morning with your veins pulsing with amphetamine courage, calling for insurrection, and watching the results on TV at noon in your office on K Street. Terry buzzed her on the intercom.

"Turn on Fox News. You just missed a great helicopter shot of some kid chucking a Molotov cocktail at a police riot vehicle. They just turned the water cannon on him. He's down. . . . *Oooo. Ouch.* That boy's not throwing anything more anytime soon. Those Florida troopers, they do *not* mess around. By the way, you'll be pleased to hear that the governor is considering calling in the National Guard— Excuse me. That's my phone. It's probably our most lucrative client, calling to cancel their account. Call you right back."

Cass watched numbly. She saw the words *"Boomsday Rage"* appear at the bottom of the CNN screen; felt a rumbling in her tummy. The phones began to ring. They didn't stop.

She was on the phone with a producer for one of the networks when her secretary buzzed to say that "two men from the FBI are here to see you." Terry, already alert, buzzed her and told her under no circumstances to say anything until his lawyer arrived.

As she gathered her thoughts, Cass reflected that there was probably no better place than here to face the storm. As Terry liked (privately) to say, "Disasters R Us."

She was in the middle of not answering the third or perhaps fourth question put to her by the two extremely unsmiling FBI agents when Terry walked into her office. The agents asked him to leave; he told them politely it was his firm and if they didn't like his company, *they* could leave. Or they could remain and meet Allen Snyder, Esquire. *The* Allen Snyder. Of Hogan and Hartson. The name was familiar? Surely? Friend of the director of the FBI? Well, ha, friend of everyone. The Man to See. Rumored to be on the short list for the U.S. Court of Appeals for the Dist—

"Okay, Mr. Tucker," said one of the agents wearily. "We get it. Mr. Snyder is an eminent personage."

The four of them sat around in awkward silence ("Would you two like some coffee?" "No, thank you." "Water?" "No . . ."), waiting for the great man's arrival, which came twenty minutes or so later, to the vast relief of everyone—especially Cass, who was trying not to hyperventilate. How embarrassing is that—passing out in front of your boss and the FBI?

No one likes lawyers until you need one, at which point they assume the raiment of knights. Despite their impatience with Terry's trumpet fanfare buildup, the agents instinctively recognized that they were now dealing with a lion of the bar. For his part, Mr. Snyder was gentle, courtly, soft-spoken, and professional. There was no "As I said to your boss last night while we were skinny-dipping in the White House pool with the president and the chief justice of the Supreme Court" or any of the usual Washington chest thumping and pecker flexing. Straight to the point, barely above a whisper: "So, gentlemen, how can we resolve the situation?" *Brilliant,* Cass thought, *the way he embeds optimism in the very gambit.* It was simply a "situation" in need of "resolve." Nothing so serious as, say, felonious incitement to violence against persons and property. Nothing of the sort.

One of the agents handed Mr. Snyder a printout of Cass's increasingly legendary 4:02 a.m. blog posting, explicitly inciting the furious disenfranchised youth of America to visit violence upon the nation's . . . golf courses. Well, Mr. Snyder said, that's certainly very interesting, and we'll all want to take a closer look, but it has hardly been established that Ms. Devine wrote this. He was no computer expert, but it seemed to him that anyone with rudimentary knowledge of the Internet could hack into a mainframe and send out postings under his client's name. And even so, under the various statutes of the law, it was very far from clear, from the wording of the posting, that the person who actually wrote it was specifically urging acts of violence. "Actions" here could be understood to mean, well, a number of things, including *peaceful* demonstrations. Protected constitutionally under the First Amendment to the Constitution, providing for rights of assembly.

The agents had no ready reply to this inpenetrable fog-bank of legalism. Cass started to say something, but Terry shot her a glance that said, *This is costing me $700 an hour—shut up.*

The agents, perhaps concluding that they were for the time being outgunned and needed to return to the J. Edgar Hoover Building in order to get bigger ones, gave their cards to Mr. Snyder and, with pointed sidelong glances at his somewhat trembly client, stated firmly that she should not leave the city limits of Washington, D.C., until their investigation was completed.

They were almost out the door when the client said, "No, wait." All heads turned. She said, "Mr. Snyder, thank you. That was really, really great, and I really, really appreciate it. But the fact is, I wrote the posting. I did urge people to, you know, sort of . . . rise up. I am sorry about the Molotov cocktail. I didn't ask them to do that. I mean, specifically. . . ."

Washington legal lore has it that it was the only time Allen Snyder, quintessence of legal probity and cool, ever groaned audibly. Terry was merely speechless.

As the agents led Cass away, she found herself thinking, *So this is what handcuffs feel like.* Funny what comes to mind in such moments. Fortunately, there were no clients in the reception area.

Chapter 9

Cass's arrest for "felonious incitement to cause damage to persons and property" had the effect she was counting on: celebrity. But with an agenda. A culture polysaturated with Paris Hilton, Britney Spears, and Lindsay Lohan craves the occasional serving of protein. This Cassandra provided. She was young, she was pretty, she was blond, she had something to say, and it had nothing to do with launching a new fragrance or singing career. By the time Allen Snyder had gotten her out on bail, she was in all the news broadcasts and on the front pages of most of the country's newspapers. Headlines ranged from the sober:

Blogger Who Called For Social Security Protest "Actions" Is Arrested by FBI

to the not:

"BOOMSDAY" CHICK TO FEDS: TAX *THIS*!

Her apartment was staked out by the media, as was, to Terry's nondelight, the K Street entrance to the offices of Tucker Strategic Communications.

"Well," he said over the phone in the resigned yet hopeful manner of his breed, the PR operative who knows that not every disaster can be made to seem a misunderstood victory, "maybe they'll think it's something to do with the neighbors." He meant the Society for the Relocation and Assistance of Displaced Muslim Persons one floor down: the CIA unit in charge of "renditions" of suspected Islamic terrorists, whom they grabbed off the streets, tossed into the back of Gulfstream jets, and whisked off to countries where "interrogation" was still an honorable and competitive profession. The society's actual function had been revealed by *The New York Times* a month earlier. But, alas, the media were here for Cassandra, not them.

"You might as well hang out at my place until we figure out the next step," Terry said. "Allen's kind of confused at this point. He's generally more used to clients who are trying to stay *out* of jail."

"I know," Cass said. "I'm really sorry. But I can't urge the people to rise up and then hide behind lawyers."

" 'The people'? You going Commie on me?"

"*No, Terry.*"

"It's that damn Rand broad. Did you see the *Times* today? That's what they called you: 'Ayn Rand of the Blogosphere.' Oh, Jesus, there's another camera truck pulling up. There's gotta be fifty people out front. Wonderful publicity for the firm. Wonderful."

"Why don't you have the mink ranchers send over some minks and unleash them."

"Not a bad idea. I'll see you later. Try not to pour any more gasoline on the fire until I get home. . . . Cassandra? . . . Hello? You listening?"

She returned to her battle station at the computer. CASSANDRA's mainframe server in Columbus, Ohio, was overwhelmed. They'd had to switch over to higher-capacity servers. When CASSANDRA came back online, Cass saw that she had 2.6 million e-mails awaiting her. The thought of reading them made her suddenly feel very tired.

Her cell phone began to chirrup with calls from bookers for the TV shows. Allen had begged her—instructed her, actually—to refrain from public comment. But she found herself saying yes to the network news, yes to *The NewsHour with Jim Lehrer,* yes to *Hardball* with Chris Matthews. Yes, yes, yes to everyone—a regular Molly Bloom.

What's the point of starting a revolution, she thought, *if you're going to dodge the spotlight?*

When Terry arrived home, exhausted and annoyed after having to use the Dumpster exit of his office building, he called out to her.

No answer. He found the note, taped to the refrigerator: "TURN ON TV. LOVE, C. P.S. Sorry (I know I keep saying that)."

Terry poured himself a large snifter of his thirty-year-old Scotch, girded his loins, and turned on the TV. He recited his mantra from Dorothy Parker: "What fresh hell is this?" The world would always provide.

"It is quiet, finally, in Florida tonight, following twenty-four hours of mayhem and protest at several golf communities. The incidents were sparked when this woman, twenty-nine-year-old Cassandra Devine, a Washington-based public relations executive . . ."

Terry let out a low moan. But at least they hadn't mentioned the name.

". . . urged young people who are angry about the recent Senate vote to raise Social Security payroll taxes to take, quote, actions. The FBI arrested Devine, and we hear tonight that she will be formally charged with incitement to commit violence. I spoke to her earlier today. . . .

"Ms. Devine, did you in fact urge people to commit violence?"

"Not explicitly, but in effect, yes. I won't hide behind legalistic terms. Sure I was inciting them. And tonight, Brian, I'm urging young people in the United States to protest the hopeless fiscal irresponsibility of the United States government. That Senate vote was an abomination. It was a vote to take food off my generation's table in order to feather the nests of aging, self-indulgent, pampered Baby Boomers. What I'm saying is we're not going to sit still while they bankrupt us."

"But don't Americans have the opportunity to protest the government at the polls, on election day?"

"Theoretically, yeah. But you don't *get* real change until you make a loud noise. Until you sit down in the middle of the street and block traffic. You wouldn't have had the Civil Rights Act of 1964 without the protest marches. You wouldn't have had a women's movement without those protests. We wouldn't have gotten out of Vietnam without the demonstrations. And we aren't going to get the Congress to act responsibly, to stop piling up endless debt and entitlements and passing it all on to the next generation, without a little dancin' in the street."

"What are you specifically calling for?"

"I'm calling on every member of my generation to take their iPods out of their ears and send the U.S. government a message. Not a text message, either. It's simple. If the government can withhold our money, then *we* can withhold our money."

"By that you mean—"

"A tax revolt, Brian. I'm calling on members of my generation to stop paying taxes."

Terry reached her on her cell phone as she was shuttling to her next TV appearance, in the back of a town car.

"I know, I know," she said. "Sorry."

"Damn fine job, Bob." It was a line Terry used around the office when particularly displeased by someone's work. They were the words uttered by the captain of a supertanker after regaining the bridge only to find that his inebriated third mate, a man named Bob, had run it up on a reef, spilling one hundred thousand barrels of crude oil into a fragile ecosystem, resulting in the extinction of several rare species and $10 billion in lawsuits.

"Allen called," Terry said. "Your lawyer. The one who told you not to talk to the press? He's looking up the actual statute. Something to do with advocating overthrow of the U.S. government. He said he'll have it by morning. At your arraignment. Oh, and your mom called. She tried you, but your cell phone was off. I told her you were in a TV studio hammering nails into your coffin. She too is thrilled at the prospect of your spending your adult life in prison. So, what act of self-destruction do you have planned next? It's only seven. You ought to be able to fit three or four more career-ending moments in time to make the eleven o'clock news."

"Keep your TV on. . . . What's that?"

"I'm filling my glass with more Scotch. To the brim. Maybe I'll mix it with sleeping pills. That works, doesn't it?"

"Save some for me."

"What do you know. This Scotch, it's older than you."

Cassandra's arraignment the next day at the United States Courthouse drew a big media crowd. As Terry said to her once they'd made it inside, "When it comes to getting your message out there, there's really nothing like being formally charged with attempting to overthrow the government."

The valiant but peeved Allen Snyder explained to Cassandra that normally they would have prosecuted her only for counseling people to violate the tax laws (26 U.S.C. section 7206). But because of the increasingly dire situation—the stock market had lost a thousand points in one week; the dollar had lost 15 percent against the euro—the government was in a sour and paranoid mood. The decision had been made to throw the proverbial book at her and to charge her under 18 U.S.C. section 2385 ("Advocating Overthrow of Government").

The U.S. attorney told the judge that Cass should be held in custody as a flight risk. Attorney Snyder did not put up much of a counterargument.

"Aren't you going to say something to the judge?" she said.

"To be honest with you," Snyder whispered, "I think I'd rather you were somewhere you didn't have access to a microphone."

"What is this, a time-out?"

Thus Cassandra found herself exchanging her K Street suit for an orange jumpsuit and shackles. As she was helped into the prisoner transport van, she gave the photographers a V-for-victory sign. The shackles kept her hands at waist level. One reporter noted that her hands "looked like two chained birds attempting to take flight." The gesture appeared on the cover of the next week's Time with the cover line "She's Not Gonna Take It!"

On Cassandra's first night in detention, four dozen gated Boomer retirement communities around the country were attacked by youth mobs, causing various state governors to have to call out the National Guard. As National Guard units were now massively deployed around the world—in Iraq, Iran, Syria, Bosnia, Bolivia, Quebec, Nagorno-Karabakh, and the Comoro Islands—the incidents caused a tremendous strain, along with renewed calls for bringing the troops home.

"This Boomsday business," the White House chief of staff said to the president, "is getting out of hand, don't you think?"

Allen Snyder visited Cassandra at the Alexandria Detention Center, along with Terry.

"I've got some good news for you," he said. "Some very good news. They're prepared to drop the overthrow-the-government charge. And they'll consider reducing the advocating-tax-revolt charge. Provided you cease and desist. They're asking us—you—to sign a statement saying that you didn't realize that what you were advocating was in violation of federal law."

"That's all?"

"No. You're being sued by the owners of the gated retirement communities that were assaulted. Willful incitement to destroy property. So far it comes to a hundred and fifty million in damages. Most of it for repairing the golf greens."

"Solidarity's revolt began in a Gdansk shipyard," Cass said. "This one seems to be teeing off from a golf course."

"I'd seriously consider taking the government up on their offer. They're nervous right now. They've got better things to do. If we say no at this point, they could very well dig in their heels. Once they do that . . . You must understand this is a very serious charge, overthrowing the government. Technically it's a capital offense. They wouldn't try for the death penalty. But they might go for the maximum sentence."

"Which would be . . . ?"

"Life without parole."

"Um," Cassandra said. "Not optimal."

Terry said, "Look, kiddo, you made the cover of *Time*. Let's declare victory and take the rest of the week off."

"That's not why I'm doing this. *Kiddo*."

"You want to spend the rest of your life here? Wearing orange?"

"No. But I have to spend the rest of my life with myself one way or the other, and I'd rather not spend it detesting myself for going back on what I believe in."

Terry had spent more time wading through swampy bottomland than standing tall on the moral high ground. He made a despairing grunt.

"Sorry," she said.

"Would you stop saying that?" Terry said. He looked completely helpless.

She smiled at him. "Smuggle me in some Scotch? The stuff they serve in here can't be even thirty days old."

Chapter 10

It had been a few months since Terry had spoken with Senator Randolph K. Jepperson of the great state of Massachusetts.

Randy had been disappointed in his first attempt to win a Senate seat, the year after the incident in Bosnia. Terry's herculean efforts to make him into an icon of American heroism had largely succeeded, and going into the final weeks of the campaign, Randy held a small lead in the polls.

Cass, working for Terry on other client accounts, had declined all press queries pertaining to the Bosnian misadventure. But the pilot of the army Blackhawk helicopter that had plucked them from the minefield did offer a comment when a reporter finally tracked him down. He had retired from the army and was thus no longer restrained by military discipline and discretion. "I never did understand," he said, "what that gold-plated imbecile was doing driving a vehicle in the middle of a f——— minefield."

"Gold-plated imbecile" is not a term one wants applied to oneself in the final days of a fiercely contested political race, especially coming from the lips of a decorated former U.S. military officer. His opponent plastered it on every bumper sticker, website, TV commercial, and leaflet. Randy lost by seven thousand votes.

People around Randolph K. Jepperson remarked on the change that came over him. He went into what is usually called "seclusion," with no movie-star girlfriend or ex-rocker's wife. When he emerged, he had a look in his eyes that one staffer called "kinda spooky."

On his first day back in Congress, he fired everyone in his office, including Lillian, who for once was correct in not finding any humor in the situation. He replaced his loyal staff with the equivalent of Capitol Hill mercenaries. He lured away seasoned pros from other congressional offices, paying above-standard salaries. He hired expensive lobbyists and operatives from K Street; trade association sharks and hired guns; legislative dogs of war. By the time the restaffing was complete, his House colleagues were referring to his office as "the Death Star."

When Randy called Terry several weeks after his defeat, Terry assumed it was to fire him, too. But instead he told him, in a voice that Terry also thought kinda spooky, "Next time, we win. Whatever. It. Takes."

A year later, Randy's mother, last empress of the Jepperson dynasty, passed away after choking to death on a hairball from one of her eight Pomeranians. The butler was either unskilled at the Heimlich maneuver or—some said—had let nature take its course.

The governor issued a proclamation. The funeral was a state occasion. Throughout the service, Randy stared at the casket with what some found an inappropriate look.

"Did you see his expression," said Mrs. Gardner Peabody Cabot at the reception afterward, "while he was tossing in the first spadeful of earth?"

"And the way he kept *on* shoveling," said Mrs. Templeton Lowell Scrodworthy.

It was just as well no one knew that Terry Tucker had had to talk Randy into attending.

"Put it this way," he told his client. "How many questions do you want, next time you run, about why you didn't attend your own mother's funeral? What are we going to say? That you couldn't miss the vote on extending the debt ceiling?"

Four years later, Randy ran again for the Senate, this time against the venerable senator Bascombe Smithers. "BS," as he was called, was an affable if somewhat pointless senior statesman then serving his sixth term in the Senate and happy to serve a seventh "if the good people of this great commonwealth still want me." He had never said an ill word of anyone (or gotten much accomplished by way of legislation) and was generally beloved by his colleagues for being one of the last of his breed to put aside partisan politics at six sharp every evening and pour the bourbon freely while reminiscing about the days when, as majority leader, Lyndon Johnson would pinch the behinds of the Senate elevator operators. In today's hyperpartisan atmosphere, such bonding protocols have gone by the wayside, along with pinching the behinds of comely female elevator operators. The bottoms of Senate pages are still available.

Randy painted a target on Bascombe Smithers's chest, turned to his campaign operatives, and said, "Commence firing. Fire at will."

Randy's people painted BS as a feckless drunk, tool of special interests, groper of underage women, comforter of terrorists, vile slaughterer of helpless animals (he went on the occasional pheasant hunt), and receiver of stolen property (someone on his staff had bought on eBay a vintage baseball card whose ownership was contested); in the narrative of Randy's campaign, good old Senator BS deserved not only to lose for these odious crimes against humanity, but also to be dragged from the Capitol building and strung up from the tallest tree, his body left as carrion for crows.

Randy won by two thousand votes, having spent over $46 million of his dear departed mother's inheritance. (It worked out to $79 per vote.) His acceptance speech on the night of his election put one pundit in mind of "Mussolini addressing a crowd from a balcony on Beacon Hill."

"I take it," Senator Randy said before Terry had sat down, "that this concerns our mutual friend. She looked a bit peaked on the television, but then I suppose the prospect of prison will do that to a person. Build yourself a drink from the bar. So, just *how* may I render assistance?"

"You're on the Judiciary Committee," Terry said, leaving the rest for the senator to fill in. *So—call the fucking Attorney General.*

"Ah. You want me to . . . intervene?" He said the word as if holding it with tongs.

"Yes, Randy."

Randy sat back, lifted his artificial leg, and rested it on a leather ottoman kept for that very purpose.

"It's not as though I don't have some history with the lady. I did try to do the decent thing back then."

"After driving her into a minefield?"

The kinda spooky look came into Randy's eyes. "I paid a price for that myself."

"Yeah. And now you're in the Senate and she's in jail, looking at life without parole."

"Which I regret, but I hardly put her there."

"But you *can* get her out."

"Even if I wanted to, I couldn't. Look here, old bean, I'm on thin ice as it is. I'm the most detested member of the United States Senate, according to *Washingtonian* magazine. They put it on the cover: THE MOST HATED MAN ON CAPITOL HILL. You know what I say to that? *Oderint dum metuant.*"

"You're going to have to translate that for me. I didn't go to Gratin."

"It's Groton. Means 'Let them hate, so long as they fear.' Cato. *Quite* one of my favorite sayings. Do you know where I first saw it? On a needlepoint pillow. In my mother's parlor."

"Fascinating. You're missing the big picture."

"*Moi?*"

"This kid's your ticket to the top."

Randy leaned back in his chair. "And just how do you figure that?"

"Take a look." Terry took out his laptop. He and Randy pored through charts of polling data. "Look at those figures for the eighteen to thirty age group," Terry said. "I've never seen them this solid. Sixty-five to *eighty* percent. This is going to be the hot-button issue in the next presidential race. Assuming this yo-yo in the White House doesn't get us into another war." The United States was currently engaged in six wars. The military was stretched to such a point that it was now safe for countries to *invite* the United States

to attack them. The latest humiliation was Bolivia's unilateral declaration of war.

Randy puffed out his cheeks contemplatively. "If I were to per-
form this . . . act of mercy, there would hardly be any point in doing it
quietly."

Terry closed his laptop and grinned. "You know what I like about
you, Senator?"

"My checkbook?"

"No. With most clients, I have to explain. Never with you."

"That's"—Senator Randy smiled—"because I went to Gratin. You
do understand that we could all go down in flames if this thing turns
on us? But I do believe it would be the most *gorgeous* fire."

The next day, on the floor of the U.S. Senate with three other senators
present, one of them asleep and the other two twiddling with their
BlackBerrys, Randolph K. Jepperson stood at his desk and in his best
senatorial voice said, "Mr. President, I rise to protest an outrageous
wrong, perpetuated upon our children, and our children's children,
from this very chamber, in the heart of what was once a country with
a heart. . . ."

Terry didn't want to be observed sitting in the Senate gallery, so he
watched his words being uttered on TV, back at the office.

One of his friends, a lobbyist for the insecticide industry, called. "I'm
watching your boy He's-No-Jefferson on C-SPAN yapping about some
Social Security 'reparations' bill he's sponsoring? What's that about?"

"Some notion he's got," Terry said matter-of-factly. "I like it. Idea
is that kids are getting fucked on Social Security, so he's proposing a
moratorium. No one under thirty has to pay in. The second part is
Congress has to permanently fix the system, make it solvent, make it
pay for itself, instead of this fucking Ponzi scheme we've got, where the
debt just gets handed on to the next generation. If Congress doesn't,
then the moratorium continues. I like it. And I think it's going to be
hotter than a chili pepper in the presidential."

"Oh, sure," his friend snorted, "that's got a *real* good chance."

"It's the fate of many propositions," Terry said, "to begin as heresies and end as truths. I read that somewhere, anyway."

"Yeah, well, you send me a postcard when it becomes a truth. Say, listen, we gotta do a PSA on this mesothamalide-7 thing because we're getting clobbered by the fucking bird huggers."

"I told you," Terry said, "you gotta rename that shit. It sounds like something they use in concentration camps. Call it . . . I don't know, something like poly . . . poly-pepto . . . perfumo-honeysuckle-number nine. Something harmless. Look up what they put in ice cream and call it that."

"It's *chemicals,* Terry. We can't rename chemicals."

"Then brand it. Call it 'Bug-Away' or 'Bug-a-Boo' or—I got it—'Bug-a-Bye.' Something cute. I gotta go, Larry. My guy's on the floor here, making a major policy statement. Doesn't happen every day. Call you later."

Randy's speech might as well have been a pebble dropped into the middle of the Atlantic Ocean for all the coverage it got. But it set the stage for what Terry called "the gathering storm."

The next day, Randy showed up outside the Alexandria Detention Center and held an "impromptu" press conference—prearranged by Terry—in which he called on the government to release Cassandra Devine, pending her trial.

"The whole world is watching," he intoned gravely. It was a bit of an exaggeration. But a lot of people had gathered outside the detention center, several hundred of Cass's supporters. One person who *was* watching on TV was Bucky Trumble, chief political counselor to the president of the United States, and he was having a bad day. The secretary of the Treasury had just informed him that the Bank of China had declined the new issue of U.S. Treasury bills.

Seeing Randy on CNN, wagging his finger in the general direction of the White House, he thought, *What the hell is he doing getting involved in this?*

Chapter 11

Randy's speech, delivered outside the detention center, was a reprise of his Senate speech the day before, only, as one pundit observed, "smothered in hot sauce." The crowd cheered and roared, made V-signs, and shouted for Cass to be released. Even Terry was impressed, and those of the PR persuasion are not, easily.

"I thought you were going to take off your leg and shake it at the feds," he said when they were back in the van that served as the mobile headquarters for the Free Cassandra campaign.

"You know," Randy said, swigging bottled water like a prizefighter between rounds, "the thought actually crossed my mind."

"Do me a favor and don't, if it crosses again. You're doing just fine. I wonder if she was watching."

On the other side of the walls of the detention center, Cass was playing hearts with a reporter for *The New York Times*. The reporter was a fellow inmate. There were quite a few reporters "on the inside" these days, so many of them that they'd formed their own prison gang. They called themselves "Pulitzer Nation" and sported henna tattoos and do-rags made from expensive hosiery. Cass's card-playing partner was a *Times* reporter who had revealed in her "Letter from Washington" that the CIA had planted a chef inside the French embassy in Washington—no mean feat—who was putting edible listening devices in the *torchons de foie gras* at state dinners. She was refusing to reveal her source.

"Yo, bitch, Devine," shouted one of the reporter's colleagues, an op-ed columnist who had declined to testify before a grand jury that had been impaneled twenty years ago to investigate whether a member of the cabinet (now deceased) had asked a waitress (now living in Argentina) at a restaurant (defunct) for her phone number (since disconnected). "Check it *out*."

She pointed to the TV monitor bolted to the wall of the so-called playroom. Cass looked up. There was Senator Randolph K. Jepperson, giving a speech to a crowd holding up signs with her name.

"Looks like someone's got herself a white knight on the outside," said the op-ed columnist. "Isn't he the one you did whuppety-do with back in Bosnia?"

"Define whuppety-do," said Cass.

"He just called you the conscience of your generation."

"Damnit girl, *knew* you had the queen."

"Wish someone would call *me* the conscience of my generation," said a society reporter for *The Washington Post* who was serving three-to-five for not revealing her source. "You sleep with him?"

"Please. What a question."

"Prisoners are supposed to share confidences. We're all in here together."

"No. I didn't. But the earth did move."

"He's cute—in a scary sort of way. Didn't he date what's-er-name, the Tegucigalpa Tamale?"

Cass watched Randy on TV as she shuffled the deck. Had to be Terry's handiwork.

By nightfall, the footage of Randy's speech had caused the crowd to swell to thousands. Terry orchestrated the chanting from the van by radio.

"Just like the sixties," he said, looking out the van's one-way windows, "only cleaner. Where are you going?" he said to Randy, who was opening the door.

"To mingle," he said, "with my people."

"Don't get yourself overexposed."

"Overexposed?" Randy chuckled. "Don't know the meaning of the word."

The moment Randy emerged from the van, he was swallowed up in an admiring scrum of twenty-somethings carrying signs.

FREE CASS!

HELL, NO, WE WON'T PAY!

BOOMSDAY NOW!

CASS WAS RIGHT!

IT'S THE DEFICIT, STUPID!

SOCIAL SECURITY = DEATH

Terry watched him get swallowed up in the throng until he was only a head illuminated by bright TV lights. There were three TV monitors inside the van, so he could watch him be interviewed live.

A reporter from the Fox network thrust a microphone at Randy.

"Senator, one of your colleagues, Senator Meltinghausen, says you're a, quote, craven opportunist. Isn't that harsh language for such a normally collegial body like the Senate?"

"I don't know about craven." Randy smiled. "Certainly I crave justice. And if by 'opportunist,' my very good friend from the great state of Virginia means that I believe in seizing every opportunity to repair our broken government, then yes, put me down as an opportunist. By all means. But the important thing here, Chris—if I may—is to . . ."

Terry sat back with the satisfaction of a mentor who has seen a pupil come fully into his own. Always a bittersweet feeling. He reminded himself sternly that this was no time for nostalgia or its evil stepsister, complacency. If anything, it was the moment of maximum danger, the moment when the client thinks *he can do it all by himself.* Washington was littered with the bleached bones of many who had succumbed to that form of hubris.

"What are you saying? We just let her go?"

President Riley Peacham was in no good temper. The economic

situation had the government in crisis mode. No one was getting much sleep. "It'll look like we're caving."

"We *are* caving," said his chief political counselor, Bucky Trumble. "That's exactly what we're doing."

The president stared expressionlessly across the expanse of his desk, made from recovered planks from the USS *Maine,* sunk in Havana harbor. In retrospect, it was perhaps an inapt desk to have chosen from the government's attic.

"What am I missing here?" he said.

"The e-mail is running nine to one against us on this."

"She's advising people not to pay their taxes. For God's sake. We're having enough trouble raising revenue as it is."

Bucky Trumble explained that the attorney general was not confident of convicting Cass in the event she mounted a vigorous defense on First Amendment grounds.

"Then how will it look? We'll have invested our prestige—what's left of it—on throwing the book at some twenty-something blogger chick. Who'll probably walk out of court giving us the finger. Ask yourself, Do you really want that douchebag Randy Jepperson in our face? I'd rather eat caterpillars off a hot sidewalk. Now look at him— Pied Piper to the just-out-of-diapers generation. He's milking this thing like a Jersey cow. His PR guy, Tucker, has his fingerprints all over the udder. The girl, Devine—she works for him. This thing's more incestuous than an Arkansas family reunion. I say get out the ten-foot pole and don't touch it. We're going to have a hard enough reelection campaign as it is."

"What's motivating this woman? Why's she got her panties in such a damn knot, anyway?"

"She was the one who was with Jepperson in Bosnia when he lost his leg. I talked to someone in the Joint Chiefs shop. Word is they were doing it in a Humvee in the middle of a minefield. She took an early discharge rather than a court-martial."

"Women in uniform," the president snorted. "God save us."

"Well, now she's *out* of uniform and raising hell. So. What do you want to do? Make a martyr out of her?"

The president hesitated, to give the impression that he hadn't yet made up his mind.

"All right," he finally said, affecting a Solomonic aura. "Tell Killebrew to make it go away."

"Good call, chief." Bucky Trumble always complimented the president for taking his advice.

Early the next evening, after a terse nolle prosequi—Latin for "We think we'd lose the case, so we're dropping it"—announcement from the Justice Department at four forty-five p.m., Cass was released from detention. A thousand people cheered her with V-signs as she drove off. Pulitzer Nation gave her a going-away do-rag from Victoria's Secret.

"Should we try to lose them?" Cass said. They were being followed by at least four, possibly more, cars full of news photographers. She'd just gotten off the phone with her weepy mother.

"Ix-nay," Terry said. "Just what we need, a high-speed car chase. We'll do an availability when we get to Randy's. They'll go away after that. I think."

"Why do we have to go to Randy's? I want to go home."

"Because he wants us to. And because he's the reason your ass is not still back there."

"You had to involve him?"

Terry rolled his eyes. "He's a United States senator. If you've got any others willing to stand up and shout on your behalf, by all means send 'em to me."

"Now I owe him."

"Count your blessings, Miss Life Without Parole. And smile for the cameras. Say a few words. We're looking for a twenty-second bite on how good it is to be out, how good it is your message is getting out—"

"Are you telling me how to do a press availability?"

"Your lawyer, a decent guy, by the way, is on Prozac because of you. I'll be standing behind you with a gun pointed at your back. So stick with the script."

"I have friends in the Pulitzer Nation."

Randy lived in a large Federal-style mansion in Georgetown that in its day had been home to a future president of the United States, two distinguished ambassadors, Theodore Roosevelt's secretary of state, and a famous Georgetown hostess who conducted simultaneous affairs with a king of England, the Count of Paris, Haile Selassie, and Josephine Baker. She died, it was said, of exhaustion.

Randy greeted Cass and Terry on the front steps. There was already a horde of media gathered around, a mounted policeman to keep order.

"I'm not going to kiss him," Cass said to Terry in the car before getting out.

"No one is *asking* you to kiss him."

Randy extended a hand. She shook it, formally.

"I'd like to make a brief statement," Randy said. "First, I want to welcome Ms. Devine back to freedom." There was applause from the well-wishers. "Second, I'd like to congratulate her for her sacrifice on behalf of what she believes in and stands for. Third, I would like to congratulate the president of the United States for doing the right thing. For once." Laughter, applause. "Fourth and lastly, I'd like to say that I'm proud to be a foot soldier in this woman's army. And I look forward to being at her side in the battles to come." Applause.

Cass looked at him. He looked older than the young congressman she'd met at the airport at Turdje years ago. She had no idea where all this was going, and a thousand misgivings about him, yet she found herself oddly glad to have him at her side.

Chapter 12

Randy, Terry, and Cass plunged in. They formed a grassroots coalition, always a good thing to have. They also formed a political action committee and a 527, another good thing to have, since it gives the impression that everyone is behaving legally in the matter of raising soft money. Evincing sincerity while raising "hard money" is harder.

Cass went on TV and wrote endless thoughtful op-ed pieces and gave a blizzard of speeches to any group that would listen. Randy made thunderous orations from the Senate floor, usually to empty seats. In time the media, as is their wont, moved on.

One day, a month after her release from jail, Cass said to Terry, "Is it me, or do I sense a certain . . . ennui out there?"

"I wouldn't call it ennui," Terry said. "I'd call it boredom. Social Security reform, entitlement reform, deficits—face it, it's dry stuff. The beast is averse to dry stuff. It needs red meat. Pictures, not charts showing 'out-year revenue shortfalls.' It was more interesting when the people—as you like to call them—were ripping up golf courses and chucking Molotov cocktails at the cops. Speaking of which, Allen called. You're being sued by another gated community. It's called Pine Haven."

Cass looked depressed.

"Don't be too hard on yourself," Terry said. "You gave it a good shot. A great shot. You moved it right to the top of the agenda there for a bit. And now, kiddo, it's *time to move on*. I need your help on the insecticide account. Larry's driving me nuts."

*   *   *

Bucky Trumble was one of very few White House staffers who had "walk-in" privileges in the Oval Office. He did, however, knock before walking in.

"What is it, Bucky?" the president said suspiciously. He didn't much like the look on Trumble's face, which resembled a fallen soufflé.

Trumble took a deep breath. "Cass Devine is Frank Cohane's daughter."

The president's face went the color of New England clam chowder. "What are you telling me?"

"Just that. Devine isn't a married name. She had her name legally changed. She and Frank apparently had some falling-out. She took her mother's name."

"Oh, god*damnit.*"

"Yes." Bucky waited for the explosion he knew was coming. Sometimes it took a while to build, like a volcano.

"Jesus fucking Christ in the . . . ," the president spluttered, his face now the color of Manhattan clam chowder, "morning! You're telling me that we instructed the attorney general to spring the daughter of a major fucking *donor* to the party?"

"That would . . . unfortunately appear to be the substance of what I'm . . . yes, sir."

The president hurled his pen onto the desk with such force that it skittered off the surface and onto the carpet.

"Who *knows* about this—this twenty-four-carat calamity?"

"That's the good news, sir. No one. I mean, I suppose Frank knows, but he isn't saying anything. He's probably embarrassed by her. At any rate, this information didn't come from him."

"Who *did* it come from?"

"You don't need to know that, sir. I made some inquiries. She's Frank Cohane's daughter. They haven't spoken in years. He lives in California—"

"I goddamn well know where he lives. I've spent the goddamn night at his goddamn *house.*"

"Yes, sir. Last October. After the Countdown to Greatness event. You presented him with his Owl pin."

Owls, of course, are those who contribute over $250,000 to the national party, making them eligible for "special White House briefings by top officials," "front-row seats at inaugural festivities," "special issues bulletins," and of course the odd ambassadorship, cabinet post, or commission position.

The president made a groaning noise.

"He's donated five hundred thousand," Bucky Trumble continued. "The other quarter mil ostensibly from his wife, Lisa. Presumably *not* Cass's mother. She seemed more the . . . evil stepmother type. You presented her with a pin, too."

"This is atrocious staff work, Buck."

"I do not disagree, sir. The question is how to go forward. I'm of course willing to take the fall here."

"Goddamnit, we've got a campaign coming up. How the fuck is throwing you over the side going to help?"

"Well, I . . . if you really—"

"Rearrest her."

"Sir?"

"Throw her butt back in jail. Call Killebrew and tell him—whatever you need to tell him."

Bucky Trumble puffed out his cheeks. "I'm not sure Fred would really go for that. Rearresting someone—it's . . . um. . . . tricky."

"Happens all the time."

"It does?"

"Well, Buck, it had better goddamn well better happen *this* time."

Bucky Trumble flashed forward in time. He saw himself sitting before a grand jury as an independent prosecutor asked him, *Did the president specifically instruct you to tell the attorney general to fabricate evidence that would lead to Ms. Devine's rearrest?*

As it happened, President Peacham—who from the first moment he went into politics began to be haunted by the homophonic possibilities of his surname—was himself having a similar reverie.

"That's all, Buck," he said, leaving Bucky Trumble in the position of being unable to tell the grand jury that the president of the United States had *specifically* instructed him to commit a crime.

"Sir, I'll do what needs to be done. But I really don't think he'll go for it," Bucky tried again.

The president leaned back in his chair. "If we win reelection, how many Supreme Court vacancies do we anticipate?"

"Two, minimum. Possibly three."

"It's a bit early to have the conversation with him. And it doesn't have anything *to do* with the matter at hand. But you know, Fred Killebrew has been a helluva good AG. He'd make a helluva good Supreme Court justice. Don't you think?"

Mr. Trumble, in that same meeting with the president, did the president instruct you to offer the attorney general an appointment to the Supreme Court in return for—

"Uh . . ."

"*I* do," the president said brightly. "*I* do."

"I could . . . relay that to him. Along with—"

"I'm sure you'll handle it, Bucky. With your usual flair."

"Yes, sir."

"After they throw her cute little ass back in jail, make sure you put it out that the White House is pleased. That we always thought it was a bit hasty to let her walk."

"Fred's really not going to like that."

"Fuck him. He'll be too busy measuring himself for judicial robes to care."

It came to her late that night, sometime between two and three in the morning, while she was blogging away on CASSANDRA.

She decided *not* to post it right away—cognizant that epiphanies time-stamped "2:56 a.m." tended, in the harsher light of midday, to arouse suspicion.

First thing in the morning, she called a meeting with Randy and Terry for that afternoon. They all met in Randy's office on the Hill.

She'd prepared a quick-and-dirty PowerPoint presentation. She took them through it. They listened in silence.

"So?" she said when she was finished. "What do you think?"

Randy and Terry stared.

"You want me to introduce this?" Randy said. "In the U.S. Senate?" He began to laugh. "Cass, Cass, Cass. I have to hand it to you. You *are* a piece of work. You really had me, there."

"I'm totally serious," Cass said. "I don't think it's got a prayer. But as a meta-issue, it would force the debate like nothing else."

"Meta-issue?" Terry said. "What the fuck is a meta-issue? Is this one of your Ayn Rand deals?"

"It's got nothing to do with that. Meta means . . . you know . . . transcendent. Bigger. Higher. Beyond. Above. Metaphysics. You were the one who told me the media was bored. Well, let's wake 'em up."

Terry and Randy exchanged glances. *My God, she's serious.*

"Look at these figures." Cass called up one of her PowerPoint slides. "That's a one-month-old Gallup poll. Attitudes are shifting. Fewer and fewer people equate longevity with happiness. They're ready for something like this. And while I realize that it would never in a thousand years fly, there's evidence to suggest that it's a debate people are eager to have. Let the government dig in its heels. Fine. Then we say to them, 'All right, so what's *your* solution?' Two workers to support every retiree? They don't have a solution. Things are already starting to fall apart and they *still* don't have a solution."

"It's nuts, Cass."

"No, it's bold."

"Boldly nuts."

"Since day two at TSC you were always telling me, 'Throw long.' So. *This* is long."

Randy looked at his watch. "I hate to be the party pooper, but I've got a committee meeting. Grand seeing you both. Let's keep up the dialogue. Ta-ta."

"What'd you expect?" Terry said in the car on the way back to the office. "That he was going to agree to introduce a bill in the U.S. Senate encouraging Boomers to commit mass suicide—in order to save Social Security?"

"Not suicide. Voluntary Transitioning," Cass said.

"Whatever. What time of night did you dream *this* one up?" Terry was quiet for a moment, then said, "I'll give you this: It's definitely out-of-the-box thinking. Now if you could just apply this kind of brain sweat to Larry's insecticide—"

"Did you ever read Jonathan Swift's 'A Modest Proposal'?"

Terry sighed. "You mean at Harvard? Or was it Princeton? Remind me, which Ivy League university did I attend?"

"The *Gulliver's Travels* guy," Cass said. "You heard of him, surely."

"Yeah. So?"

"In 1729, Swift published an article proposing that the way to solve poverty in Ireland was for the poor Irish to sell their children for food."

"Today he'd make millions on the diet book. What does this have to do with your scheme? Other than also being completely insane?"

"It's the whole point. It got people's attention. It got them debating the Irish hunger problem. He was a minister. He was on the side of the poor."

"So what happened to him?"

"Well, he ended up in a sanatorium."

Terry snorted.

"He got senile. Big deal. So will you and I be, if we live long enough. Come on," she said. "You're being obtuse."

"You're advocating that the government incentivize suicide, and *I'm* being obtuse?"

"Voluntary Transitioning."

"You offer people tax breaks. To kill themselves. At age seventy."

"More if they Transition at sixty-five. Yes, a package of incentives. Free medical. Drugs—all the drugs you want. Boomers love that kind of pork. The big one is no estate tax. *Why leave it to Uncle Sam when you can leave it to the kids?* That'll get the kids on board. Terry, listen to me. I ran the numbers. By my calculations, if only twenty percent of seventy-seven million Baby Boomers go for it, Social Security, Medicare, Medicaid will be solvent. End of crisis. Tell me that's not worth debating."

Terry looked at her with the mixed pride and alarm of a mentor whose protégée has gone up to the edge of the abyss—and swan-dived into it.

"What if they sign up for it," he said, "and then when they turn seventy decide, *You know, on second thought I think I* won't *kill myself. Maybe when I'm a hundred.*"

Cass said matter-of-factly, "There'd have to be, you know, substantial penalties for non–early withdrawal."

"The 401(k) from hell? Oh, sign me up."

"Terry, you're missing the point. It's never going to get to that. Because as you and Randy so astutely point out, the Congress is never in a thousand years going to pass it. Even if they *did* pass it, the president would never sign it into law. And if he *did* sign it, the Supreme Court would rule it unconstitutional."

"So what *is* the point?"

"To force a debate! So that at the end of the day, the government will have to do *something*. Remember what Churchill said? 'Americans always do the right thing—after they've tried everything else.' "

Terry considered, then said, "Uh-uh. Pasadena. I can see explaining to our corporate clients, 'We don't actually *expect* the Congress to pass a mass suicide bill. Don't you see? It's a *meta*-issue. What are you, obtuse?' "

"Suit yourself," Cass said. "I'm taking this to the next level."

"The basement?"

That night, after putting in a few hours trying to make Larry's insecticide sound like something you'd spray on your newborn infant to make it sleep through the night, Cass went to work on her "Modest Proposal."

In the days following, she consulted with gerontologists, economists, actuaries, the Congressional Budget Office, people who'd worked at the White House Office of Management and Budget, theologians and ministers (so that she could say she had), and even someone who'd worked at a penitentiary putting people on death row to sleep (another good footnote).

As she worked furiously, there came a moment—toward dawn, as the birds began their cheeping, the sound of life primordial beginning all over again—when she looked up from her warm laptop and asked herself, *What are you* doing? But she had an answer, and soon her fingers were clicking away on the keys, fortissimo.

She was about to post it on CASSANDRA when she decided—once again—to wait and post it at a more respectable hour than 5:22 a.m. It was as she lay with her head on the pillow, drifting into postponed sleep, that the notions of volunteers came to her. She was so excited that she got out of bed, made herself a Red Bull smoothie, and paced the apartment trying to figure out this part.

Chapter 13

"From Washington, tonight, a *novel* proposal on how to solve the Social Security crisis. For that story, we go now to our correspondent, Betsy Blarkin."

"Thanks, Katie. Cassandra Devine, the twenty-nine-year-old blogger who calls herself CASSANDRA, is back in the news. Last month, she urged young people not to pay taxes and to storm the gates of Boomer retirement communities.

"At a press conference today, she unveiled a plan that, she says, would solve the problem by making the *government* solvent.

"Her solution? The government should offer incentives to retiring Boomers—to kill themselves."

" *'Americans are living longer. Okay, but why should my generation spend our lives in hock subsidizing their longevity? They want to live forever—we're saying, let them pay for it.'* "

"Under Devine's plan, the government would completely eliminate estate taxes for anyone who kills themself at age seventy. Anyone agreeing to commit suicide at age *sixty-five* would receive a *bonus,* including a two-week, all-expenses-paid 'farewell honeymoon.'

" *'Our grandparents grew up in the Depression and fought in World War Two. They were the so-called Greatest Generation. Our parents, the Baby Boomers, dodged the draft, snorted cocaine, made self-indulgence a virtue. I call them the Ungreatest Generation. Here's their chance, finally, to give something back.'* "

"Devine has even come up with a better term for suicide: 'Voluntary Transitioning.' I spoke with her earlier today after her press conference. . . .

"Ms. Devine, do you expect anyone to take this proposal of yours seriously?"

"Well, Betsy, you're interviewing me on network television, so I'd say that's a good start. If you're asking why am I proposing that Americans kill themselves in large numbers, my answer is, because of the refusal of the government, again and again, to act honestly and responsibly. When Social Security began, there were fifteen workers to support one retiree. Now there are three workers per retiree. Soon it will be two. You can run from that kind of math, but you can't hide. It means that someone my age will have to spend their entire life paying unfair taxes, just so the Boomers can hit the golf course at sixty-two and drink gin and tonics until they're ninety. What happened to the American idea of leaving your kids better off than you were? If the government has a better idea, hey, we're all for it. Put it on the table. Meanwhile, we're putting this on the table. And it's not going away."

"A number of experts that we spoke to, including Karl Kansteiner of the Rand Institute in Washington, actually *agreed* that such a measure, however drastic, would in fact solve the Social Security and U.S. budget crisis."

"The average American now lives to seventy-eight, seventy-nine years old. Many live much longer. We currently are experiencing what could be called a surplus of octogenarians, nonagenarians, and even centenarians. If the government didn't have to pay benefits to these elders, say, past the age of seventy, the savings would be vast. Enormous. Indeed, tempting. Certainly, it is not a solution for, shall we say, the faint of heart."

"Others, like Gideon Payne of the Society for the Protection of Every Ribonucleic Molecule, call Devine's idea 'morally repugnant.'"

"Have we finally reached the point where we are advocating mass murder as a national policy? This entire plan, this scheme, is an abomination in the eyes of the Almighty. I tremble for my country. This woman should be ashamed."

"Cassandra Devine doesn't appear in the least ashamed. Indeed, she seems quite determined. Katie?"

"Thank you, Betsy Blarkin in Washington, for that report. Finally, tonight, Wal-Mart announced that it has obtained permission to open a one-hundred-and-fifty-thousand-square-foot megastore on the Mall, in Washington. . . ."

"I'll take two more questions. Anne?"

"What is the president's position on her proposal?"

"What proposal? Whose proposal?"

"Voluntary Transitioning."

"No. No, no, no. I'm not going to dignify that with a response."

"What do the president's economic advisers have to say about it?"

"They don't— Look, there are *no* conversations about this . . . no one in the White House is having discussions about this. No one in the White House, or, or anywhere in the entire U.S. government—"

"Are you saying that the president isn't discussing with his advisers the Social Security crisis? The stock market fell another five hundred points yesterday on news that the Nippon Bank—"

"I didn't *say* that. Don't put words in my mouth. Please. I'll take one more."

"Has he talked to *anyone* about Voluntary Transitioning?"

"All right, that's it. We're done. This briefing is over. Thank you. Good morning."

"Maybe," Terry said to Cass as they watched it all on C-SPAN, "the line dividing reality from absurdity in this country has finally disappeared. I guess it was inevitable, the way things were going."

"I don't know," Cass said. "Maybe it just shows that people are tired of hearing the same old bullshit."

"Right. They demand fresh bullshit."

"Is it?"

Terry stared at his protégée. "Whoa. You been drinking your own Kool-Aid? I warned you about that."

"Come on. We did it. It's on the table. They're certainly talking about it."

"Oh, yeah."

"They asked me to be on *Greet the Press* this Sunday."

"Well, well. Very good. Who else they having on?"

"Director of the Office of Management and Budget. Gideon Payne."

"The White House must be pretty freaked out if they're sending the OMB director out to do battle. He'll dismiss you as a nut."

"I'll say, 'You're borrowing two billion dollars a day from foreign banks—or *were,* until they stopped lending it to you—and I'm the nut? Okay, let's hear your solution. Other than making twenty-year-olds pay for thirty years of incontinence.' I'll tell him, 'Hold on, pal. You're the budget director of a locomotive headed off the cliff, in the middle of an earthquake, on fire—' "

"Easy on the metaphors."

"Whatever. But it is a runaway train. The White House is talking about wage and price controls. They're desperate."

"They're also leaking it that it wasn't their idea to let you walk. I wouldn't go making them too mad, if I were you. And watch out for Payne."

"Payne? He's just another preacher on steroids."

"Rule number one: Don't drink your own Kool-Aid. Rule number two: Never, ever, underestimate the enemy. Gideon Payne didn't get to be Mr. Pro-Life by being an idiot."

Cass reflected. "Did he really kill his mother?"

"That's what they say. Why don't you ask him, on the air? That'll break the ice."

Cass's phone rang.

"Ms. Devine?" said the voice. "I have Senator Jepperson for you."

"Well, well. Hello, Senator."

"Cass? Voluntary Transitioning! Best euphemism I've heard since 'ethnic cleansing.' I love it. With all my heart, I love it. I knew this was a winner from the get-go."

"Randy," Cass said coolly, "when I presented it to you, you practically threw me out of your office."

"Darling girl, I had a committee meeting. On that moronic monorail that my distinguished colleague wants to build in the middle of

Alaska. *Someone* has to stand up for the caribou. Now listen up. Pay attention. I'm calling to say—I want to sponsor the bill."

"To save the caribou?"

"Screw the caribou. No, child—Voluntary Transitioning. It's big, it's bold, and I love it to death. Pardon the pun. Now you and I both know that it doesn't stand a chance of a snow cone in Dante's Hell. It redefines *reductio ad absurdum*. It's the policy equivalent of Pickett's Charge. We may go down in flames, but they'll be writing ballads about us. Oh, how I love it."

"And you want to go down in flames?"

"Honestly?"

"Randy, why do I cringe when I hear you say 'honestly'?"

"Don't be too hard on me, Cassandra. I'm disabled."

"Don't go there, Randy."

"I want to sponsor it for the same reason you came up with it. To make *waves*. To make those lily-livered weasels in the White House wet their pantalones. I'm going to get Ron Fundermunk to co-sponsor it with me. The junior senator from the great state of Oregon. You know how they are in Oregon. It says the 'Assisted Suicide State' right there on the license plate."

"Watch *Greet the Press* this Sunday," Cass said. "I'm on with Gideon Payne."

"Loathsome little toad," Randy said. "Did you know his ancestor shot my ancestor?"

"What?"

"In the Civil War."

"Sedgwick?" Cass said.

"Clever girl. He was a brilliant soldier and by accounts a lovely chappie. Distinguished himself in every battle—Antietam, the Wilderness, Gettysburg. They were getting ready for a big clash at Spotsylvania. He was inspecting the Union artillery position. There were Confederate snipers. The officers were nervous and told him he should take cover. He said, 'They couldn't hit an elephant at this distance.' His last words. Story is, the sniper who drilled him is related somehow to Gideon Payne. Give him a good kick in the macadamias for me, would you?"

*   *   *

Greet the Press was the premier Sunday morning news show. Its opening theme music consisted of trumpets and kettledrums, affecting a tone of earthshaking momentousness, as though an electronic curtain were about to rise to reveal the chief justice of the Supreme Court, a prime minister, and the pope.

The host was a genial, ruddy-faced man named Glen Waddowes. He began his career as a Benedictine monk, left the order under circumstances never entirely clarified, then became a speechwriter and ultimately chief of staff to the governor of New York. He ran for Congress, served two terms, and, with eight children to feed (he had apparently remained Catholic), accepted a job running a network news bureau, ultimately taking over *Greet the Press,* whose motto was, "Since 1955, more important than the people who appear on it."

Beneath Waddowes's jolly, rubicund exterior lurked a mind armed with brass knuckles, a shank, and a blackjack. He had famously derailed the presidential campaign of Senator Root Hollings by asking him, "Senator, with all due respect, what makes you think that a man like you has the right to run for president?"

Cass had done her homework. Still, as she sat in the greenroom before the show, her palms were clammy and her chest felt tight.

In two other corners of the greenroom, eyeing her with barely concealed disdain, sat Gideon Payne and the director of the White House Office of Management and Budget. They were carrying on polite conversation, the purpose of which was—mainly—to exclude her. The OMB director was pretending to be interested in what college Gideon Payne had attended. Gideon, for his part, was pretending not to notice that he was being flattered. As the saying goes, what flatters people most is that others feel you're worth flattering. Gideon knew he was worth it and accepted it as nothing less than his due. He was a short, fat, elegant man in his late forties. He wore his hair slicked back, gave off a warm, clovelike aroma of French cologne, had a neatly trimmed beard, carried a silver-tipped cane, and dressed in bespoke suits from Gieves & Hawkes of London.

Cass overheard him saying to the OMB director, "As I said to the president just last week . . ." She mused that the only way really to top that was to say, "As I said to the president in bed this morning . . ." But the OMB director, apparently not being able to make this boast, merely nodded and pretended to be impressed by Payne's easy familiarity with the summits of Olympus-on-the-Potomac.

They were led into a refrigerated studio by whispery production assistants, miked, foreheads blotted dry of sweat by the makeup lady—not that it was possible to sweat in these subarctic temperatures.

Waddowes arrived, preceded by a flutter of aides with earphones. He was all smiles, looking like a fifty-five-year-old altar boy who'd just had a swig from the sacramental wine cruet in the sacristy. Cass smiled back, trying not to overdo it for fear her grin would freeze in place.

Five, four, three . . . Trumpets volunteered, kettledrums beat their somber, self-important tattoo.

"Economic calamity . . . ," the host intoned over montage footage of depressed-looking traders on the floor of the stock exchange. "Retiring Baby Boomers trigger a Social Security crisis"—gray-haired sixty-somethings in golf carts, fleeing one of Cass's mobs—"and angry youths saying they're not going to pay for it anymore. . . . Foreign banks refusing to go on financing America's debt—" Segue to a shot of Japanese currency speculators shaking their heads furiously. "Have we— finally—reached the tipping point that some are now calling 'Boomsday'? Our guests on this week's *Greet the Press* . . ."

Terry had been right. The OMB director treated Cass like an unwelcome bug that had splattered on Uncle Sam's vast windshield and simply needed to be wiped away, if possible without going to the trouble of pulling the vehicle over to the side of the road.

Cass patiently and courteously countered that her generation was quite open to hearing another solution, as long as it emancipated them from having to pay the bill for the excesses of the prior ones. He announced that the White House was boldly "considering" appointing a "blue-ribbon presidential commission" to "study the problem." Cass—still polite—suggested that this was akin to being on a runaway train and appointing a commission among the passengers to "study the problem that they were about to drive off a cliff." That *being* the case, the OMB director sniffed with all his Harvard hauteur, he hardly expected a "callow PR person" to understand the complexities of a highly engineered locomotive. After all, so many moving parts . . . It went on like this until Gideon Payne, impatient of being left out of the fight, came out swinging.

"May I—might I—interject?"

"Please," Waddowes said.

"Ms. Devine is ironically named. Because her scheme to kill off America's most sacred resource—her respected elders—is nothing short of demonic."

"At least"—Cassandra smiled—"I'd be willing to give *my* mother a choice whether she lives or dies."

Across the country, fifteen million viewers gasped.

Chapter 14

Cass's assault on Gideon Payne put her back on the nation's front pages, not that she had been off them for long. It also put Gideon Payne's past back in the present, not that anyone had quite forgotten it. It was a matter of some delicacy.

Gideon's great-great-great-grandfather had, indeed, been the Confederate sharpshooter who put a .55-caliber minié ball into Randy's great-great-great-uncle at Spotsylvania in 1864. For this conspicuous bit of marksmanship—General Sedgwick was one of the better Union generals and a favorite of Grant's—Gideon's ancestor was given an engraved gold watch and $100.

After the war, he used the money to buy a hundred acres of timberland in Alabama and an old sawmill. (Cheap, in 1865.) He worked hard, prospered, and handed it over to his sons, and within half a century the family business owned tens of thousands of acres of timber forest in the South and saw and paper mills. At one time, all the Scrabble tiles, tongue suppressors, and Popsicle sticks in the United States were made from Payne pine. They also made inexpensive coffins.

Gideon's father was a kindly, rotund man who preferred to sit on the front porch and drink mint juleps rather than busy himself overly in the family business. He loved Gideon, who was born corpulent and remained so, and would dangle him endlessly on his knee and make up stories about mythical ancestors who, like the real ancestor, had performed heroic deeds on battlefields. His wife, Gideon's mother, Cassiopeia Idalia Clampp—she could hardly wait to marry and get rid of the name—was very different in nature from her husband: tall, slender, fine-looking, and angry. ("*Born* angry," her father used to say, "and she'll probably *die* angry.") Her own family fortunes dwindling, and determined not to live a life of poverty, she met her future husband one day at the Colonial Cup in Camden, South Carolina, and determined to marry him. It is not especially hard to seduce an amiable, rotund, and feckless pleasure seeker. All you have to do is lead him to the lotus patch and then to the altar while the poor beast is still in a daze. This she did with efficiency and in due course provided him an heir in the form of Gideon and a few perfunctory sisters.

She had hoped for a son in the traditional southern mold, which is to say Yankee-hating, manly, attractive, good on the back of a horse, and reasonably sober. Gideon possessed none of these qualities, except for the last. His favorite children's book was *Ferdinand the Bull,* the story of the Spanish bull who didn't want to fight in the ring and preferred to sit in a field all by himself smelling flowers. His great joy, oddly, for one of his generation (and wealth), was reading the Bible, a pastime that took root one day at age five, when his father, nestling him on his lap, read him from Judges 6, chapter 11.

"And there came an angel of the Lord, and sat under an oak which *was*"—Gideon would giggle at his father's rendition of the oddly emphasized verbs in the King James version—"in Ophrah . . . Gideon threshed wheat by the winepress, to hide it from the Midianites."

Gideon was hooked. But then it is pleasant to find your own name in a book that everyone in the world owns.

His father died when he was twelve. When the bereft child asked his rather dry-eyed mother what had caused his papa's death—it was a heart attack—his mother replied, "Eating and drinking and not getting off that *porch*." This was delivered with an icy stare, the implication being that her son was somehow complicit in his death. And that was the end of Elysium for young Gideon.

A few weeks later, she handed him a rifle and said, "It's about time you killed something." Gideon was horrified. He was sent off whimpering with one of the plantation hands with instructions not to come back without a kill.

The hand, an old colored man—as they were called then—took

pity on the poor boy and shot a possum. He proudly told the evidently suspicious Cassiopeia that her son had by his very own self shot the creature off the highest limb of a sparkleberry tree by the creek.

For weeks afterward, Cassiopeia referred to her son at the dinner table, in front of guests, as "our own little Lee Harvey Oswald." Shortly thereafter, Gideon was sent off to a military academy in Mississippi, where his physique and temperament were not in step with those of the young savages. His torments were great. He was dangled from windows, had his head immersed in toilet bowls. His knowledge of the Bible made him a figure of ridicule and earned him the nickname "Preacher Boy." One day he escaped. It could not have been called a heroic attempt inasmuch as he was found shortly, tucking into an enormous ice-cream sundae at a soda fountain in town. But he refused, absolutely, to return to what he called "that place of desolation." Cassiopeia really had no choice but to take him back. Still, she was determined to make a man of him.

To that end, she sent him to work the night shift at the Payne paper mill on the Coosoomahatchie River. In those pre-environmentalist days, paper mills emitted a noxious stink redolent of rotten eggs, sulfur, and vomit. The very thought of toiling away in this mephitic inferno appalled Gideon. He begged for reprieve. Cassiopeia would have none of it.

To compound Gideon's misery, she had him chauffeur-driven to the plant every evening. The spectacle of this butterball Fauntleroy emerging from a black Lincoln caused sniggers among his co-workers, even outright hooting. Gideon was mortified but determined to show that he had some steel inside, along with the blubber.

Every morning before setting off in the Lincoln, he saturated a handkerchief with cologne (Eau de Joie). He would hold it to his assaulted nostrils when the stench of the mill overwhelmed him. This occasioned louder hooting among his colleagues, and the nickname "Rose of Coosoomahatchie."

Gideon soldiered on bravely like a forlorn character in an Edwin Arlington Robinson poem. He learned quickly and soon worked his way up to assistant night foreman. Then, some years later, came the incident that became known ever after as "the incident."

Cassiopeia, a traditional southern lady of a certain era, enjoyed being taken on Sunday afternoon drives. This chauffeuring duty fell to her young son, Gideon, now seventeen. After Sunday dinner (lunch, in the North), the two of them would drive off in Cassiopeia's 1955 Cadillac Eldorado convertible with red leather upholstery, she in the back, holding her parasol in white-gloved hands, waving in a matriarchal fashion at the farmers and workers of the estate. These drives traditionally culminated at a promontory high above the Coosoomahatchie that looked out on a spectacular view of the Payne timberlands.

Gideon's account, sobbed out to Payne County sheriff Jubiliah Stipps, was as follows. He parked the Cadillac, as usual, on the sandy bluff, set the parking brake, and got out of the car in order to answer an urgent call of nature. While doing this, he said that he heard "an awful sound." He turned and saw the car rolling forward toward the edge of the cliff with a wide-eyed, shrieking Cassiopeia in the back. He ran ("with all my lungs, I ran") to intercept the car but was unable to reach the vehicle in time. It rolled off the bluff and came to a crunchy end three hundred feet below. Gideon's imitation of the sound of the Cadillac landing was said by all who heard it to be a masterpiece of onomatopoeia.

The only question remaining was—was he telling the truth?

The inquest was inconclusive but left open the possibility, as it was quietly put, of "mischief." The evidence, such as it was, was inconclusive. The district attorney declined to prosecute. No one wanted a scandal. His unconvincing explanation was accepted—with a collective rolling of eyes—and the matter was closed.

In fact, it was anything but "closed." Cassiopeia may not have been a popular person in Payne County, and her cruelty to Gideon was well-known. That said, matricide was "not done" in fine families in the South. Perhaps in the North, but not here.

A year later and now legally an adult, Gideon left his ancestral home, some said with hardly a look back over his shoulder. He sold his shares in Payne Enterprises, which made him relatively wealthy. He enrolled in a theological seminary, where he excelled in homiletics. He concentrated his ministry among the elderly. (Guilt, they said back home.) In the process, he came to know the owners of a home for the elderly outside Memphis. It was failing financially. He took an interest, bought it, and, displaying a genetic ability for business, turned it around and made it profitable. He bought a few more homes, turned those around. By the time he was in his mid-thirties, he owned a majority share in Elderheaven Corporation, which owned or operated nearly a hundred homes for the elderly throughout the country. Its motto was: "The next best thing to heaven." Back in Payne County, heads were shaking, but they had to admit that this was penitence on a grand—and profitable—scale.

Gideon's ministry expanded with his business. He became a defender of life not only for the elderly, but for the unborn. Invited to speak at a pro-life rally on the Mall in Washington, he gave an impressive, pulpit-pounding defense that put many in mind of a younger Billy Graham or, as one newspaper put it, a "white Al Sharpton." More invitations followed, and before long he became leader of the Protestant branch of the pro-life movement. He founded the Society for the Protection of Every Ribonucleic Molecule, SPERM. Soon it became the go-to activist pro-life vanguard. If an abortion clinic opened somewhere, SPERM was there to protest. He spoke out against stem cell research. If the family of a vent-dependent, brain-dead coma victim tried to unplug life support, SPERM was there with a court order to stop it and a howling posse of interventionist congressmen. If a state legislature debated an assisted suicide bill, Gideon himself would be there to denounce it from the steps of the statehouse. Before long, Gideon was "Mr. Life."

Because of this and Elderheaven, he also became Mr. Rich. He was a significant personage in the nation's capital, courted by presidents and by those who craved the presidency. Every so often, some smart-alecky pundit would allude to "the incident," but they did it at their peril. Retaliation followed, sure and swift. Denunciations of the pundit would pour forth from pulpits all over the land. Most punitively of all, advertising would be pulled from the offending newspaper or radio or website. All of which made Cass's remark on *Greet the Press* no mere taunt, but a formal declaration of war.

* * *

"Why didn't you just pull a knife and stab him in the neck?" Terry said, shaking his head. "Where'd you learn your debating style? From watching *World Wrestling Federation Friday Night Smackdown*?"

"Whose side are you on?" Cass said. "He called me 'demonic.'"

"He calls everyone that."

"Well, I'm not going to take that from some Mr. Chubby Ducketts southern-fried preacher who drove his mother off a cliff. Why should I kowtow to that asshole?"

"Cass—Supreme Court nominees kowtow to 'that asshole.' Powerful corporations kowtow to 'that asshole.' Corporations, by the way, that we seek to become clients of. *Presidents* kowtow to—"

"I'm not running for president. Or the Supreme Court. Whatever. We got his attention."

"Oh," Terry snorted, "yeah, I'd say we definitely accomplished that. You're probably now numero uno on Gideon Payne's shit list."

"Bring it on."

"*Please* don't say that. It's such bad karma. God might be listening."

"If Gideon Payne is God's instrument on earth, I volunteer for the next manned mission to Mars."

The phone rang. It was the junior senator from the great state of Massachusetts, Randolph K. Jepperson.

"I'm calling to say thank you."

"For what?"

"I asked you to kick that sanctimonious bag of helium in the balls. And you ripped them right off. *Bra-va.*"

"I didn't do it for you," Cass said a bit hotly. "He called me 'demonic.'"

"Oh, heavens, he calls everyone that. Anyhow, you were brilliant. Brilliant. I love you. Marry me. Now, I am not without news myself. While you were administering bastinadoes to the Reverend Payne, *I* was working feverishly to make our little 'Modest Proposal' the law of the land. I presented the idea of co-sponsoring the Voluntary Transitioning bill to the distinguished junior senator from Oregon, Ron Fundermunk. At first the blood drained from his face. I thought he might faint. Then I explained that it's a *meta*-political device. A proxy, as it were, a philosophical tool to spark spirited debate on the issue, sure in time to lead to reform of a less, shall we say, draconian kind. Sure enough, the color returned to his face. He gets it! Those Oregonians. I love them. They're so ahead of the curve. He's an educated fellow. He took philosophy in college. It's not going to alarm his constituents. He represents a state that's dying to commit suicide. He knows a brave new world when he sees one. So, Little Miss Sunshine, the bottom line is that I am calling to inform you that I have a co-sponsor for our bill."

The "our" gave Cass pause, but she had to admit it was, all in all, encouraging news.

Chapter 15

"**M**r. President," Senator Randolph K. Jepperson said, beginning his historic speech on the floor of the Senate, "I rise to introduce a bill of momentous importance and urgency."

The president pro tem nodded sleepily in return and went back to his Sudoko puzzle.

The Washington and national press corps watched with one collective eye on C-SPAN, which had thankfully relieved them of having to be physically present when politicians rose to introduce bills of momentous importance and urgency.

"Together with my distinguished and learned colleague from the great state of Oregon, we are today introducing S.322, the Voluntary Transitioning bill. This bill is coming at a time of dire national economic crisis, as seventy-seven million . . . yes, Mr. Speaker, I said *seventy-seven million* members of the Baby Boom generation are beginning to retire, playing havoc with the Treasury and creating mayhem on Wall Street. Mr. President, under the provisions of the Voluntary Transitioning bill, which I believe will take its rightful place in the historic pantheon of legislation, along with the Civil Rights Act of 1964 and the recent Alaska Monorail Transportation Act, elder Americans will be able to give something *back* to their country. And in the process, provide for their children, and their children's children, to make a better world.

"Mr. President, I surely recognize that at first glance, this bill may appear to advocate a desperate remedy to our nation's fiscal calamities. But it was a former member of this very body who, on assuming the leadership of this great nation at a time of great peril, said, 'Ask not what your country can do for you. . . .'

"Mr. President, the generation that preceded my own has been called 'the Greatest Generation.' Born into the Depression, forged in the annealing fires of the furnace of World War Two, they made themselves great indeed. The generation that followed—*my* generation, and that of many of my distinguished colleagues—might be called 'the Luckiest Generation.' Why? Because of the sacrifices made by our fathers and mothers, uncles and aunts, grandfathers and grandmothers. Meanwhile, my generation has not been idle, exactly. Perhaps we did not fight in a great war or weather a depression. But in our own way, we have contributed. We have made advances in science, in the arts, in technology. And some of us did fight in wars—perhaps not great ones, but wars nonetheless. Others of us were wounded on foreign battlefields—"

"Gimme a break," the correspondent for *The Washington Post* muttered to himself as he typed. "You drove into a minefield to get your rocks off."

"—in wars very different from the great ones fought by our forebears. Still, war is war.

"Thanks to advances made by my generation, people around the world can now find decent coffee on practically every street corner. Can send e-mails. Participate in chat rooms. Type on laptop computers. No, Mr. President, we have not been idle. But these accomplishments pale in comparison with the ones of those who went before us. And so, Mr. President, it is—truly, surely, indeed, absolutely—time for us to make the ultimate sacrifice on behalf of *our* children and give back. Give back our own lives, so that those who come after us may not become enmired indeed, enmeshed in an endless swamp of debt and misery. This, Mr. President, is truly the least we can do for our country."

Cass and Terry watched Randy's speech on TV at the Tucker offices.

"Not bad," Terry said. "A little Kennedyesque, but not bad."

"Give the man credit," Cass said. "He definitely put it on the table."

"You know he's gonna get crucified."

"Yes," Cass said, "but Randy has a tendency to rise again on the third day."

Gideon Payne had also been listening. His minions had alerted him that a speech of keen interest to the pro-life lobby was being broadcast to the world. He watched impassively, stroking his neatly groomed beard. A smile spread across his face like an oil slick. Gideon thought, *Truly the Lord is bountiful. Here is manna from heaven, and all covered in butterscotch sauce.*

Had he merely dreamed a beautiful dream, or had a United States senator just gone on national television to advocate *mass suicide* as a means of dealing with the deficit?

He gave his chinny-chin-chin a little pinch to see if it was a dream. No, his beard felt real enough under his soft fingertips. This was no dream. It was the lowest-hanging fruit in the Garden of Eden. Gideon could scarcely believe his good fortune. He himself could not have devised a more succulent fund-raising opportunity. He folded his hands across his capacious belly. His gaze wandered to his phone. He counted silently. *One, two, three . . .*

He'd only reached fourteen when it began to ring—line one, then line two, then all ten lines, lovely little green lights full of sound and fury, signifying . . . money.

Bucky Trumble did not bother to knock on the door of the Oval Office.

He said a bit breathlessly, "Jepperson just introduced a bill on the floor of the Senate that would legalize suicide in return for tax breaks. It's Devine's Transitioning scheme repackaged as legislation. And he got Fundermunk to co-sponsor it."

President Peacham barely looked up from his desk. "The ones committing suicide are Jepperson and Fundermunk. Hardly know how we'll survive without 'em. Screwy fucking idea."

"I'm not so sure, Mr. President."

"Why aren't you?"

"Because, sir, the White House is getting so many e-mails in support of their 'screwy fucking idea' that our servers are crashing. The switchboard's flooded, too."

President Peacham looked up. "What are you saying?"

"They're from kids, mostly. The under-thirties. A lot of it may be generating from her blog. But they're going for it, and they're going for it big-time. We'll know more. I'm monitoring." Bucky walked in a circle as he talked excitedly. "We'll know more. I've got Sid Fiddich working the Hill, see what he can—"

"Will you stand still, for chrissake. You're making me dizzy. If you want to exercise, go to the goddamn gym."

"This thing's a can of worms. A big can. Our numbers are bad enough as is. We're going to need the eighteen-to-thirties next November. Meanwhile, you can't—there is no *way* we are going to support a legal suicide bill. I don't care how bad the crisis is. Meanwhile, this is going to raise *her* profile big-time. Everyone knows this was her idea."

"In other words . . ."

"In other words, Mr. President, it is now officially too late to re-arrest this chick."

For that much, Bucky Trumble was in fact grateful. He had not been looking forward to bribing the nation's top law enforcement official to commit breach of justice by dangling the promise of a Supreme Court appointment in a second term that at this point was looking elusive at best.

The president let out a lungful of disappointed air. "Well, we'll just have to tough it out, won't we? Blame it on Fred. If they come after us, you can just throw up your hands and say, 'I had no *idea* she was Frank Cohane's daughter. President sure as hell didn't.'" He drummed the desk with his fingers. "What in the hell is Jepperson up to, anyway, sponsoring this piece-of-shit legislation?"

"He's coming after us, is what he's doing. It's a way of making us look bad for not doing anything on Social Security reform."

"Jesus Christ on a pogo stick. No one *can do anything about Social Security reform!* It can't be done. Period."

"Tell that to the under-thirties. Tell it to Jepperson. He's playing it for all it's worth. I think he's going to challenge us for the nomination."

"Randolph Jepperson? I'll kick his overbred ass back across the Charles River so fast his bow tie will spin."

"I wouldn't underrate him. He can sound like a rich boy, but he's a mean son of a bitch. Look what he did to poor old BS Smithers. And he's rich. Real rich."

"I'm not afraid of that candy-ass. I'll tear off his prosthetic leg and beat him to death with it. On national television."

"That'll get us the disabled vote. Look, Mr. President, we need to manage this. Let's see how it plays out. You know who'd be good to have on our side? Gideon Payne."

"Sweet Jesus. Don't even—"

"Hear me out—"

"Damnit, Bucky. Last time that goateed butterball was in here, he lectured me—*me*—for a full fifteen minutes on why I needed to intervene in that vegetable case down in Georgia. Christ in a refrigerator, the woman'd been in a coma for fifteen years. She had a flatter brain scan than a three-thousand-year-old Egyptian mummy. And he wanted me to issue an executive order to plug her back in. Who appointed Gideon fucking Payne the conscience of the nation anyhow? Hell, he killed his own goddamn mother, didn't he?"

"I don't much personally care for him, either, Mr. President, but slice him or dice him, he *is* Mr. Pro-Life. I'm saying let's make him an ally. Let's at least not have him as an enemy. Remember the Godfather's rule: Keep your friends close, your enemies—"

"Damnit, Bucky, every time you quote that at me, you're about to drag some *asshole* in here and make me kiss his ass. I'm president of the U.S.! *My* ass is the one that oughta be kissed! What the hell's the point of being president, anyway? Been so long since anyone kissed my butt, I wouldn't know where to find it at this point."

"Feeling better, sir?"

"Yes," President Peacham barked. "I goddamn well *do*."

"Shall we say three o'clock, then? Today?"

"Get the hell outta here."

Bucky Trumble stood his ground.

"All right. All right. Bring the little turdball in. I'll kiss his ass. Then I'll go out on Pennsylvania Avenue and kiss all the tourists' asses. Jesus Christ. Goddamn job isn't worth a—"

"Thank you, sir," Bucky Trumble said, leaving quickly.

Frank Cohane's office at Applied Predictive Actuarial Technologies looked out over a coastal California vista redolent of eucalyptus and kelp.

Some days he could hear the contented bellowing of sea lions after they'd been gorging on schools of squid. But for the occasional great white shark, life for them was good; for himself, Frank mused, life was very, very good.

He was a tightly focused man, but he sometimes allowed himself to muse on that anxious time all those years ago, after he'd quit Electric Boat to work on the first start-up. Seemed like another century. Actually, it *was* another century—another millennium, for that matter.

For a time, Frank had regretted—even felt a bit guilty—about secretly taking out the second mortgage on the house to finance the start-up. But his motives had been pure: to support his family. It was Helen who stormed out of the house with the kids and filed for divorce. It was *her* decision. There he was, working himself to death, for her, for the kids, and she'd acted as if it were the end of the world.

He admitted now to a certain retaliatory pleasure in how the timing had worked out in the end. If Helen had waited a few months more before filing for divorce, she'd be a very wealthy woman now instead of teaching high school in New London and living on a monthly alimony of $1,500. The start-up took longer than planned—they all do—but after Frank and his two partners took it public, they'd split a handsome $540 million.

Shoulda hung in there a little longer, honey.

For a time, he had felt bad about Cass. Spending her Yale tuition money. That . . . *did* rub his conscience wrong. But he'd made it up to her. And then some. He calculated how many shares in the company her tuition money would have bought. That $33,000 was worth $27 million. He'd written out a check and sent it to her. *Twenty-seven million dollars!* And what had she done? Sent it back to him, ripped into little pieces. She had her mother's Devine genes. And for good measure—just to let him know what a prick she thought he was—she'd changed her name legally to Helen's maiden name. From that moment on, Frank Cohane decided, *Okay, Cassie, we're even.* He wasn't going to spend the rest of his very nice life wringing his hands over two pissed-off Irish women.

Now Frank had a second family—and frankly, it was an improvement over the previous one. A *vast* improvement. He had a new wife, Lisa, a hard-body former tennis pro, who, unlike lumpy softbody wife version 1.0, liked to have sex so much and so often that he now routinely took one of those long-lasting erection pills. The only downside was that if an even mildly erotic thought crossed his mind any time during the day, the affected gland responded like an overwound jack-in-the-box. This was not ideal when, say, standing onstage at the annual shareholders meeting giving his pep talk. But the upside—*rrrrrrrrowl.*

Lisa did, he thought sighingly, come with an encumbrance in the form of a teenage son, Boyd, by the previous marriage to that moron restaurant manager. The kid was harmless, though not much in the conversation department. Lisa had the notion that the boy would be greatly improved by sending him east to college. In California, Frank noticed, "east" was synonymous with certain things, like "education" or, as Boyd put it, "learning shit."

Frank was all in favor of sending him 2,500 miles away—in any compass direction, for that matter. Lisa announced that the only place to send him was Yale. He wondered: Had she gotten the notion because of Cass? When she told him this, he burst out laughing, a fit of spontaneous mirth that did not sit well with the second Mrs. Frank Cohane. He explained that with Boyd's grades and SAT scores, his chances of getting into Yale were approximately those of launching a spitball to the moon.

Lisa had another approach in mind, so Frank Cohane found himself fulfilling his promise of building Yale a new football stadium, albeit for a different child. Yale's cheer was "Boola boola" (whatever the hell that meant). To Frank, it rhymed suspiciously with "Moolah moolah."

Meanwhile, Frank had made other improvements to his life. His company had a fleet of half a dozen jets, and he personally had just taken delivery of a nifty little toy called a Javelin, a civilian-version fighter jet with a top speed of Mach .9. On the ground, he drove a Ferrari Enzo. He owned a 275-foot motor yacht that had just appeared on the cover of *Vulgar Yacht Quarterly* and a new twelve-meter sailboat that he was skippering in the trials for the upcoming America's Cup race.

His previous twelve-meter, an experimental marvel of high technology, had proved a bit too high-tech. Its revolutionary carbon-, Kevlar-, and PVC-core–epoxy composite hull had, one day in five-foot seas and thirty-knot winds in the Tasman Sea, suddenly splintered into about five thousand pieces. Three crew members had drowned. Back on the dock, he had made an unwise comment to a reporter ("Now I've gotta break in three new winch monkeys").

The quote went around the planet in about ten seconds, earning Frank a profile titled "Sportsman of the Year" in *Time* magazine. The Internet reveled in his disgrace. When he Googled his own name, the top ten thousand hits had to do with his ill-advised quote. But it spawned a brainstorm.

When he got home, he called in his top programmers and gave them their orders. Within a month, they'd developed something called Spider Repellent™ software. It was so simple, he wondered why no one had thought of it before. You loaded the software and typed in the search words. Say you'd been arrested for drunk driving or soliciting a prostitute, or you'd been in a gossip page biting the ear of some pretty young thing in a nightclub. Or, for that matter, you had been charged by the SEC with swindling your shareholders. You typed in your name, along with "drunk driving" or "prostitute" or "ear" or "embezzling." Spider Repellent™ found all the references to you on the Web and—*deleted them*. Simple. Brilliant. Lucrative. Spider Repellent™ was making

Frank's company jillions. His biggest customers were celebrities and rich people who behaved badly, and there were plenty of those.

Now Frank Googled his own name and "winch monkeys." Google reported back, "No matches."

Sure, people in the racing world remembered his gaffe, but it was a long time ago now. And in the brave new world of the Internet, if it wasn't on Google, it didn't exist. He had a new boat, and he was going to kick ass with it in the Capetown-to-Rio Rolex Challenge.

This pleasant California morning—they were all pleasant, California mornings—Frank was checking the news on the Internet.

A few paragraphs into the story about Senator Randolph K. Jepperson's Voluntary Transitioning bill, he saw a reference to Cass Devine. It occurred to him that he should probably be grateful for the difference in their surnames. There was no advantage to being publicly known as the father of the poster girl for the burn down Boomer retirement communities movement. Frank wasn't about to volunteer (to use her word) their consanguinity. Some people knew but didn't bring it up around him—and never around Lisa.

She had never met Cass. Frank was just on the verge of asking her to become Mrs. Frank Cohane (version 2.0) when Cass got herself blown up in Bosnia with Congressman Jepperson. The incident caused Frank a mixture of guilt and alarm—guilt because she was there because of him, alarm because . . . was she really in a minefield *screwing* this guy? It wasn't long before the guilt and alarm had congealed into annoyance at Cass. That should have been a happy time for him: new family, new fortune. Lisa confirmed his annoyance, and in time her feelings toward Cass were about the temperature of liquid nitrogen.

One day, not long after he and Lisa were married, Frank mentioned the fact that Cass had changed her name to Devine. Lisa said that Boyd would be *proud* to have the name Cohane.

Frank was frankly not overly fond of his stepson, but Lisa kept on him about it, so he eventually adopted Boyd legally—after instructing his lawyers to make certain changes in his will.

On this sparkling California morning, as Frank looked out on his peaceable kingdom and read about events back east, it crossed his mind that this screwball bill of Jepperson and Cass's could somehow affect RIP-ware, his latest software brainstorm.

RIP-ware was the company nickname for a software program that, if all went according to plan, would make Frank Cohane one of the richest men on the planet. Its actual name was Bio-Actuarial Dyna-Metric Age Predicator (BADMAP), and because of its vast potential, few people outside the company knew about it. Frank had invested a huge chunk of his fortune in it.

It worked this way: A person's DNA profile, family history, mental history, lifestyle profile, every variable—how many trips to the grocery per week, how many airplane flights, hobbies, food, booze, number of times per month you had sex and with whom, everything down to what color socks you put on in the morning—were all fed into the software. RIP-ware would then calculate and predict how and when you'd die. In the testing, they had programmed it retroactively with the DNA and lifestyle profile of thousands of people who had already died. RIP-ware predicted their deaths with an accuracy of 99.07 percent. In a simulation, it predicted the death of Elvis Presley—just four months from the actual date of his demise. The ultimate "killer app."

Insurance companies had been working on similar programs. What a windfall it would be for them if they could sell life insurance to someone they knew was going to live another forty years—and conversely *decline* life insurance to someone the computer predicted would be pushing up daisies within two years.

Another field of vast potential were the old folks' homes. Typically, these demanded that a prospective resident turn over his or her entire net worth in return for perpetual care. You could live two years or twenty years; that was their gamble. But if a nursing home knew, in advance, that John Q. Smith was going to have a fatal heart attack in 2.3 years while watching an ad for toenail fungus ointment on the evening news, they would much rather have his nest egg as advance payment than that of, say, Jane Q. Jones, who RIP-ware predicted would live another twenty-five years and die at the ripe old age of 105. Frank was already in negotiation with a huge national chain of nursing homes called Elderheaven. The majority shareholder was that fat little pro-life guy Gideon Payne. Cass had just gone after him on that Sunday morning TV show recently. Small world. Meanwhile, RIP-ware was being marketed to companies very discreetly. Its high accuracy was nowhere referred to in company documents. As far as the broader world knew, it was simply "acturial enhancement software that assists companies in certain market sectors with paperwork reduction and simplification."

But now a United States senator had proposed on the floor of the Senate that Americans should be allowed to decide for *themselves* when they died—and, morever, be compensated for it by the government. Frank detected a blip on the radar.

He called up the video of Jepperson's speech on his computer, listened for a few minutes. He studied the face on the screen. Good-looking. A bit effete, aristocratic. You could tell at one hundred yards the guy came from money. More than a little pompous—who did he think he was? Sounded like he was practicing giving his presidential inaugural speech.

And suddenly Frank found himself wondering: *Is my daughter screwing this guy?*

In one of the last good talks around the family kitchen table that he had with Cass, she had told him that she was still a virgin. She was just eighteen. Then she went off to the military, and then they had the falling-out—in absentia, when she found out about the mortgage—so the two of them had never had the father-daughter talk about . . . boys.

After the incident in Bosnia, there were hints in the media—more than hints, if you considered one of the tabloid headlines: DID THE EARTH MOVE FOR YOU, TOO, DEAR?—about what they were doing in the minefield in the first place. Then Cass went to work for the guy in Washington. And now here he was championing her national suicide scheme. She *had* to be sleeping with him.

He tried to shrug it off, but Frank Cohane found himself unaccountably curious.

Had to be.

He certainly had the means to find out. He had Washington connections. Hell, he had the town wired. He was an Owl—a major donor to the party. A big, snowy Owl. He and Lisa had spent a night in the Lincoln Bedroom—doing things that old Abe and Mary Todd Lincoln never dreamed of. They'd sat one row behind the president and Mrs. Peacham at the inaugural parade. They'd been in the presidential box at the Kennedy Center. And once a month, his private line or private cell phone would ring and he'd hear those sweet words: "This is the White House operator trying to reach Mr. Frank Cohane." And on would come the voice of Bucky Trumble, chief political counselor to the president of the United States, his closest adviser.

The last time he called it was to say, "The president and I were talking about you in the Oval this morning." The Oval. It was all bullshit, Frank knew. With these political guys, it was almost *all* bullshit. But high-level bullshit. And ear-pleasing bullshit all the same. And what Bucky had gone on to say was most definitely pleasant: "He's got you in mind for a significant ambassadorial posting. Don't let on I told you, okay? He'll want it to be *his* surprise."

Frank had run that one, too, through his bullshit meter. What exactly constituted a "significant" ambassadorial posting? London? Paris? Tokyo? Those were *his* definitions of significant. Moscow? Dreary. And without a cold war going on, somewhat pointless. You'd go broke trying to sell RIP-ware in a country where the average male died at fifty-seven—of either alcoholism, lung cancer, or a bullet. He did not particularly relish the idea of four years playing wet nurse to a parade of U.S. oil executives looking for preferential leases in the Novaya Zemlya trough.

Ireland? Pointless. Appealing in a way, since his great-grandfather had come over and spent his life working in a coal yard in South Boston. You probably didn't have to spend too much actual time *in* Ireland. But then the Irish press would hate you.

He ran it by Lisa that night after some cosmic coitus. (She was working their way through the third edition of *The Joy of Sex* and had found a position called "la grande morte.") Her only comment—about the ambassadorship—was, "I wouldn't have to, like, learn a language or anything?"

That would be one advantage to London or Dublin, Frank

considered. Then he thought of all the paperwork. His fellow Owl Steve Metcalf had been nominated to be ambassador to some utterly pointless country in Africa and had spent $150,000 on lawyers filling out the four-hundred-page financial disclosure form—"Please list *all* stock and securities traded in the last 40 years"—only to be humiliated in front of some grandstanding senator who asked Steve what countries his country shared borders with. *Uh . . . well, Senator, I'm certain that the embassy has people who, uh, stay on top of issues of that, uh, nature.* A bit embarrassing, considering that the country was an island. Steve never quite recovered socially.

Frank was in the process of mentally writing off an ambassadorship when his private phone rang. "This is the White House operator . . ."

"Frank? Bucky Trumble!"

They always managed to announce their names with a little trumpet blast, frank recognition of, and unbridled joy in, their own importance.

"The president and I were just talking about you. He asked me to give you a call, in fact. . . ."

Chapter 16

Randy's speech on the floor of the Senate had the predictable effect: It got him on the nation's front pages and the evening news. The *Times* denounced him in unusually harsh personal terms. ("It appears that the junior senator from Massachusetts may have left more than one body part in the muddy fields of Bosnia.")

But it also got him invited on the late-night shows, which, studies now showed, provided over 80 percent of the nation's youth with 100 percent of their political information. The idea of aging, self-indulgent Boomers killing themselves rather than becoming an oppressive financial burden to their children and the nation was not anathema to these young viewers. In fact, to them it sounded like a darn good idea. They especially liked the part where the government would eliminate all death taxes so Mom and Dad's money could flow straight to them.

Cass accompanied Randy to New York City for the Letterman and Jon Stewart and Colbert shows and to Los Angeles for the Jay Leno show. Randy might excite vituperation in older, more serious-minded TV hosts, but to them, he was a million-dollar gift certificate, proof of the existence of a bemused, smiling God. They loved him.

Letterman asked, "Aren't *you* the one committing suicide here?"

Randy replied, "Maybe. But if I can convince a majority of the U.S. Senate to commit suicide along with me, this country would be a whole lot better off." They loved everything about Randy: his funny accent, his wealth, the fact that his colleagues hated him, his screwball idea, even his fake leg, which he obligingly removed on the Jon Stewart program. "This is where I hide the tequila," he said. Cass, looking on from the greenroom, smiled at the precision and deftness with which Randy was rendering the lines she had written for him. As media training went, this was as good as it got. She'd come a very long way from teaching disgraced hospital owners how to spin. Her CASSANDRA blog was getting so much traffic that she had had to hire a staff of five just to keep it fresh. A woman from IBM—the head of its entire corporate communications department—had called to say she wanted to have lunch with Cass at someplace in Manhattan named Michael's to explore "possible strategic synergies."

Within a week of Randy's TV blitz, the media was treating Voluntary Transitioning, if not with respect, with less reflexive derision. Adjectives such as "outrageous" and "despicable" and "unthinkable" that had been initially Velcroed to the phrase were now replaced by "bold" and "revolutionary" and "dire yet deserving of discussion."

An editorial in *The Washington Post* made the paradigm shift official: "Whatever else Senator Jepperson is up to, we're beginning to suspect that his real intention all along was to force the issue of Social Security to the forefront of a Congress that has been in continual denial, even amid crisis and collapse, and that much, Mr. Jepperson has emphatically accomplished."

One night in New York during their media tour, Randy summoned Cass to his hotel room, ostensibly to go over the next day's schedule. It was late, and she very well could have begged off, but she went. When she walked in, the lights were turned down low, Patsy Cline was singing "Three Cigarettes in an Ashtray" over Randy's iPod speaker, and she saw the neck of a bottle of Dom Pérignon protruding from a frosted ice bucket in a way that seemed, well, suggestive.

There was Randy, sitting on the edge of the bed, wearing an expensive silk kimono.

"You wouldn't make a one-legged man chase you round the room, would you?" He smiled.

Cass had known something like this was going to happen. There had been a few signals. A few dinners, just the two of them, legs—his good one, that is—accidentally grazing against hers under the table.

Her feelings for this peculiar man were complicated. But he made her laugh, and he was not dull. And he wasn't bad-looking. And he was rich. And not married. And evidently running for president.

A few days ago, she'd said to him, "Why do you want to be president?" He'd told her about the day of his acid epiphany in the lobby of the JFK Library.

"You want to be president because of an acid trip you took?" she'd said.

"It's not such a bad reason, really. Have you ever taken acid?"

"No," Cass said. "My life is enough like an acid trip as it is. When you do announce, let's leave out this epiphany, shall we?"

"Why?"

"I'm not sure the country is ready for a candidate who says he wants to be president because he swallowed a triple dose of LSD while staring at a photograph of John F. Kennedy. But I could be wrong."

"I think the country would welcome it."

"Well, we could find out. If you're wrong, at least it will be over quickly. Like by noon the first day."

Randy considered. "You could be right. And that's a pity. I think there's a hunger out there for the truth. That's why I think we've come so far with this nutty idea of yours. It's so *fresh*."

"You do this pronoun shift. You may not even be aware of it. If it's a 'bold idea,' it's 'ours.' If it's a 'nutty idea,' it's 'yours.' "

"Grammar Nazi. Would it be enough to say I want to be president to . . ."

"I'm listening."

Randy said, "I was about to say, 'To give something back,' but it sounds so pathetic. What it really boils down to is, I'd like to be in charge for just five minutes. Balance the books. Get us out of debt. Be nice to our friends, tell our enemies to fuck off. Clean up the air and water. Throw corporate crooks in the clink. Put the dignity back in government. Fix things. What else . . . ? Can't have Arabs blowing up our buildings, certainly, but I now know that we don't need to be sending armies everywhere. Among other things, it's *expensive.* . . ."

"I'm sorry, were you talking? I went to sleep after 'balance the books.'"

"It's not that bad. What do you want me to say? 'Bind up the nation's wounds, with charity toward all and malice toward none'?"

"I think we need to work on it."

"*Evidament.*" Randy sighed.

"No French."

"Quite right. *Muchas gracias. Qué bonita es este burrito.*"

Now here they were in a hotel suite that was decorated for sex. She'd finally run out of reasons not to go to bed with him. She looked at him sitting on the bed and said, "It's been a long day. I don't think I have the energy to run."

"Glad to hear it. Why don't you walk that bottle of Dom Pérignon over here. Damn thing cost three hundred and fifteen bucks in room service. Reckon we might as well drink it."

Cass brought it over and sat on the bed. "That may be the only time in history the words *reckon* and *Dom Pérignon* have been used in a single sentence."

"I'm just a simple boy from Boston," Randy said, twisting off the cork with the expertise of a three-star sommelier. "You remember that beer we drank in Bosnia? Right before I got us blown up?"

"The beer *you* drank. I was on duty."

"It wasn't that bad, really. But this will be better. Certainly ought to be, at these prices."

"Do rich people also complain about prices?"

"Always. It's how they got rich."

He poured the Champagne into their glasses. The tiny bubbles tickled on the way down.

He put his chin on her shoulder. "Want to watch a dirty movie on the television?"

Cass said, "Sure, but do you really want an item appearing on Page Six of the *Post* the day after tomorrow about how *Latex Ladies Three* was charged to the hotel bill of a certain senator?"

"Good thinking, Devine. You're a good handler." He leaned forward and kissed her on the lips. "Want to be part of my *brain* trust?"

"I don't know." Cass kissed him back. "What's in it for me?"

"Expensive French Champagne? We'll start you off in the secretarial pool. Can you type?"

Successful, busy men are by nature impatient, and though Frank Cohane found it pleasant enough to listen to Bucky Trumble go on and on about how much the president appreciated his efforts in recruiting more big-donor Owls to the party, he was thinking: *Can we move along to the part where I get a "significant" ambassadorship?*

Instead, Bucky cleared his throat and said, "Frank, I need to speak with you about something. On a discreet basis."

"Okay."

"It concerns Cassandra Devine."

Frank's stomach muscles contracted. "Yeah?"

Bucky cleared his throat again. "I believe you two are . . ."

"Related. Yeah. She's my daughter."

"Right." Awkward silence. "That was our information as well."

"We're not in touch. It's been many years."

"I guess that would account for your not having brought it up."

"Bring *what* up? I said, I haven't talked to her in—hell, this century."

Another silence. "What I'm about to tell you is highly sensitive information."

"We keep secrets here, too, Bucky."

"You're aware she was arrested and charged with a very serious crime."

"It was on the cover of *Time,* and she's, ah, my daughter, so—yeah."

"The government—that is, the attorney general—decided not to pursue the charges, on the strictly legal grounds that successfully prosecuting her would in all likelihood prove difficult."

"Uh-huh." *Where was this going?*

"So she walked out of jail a free woman. It only *then* came to our attention—that is, the president's and mine—that she was the daughter of one of our most valued donors."

"I don't know how many ways to say it, Buck. We haven't seen each other in—"

"That's not really the issue." Pregnant pause. "*Is* it, Frank?"

"It is as far as I'm concerned."

"Let me tell you how we see it. If I may?"

"Shoot."

"Let me state clearly and absolutely that the White House did not influence the decision of the attorney general. But the AG *is* a cabinet officer in this administration. So you have a situation where as far as the media would view it . . . the government decided not to prosecute the daughter of a major party donor."

"I didn't ask you for any favors for her."

"No, you didn't. You absolutely didn't. And the president and I appreciate that. We do. Still and all, Frank, it might have been helpful if you'd given us a little, you know, heads-up that this radioactive young lady was—your daughter."

It had been a long time since anyone had criticized Frank Cohane, even mildly. (Except his wife, who exercised high, middle, and low rights of spousal criticism.) He was tempted to tell Bucky Trumble that if he felt that way, he could return Frank's half-million-dollar donation.

But people, even very successful ones, tend not to speak that way to someone who sits at the right hand of the president of the United States, a position that for all its many faults still packs a nasty punch. Especially when they've told their wives that they're about to be appointed to the Court of St. James's and they'll be presenting their credentials to the queen of England. And probably staying over at Buckingham Palace for dinner.

"I'm . . ." Frank reached for the word. What *was* the word, anyway? "*Sorry* if . . . I've been busy as hell here. We're launching a new software, and I've been focused 24/7 on . . ."

Bucky let him prattle on a bit and then said, "I understand. But sooner or later the media are going to make the connection. So the question really is, where do we go from here?"

The sentence hovered between the two men like a malignant hummingbird. Frank saw the "significant" ambassadorship he wasn't even sure he wanted suddenly going *pfffut*. Which, human nature being what it is, suddenly made him crave it above all earthly things. He saw himself explaining to Lisa that she would not, in fact, be dining with the queen and Prince Philip.

Then Bucky said, "I have some thoughts. May I share them with you?"

"Yeah," said Frank. "Sure."

"We were thinking that if *you* brought the connection to the media's attention, in such a way as to demonstrate that you're opposed to what she stands for and did . . . that that might solve the immediate problem."

The third long silence of their conversation settled in.

"In other words, you want me to publicly denounce my daughter?"

" 'Denounce' is a loaded term. Let's say *distance*. As long as you make it clear that you don't approve of what she did, and clarify that you haven't even been on speaking terms for—since the last century. I think that would do it."

A roar of sea lions suddenly broke in through Frank's open window and into Frank's speakerphone.

"What in the name of God was that?" Bucky said.

"Sea lions. They probably saw a great white."

"Where were we?"

"You want me to distance myself from my daughter."

"I'd sure rather that than us have to distance ourselves from you. The president values you. I can't emphasize that enough. He talks about you all the time. I've gotta go. Will you think about it and get back to me one way or the other? And Frank?"

"Yeah?"

"Let's not put any of this in e-mail, okay?"

"Of course."

"Oh, there is one *other* thing you could do. I know it would mean a great deal to the president. . . ."

Chapter 17

Gideon Payne was of course delighted to receive an invitation to the White House for a one-on-one with the president, but he was suspicious.

Bucky Trumble had told him over the phone that the president desired "to get the benefit of your wise counsel and maybe even a private prayer session over this Transitioning business." Prayer session? *My, my, my,* as Gideon was wont to say, *how the wicked do lie.*

Gideon did not trust Mr. Buckminster Trumble, and he did not like President Riley Peacham. The occasion of his last visit to the Oval Office had been an attempt to get the president to intercede personally on behalf of Mrs. Delbianco, his latest Lazarus. "Lazarus" was Gideon's private term for hopeless coma cases who were about to be unplugged from life support. They were a most lucrative segment of SPERM's fund-raising. And made for the most poignant photo ops.

The meeting had gone . . . "uncomfortably" would be the best word. President Peacham squirmed and frowned and fidgeted throughout Gideon's rather inspired monologue about the need to keep poor Mrs. Delbianco alive. Never mind that the woman was in her seventeenth comatose year and had been pronounced brain-dead and permanently vegetative by several dozen specialists; or that twenty-three judges had approved the family's request to remove life support. Life is life, the most precious gift of the Almighty, even if it just, well, *lies* there growing fingernails.

What made the case worthy of presidential intercession—where Gideon was concerned—was the fact that a hospice worker reported seeing a recurring rash on Mrs. Delbianco's stomach in the shape of the Virgin Mary. When a hospice worker informs a local newspaper that a rash in the shape of the Madonna is visible on the stomach of a woman about to be unplugged from life support, it is a certain thing that the hospice worker will snap a photo of it and sell it to the tabloids for almost as much as a picture of a newborn celebrity baby. And that other newspapers will reprint it and that national attention will follow. And with it, Gideon Payne.

Gideon did not succeed in getting President Peacham to intervene; the around-the-clock prayer vigil outside the hospice that he and his friend Monsignor Massimo Montefeltro organized kept Mrs. Delbianco front and center up to the moment of her last exhalation.

Unfortunately, a few months later the hospice worker was arrested for credit card fraud and revealed that she had created the image of the Virgin on Mrs. Delbianco's stomach herself with benzocaine ointment, to which poor Mrs. Delbianco was allergic. All rather embarrassing, to be sure, but—Gideon insisted—beside the point. Did not the Lord work in mysterious ways? Could He not have directed the hospice worker to paint the image? Who can know the workings of the Almighty? Gideon didn't flinch. He valiantly defended the worker as a heroine who had done what she could to save a life. Some even suggested that he himself was behind the dermatological hoax. To which he tut-tutted, "My, my, my, how the wicked do lie."

But this time, the White House had called *him*.

The president went briskly through the motions of pretending to be honored that Gideon should carve time out of his busy schedule to visit with the most powerful man on earth.

"What do you make of Jepperson's Transitioning bill?" he asked.

"I view it, Mr. President, as an abomination. To quote Jefferson, as opposed to Jepperson, 'When I consider that God is just, I tremble for my country.'"

The president cast a sidelong glance at Bucky by way of signaling his aide, *Don't let him start rambling on about Jefferson, for God's sake.*

"Yeah," the president said. "That's pretty much how we view it. Hell of a thing. And a hell of a different thing than that woman with the Virgin Mary tattooed on her stomach. We don't think you had anything to do with that, by the way."

"Thank you, sir," Gideon said heavily. "That's most generous of you. Of course, the real issue with respect to Mrs. Del—"

Bucky Trumble leapt in. "Mr. President, Gideon is the preeminent moral authority in this country in the matter of the sanctity of life. I don't think anyone disputes that."

"I sure as hell don't dispute it. I know. That's why we need him. That's why we called him in."

Gideon thought, *Why all this slathering on of butter? What do they want, these two sinners?* But opportunity trumps suspicion. Gideon had been in Washington long enough to know that when powerful people need something from you, it is accompanied by the sound of a very large dinner bell.

"You've seen the polls," the president said. "The kids, the eighteen-to-thirty-year-olds, they're going for it. In a big way."

"Is it any surprise, Mr. President," Gideon said, "that the young people of this country should be so easily led astray, when we have failed them so profoundly in moral leadership?"

The president frowned.

Gideon added, "I did not mean by that *you* personally, sir."

"Uh, no. No."

"I mean that we as a society have failed them. For what have we offered them but a false banquet of materialism? Video games, pornography, filth, copulation, fast food, downloads, uploads. 'Thou hast prepared for me a feast, yet I hunger. My soul *thirsteth* for the Lord.'"

"Right," the president said. "That's why we need to come out swinging. *Crush* this cocksucker."

Gideon stiffened. He was, after all, a reverend. People, even presidents, weren't supposed to talk this way. He shot Bucky Trumble a perturbed look. Bucky shot back a look that said, *Suck it up, pal. He's the president of the United States.*

"Grab him by the throat," the president continued. "Kick him in the nuts, cut off his dick, put his head on a pike . . ."

Gideon cleared his throat. "Ah. I have spoken out against—"

"You know who's behind all this, don't you?" The president leaned forward, eyes blazing, setting the hook.

A look of solemnity came over Gideon's face.

"Yes, sir, I do. The ever so inaptly named Miss Devine."

President Peacham shook his head in disgust. "What she did to you on that TV show. It was inexcusable. Atrocious. Uncalled for. If she'd done that to me, I'd have reached over, grabbed her by the hair, and slammed her goddamn head on the table."

Gideon shifted in his seat. It was awkward enough to have the matter of your having supposedly killed your own mother brought up in the Oval Office, by the president. Was he also suggesting that Gideon had been . . . cowardly on the TV show?

"I do appreciate that sentiment, sir," he murmured.

"Ugly business. Fucking ugly."

Gideon was speechless.

The president said, "Hell, Gideon, I'm a sinner and a salty man. I apologize. But this is how I talk. Among—*friends*."

"I thank you, sir, for your friendship."

Bucky Trumble leaned forward and said, "The president and I were hoping that you, Gideon, will take the lead against Jepperson."

"Well, as I say, I am speaking out. I have hardly been idle. But, sir, why not take the lead yourself?"

"Gideon, listen to me," the president said, lowering his voice and boring in like a drill. "I am up to my ass in alligators. I got a collapsing economy. Foreign banks are using the U.S. dollar to wipe their asses. I'm fighting four wars—and looks like another on the way, in goddamn *Nepal*. Someone tell me what in hell we're doing in *Nepal*. I got melting ice caps on both poles. Florida just lost another two feet of waterfront. Hundred square miles of Mississippi just went under. They just found another tunnel under the Mexican border, this one a four-lane highway, for Christ's sweet sake. I got a drought in the West the Interior Department says is going to make Colorado and Wyoming into another dust bowl. Pakistan and India are going at each other like a couple of wet cats, and don't get me started on that hairball maniac in North Korea. CIA's telling me Israel's preparing to launch nuclear weapons at fucking Mecca. Mecca! Gideon, I don't have *time* to take on a one-legged senator who says the solution to Social Security is for us to kill ourselves at age seventy. Shit, the way I'm feeling now, *I* may shoot myself. And I may not *wait* until I'm seventy."

It was flattering to have the most powerful man in the world supplicate in this fashion. But there was something just a tad smelly about it all. He was leaving something out.

"Mr. President," Gideon said, "with all *due* respect, why—really—do you want me to take the lead on this?"

The president leaned back in his chair. He nodded as if in acknowledgment of defeat. Then he smiled, looked over at Bucky Trumble, and said to Bucky, "I told you he was smart. Didn't I tell you?"

"You did, boss. You did."

The president, calmer now, said to Gideon, "Look here. If *I* take the lead on this, all it's going to accomplish is to empower the cocksucker. Don't you see? His numbers'll jump. He's going at the president! It'll make it a *political* issue instead of moral issue. Which is what it is. That's why you're the only one who can do it. And I'll back you with everything short of air strikes."

"What exactly do you propose, Mr. President?"

"Buck," the president grunted.

"There's certain information about Jepperson and this woman Devine that you might find useful in this debate."

Gideon's eyebrows arched like stretching cats. He stroked his beard with moist, scented fingertips. His lips pursed. *Oh my, oh my.* Yet a voice whispered, *Careful, son. You're in the lion's den, and the beasts do* raven.

"What *kind* of information?" he said cautiously.

"The kind," the president said, leaning forward, suddenly every bit the commander in chief, aiming soul-seeking missiles into Gideon's eyes, "that causes *tides* to turn. Let me pay you a compliment: We didn't call you in here just to fuck around."

Good Lord, Gideon thought. *What* had *this man eaten for breakfast? Flapjacks with nitroglycerin syrup?* Another thought came to mind: *Were they recording this? You never knew with the White*

House. But then why record yourself in the act of offering dirt to a man of impeccable moral rectitude? Impeccable, that is, apart from the business about killing Mother.

"I would like to consider it," Gideon said nervously. "I would like to *pray* on it."

The president's look of cold command suddenly congealed into panicked horror at the prospect that Gideon was about to invite him to get on his knees in the Oval Office and pray with him. He'd done that the last time with the "Stomach Madonna" woman, as the tabloid press had unfortunately dubbed Mrs. Delbianco.

Sensing the president's discomfiture, Gideon added quickly, "In the privacy of my own heart."

The president sighed with relief. "Of course. If there's anything we can do for you in the meantime . . ."

Bucky shot the president a cautionary look—too late.

"There *is* something, actually," Gideon said.

"Oh?" the president said, as if delighted to hear it.

"The memorial to the forty-three million."

"Oh. Right." *Shit.*

For years, Gideon had been petitioning various congressmen and senators for a memorial on the Washington Mall to the 43 million unborn souls since the Supreme Court's *Roe v. Wade* ruling in 1973.

"Well"—the president stood, smiling broadly and extending his hand—"we will certainly give that *our* prayerful thought."

Chapter 18

Cass had come up with the notion of a television and Internet advertising campaign to stigmatize old age. This would, theoretically, nudge voters toward greater acceptance of Voluntary Transitioning. Randy loved the idea and, in the spirit of the thing, volunteered to pay for it out of his own deep pockets. Terry was less enthusiastic, for practical reasons.

"Cass," he said, "some of our best clients are CEOs in their sixties, some in their seventies. You really want to run public service announcements on TV telling them they're selfish bastards and should kill themselves? Speaking as the founder of Tucker Strategic Communications—and incidentally as your *employer*—let me just say that this company is not out to commit suicide."

"Terry," Cass said, "we're not urging our *clients* to Transition."

Terry furrowed his brow and clicked on one of the storyboard slides in the PowerPoint presentation Cass had prepared. He read aloud:

"Spot number four. 'Resource hogs'? Now we're calling old people resource hogs?"

"Problem?" Cass said matter-of-factly.

"Well—it's a little *harsh,* isn't it? I never thought of Grandma and Grandpa as resource hogs. What happened to *meta*?"

"Terry, Terry, Terry, we're simply making the point that nonproductive longevity only consumes resources that would be better spent on younger generations, who are currently being crippled with passed-along debt as a result of—"

"Thank you, Ayn Rand."

"Okay." She smiled. "So, no problem?"

"What about this one?" Terry punched up another slide: "'Wrinklies'? We're calling them Wrinklies?"

"I wasn't *going* to put that on TV."

"That's a relief," Terry snorted.

"I'm going to plant it," she said brightly. "Have a third party send it into CASSANDRA and then make it our own. I think the kids'll go for it in a big way. '*Wrinklies. Ew, gross! So* heinous.'"

"Was Einstein a Wrinkly? Eleanor Roosevelt . . . Helen Keller?"

"*They* gave something back. Einstein showed us how to blow ourselves up. Now that's what I call transitioning."

Terry gave her a worried look. But on she went. "This campaign is about self-indulgent aging Boomers who are wrecking the U.S. economy and economically enslaving the next generations. This is not about *The Miracle Worker* or Eleanor Roosevelt. Though she really *was* wrinkly. Will you please just chill?"

"You're kidding, right?"

"Yes. For heaven's sake."

"I couldn't tell. This one . . ." He clicked on another slide. Up came an image of a group of gaunt, hungry-looking youths staring hollow-eyed at a large empty bird's nest. The caption read: "What kind of nest egg will *you* leave them?"

"I guess it works," he said. "But kind of a downer, though."

"It's *supposed* to be. What's eating you? It's like you're suddenly a double agent working for the American Association of Resource Hogs."

Terry sighed. "I don't know. This is starting to give me the creeps. Urging old people to kill themselves. Norman Rockwell it ain't."

"Omigod, Terry."

"What?"

"That's it! You are such a genius." Cass hugged him. "You really are. It's *beyond* brilliant. I can't even discuss it."

"What are you talking about?"

"*Norman Rockwell.*" Cass snapped her laptop shut and dashed out of the conference room, leaving Terry to shake his head and go back to work.

* * *

Two days later, she burst into his office with the laptop, smiling like a cat that had just swallowed an entire cage of parakeets. He hadn't seen her look this happy—ever.

She put the laptop in front of him, fired it up, and clicked on the "Start Slideshow" icon.

Terry watched.

Cass had hired a computer graphic artist to duplicate Norman Rockwell's sliced-bread, rooster-crowing, soda-fountain, friendly-cop, Thanksgiving-turkey America—only on the theme of Voluntary Transitioning.

The first slide showed a man and wife in their seventies, holding hands, smiling as though they were embarking on an ocean cruise. They were walking into the doorway of a homey, gingerbread-style house whose address might be 15 Maple Street. Above the doorway was a bright yellow sign that read, VOLUNTARY TRANSITIONING CEN-TER—WELCOME, SENIORS!

The next illustration showed a pair of perfectly healthy-looking people in their mid-sixties thumbing their noses at a frustrated-looking Grim Reaper. The caption read, WE'LL DO IT ON OUR TIMETABLE, THANKS—NOT YOURS!

There were half a dozen illustrations. The last one showed an elderly man in a comfy, fluffy bed attended by an attractive and shapely nurse dressed in a traditional starched uniform. The man was smiling sleepily. The nurse was smiling back at him as she adjusted the valve of an IV drip running into his arm. The caption read, OFF TO A HEAV-ENLY REST!

Terry looked up at Cass, who was still beaming.

"Well?"

"I'm speechless."

"Aren't they fabulous?"

"Lethal injection never looked so warm and fuzzy. A happy occasion for the whole family. I'm sure the Rockwell estate will be thrilled."

"You were so right. It needed to be uplifting. Randy loved them."

"Did he? How is Randolph of Bosnia?"

"Ooh," Cass said, "do I sense a note of—something? Hel-*lo*," she said. "Who was it that kept telling me to get laid?"

"He's a client. And what is Tucker's first law?"

"No *schtupping* the clients. Yeah, yeah. Well, I mean, I figured this is different."

"How, exactly?"

"Among other things, I knew him before he was a client. Why are you being such a hard-ass about this?"

"Because I don't *like* Randy."

"Okay. So. Don't sleep with him."

"I think you're getting *way* wound around the axle," Terry said. "I've seen it happen before. Young, impressionable account execs— they go over to the client side. They drink the Kool-Aid. You end up having to deprogram them. I've seen it happen to the best minds of my generation."

"Thank you, Allen Ginsberg. No one was focused on this before I came along. Now everyone's talking about it. It's *my* friggin' Kool-Aid."

"And you're drunk on it. Resource hogs. Wrinklies. Norman Rockwell goes to Auschwitz?"

Cass looked down at the floor. She said quietly, "I'm just trying to get a debate going about the future of Social Security."

"All right," Terry said. "I don't want you to get hurt. I've been around politicians way longer than you have. When push comes to shove, trust me—it's you over the side first, not them. Wait a minute. Why am I even having to tell you this? *He blew you up in a minefield!*"

"Yeah, and he's the one limping for the rest of his life. Give the man a break. If you don't like my Norman Rockwell thing, I'm open to suggestions."

Terry considered. "Why not celebrity endorsements? Like the milk ads, only they're drinking poison. They've got little purple hemlock stains on their upper lips. 'Got Transitioning?'"

Cass smiled. "You can't help it, can you. Even when you're being a total jerk, you're brilliant."

"Either you've had too much Red Bull," Terry said, "or you've gone over to the dark side. Either way, you're grounded. Lose Norman Rockwell."

"This is no time for timidity."

"That's right," Terry said. "Next Tuesday is the time for timidity."

It was an old joke between them. On any given day on Capitol Hill, someone said, "Now is not the time for partisanship"—usually when he or she was about to be crushed by the opposition. Whenever Terry or Cass spotted the quote in the paper, one rushed to e-mail it to the other first. Whoever spotted it second had to pay for drinks that night.

"I've gotta go," Cass said. "I've got a meeting on the Hill with Randy."

"Tell Ahab I said hi."

"That is so funny. I am, like, *paralyzed* with laughter."

But in the elevator down to the lobby, Cass found herself wondering if she was, in fact, crossing some Rubicon of weirdness. She looked idly at her shoes. They *looked* dry.

She was disappointed, even quietly furious, over Terry's reaction to the Norman Rockwell campaign. He might at least have said it was clever. Maybe it was a passion deficit on his part. Terry was a generation older than Cass. He could hardly be expected to muster the zest she was bringing to this issue. *He's also completely jealous,* she told herself. *"Ahab." Honestly. Let's all breathe into a bag and get on with it, shall we?* One of the colonels in Bosnia used to say that.

As the elevator doors dinged open, she forced a shrug. *Whatever. Thank God,* she thought, *for "Whatever."* "Whatever" could stop any unwelcome thought in its tracks. *To be or not to be. Whatever. We have nothing to fear but fear itself. Whatever. Mission accomplished. Whatever.* It was the philosophical equivalent of a Jersey barrier. Maybe she'd have it inscribed on her tombstone: *Here lies Cassandra Devine. Whatever.* So very *meta.* Like Transitioning.

Her BlackBerry began humming like an epileptic bumblebee. A news alert. She read: FATHER OF TRANSITIONING DIVA CASSANDRA DEVINE BLASTS OWN DAUGHTER.

She stopped. Took a deep breath. Stared at the display. Scrolled down:

Billionaire California hi-tech wizard Franklin Cohane says his daughter Cassandra Devine, originator of Senator Randolph Jepperson's "Voluntary Transitioning" scheme to save Social Security, gives him "the willies."

"She's clearly dealing with some issues," said Cohane. "It's not pretty to watch."

Cohane, who made his first fortune developing a package tracking technology which he sold to FedEx for $540 million, said he was taking the unusual step of criticizing his daughter because he found her proposal to offer seniors incentives to kill themselves "morally repellent."

He is a member of President Peacham's "Owl Nest" of major donors. To be an Owl, a person must donate at least $250,000 to the national party.

He said he had never discussed his daughter with the President or his staff, but wishes "the Attorney General had prosecuted her to the full extent of the law: Tearing up golf courses is a very serious crime, to say nothing of trying to overthrow the government."

Cohane said he had not spoken with his daughter in nearly ten years, after a "family squabble," and that she had rebuffed his several attempts at reconciliation, including a "mind-boggling" cash gift.

"She's an angry kid," he said. "I feel sorry for her. She's all screwed up."

He said he was coming forward because he was in the process of "increasing my visibility at the national level" and wanted to "publicly distance myself from someone I happen to be related to but am in no way associated with."

Cass stood in the marble lobby listening to the sound of her heart. She didn't know quite how long she'd been there, not moving, and then she heard a distant voice, ever so familiar to her. It was yelling insistently in her ear, shouting at her, screaming, bellowing: *All right, girls—let's put on our big-girl panties and move it!!!*

It was the voice of her drill instructor at Fort Jackson. *There's something to be said for basic infantry training,* Cass thought as she headed out the door onto the shimmering heat of K Street. Too bad they didn't issue M-16s in civilian life. She'd have used it.

Gideon Payne, hat in hand, mopped his moist brow—Lord, it was warm—and pressed the doorbell to the attractive redbrick house on Dumbarton Street in Georgetown. A servant dressed in a white jacket opened the door almost immediately.

"*Signor Payne! Buon giorno.*"

"*Buon giorno,* and how are *you* today, Michelangelo?" Gideon loved calling a living human being Michelangelo, even if it was only a butler. The interior was blessedly cool.

"Monsignor is expecting you, signor."

He led Gideon across the highly polished creaking floor that had in its day absorbed the footfalls of a Supreme Court justice, an ambassador, and various cabinet members of various administrations. It was over 150 years old and had high ceilings and a graceful curving staircase above an eighteenth-century Italian fountain that burbled softly. Lustrous oil paintings with religious themes hung on the walls. In a niche stood a minor but rather good Saint Sebastian by Donatello. Michelangelo opened the twin doors to the study.

Gideon's host, seated behind a museum-piece rosewood desk, rose and smiled broadly. He was a handsome man in his early fifties, tall and dark, beautifully tanned, graying about the temples, with an athletic build. He was gorgeously accoutred in the raiment of a monsignor of the Roman Catholic Church. Around his neck hung an especially fine silver chain and crucifix that had once adorned the sternum of Giovanni Maria Mastai-Ferretti, future Pope Pius IX and promulgator of the doctrines of the immaculate conception and papal infallibility. A family keepsake.

"Geedeon."

"Massimo."

The two men embraced warmly. Gideon's friendship with Monsignor Montefeltro went back years, but they had really bonded during the affair of the Stomach Madonna.

As a good Southern Baptist, Gideon had been brought up to despise papists and popery. But as a canny Washington operator, he knew the value of coalition building. From his earliest days at SPERM, he had reached out to the Roman Catholic Church to make common cause. They were natural allies in this war. Monsignor Montefeltro had been posted to Washington as its number two, a sort of shadow papal nuncio. The actual papal nuncio was Rudolfo Cardinal Moro-Lusardi, the pope's ambassador. Massimo reported not to him, but directly to the Vatican. For his part, Massimo Montefeltro viewed American Baptists as (barely) more evolved than swamp creatures; but as a Jesuit-trained diplomat, he was acutely aware of the value of a man like Gideon Payne. The odd thing was that these two dissimilar men actually liked each other.

They recognized in each other a kindred risibility, ecclesiastical equivalents of the famous remark by the skeptic who said he didn't understand why two psychiatrists, meeting each other on the street, didn't burst out laughing. It wasn't that Gideon and Monsignor Montefeltro believed they were part of a joke, but that they were mutually conscious of their own outrageousness: two splendid peacocks in the service of Christ.

They admired each other's sartorial style. Gideon was fascinated by the Roman Catholic Church's ecclesiastical garbs and vestments. He had in him a bit of Miniver Cheevy's yearning for "the medieval grace of iron clothing." He would listen to Monsignor Montefeltro for hours as he talked in detail about the finer points of stoles, soutanes, phelonions, and cinctures. After a particularly engrossing description of the holy father's new Lenten chasuble, spun from Persian silkworms and woven with ground Badakshan lapis lazuli, Gideon sighed with wonder and declared, "How very drab by contrast are my own brethren!"

Monsignor Montefeltro smiled and rattled off the names of half a dozen Southern Baptist televangelists whose combined incomes were larger than the gross domestic product of Delaware and who dressed like archangelic pimps. Gideon's own attire—floppy-rimmed Borsalino, silver-tipped cane, high starched collar, cravat, velvet vest, gold chain, and watch fob—itself suggested a Natchez riverboat gambler who was trying to maintain a low profile while visiting up north and not quite succeeding, on purpose. Both men wore rings on the pinky finger. Gideon was envious of the fact that by protocol, Monsignor Montefeltro was entitled to have his kissed. Gideon meanwhile could offer other portions of himself for the same office.

Monsignor Montefeltro had risen to prominence by courting wealthy American Catholic widows, persuading them that the path to sainthood lay in leaving their (husbands') fortunes to the church. He had to date brought in a total of over $500 million for Mother Church. In recognition of this service, he received a living allowance that would certainly have given St. Francis of Assisi pause, if not an embolism, and for his base of operations, so to speak, the Georgetown town house, which could not by any means have been called monastic.

"I saw you on the television," Monsignor Montefeltro said. "You were *very* good, Geedeon. But that woman! *Dio mio.*"

"Oh, Massimo, it was a catastrophe," Gideon said. "An epic catastrophe." There were few others to whom he would have made such a frank admission.

Montefeltro smiled. "Still, you were very good. At least you didn't *murder* her for the cameras." Montefeltro's English was actually Oxford level—he was, in fact, fluent in seven languages—but he found it expedient, especially with the widows, to employ a slightly flawed syntax and accent and sometimes forgot to switch back to his normally impeccable English.

Both men laughed.

"Next time, I will. It is that woman that I have come to discuss."

"Then you must stay for dinner," said the monsignor, "for I have the feeling that you have very much to relate to me."

Chapter 19

"**W**onderful news," said the junior senator from the great state of Massachusetts as Cass entered his office. "We lined up two more— Hey, what happened to you? You look like you ran into a tornado."

Whatever the right metaphor, Cass did look at a minimum out of sorts. Her eyes were red and puffy. She had gotten out of the cab to walk up Capitol Hill to try to clear her head and then burst into tears by the Robert A. Taft Memorial and Carillon, a well-known D.C. locale for emotional outbursts. She had a good sob lasting fifteen minutes, all the time trying to conjure the voice of the drill instructor from basic training to shake her out of it.

"I'm okay," she announced with defiance. "I'm *fine*. I am totally . . . fine."

"Then why is your chin doing that quivering thing?"

"Because my father," she said in a voice loud enough to carry into the outer office, *"is an asshole."*

Randy said in an even voice, "Well, I rather thought *that* was established a long time ago."

She handed him the BlackBerry and commanded, "Scroll."

"Sweet cakes, you know I hate these damn things. Couldn't you just tell me in your own wo—"

"Scroll."

"All right, all right, keep your knickers on."

He read it, groaned, and tossed the device onto his desk. "At least he's consistent. What a prick. Sorry, pumpkin. Now look, we got two more votes. They ate up the 'meta' business. The smart ones get it right off. The dumb ones, forget it. It really is in that regard *representative,* the Congress. Remember what Senator Hruska said about—"

"Excuse me," Cass said. "Are we finished consoling me and now on to Senator Jepperson's thoughts of the day?"

"I was just musing," Randy said. "I agree with you. He's a complete penis-head, your father. It's a wonder you don't have an eating disorder. How are we coming on the Wrinklies campaign?"

Cass sighed. "Can we talk about my prick father for *just* two more minutes? Then I promise I'll spend the rest of my life on you. I'll never mention myself again."

"All right, on that condition."

"You know, I can never tell if you're being serious," Cass said.

"Neither can I," Randy said.

"Look at it," Cass said. "There's something weird about the timing. Why attack me publicly now? It's almost as if it's orchestrated. But who would orchestrate it?" She considered. "The White House?"

"Darling, don't get me wrong, but the White House might have other things on their mind."

"Like Massachusetts senators?"

"Well . . ."

"As a matter of fact, you may have a point. The White House has staked out an anti-Transitioning position. So, darling"—Cass grinned theatrically at Randy—"it might be about you after all. Happy now?"

A look of quiet alarm came over Randy's face. "Go on."

"Frank's a big Owl, big fund-raiser for the party. Probably wants to be an ambassador or something in the second term. At least, his wife probably wants it. He comes out swinging against me. I'm—sorry to dwell on me for a moment—*somewhat* identified as the person who came up with your big idea. So the White House tells him, Go after her. That'll hurt Jepperson. It's plausible. It's *one* explanation. Unless Daddy Dearest just woke up one morning, drank his fresh-squeezed orange juice, and said, 'I think I'll call my daughter morally repellent today.' I wonder . . ."

"What?" Randy said, now all attention and fearful that he was going to find himself within the blast radius of the Cohane family saga. No one wants to be collateral damage in someone else's personal tragedy, especially if you're running for president.

". . . what else they're planning," Cass said.

Randy picked up the phone and said, "Send Mike Speck in, would you?"

A few minutes later, Mike Speck entered. Speck was a former Secret Service agent who handled what Randy called his "special legislative assignments." Randy had brought him aboard his Death Star staff at the beginning of his second, scorched-earth Senate campaign. As Randy described what he called "the problem" to the stony-faced, laconic Speck, Cass almost felt a twinge of concern for her father, knowing that this scary-looking man was headed his way. This was surely the senatorial equivalent of sending Luca Brasi to make someone an offer they couldn't refuse.

After Speck left, not having uttered more than three words, Cass said, "He's not going to break my father's legs or anything, is he?"

"Maybe a pinky or two." Randy had already moved on to the next thing. Cass found him very focused these days. "Okay. *Now*—how's the Wrinklies campaign coming?"

"Terry wasn't hot for it. He hated it, actually."

Randy rolled his eyes. "Well, Terry isn't paying for it, is he? How soon can you get it up and running? We got momentum going here, kiddo. Have you seen the latest numbers? Who was it said it's the customary fate of new truths to begin as heresies and end as superstitions?"

"Huxley. Thomas, not the one who wrote *Brave New World*."

She had seen the numbers, and they were trending—"creeping" might be the better term—their way.

There had been more violence. The latest incidents had been triggered when the Florida State Legislature passed a law exempting mausoleums from state sales tax. As Boomers faced the inevitability of death, despite their healthy diets and exercise and yoga and not smoking and drinking pomegranate juice every morning, they had started to build themselves mausoleums. As with the mansions they had erected in life, so in death they planned to—sprawl.

American passions have a certain viral quality. Competitiveness had entered in. Vast mausoleums were going up all over the state, with features that not even old King Mausolus could have envisioned: "grieving rooms" for the visiting relatives, with music playing twenty-four hours a day (in the event the bereaved felt like stopping by at three a.m. for a quiet sob after hitting the International House of Pancakes); theaters with padded seats where the bereaved could watch home movies of the dearly departed. An entire new industry had sprung up around just that: companies that made epic documentaries about you, complete with interviews, testimonials, animations, sound tracks. One aging Boomer—owner of a string of foreign car dealerships—had commissioned an IMAX film of his (not all that interesting) life, to be shown in perpetuity on the walls of his 360-degree mausoleum. Other Boomers were channeling their intimations of mortality into art: commissioning paintings that celebrated their lives, to hang for all eternity in climate-controlled air beside their remains. Carl Hiaasen of the *Miami Herald* expressed the opinion that it might just be simpler to wall them up in their mansions, "preferably alive." Vast sums of money were being spent on this literal decadence. In due course, the Florida Mortuary Builders Association petitioned the legislature for "special variance"—in other words, tax exemption. The measure passed in midnight session, when no one was looking.

To offset the revenue loss, lawmakers quietly voted during the same session to increase the sales tax on soda, beer, skateboards, video games, and the hypercaffeinated beverages so favored by the youth of the Gator State. (The legislature was banking that they were too brain-dead to notice that their taxes were being raised.) When this news was revealed in the harsh light of day—and the Florida sun can be pretty harsh—it was not greeted with enthusiasm by younger Floridians, who vented their rage by assaulting and defacing the more extravagant mausoleums. Governor George P. Bush once again had to call out the National Guard. The pictures on television of bayonet-wielding soldiers guarding enormous Boomer tombs at the public expense made Transitioning an increasingly attractive proposition. So, yes, Cass had seen the numbers, and Randy was right: There was momentum out there.

"Randy," she said.

"Um?" He was scribbling notes for his speech that night to ABBA—the Association of Baby Boomer Advocates.

"We're not actually expecting Transitioning to . . ."

"Hmm . . ."

"Pass?"

Randy took off his reading glasses and rubbed his eyes. "If you'd asked me that a month ago, I'd have said it was likelier that icicles would form in hell. But you know, we're getting more and more votes. Just as long as we keep giving away the store, mind you." He chuckled mirthlessly. "But at the end of the day?" He sniffed philosophically. "Nah. Not a chance. On the other hand, this *is* America. Our national motto ought to be: 'Since 1620, anything possible, indeed likely.'" He began to hum the words to the Billie Holiday song: "The difficult we'll do right now, the impossible will take a little whi-ile . . ." He said, "That was the Seabees motto in World War Two. Well, point is, we're making a fine nuisance of ourselves. A very fine nuisance," he murmured, looking over his text. "I'm told the White House is passing peach pits over this. They're going to have to deal with Randolph K. Jepperson sooner or later." He handed her the legal pad. "Want to run this through your washer-dryer? It's my speech to ABBA. ABBA. Can you imagine naming yourself that? *Mamma mia.*"

"I've created a monster," Cass said.

"No, darling." Randy smiled. "Mother created the monster. You merely added a few finishing touches."

ABBA had formed a few years earlier when a faction of members of the American Association of Retired Persons decided that aging Boomers needed their own lobby. The split with AARP had been contentious and litigious. Given its demographics—77 million, average household income of $58,000—it had quickly become a formidable lobby. Its guiding philosophy was: "From cradle to grave, special in every way."

ABBA's headquarters on Massachusetts Avenue near Dupont Circle had been designed by the architect Renzo Nolento at a cost the organization preferred not to discuss in public. The building's lobby consisted of an elliptical atrium with brushed steel walls. In an interview with

Architectural Digest, Nolento revealed that he had been inspired by the platinum stainless steel finish of the Sub-Zero refrigerators popular among ABBA's membership. "I wanted to express a certain coldness," he said, "but also a forcefulness that conveys the idea 'Don't fool around with us because we are *very* powerful, okay?' " The metallic walls were inscribed, "Ask not, what can your country do for you. Ask, what has your country done for you lately?"

Randy whispered to Cass as they were escorted to the greenroom behind the stage, "Here we are again—behind enemy lines."

He and Cass had debated whether he should accept the invitation to speak to ABBA. The Boomer membership was not particularly happy that Senator Jepperson's chief adviser, Cass, had been inciting youth mobs to attack their retirement communities. But recognizing the value of getting ABBA "on board" in the Transitioning debate, Randy had been in quiet talks with the leadership. People might not smoke anymore, but the "smoke-filled rooms" lived on one way or the other. And in the spirit of those locales, he had, in the manner of his ilk, been making certain promises.

Among others, Randy had pledged his support for the cosmetic surgery benefit ABBA had been lobbying for, along with a Segway "cost defrayal" so that creaky-kneed (or just plain lazy) Boomers could deduct the full cost of these devices that were now ferrying so many of them around the nation's sidewalks and malls. He'd also agreed to support other ABBA legislative goals: a federal acid reflux initiative; a grandchild day care initiative; visa requirement waivers for elder care; and a sure-to-be-controversial subsidy for giant flat-screen plasma TVs (for Boomers with deteriorating eyesight).

Randy had been busy. What he had *not* done was inform Cass of the full extent of his private deal making. She, destroyer of golf courses and assailer of gated communities, disturber of the Boomer peace, may have been "behind enemy lines" tonight, but Randy was among new friends.

Mitch Glint, ABBA's executive director, stopped by to pay his respects. He extended a somewhat cool handshake to Cass, but a hearty one to Randy. They talked for a few minutes. As he left, he said, "We'll talk more about those other things."

"What 'other things'?" Cass said when they were alone.

"Oh, nothing. Just been keeping the lines of communication open."

"I thought I was your communications person."

"And so you are, so you are. Fill you in later. Need to focus on my speech. Got to be on my toes now, or this crowd'll have my guts for garters."

She watched from backstage, through a partition in the curtains. Normally, Randy hardly limped at all. But when he was walking out onto a stage, he could make himself look like someone dragging out of the surf onto the beach after having his leg gnawed off by a shark.

That's my boy, Cass thought.

Randy began, "When I was lying in the hospital bed after the explosion . . ."

She'd heard that before, many times.

". . . thinking about the far greater sacrifices made by other Americans . . ."

Her mind wandered. She felt, sitting there in the shadows, like a political wife listening to the same speech for the four hundredth time. At least she wasn't out there onstage where you had to force a smile. They must get the zygomaticus muscle equivalent of carpal tunnel syndrome, the wives.

". . . no time for partisanship . . ."

She thought of Terry.

". . . not a Republican issue or a Democratic issue . . ."

Cass's lips moved silently: . . . *but an American issue.* . . .

". . . but an American issue. . . ."

She was texting on the BlackBerry when she became vaguely aware, as if some bat had suddenly appeared and was flitting about in the backstage darkness, that Randy was uttering words she did not at all remember reading in the text she had written for him.

"For our agenda is very much *your* agenda."

What?

"Indeed, there are more things that join us than separate us."

What was he talking about? ABBA was the principal lobby for the enemy, the most self-indulgent, self-centered population cohort in human history, with the possible exception of the twelve Caesars.

She looked up from her BlackBerry and stared at the spotlit figure onstage. His right arm was raised in a pantomime of a Greek statue, index finger pointed upward as if to imply some spiritual connectedness with, or sponsorship of, the heavens, or perhaps some passing American eagle, or, failing that, the auditorium roof.

"Ronald Reagan used to say that the nine scariest words in the English language were 'I'm from the government, and I'm here to help.'"

An amused murmur rippled through the audience.

"Well, ladies and gentlemen . . ."

Where is this going? Cass thought, curiosity turning urgent. She was on her feet now, subconsciously looking about for a long hook.

". . . I *am* from the government. Run—while you have the chance!"

The audience laughed. Cass relaxed slightly. Speechwriters are fundamentally Calvinist: They become nervous if their principals exhibit free will and depart from the prepared text.

"Whatever you thought of his politics, Ronald Reagan was a great man. A courageous man. He took an assassin's bullet and joked to the doctors as they desperately worked to save his life. He survived and saw through his presidency. He outlived many of his adversaries and contemporaries. Survived—but for what? Only to come down with Alzheimer's disease. To die a long, lingering, and inglorious death. Was this any way to go? I think the answer must be—no. No way. No way. At all."

Cass snuck to the edge of the curtain to peer out at the audience. They were stone silent, eyes fixed on Randy. She couldn't tell what they were collectively thinking, but they weren't coughing or fidgeting or furtively BlackBerrying.

"My fellow Americans, we are all of us going to make the Great Transition. We can inject ourselves full of drugs, have doctors replace our organs, change our blood, become bionic Frankensteins. But we were born with expiration dates stamped on our DNA. We can fool some of the diseases some of the time, but we can't fool all of them all of the time. We are all of us sooner or later going to cross the river and rest in the shade on the other side. And just as this generation has always contrived to get the very best from life, so too can it aspire to wring the best from death. My fellow Americans, as Country Joe and the Fish, balladeers of our youth, put it so memorably, albeit in a slightly different context, 'Whoopee! We're all gonna die!' Indeed. So I put it to you: Why not do it the way we've lived our lives—on *our* terms? Why—I put it to you—not do it on *our* timetable? And finally, I put it to you, my fellow Americans—indeed, my fellow Boomers—if we are going to make the ultimate sacrifice, isn't the least our govern-ment can do for us is show a little *gratitude*?"

The audience applauded warmly when he finished. A few even stood. Mike Glint came out onstage to thank him and to tell the crowd that he had demonstrated that he was "someone we can work with."

"Well?" Randy said when the two of them were in the car. Cass had been somewhat quiet. He had the exhausted but exhilarated air of a politician who has just heard the sound of a thousand hands clapping. "Was it good for you, too?"

"Yeah," Cass said coolly. "I had multiple orgasms."

"Well, what on earth is eating you? In case you didn't notice, I just killed."

"You've been doing deals."

"Just a little back-channel dialoguing."

"I knew you'd do it."

"Don't be a downer, darling. Come on—they ate it up. Veni, vidi, vici. Let's go roast an ox, drink the best wine in Gaul."

"Which of our fundamental principles did you trade away first? No, don't tell me. Let me read about it in *The Washington Post*."

"Cassandra. We have to do business with these folks."

"No, we don't. God—you're such a . . ."

"What?"

"*Senator*."

"I didn't realize," Randy said archly, "that it was a term of opprobrium."

Chapter 20

Cass didn't have to wait long. Three days later, ABBA announced that it would support Senator Jepperson's Voluntary Transitioning proposal, and co-sponsor Senator Fundermunk of Oregon had disappeared into a northwest mist. "With the proviso," as Mitch Glint said at his press conference, "that the final legislation reflects ABBA's input."

In Washington, "input" means "demands." ABBA's input consisted of several truckloads of Boomer pork. Cass read down the list with mounting despair: a Botox subsidy? Tax deductions for—Segways? Grandchild day care allowance? The blood throbbed in her temples. Then she came to the real eyebrow raiser: "Mr. Glint further said that Senator Jepperson had 'indicated a willingness to raise the threshold age of Transitioning from 70 to 75.'"

He gave it all away, she thought. *He gave away the entire store.*

She angrily punched the speed-dial button on her cell phone. His emergency cell number, to be used only in the event of a nuclear strike or his receiving the Nobel Peace Prize. Randy answered in a whisper, indicating that he was on the Senate floor. The Senate, bowing to OmniTel, the powerful cell phone and PDA lobby, had relaxed the rules so that senators and congressmen were now permitted to use phones on the floor, even during speeches. They were still banned during the joint session for the president's State of the Union address, but OmniTel's lobbyists were working on it.

"Before you go getting varicose veins," Randy said, "would you like to hear the good news?"

"There is no good news," Cass said. "Don't you realize what you've done? You've made Transitioning completely pointless, even as a meta-issue. Under the Jepperson plan, it will now *cost* the Treasury."

"Are you finished?"

"No. Not nearly."

"Would you please lower your voice? They can hear you clear across the aisle. Hush. As of this morning, and as a direct result of my willingness to meet them halfway—"

"Halfway? Halfway? Are you kidding? You met them in your own end zone!"

"May I continue? We now have thirty-five votes for Transitioning. Barzine and Wanamaker just came aboard. And Quimby says he'll vote for it. The older senators have been taking in so much in campaign contributions from ABBA, they now have no choice but to come aboard. Isn't that marvelous? Of course, with Quimby you never know how he's going to actually vote. Silly old ass. . . ."

"Randy," Cass pleaded in a calmer tone of voice, "these concessions . . . if you raise the age to seventy-five—don't you see, it's meaningless? There won't be any savings. There's no point—"

"Darling. Darling. It's a meta-issue."

"That's not the point."

"We'll fine-tune it. Don't worry. I've got to go. Call me later. I've got some interesting news for you."

"I don't want any more news from you."

"My man Speck checked in. I think you'll want to hear it."

Cass pressed "End." "End" was the new hang-up.

She wanted to reach through the phone and strangle him on the floor of the U.S. Senate. She was so mad, she didn't care what his myrmidon Speck had to report.

ABBA's endorsement of Transitioning made the front page. Randy's proposal that Americans kill themselves in return for tax breaks, a bill that had begun as a turd in the Capitol Hill punch bowl, had now attracted the support of one-third of the U.S. Senate. And this made Randy front-page news.

JEPPERSON EMERGES AS SURPRISING FORCE
IN DEBATE OVER "VOLUNTARY TRANSITIONING"

Within several days, there were more headlines:

WHITE HOUSE SAID TO VIEW JEPPERSON
AS SPOILER IN COMING CAMPAIGN

JEPPERSON DOES NOT RULE OUT
POSSIBLE PRESIDENTIAL RUN

"Was this ABBA deal *your* idea?" Terry said, standing in the doorway of Cass's office, holding a Styrofoam cup of coffee.

"No," Cass snapped.

"Just asking. Have we not had our morning Prozac?"

"He totally sandbagged me."

"Surprise. Did you see the story about how he's thinking of running for—"

"*Yes.*"

Terry closed the door and sat in front of Cass's desk. "Are you pissed off specifically at me, or just with the human race in general?"

"I'm mad at myself."

"For putting your trust in a politician? Or for—"

"Go ahead," she groaned. "For sleeping with him? It just happened. It does *happen,* you know. You're on the road and—"

"The road," Terry said. "That's good. The road did it."

"You're not helping."

"Well, look at it this way. You fucked him before he fucked you. Does that help?"

"Thanks," Cass said. "I feel so much better."

"Do you want me to hire you a grief counselor? Do you know what those people make? Weird niche, when you think about it. What do they do, come to work every morning hoping there's been a plane crash?" Terry said hesitantly, "You, uh, saw about Gideon Payne?"

"No."

"Oh. He . . . What a fat little dick."

"Just tell me."

"He gave a speech last night in West Virginia. Wheeling. Traditional venue for dramatic speeches. Your name came up."

"Terry, you're burying the lead."

"Oh, he said he had some evidence that you and Randy were, uh, doing some pretty hot and heavy fact-finding in the minefield. Also, he called you 'Joan of Dark.' "

"Hm," Cass said, "not a bad line."

"I'm sure someone thought it up for him."

"Yes," Cass said. "Someone clever. What evidence?"

"Ignore it. He's just trying to get back at you for calling him a mother killer."

"Don't be avuncular," Cass said, "or I'll cry."

"Change of subject. So. Our boy wants to be president. Did he mention this while you two were playing hide the salami?"

"That's completely heinous."

"Give these guys one good headline and suddenly they're hearing a chorus of voices. A call he cannot—must not—ignore. The will of the people."

"I don't see it, personally. And I'm not being disloyal saying that."

Terry snorted. "No. But I wouldn't exclude it. It's America. Land of the free, home of the strange. In 1991—you were in diapers—the president of the United States had an approval rating of ninety percent. He'd just won a spectacular war in the Persian Gulf. Eighteen months later, he lost reelection to a horny governor from Arkansas."

"Thank you. I heard something about it. Your point being?"

"American history is one accident after another. But with the right management . . . the right handling . . ."

"Terry—the man just sold me down the Mississippi River. Why would I want to help him become president?"

"So he's an opportunist. How does that differentiate him from ninety-five percent of people who run for president?"

"I thought my generation was supposed to be the cynical one."

Terry said, "I've spent my entire professional life making chicken shit into chicken salad. I'm almost fifty. I hear the flip-flop feet of the Grim Reaper approaching. It's time. I want to work with—turkey shit."

"There's a life goal for you."

Terry shrugged. "Cass, I'm a PR man. This could be my shot."

"Can't you find someone, I don't know, *worthy*?"

"I bet I hate him every bit as much as you do. More."

"This is your justification for wanting to help elect him president of the United States?"

"Didn't you ever want to do something major in your life?"

"I can't believe you just asked me that. I was on the cover of *Time* magazine. Voice of her generation? Hello? Remember?"

"I misspoke. I retract. My prior statement is inoperative. I apologize. Come on. I always wanted to do this. You know, put someone over the top. Play in the big leagues. So. Here's my chance."

"Be my guest. I'd sooner eat caterpillars off a hot sidewalk."

"Where did you pick that up?"

Cass shrugged. "Randy."

"So he fiddled a bit with Transitioning. But look, he got thirty-five senators."

"Stop spinning me. Friends don't spin friends."

Terry leaned across her desk. "So he cut a few deals. Did you skip Civics 101? They *all* do that. So we say to him, 'Look, asshole, we got you this far. We'll get you all the way. Meanwhile, here's what we want in return.'"

"What do we want?" Cass said.

"I don't know," Terry said. "We'll think of something."

"Cass! Come in, sweetheart. I've been thinking about you."

Randy's Senate office, like most, was spacious, and it took some time to cross from the threshold to his desk, which normally gave the senator time to rise to his feet and greet his visitor. But Randy did not rise to greet Cass. Some . . . protocol shift had taken place since her last visit here, the day of the fateful ABBA speech. Not only did he not rise to greet her, but he went back to his paperwork.

"Sit, sit," he said, still not looking up.

"Am I . . . interrupting?" she said a bit coolly.

"You? Never! Thanks for coming by."

"Did you really just say to me, 'Thanks for coming by'?" she said.

"Hm? Problem?"

"No problem. Only, it's just the sort of thing that senators more typically say to, I don't know, Barnstable County Teacher of the Year or some undersecretary of housing and urban development."

"Still mad, are we?"

"Why would I be mad? Just because you completely rewrote the Transitioning bill without bothering to tell me?"

"Look, sweetkins, there's the real world, and then there's the U.S. Senate. We have a chance to carry this thing into the end zone."

"Whose end zone, Mr. Flutie?"

Randy gave her an exasperated look, as though only her recalcitrance stood in the way of acknowledging his political genius. "I don't know how else to put it. We *need* the Boomers."

"I thought the whole point was to oppose the Boomers."

"Same thing. But you want them inside the tent pissing out, not on the outside pissing in."

Cass stared. "Are we quoting Jefferson or Madison?"

"Do you want this bill to pass or not?"

"At this point, no. You've taken my meta-issue and turned it into a Boomer pork sausage. That's not why I signed up."

"I'm sorry that the democratic process doesn't measure up to your high standards. Give my regards to Aristotle and Pericles."

He had the kinda spooky look.

Cass stood. "Well, good luck."

"Where are you going?" he said, looking suddenly more human.

"I'm not 'going.' I'm fleeing."

"Oh, sit down, Cass. Come on. We can work this thing out."

"I'm not a lobby, Randy."

He smiled. "No. I got that." He stood and hopped around the desk to her. Cass realized that was why he hadn't stood. He wasn't wearing his prosthesis. She began to giggle.

"Sorry," she said. "It's . . . just . . . whatever."

"Making fun of cripples. And you all full of umbrage."

He hopped over to the door and locked it.

Sometime later, both of them lying on the big leather couch, she said, "You heard about Gideon Payne's speech?"

"I did," Randy said. "I was thinking of going to his office personally and breaking his nose, but my handlers advise against it. There are certain drawbacks to being a senator. Plus there's the business about his ancestor shooting my ancestor. It would only look like some preposterous blood feud. Not quite the attitude of dignity one strives for if you're thinking of running for president. I suppose I could hire a sniper. That *would* even the historical score."

"Is it something we need to worry about?"

"Shouldn't think. There isn't any evidence. We weren't lap dancing in the minefield." He smiled. "Hardly had time."

"He called me Joan of Dark."

"I saw. Good line, actually."

"Um-hum."

"You'll come up with a good counterpunch, darling," Randy said.

"I was thinking of 'fat little fuck.' What do you think?"

"I like it. It's witty, but it also has substance. Anyway—change of subject—my man Speck reported in. I'm afraid you're not going to like what he found out. This has to be absolutely confidential, yes?"

"No. I thought I'd tell *The New York Times*."

"He's former Secret Service, so he has access to all sorts of . . . No point in going into it, but he's an absolute pit bull, let me tell you. During the last campaign . . . well, never mind."

"You're babbling."

"Darling, I'm in a state of postcoital bliss. Drowning in endorphins. Of course I'm babbling. It seems there were a number of phone calls between your father's very private phone line and the White House."

Cass froze. "Why wouldn't there be? He's a big donor. He's an Owl. . . ."

"Yes, but most of these were made in the days just before your dear old pater announced to the press that you were . . ."

" 'Morally repellent'?"

" 'Fraid so. Sorry."

Cass thought. "Still doesn't mean—"

"Cass. Now who's giving whom the reality check? But let's look at it analytically."

"Beats looking at it emotionally."

"Quite. Let's assume they asked him to denounce you. Why? Cui bono. Them—has to be. In any White House, it's always about them." Randy considered. "Can't quite parse it, but it must have something to do with sparing the White House some embarrassment. It's as if they wanted Frank to publicly identify himself as your dad." He thought. "Of course. That's it. It's quite obvious. Want to take it from there?"

"The media hadn't yet connected the two of us. He'd been lying low. We don't have the same surnames. He's a big donor to the White House, and I'm the Molotov cocktail thrower. And the Justice Department lets me go."

"Clever girl. See what sex does for the brain?"

Cass sighed. "Boy. Regular nest of vipers, isn't it?"

"It's Washington, darling. The shining city upon the hill. Beacon of democracy. Last and best hope of mankind. And you wonder why I have to cut a few deals?"

"Whoa. Bait and switch. You're not off that meat hook yet."

"We'll discuss it. Meanwhile, that's not all my man Speck found out. Does the term 'RIP-ware' ring any bells?"

Chapter 21

The president's mood, already foul, was not improved by Bucky Trumble informing him, during the regular seven a.m. political briefing, that Senator Randolph K. Jepperson was now "not ruling out" a presidential bid. This brought the total number of presidential challengers to—five. It is unpleasant to have this many people publicly expressing the desire to have your job.

"For fuck's sake," the president exploded, sending a gust of hurricane-force, caffeinated breath across his desk at Bucky. "Is there anyone out there who *isn't* planning to run against me? Isn't it hard enough trying to keep this goddamn fucking country"—Bucky Trumble lived in terror that the president, a salty speaker, would one day publicly refer to the United States as "this goddamn fucking country"—"together without having to run a goddamn *primary* campaign? Jesus, Mary, and Joseph, now you're telling me I'm going to have to haul my ass back to New Hampshire in the dead of fucking winter so I can defend myself in some goddamn high school auditorium debate against a bunch of shitheads?"

"Uh, well, sir—"

"How in the hell did it come to this? Someone tell me! You tell me!"

Bucky Trumble trembled.

"It's that fucking Devine woman," the president continued, sending another shock wave of air across the room. "Should have Transitioned *her* ass when we had the chance. But *someone* thought it would be a *brilliant* idea to let her walk!"

"It hasn't played out fully yet, sir," Bucky said. "I'm efforting it very hard. By the way, you saw that Gideon went public with the, ah, 'evidence' we, ah, conveyed to him?"

"I saw," the president grunted. "He goddamn well better not trace it back to us. Evidence. It's thinner'n piss on slate."

The "evidence" that the president of the United States and his political counselor had armed Gideon with against his tormentor Cassandra Devine and—by extension—their tormentor Senator Jepperson was in fact thin. One of the crew members of the helicopter that plucked them wounded from the Bosnia minefield had gotten drunk a few months later and told a U.S. embassy staffer in a bar in Turdje that "they were definitely fucking each other's brains out."

This bit of bar talk was flatly contradicted by Cass's frantic radio reports to base that they were under attack and required assistance. But the embassy officer had duly reported in a cable to the State Department what the drunken warrant officer had told her. From there it was duly leaked to the White House by a deputy assistant secretary of state seeking to curry favor and get a promotion.

It was very far from the kind of information that, as the president had put it to Gideon, "causes tides to turn." But it was enough to pass the muster of Gideon, who in any event was thirsting for revenge against Cass.

The president and Bucky had shown Gideon the State Department cable but refused to give him a copy of it. In Gideon's speech in Wheeling, a historical platform for speeches purporting to reveal shocking State Department information, Gideon only said—but said with great umbrage and conviction—that he had "seen proof positive that Corporal Devine and Congressman Jepperson were doing more than fact-finding."

Bucky said, "The media's eating it up."

The president said, "Well, let's hope he doesn't give up his sources."

"He also called her 'Joan of Dark.' Wish I'd thought of that. Sir, the whip count on the Transitioning bill, it's worrisome. Jepperson's gotten thirty-five senators aboard."

"This thing isn't going to fly. You know that."

"That's not what concerns me. Jepperson's using it as a spring-board. A trampoline. We need to remove the trampoline. And with regard to that, I . . . had a thought."

"Go ahead," said the president, managing to sound bored. He wasn't, but he found it kept people on their toes.

Bucky explained his idea. The president pretended to be listening with only one ear. When Bucky was finished, the president snorted, stared, pursed his lips, rubbed his chin, nose, tugged on an earlobe.

"Not bad," he said, "but won't Gideon shit his britches if we do that?"

"Not if we tell him—on a confidential basis—exactly what we're up to. And . . . throw in a memorial on the Mall."

"Ah, goddamnit, Buck, I don't want to look out my bedroom win-dow onto the Mall and see some memorial to forty goddamn million fetuses. For crying out loud. It's undignified."

"It won't ever get to that. All you have to do is put it out quietly that you're not entirely opposed to it. Tell him you'll call in the senators and congressmen who sit on the Mall Memorial Commission and . . . for-get about it. By then the election will be over and it won't matter what we've promised Gideon. We'll tell him we tried. Have him to Camp David for a weekend, that'll shut him up."

"I'm not spending a weekend with him at Camp David or any-where. But all right. I like it. Tee it up."

"Yes, sir." It was the first time Bucky Trumble had relaxed in months.

Randy had never been to the Oval Office before. Riding down Capitol Hill in the car the White House had sent for him, he couldn't resist daydreaming about a day in the future when he might find himself being driven to the White House in an even bigger car. With Secret Service agents running alongside. Sweating.

The car was turning into the southwest gate, slowing as the uni-formed Secret Service men approached.

Bucky Trumble, the president's chief political counselor, deputy chief of staff, and most trusted aide, the second most powerful man in the country, had called Randy the day before—personally—to congratulate him on the success he was having with his Transitioning bill. Trumble said to him, "The president would like to meet with you."

At first, Randy affected aloofness. "What about, exactly?"

Bucky said, "The president admires the way you've stewarded this issue. As you know, we're on the other side of it. But he's been impressed by the way you've carried the ball. *Very* impressed, you might say."

Randy, now all jelly, said, "Tell the president that while we may not agree on some things, I have the deepest personal respect for him."

"I'll let you tell him that yourself," Bucky said brightly. Time to set the hook. "Senator, may I pay you the compliment of candor?"

"Uh, sure. Of course."

"I must ask for your total discretion."

"You have it," Randy said, flush with curiosity.

Bucky lowered his voice to just above audible, which guarantees intent listening. "The president is keeping his options open with respect to the vice president being his running mate again in the election. In the event . . ." He let the words dangle like mistletoe. "He may choose to designate another running mate."

Randy worried that Bucky might hear his heart going *thump-thump, thump-thump*. "Yes . . ."

"That is not the ostensible purpose of your visit. But strictly between you and me, that is the unostensible purpose for it." Bucky laughed softly. "I'm sorry to be so gosh darn elliptical."

Randy was by now sitting bolt upright at his desk. "I understand," he said solemnly.

"Three o'clock tomorrow?"

"You betcha!"

Randy chided himself for sounding so eager. As a card-carrying member of the WASPocracy, he was good at the old languor; but here his training had, alas, failed him.

He was about to summon the staff and tell them about the call, but then, fearful that they might leak it and blow it for him, he decided to keep it to himself for now. He yearned to tell Cass but worried that she'd tell Terry, and he didn't trust Terry not to blab it all over town. Those PR types were always trying to impress.

He scarcely slept a wink that night.

And so the next day, he found himself walking across the threshold of the Oval Office, omphalos of history, anvil of ambition, and, unbeknownst to him, a large, irregularly shaped trapdoor.

The president gave him his thousand-watt smile and rushed to intercept him as he walked in. Randy's limp became exaggerated as he walked to greet the commander in chief.

How kind of Randy to come on such short notice. Long been an admirer. Hell of a thing he'd done back there in Bosnia. Amazing the way he'd focused the national attention on Social Security reform. Coffee? Will you sit for a moment? Wish we'd done this sooner. Bucky, why'd you take so damn long to invite Randy down here? You falling asleep on the job? Bucky smiled. All my fault, boss. All my fault.

"May I call you Randy?"

"Yes, sir."

"Randy, I've got a job for you."

Randy thought, *That was fast.*

"This Transitioning thing."

"Oh? Yes?" Randy said cautiously.

"You know—and I know—and everyone knows, it isn't going to fly."

"Well"—Randy smiled—"I wouldn't be too absolutely certain of that, Mr. President. We're getting more votes every—"

"*I* would." The president had a strong physical presence. His staff called it "the death stare." It was an accurate name.

"Thirty-five senators have—"

"Doesn't mean shit. They're supporting because they know it'll never pass. Even if it did, you've already gutted it of any positive fiscal impact by handing out all that Boomer pork." He chuckled. "Subsidies for Segways? That's some major oinking."

Randy shifted in his chair and was about to assert himself when the president put a hand on his shoulder and said, "But I will tell you—I like your style. I've been in this business a long time. There's amateurs, there's pros, and then there's thoroughbreds. The ones born to run.

That's you. You were put on this green earth to be a politician." The president leaned back as if weary from having unburdened himself of such a momentous observation. He looked over at Bucky in a gruff, almost accusatory way and demanded, "Did you tell Randy what I had in mind?"

"No, sir."

"Don't bullshit me, Bucky. I can always tell."

"I didn't, sir."

The president looked back at Randy, who at this point was a thoroughly confused thoroughbred. A growly smile spread across the president's face. He said, "I bet he's lying to me. He always does. But it doesn't matter. What does matter is you've got to keep what I'm about to tell you to yourself and only yourself. That includes pillow talk." The president extended his hand. "Can I count on you?" Randy shook his hand and nodded wordlessly.

"All right. Now, I may be looking for a new running mate. I haven't decided yet. But I may."

"I see."

"Bucky here thinks you'd be a real asset. I'm inclined to agree with him."

Randy stared, mute.

"However," the president continued, "there's a problem. This Transitioning business."

Randy stiffened. "I can't just drop it. Nor will I."

"Wouldn't expect you to. Wouldn't ask you to. Wouldn't ever ask a man, especially a man who left a leg behind in a war zone, to throw away his principles just for the sake of advancing his career."

Randy said, "I'm not sure I'm following you, sir."

The president leaned in closely. "Look here, son. Now, sooner or later, this silly Transitioning business is going to blow up in your face. You'll look like you just bit down on an exploding cigar." The president glanced at Randy's leg. "I mean . . . Hear me out. You're not going to get the votes. And then where will you be? You'll just be the poster boy for suicide. You can call it 'Transitioning' or whatever the hell you want. It's still legalized suicide, never mind all that shineola about how it's all for the common good. Even if you did get the votes, I'd veto it faster'n you can take a morning crap. I promise you that. Now, I can't *have* for a running mate someone whose name is synonymous with 'lethal injection.' We've got to put some daylight between you and this bill. Like you said, you can't just walk away from it. You need an exit strategy. Some way where you *can* walk away from it and still have your integrity. And once that's done, I believe you would make me a fine running mate. You're young, good-looking, a regular Pied Piper with the kids. And we're going to need them. Yes, you remind me a bit of John F. Kennedy. You with me, Randy?"

"I think so, sir."

"Sure you are." The president smiled. "Hell, you went to Harvard. Now, the way it would work, I would come out and make a public statement, say, 'Look here, I don't like the idea of people jumping off bridges in return for tax breaks. It's un-American. But I recognize that we live in damn hard times—and we got to do something about it.' "

Bucky Trumble nodded. "That's right."

"I'd say, 'I'm a reasonable man. I'm willing to listen to both sides of the argument. So I am going to' "—the president paused for dramatic effect—" 'appoint a blue-ribbon Presidential Commission on Transitioning. I'm going to call together all the best minds in the country—starting with Senator Randolph K. Jepperson of Massachusetts, who I suppose knows as much about this issue as anyone on the planet.' Naturally, we'll have to have other people of diverse views. But you'll be my first pick. My"—he grinned—"eyes and ears. I'll say, 'I am asking these distinguished Americans to deliver me their report. And at that point I will make up my mind as to whether this proposed solution truly represents this country's best chance at solving this most dire dilemma.' Still with me, Randy?"

Randy nodded.

"Now, what'll happen is you'll be front and center, with daily TV coverage. Only now instead of looking like the poster boy for mass suicide, you'll be the voice of reason. You'll get to say in front of cameras—with everyone watching—as you interview witnesses, 'Well, hm,

I don't know, maybe this *isn't* the answer, after all. Maybe there is a better way.' I see headlines. JEPPERSON EMERGES AS MODERATING VOICE ON TRANSITION COMMISSION. I see another headline. Want to hear it?"

Randy nodded.

"WHITE HOUSE SAID TO BE IMPRESSED BY JEPPERSON PERFOR-MANCE ON COMMISSION."

"WHITE HOUSE *DAZZLED*," Bucky corrected.

The president smiled. "You want to hear one more? PEACHAM ASKS JEPPERSON TO BE RUNNING MATE. Do you like that headline, Randy? Do you?"

A little voice inside Randy was shouting, *Look out!* but what came out of his mouth was, "I believe so. Yes."

The president leaned back with a contented air. He looked over at Bucky. "What about you, Buck? You like that headline?"

"I like it a lot."

The president stood, extended his hand, and said, "Okay, then, pardner. See you round the corral."

It was only later that Randy would note the conjunction of the words *okay* and *corral* in the sentence.

Cass was cooking dinner for the two of them—a rare thing in these busy days—in Randy's Georgetown manse. She had the TV on as she worked. She heard the anchor say, "And the White House today an-nounced that it was appointing a special Presidential Commission on Transitioning . . ." She looked up from her soft-shell crabs.

The phone rang. It was Terry, saying, "Turn on the TV."

"It's on."

"What do you know about this?" he asked.

"Nothing."

"Where's the junior senator from the great state of Massa-chusetts?"

"He's on his way. I'm cooking dinner for him."

"What are you making?"

"Soft-shell crabs."

"What are you cooking them in?"

"Skillet. Why?"

"Well, when he walks in the door, hit him in the face with it. He's *on* the commission. It was just announced."

"What? Impossible. He'd have said something."

She heard the door open. "Randy?" she called. "Is that you?"

"Hi, darling. Are you in the kitchen?" His voice had a foreign upbeat quality to it.

Cass said to Terry, "I don't believe this. Call you back."

"Kill him," said Terry.

"Yum! Soft-shells! I love soft-shells. How was your day, sweetie?" He gave her a kiss on the cheek.

"Fine. How was your day? Darling."

"Gosh. Busy. Listen—great news."

Cass sliced tomatoes. It kept her from disemboweling Randy with the knife.

Randy said, "You won't believe it."

"I've seen a few things in my time. Try me."

"I got the White House to appoint a commission on Transitioning."

Cass stared.

He added, "It's unbelievably good news for our side."

"A presidential commission," Cass said somewhat coolly. "Boy. Those don't come along just every day."

"It wasn't easy, let me tell you. Had to twist quite a few arms. Bucky Trumble is one tough cookie. I had half an hour's face time in the Oval with the president."

"Really? Well, you have been a busy boy," Cass said, clutching her knife, reminding herself that killing a U.S. senator was a federal crime.

"Aren't you pleased? You don't sound pleased."

Cass adopted a pensive attitude. "Didn't you tell me that presidential commissions were what they appointed when they didn't want to do anything about something, while giving the illusion that they do?"

"*Moi?* Did I? I don't remember that. No. No, no. Au contraire.

Commissions are—my gosh, if you want to shine a light on something, there's no better way. Darling, you don't seem to grasp what marvelous news this is: a presidential commission. Blue-ribbon. You might be a little enthusiastic."

"Let's review," Cass said. "You've gone from hating the idea, to championing the idea, to giving away the idea, to sitting on a commission to discuss the idea. It's not quite the 'take that hill' brand of leadership, is it?"

Randy said, "I'm going to be more than just a commissioner." He chuckled. "Don't you doubt that. The White House is . . . This is really-really-really between us, okay? . . . The White House is on *our side*."

"Really?" said Cass. "Funny. You wouldn't think so, the way they've attacked the idea day after day. Not to mention encouraging my father to denounce me."

"Darling. They can hardly come right out and say they like it. Presidents can't just endorse mass suicide. It's not presidential."

"Yes, that seems to be the general case in this town. Everyone walking around wishing they could say what they really believe."

"I'm starved. Let me go wash up."

"Yes," Cass said. "You'd better, if you've been at the White House."

He ignored it and gave her a peck kiss on the cheek and toodled off.

Cass called Terry. "Should I use the nine-inch skillet on him or the twelve-inch?"

"The twelve-inch," Terry said. "They just announced Gideon Payne is on the commission."

Chapter 22

Dinner was not a success, and through no fault of the food. Cass served the crabs, along with dilled new potatoes and fresh tomatoes in balsamic vinegar, onto Randy's lap. She then stormed out of the mansion, giving the ancient door such a satisfyingly good slam that the stained glass transom rattled. She drove back to her apartment and hunkered down in front of her computer in a Red Bull rage. When the going gets tough, the tough get blogging.

There was a lot to do. She had to respond to Gideon's charge about the Bosnian "evidence." Once that was done, she would have to explain to her millions of loyal followers—followers who were depending on her—why their maximum leader, the senator from the great state of Massachusetts, Randolph "Let's Make a Deal" Jepperson, had apparently sold them all down the river for some unspecified mess of pottage. The proximate cause of her dumping the delicious meal onto his lap was his refusal to tell her exactly what devil's bargain he had entered into with the White House (in return for selling her out). Then there were thousands of e-mails wanting to know about her father's denunciation of her. She sighed. She was tired. Should she take a Ritalin? It would be a long night. But it was good to be back in the cockpit. In cyberspace, everyone can hear you scream.

The phone rang and rang. Randy. She answered four times, each with, "Fuck off," and hung up. The fifth time, she picked up and listened. A strained voice said, "I'm all in favor of screwing, but can we at least do it in bed and not over the phone?"

"I'm glad you called," she said. "I need your help with the wording of this posting for CASSANDRA. See what you think: 'Senator Sells Soul to Lowest Bidder. . . .' Do you like it?"

"Cass—"

"Originally I had 'Highest Bidder,' but I changed it to 'Lowest.' I'm not sure what it means, but I like it. It says 'sleazy.' That's just the headline. Do you want to hear the whole post?"

Randy said, "Cass, will you please calm down?"

"Too late. I've drunk three Red Bulls."

"Well, take a pill. You're coming unhinged. You're completely mis-interpreting this. I'm telling you, it's a coup what I've pulled off."

"What did they promise you?"

Randy had been in Washington long enough to lie smoothly, but he couldn't quite bring himself to do it to her. Anyway, she wouldn't believe him. Once you've slept with a woman, it's harder to lie to her, despite the necessity. "That Transitioning would get a good full hear-ing, with all sides represented, in the plain light of day. You have to understand, Cass, this is the way to go."

"I can't even discuss it. And please, spare me a lecture on 'How Our Democracy Works.' It's a good thing it was your ancestor and not you who worked on the Declaration of Independence. You'd have put in a clause reimbursing King George for the tea they dumped in Boston Harbor."

"What do you want me to do? Get down on my one good knee and beg forgiveness?"

"A new record. Less than a minute into the conversation and you've played the amputee card. I'm beginning to wonder if it's your leg you left over there or two other parts."

"That's not very nice."

"Sorry. No, actually I'm not sorry."

"All right. Start over. I'm sorry I didn't consult with you first."

"You should have."

"I know. You're right. I'm pathetic."

"More."

"How can I ever forgive myself? I should have told the president, 'I have to check with my girlfriend first.' "

"Girlfriend? You mean the one you got the whole idea from in the first place?"

"Intellectual partner. Soul mate. *Anam cara*."

"What?"

"It's Celtic. A good thing. Trust me."

"Trust is the issue here, Randy."

"I'm sorry. Okay? I am truly, sincerely sorry."

"Try practicing in front of a mirror. Call me in the morning."

"I will. But no blogging, okay? Promise? . . . Cass? . . . *Ca-ass?*"

Cass and Terry were working on a PowerPoint presentation for a client who was looking to get a fat government subsidy for distilling automobile fuel out of used fast-food restaurant fry grease when the senator from the great state of Massachusetts walked in, looking somewhat less great than his state. He was limping, Cass noticed, and for once it had the look of sincerity. He slumped wordlessly into a chair.

"Did you really," he said to Cass, rubbing his forehead, "have to say that about me on your website?"

Terry looked at Cass.

She explained, "I quoted Groucho Marx: 'I've got principles. And if you don't like those, I've got others.'"

"Sounds about right," Terry snorted.

"Before you two swoop down and begin feasting on my carcass," Randy said, "I've got something to say."

"If it's your *Ich bin ein asshole* speech," Terry said, "I'm all ears."

"Finished?" Randy said. "I called Bucky Trumble this morning, and I gave him what-for."

Terry said to Cass, "'What-for'? Is that WASP-talk?"

"I said to him, 'How could you put Gideon Payne on the commission when just the other day he suggested that Cass and I were . . . *screwing* in a minefield?' He said they had to put him on. I told him in no uncertain terms that I was not pleased."

Cass said, "I bet that had him quaking in his loafers."

"I'm trying," Randy said, "to make amends."

"Why don't you tell us what deal you struck with them in return for this abortion."

Randy glanced at Terry, then at Cass with a look of *Not in front of the children.*

"Is he suggesting," Terry said to Cass, "that I leave—my own office?"

Cass said, "Randy. What do I have to do—toss a stick of dynamite down your throat? Just tell us."

"This stays in this room. They're thinking of dumping Laney. And when they do, they'll make me VP."

Cass and Terry stared.

"They were *very* impressed with the way I've handled the Transitioning bill."

Still no reaction from Cass and Terry.

"He said I remind him of JFK."

Cass and Terry reacted. They burst out laughing.

"You, uh," Cass said, trying to compose herself, "got this in writing?"

"Of course not. It's a deep, deep secret. Which I'm counting on you two to keep. So don't, please, blow it for me."

"Wouldn't dream of it. Well, at least I got it right that you sold out to the lowest bidder."

"Lowest bidder? They're offering me the vice presidency! You make it sound like I won ten dollars in some county fair for growing the second biggest cucumber."

"More like for laying the biggest egg. There wasn't much point left to Transitioning after your Boomer pork giveaway spree. And now you've thrown the rest of it down the drain for a slot on some idiot commission."

Randy glowered.

"And you can cool it with the 'kinda spooky' look. You look like a poodle pretending to be a Rottweiler."

For a few seconds, Randy looked as though he might take off his leg and start smashing furniture. Then the air went out of him. His muscles untensed. Suddenly he looked like a schoolboy who'd run out of excuses. Cass was almost moved to comfort him.

"I guess I have made a bit of a pig's breakfast of it," Randy said, chewing on a fingernail.

"There," Cass said. "See? Telling the truth is like riding a bicycle. No matter how out of practice you are, it'll come back to you."

"I don't suppose you two would help me clean up the breakfast?"

Cass and Terry looked at each other.

Randy added, "On a professional basis, of course."

"Oh," Terry snorted, "definitely."

Randy said, "I can't do this without you."

"What about that crack ninja Senate staff of yours?"

"I don't like them. I don't trust them. They scare me."

Cass said, "I work for Terry. It's up to him."

"In that case," Randy said, "I'm done for."

Terry said, "Are you capable of following instructions?"

"Within reason," Randy said, reverting to aristocratic mode.

It was Cass, not Terry, who issued Randy his first instruction: to call Bucky Trumble and tell him that if Gideon Payne was going to be on the presidential commission, then so was Cassandra Devine. When she got Bucky on the phone, he resisted, but Randy, with Cass hovering over him, informed the president's chief counselor that he didn't really have a choice in the matter.

The ring tone of Gideon Payne's cell phone was programmed to the sound of church bells tolling "Hallelujah." All day long it had sounded like Easter Sunday.

A number of his callers were incredulous that he had accepted a job on a commission appointed to study the feasibility of legalizing mass suicide. Many of these were big SPERM donors. Gideon patiently explained that he was now in a position to influence—or as he put it, "determine"—the outcome. He did not reveal the precise terms of his deal with the president. But he hinted heavily that before long they would be hearing a message of support from the White House about SPERM's long cherished memorial on the Mall to the 43 million unborn. To this reassurance, he added, with a coy little chortle, that with him on the commission, Transitioning now stood as much chance of becoming national policy as a snowball in the infernal region.

Gideon did not have much chance to wallow in his new position. The next day, a sheepish-sounding Bucky Trumble called him to say that, uh, well, it seems that Cassandra Devine is also going to be on the commission.

"This is monstrous!" Gideon exploded. "She's the *architect* of this fiendish scheme! It's like putting Adolf Hitler on the board of B'nai B'rith!"

Bucky equivocated to the overheated reverend that, much as he wanted to, he was unable to remove the dreadful woman from the commission. In soothing tones, he said that he and the president had "full confidence" in Gideon's ability to "decisively influence" the commission.

"The president is counting on you," Bucky said. "You're our man on the commission."

"What about my memorial?" Gideon demanded sulkily.

"Gideon. If we don't get the president reelected, there won't *be* a memorial. If Jepperson and that terrible woman prevail . . . well, I shudder."

"I still want a statement for the record of the president's support."

"The announcement is being drafted even as we speak."

Late the next Friday afternoon, when even an announcement that the United States was preemptively launching a nuclear war might be overlooked by the media, the White House issued a statement saying that it had "no objection in principle" to a "life memorial in a suitable locale within the nation's capital."

Gideon telephoned the White House to express his displeasure at this tepid declaration of support. Bucky assured him that the president would make his memorial "a priority" in the second term. On hanging up, Bucky Trumble wondered if he had done the right thing by inviting Gideon into his tent. His days were full enough without being on the receiving end of half a dozen daily hysterical phone calls from a steam-driven man o' god. Gideon's high-pitched voice was far from dulcet, even on an otherwise calm day.

*   *   *

Gideon and Monsignor Montefeltro met for a glass of 1997 Brunello di Montalcino to discuss strategy. The monsignor kept a superb cellar beneath his Georgetown home. Bottles from this happy catacomb had lubricated the pen hands of many a wealthy Catholic widow as they signed away vast tranches of their substance to Mother Church. How well the Lord would be pleased with them. Don't forget to sign here, too. And initial here.

Gideon shared with the monsignor every jot and tittle of his deal with the White House. Montefeltro was himself a man thoroughly versed in hierarchies, a denizen of one of the world's most ancient bureaucracies. Gideon craved his advice.

"Bucky Trumble, he sounds a very clever fellow," he said, pouring Gideon a second glass. "But since he is a clever fellow, you must be vigilant, Geedeon."

"Oh, to be sure," Gideon said sipping the wine, "to be sure."

"Do you believe Bucky Trumble when he tells you the president will make the memorial a priority in his next term of office? After he is reelected, he won't need quite so much from his old friends and supporters."

"Massimo," Gideon said, "no more, thank you, it's delicious, just delicious, but I'll be three sheets to the wind. Of *course* they're lying to me. How they *do* lie. But don't suppose for one second that they're going to play me for the fool. Gideon Payne did not fall off the back of a sweet potato truck. No, no, no. At the appropriate time, between the national political convention in August and the start of the general election on Labor Day, I will insist that they make the memorial a campaign issue. I will insist on a written declaration." Gideon pursed his wine-moist lips.

"There is a matter I must share with you," the monsignor said. "There was a meeting at the Vatican some days ago. On the subject of the American Transitioning bill. There is a group of some cardinals. Very orthodox, very doctrinal, very severe. The chief of them is Cardinal Restempopo-Bandolini. He is very important in the Vatican. Really, he is the semipope. Very powerful. What I will tell you now must sound very old-fashioned, but these cardinals, they see in this Transitioning an opportunity. At this meeting—this is very secret, Geedeon—they urged the holy father to issue a bull."

"A . . . what, Massimo?"

"A bull of excommunication, against any American Catholic who supports such a bill. Or who even votes for any politician who supports such a bill."

"Excommunication. You mean, you get tossed out of the church?"

"Yes. Forbidden from sacraments. Like I say, it's very old-fashioned. To me, honestly, Geedeon, I think it's too much. But they are very powerful, these cardinals. And I fear the holy father will listen to them. What will be the reaction of America in such an event?"

Gideon drew a deep breath. It was exhilarating to hear this news, and from the lips of someone intimately familiar with the innermost thinking of Rome, but—great God . . . a papal *bull*? Didn't that go out with the Borgia popes?

"Massimo," he said gravely, "I'm most grateful and honored that you have shared this confidence with me. But I must tell you, I am not certain that that is the way to proceed here. I'm sure you know your flock better than I do, but Americans don't cotton to the idea of—"

"Cotton?"

"Sorry. Southern expression. Americans don't like being told what to do by a—you'll forgive me—foreigner."

Monsignor Montefeltro said, "Geedeon. The pope is not 'foreign.' He is the universal church."

"Yes, yes, I understand that. And I have only the highest respect. I'm only saying that if the pope issues some bull—and by the way, 'bull' is a pretty pungent term here; indeed, I fear for the puns that will result—but if the pope goes issuing bulls, it could upset things quite a bit."

"I would say, from the perspective of Rome, things are already very upset in America, Geedeon. But I understand what you are saying, and I will of course relay this to Rome."

"This Transitioning is going to be deader than a run-over raccoon. I'll see to that. You tell your cardinals that Cardinal Gideon is on the case." He winked. "Delicious wine, by the way."

"There is a case of it in your car." Monsignor Montefeltro smiled.

"Your generosity leaves me speechless."

Chapter 23

*W*hat now? Frank Cohane thought, seeing his daughter's name pop up on his Google news alert page yet again. She was the Terminator. He read aloud.

Appointed to the Transitioning commission. For chrissakes. Her and her senator boyfriend Jepperson.

In due course, Bucky Trumble called to give him a heads-up about the commission. He told Frank there was more to it than met the eye. He wouldn't say any more, only that they'd put Gideon Payne on it, as a "firewall." He hinted that they'd tricked Jepperson into serving on it so as to reduce his visibility as Mr. Transitioning Champion.

Frank had complex views about Gideon Payne. Deep down, he couldn't stand the man. He had no taste for southern Bible-thumpers. This one was always in the news, yammering about building some grotesque monument to fetuses—fetuses!—on the Mall in Washington or showing up at the bedside of people who'd been declared brain-dead twenty years ago, with a media posse in tow, calling down thunder and federal intervention.

Which made it all the more strange that Frank Cohane found himself in business with Gideon Payne. The (highly confidential) negotiation with Elderheaven had gone through. Gideon's string of old folks' homes were RIP-ware's first client. Every prospective resident at Elderheaven was required to submit to the RIP-ware questionnaire (DNA, family history, lifestyle). Elderheaven was quietly turning away anyone for whom RIP-ware was predicting longevity and accepting the ones who had only a few years left, while pocketing their entire life savings.

In the six months since Elderheaven had begun using RIP-ware in its applications process, the mortality rate of Elderheaven had shot up 37 percent. Profits were up 50 percent!

Frank, who was as canny a businessman as he was an engineer, had insisted on a 10 percent share of Elderheaven profits. Everyone was making a killing.

For this reason, Frank Cohane kept his personal feelings about Gideon Payne to himself. As for Gideon, it had come as a bit of a shock to him when he realized that RIP-ware's owner was the father of his archenemy, Cassandra Devine. But he was greatly mollified by Frank's denunciation of her as morally repellent. He told Frank, "I'm sure she takes after her mother."

Frank had watched the famous episode of *Greet the Press* where Cass told Gideon she wasn't about to be lectured by someone who'd run his own mother off a cliff. He'd had a good laugh at that. A scrapper, his little girl. He reflected, with mixed emotions, that he had no doubt played a role in that aspect of her development.

Now he found himself thinking back to the call a few weeks ago from Bucky Trumble, asking him to denounce her publicly: *The president would very much appreciate it if . . .* Hell of a thing to ask a father to do.

The White House drafted his talking points. *Morally repellent? Jeez, Bucky, that's a bit . . . harsh, isn't it?* Bucky said, *Look, Frank, if you're going to do it,* do it. He gave in. But Frank had taped Bucky's phone call. He taped all his calls. In life as in engineering, Frank Cohane believed in zero tolerance.

A week later, his security people reported a hack into Applied Predictive Actuarial Technologies' phone system. The weird part was that they'd traced it to a server in Winchester, Virginia, maintained by an obscure division of the U.S. Treasury Department. Why was the government suddenly interested in his company's phone calls? Then he thought: *Is it possible Bucky Trumble has something to do with it?* Did he suspect that Frank had taped their phone call? Was he trying to send Frank a warning?

Concentrate, Frank told himself. *RIP-ware. RIP-ware. RIP-ware. It's going to make you one of the richest people on the planet.*

His cell phone rang. The caller ID said: *LISA*. He hesitated before answering.

"Yeah, Leese?" he said, trying to sound hurried so as to keep the conversation short. "What? . . . When? . . . Jesus, Lisa. What does he think college is? A four-year-long wet T-shirt contest, for chrissake? I told you it was crazy to send him to Yale. He couldn't get into . . . I'm not being hard on him. I'm being realistic. I haven't said one goddamn word to him. Not that he'd understand if I did. You're right I'm pissed off. Cost me ten million dollars to get that nitwit into . . . I didn't mean it that way. . . . Lisa . . . Lisa . . . will you . . . Well, fuck you, too!" Frank Cohane hurled the cell phone across his office.

In the distance, a sea lion surfeited on salmon bellowed.

Randy and Cass were in bed. For all his flaws, it was good to be back there with him. Dear Randy. He was so obvious, but in men it can be a kind of saving grace. Transparency confers absolution.

Cass lay next to him, head nestled against his shoulder, fingers idly twirling a strand of his sandy-colored hair. She was happy and at peace. She'd missed this more than she cared to admit.

Randy said, "I heard some more from my guy Speck." *Odd choice of pillow talk,* she thought.

"Um?"

"So guess who flunked out of Yale?"

"George W. Bush?" she said, not terribly interested.

"Your stepbrother. What's-'is-name. Byrd. Boyd."

Cass wasn't sure how to process the information. "I never thought of him as my stepbrother. I've never even met him."

"Quite the party animal, it would seem."

She felt a twinge of indecent curiosity. "Randy, why would your guy Speck be investigating my stepbrother?"

"You know how it is. You point these guys in a direction and they keep going. They don't stop. You do want to keep track of all the pieces."

"Why is Boyd a piece?"

"Well," Randy said, "your father more or less declared war on you. Calling you morally repellent. Know thy enemy, I always say. The Jepperson family motto is, 'Don't be caught with your pants down.' Goes back to Baron Guy de Jepperson. Fourteenth century. Or was it thirteenth?"

"I'm not sure I think of some seventeen-year-old college kid as my 'enemy.' "

"Eighteen. And he's an ex–college kid. His mother—your step-mother—now *she's* a piece of work, I hear."

"Do we have to talk about this now?"

"Former tennis pro," Randy said. "What *is* it about tennis pros? You know the type."

"Not really," Cass said, rolling over and staring up at the ceiling. "I never spent any time at country clubs. So, tell me, what kind of moral deficiency is implicit in the job description for 'tennis pro'? Shoplifting? Serial murder? Terrorism?"

"They're rather keen at the networking. She'll make a dandy ambassador's wife."

Cass flumped a pillow and sat up. "You're awfully informed about all this."

"It's my business."

"Why is it your business?"

"Darling girl. I'm trying to protect you. Don't you want to be protected?"

"Are you serious? In this relationship, who protects whom?"

Randy shrugged. "Knowledge is power. These people are out to get you."

"Are you familiar with the word *buzz kill*?"

"Military term?"

"No, sweetheart. It's what people my age say after they've made love to someone and they're lying in their arms thinking soft, wonderful, dreamy, lilac-scented thoughts, and suddenly their lover announces that his private investigator and personal executioner has learned that some stepbrother they've never met and don't even care to know has been kicked out of a college that they got into once without their asshole father donating ten million dollars to it and that the evil stepmother now wants the asshole dad to give huge amounts of money to a corrupt U.S. president so that she can become an ambassador's wife. And suddenly she's gone from warm and fuzzy to cold and trembling. Buzz kill. It's in the dictionary, under B. You could look it up."

"Good word." He rolled toward her. "Can we . . ."

"What?"

"Go back to the buzz?"

"Yes," Cass said, rolling back to him, "I like that part."

The first meeting of the Commission on Transitioning and Tax Alleviation was gaveled to order.

There were several dozen commissioners, roughly the number required to satisfy every special interest group clamoring to have "input" into the question of whether Americans should be allowed to kill themselves in return for a tax break.

ABBA was of course represented, as were various other Boomer advocate groups: the National Organization of Baby Boomers (NOBB); the Association for the Economic Enhancement of Persons Born Between 1946 and 1964 (AEEPBB46–64, one of the more unwieldy lobby acronyms, but still not an organization to be trifled with). Also present were representatives of the Mortuary Association of North America (MANA); the National Association of Lethal Injectionists (NALI); the Reverend Gideon Payne of SPERM; the Association of Floridian Assisted Living Facilities (AFALF); the American Association of Actuaries; the Botox Institute; the Organ Transplanters Network of North America (ONTNA); the National American Body Part Exchange Network (NABPEN); the American Golf Cart Manufacturers Association, which had formed a kind of alliance with the Segway Owners of America (also present); the American Association of Expensive Estate Attorneys; the Canadian Association of Providers of Cheap but Not Altogether Reliable Pharmaceuticals, an increasingly powerful voice in Washington, despite being based in Ottawa; Senator Randolph K. Jepperson; and Ms. Cassandra Devine, representing the eponymous CASSANDRA. The chairman had taken care to seat her at the opposite end of the semicircular dais from Gideon Payne.

"Mr. Chairman," Gideon said as soon as Randy had gaveled the first meeting to order, "may I be recognized?"

"Yes, Reverend Payne."

"I move that we commence our deliberations with a prayer."

"Reverend Payne," said the chair, "I'm sure that we are all in our own ways prayerful that we will conduct our hearing in a—"

"That being the case, then may I proceed to ask Almighty God's blessing upon our work?"

Cass raised her hand. "Mr. Chairman?"

"Yes, Ms. Devine?"

"I second the motion."

"You do?" There were puzzled looks all around.

"Yes. If the gentleman from SPERM is in need of spiritual assistance, who are we to deny it to him? If I'd done the things he's done, I'd certainly want the Almighty's forgiveness—"

"Mr. Chairman!" Gideon, now the color of a canned Harvard beet, shouted, "I did not come here to be insulted by someone who advocates mass murdering to solve a budgetary problem!"

The chair tapped his gavel wearily. "Reverend Payne, Ms. Devine. Please. We have a great deal to do."

"I demand an apology," Gideon said.

"I apologize," Cassandra said. "It was insensitive of me to bring up Mr. Payne's past in such an insensitive manner."

"Mr. Chairman! I will not be insulted!"

Tap-tap-tap-tap-tap-tap. TAP.

"Please."

SPARKS FLY AT OPENING SESSION
OF TRANSITION COMMISSION HEARING

Frank Cohane was in no good mood. His private jet couldn't land at Tweed–New Haven Airport because the runway wasn't long enough, so his pilot had to put down in Bridgeport, half an hour from Yale.

With the upcoming roll-out of RIP-ware, he had a thousand better things to do. Make that a thousand and one.

This was, needless to say, Lisa's idea. Idea? More of an order. *Go out there and tell them if they don't take Boyd back,* you're *taking your ten million dollars back!*

Frank Cohane, billionaire, wizard of technology, hotshot entrepreneur, yachtsman, friend of and adviser to the president of the United States, future secretary of the United States Treasury, did not enjoy being given commands by a former tennis pro, no matter how good the sex was.

Why had he remarried? What possessed him? If he'd only waited a little longer, his dick would no longer have been in charge.

The president of Yale greeted Frank in his office in Woodbridge Hall. He was a mild, pleasant man, an economist by training, amiable, polished, at ease in any situation. When two men at the top of their various professions meet, they don't waste each other's time inquiring about the other's golf handicap.

"Frank," the president said, "this isn't a question of blame. In the end, it probably wasn't fair to Boyd to expect that he would—that it would work out for him here. He'd probably be much better off—much happier—at some other college."

Frank nodded. "He'd be happier smoking marijuana twenty-four hours a day, playing video games, and downloading porn. But that's not why I'm here."

The president frowned. "Don't sell him short. He's a good kid. I think he's just overwhelmed here."

"How much?"

"How much . . . what, Frank?"

"To reenroll him."

"I don't think that's"—the president sighed—"the right approach."

"Another ten. Done?"

The president stared, mouth open.

"Fifteen, then," Frank said. He rose before the president could let out so much as a croak and gave him a California grin. He thrust out his hand. "It'll be wired to you by noon. Great to see you. Keep up the terrific work. I like your office. Fabulous ceilings." And with that he was out the door, leaving the president of Yale speechless and, really, helpless.

Frank wanted to get back to the plane and wheels up without spending another minute there. He felt as though he had just pulled off some sort of crime and was eager to flee. But he knew Lisa would demand to know if he'd seen Boyd, and there would be a scene if he hadn't. So he made his way to Boyd's room in Jonathan Edwards College, one of the prettier residential colleges at Yale. He found Boyd putting things into cardboard boxes.

"You can put that stuff back," Frank said. "You're reenrolled."

Boyd gave him a perplexed look. "But they—"

"It's done. You're back in."

Boyd gave no indication as to whether this was good news to him. But then he was not a very expressive young man.

"Boyd . . . ," Frank said, noticing a colorful tubular plastic object on the table, with a mouthpiece at one end and a bowlful of dark, impacted ash on the other. The center of the vessel contained a quantity of liquid that might have been—he guessed—crème de menthe, through which several hundred cubic feet of smoke had been filtered. "What is that?"

"Science project?"

"Really. Uh-huh. What is the name of the course that you're doing this . . . project for?"

"Fluid dynamics?"

"Fluid dynamics. Terrific. So this would be to measure the effects of, say, Prandtl-Glauert condensation?"

"Right," Boyd said. "Definitely."

"Well, it's wonderful that you're buckling down. Boyd . . ."

"Yeah?"

"Nothing," Frank said. "Call your mother, would you? Just tell her we had a good talk. Would you do that for me?"

"Cool. No problemo."

"Do you need money?"

"Yeah," Boyd said, brightening. "Sure."

Frank stripped five hundred-dollar bills off his billfold.

"Hey, thanks, Frank."

"Good to see you, Boyd."

Twenty-five million dollars. Twenty-five million five *hundred* dollars. But look at how seriously he was applying himself to . . . fluid dynamics. Learning all about Prandtl-Glauert condensation. What a wonderful addition he would someday make to the Cohane Aviation Division.

Chapter 24

The national situation continued to decline: plunging stock market, soaring prices, inflation running at 18 percent. This last factor, combined with six consecutive quarters of negative growth, officially signaled stagflation. The U.S. Treasury was furiously printing dollars, while the dollar itself had lost 40 percent of its value over the last six months. The Federal Reserve, meanwhile, had announced yet another hike in the prime rate, to 14 percent. Amid this calamitous economic news, the Congress adamantly—some said magnificently—refused to cut federal spending, with the result that the year's deficit was now projected at $1.1 trillion.

The foreign situation was encouraging. U.S. and Mexican troops were now taking potshots at each other across the border, inasmuch as Mexico had declared a *destino manifesto* policy of free emigration. The border to the North was similarly vexed. In the wake of the U.S. embargo on Canadian lumber, paper goods, gypsum, and beer, rogue units of Canadian Mounted Police were now harassing American truckers—on the *American* side of the border. In the Persian Gulf, never a quiescent body of water for Uncle Sam, U.S. Navy ships were blockading the Strait of Hormuz in an effort to drive up the price of Alaskan crude oil. (A bold move, to be sure, initiated by the Alaskan congressional delegation, now wielding disproportionate influence in the Capitol.) Meanwhile, a small but powerful cabal calling themselves the "geo-cons" were clamoring for U.S. military intervention in Tahiti, Taiwan, Tashkent, Tibet, and any other country whose name began with the letter *T*.

Amid this tumult, President Peacham set about the business of running for reelection. By all indications, it was going to be an uphill battle. Thus far, the best his people had been able to come up with by way of a campaign slogan was, "He's doing his best. Really."

Randy and Cass went about the business of the Transitioning commission. Cass was engaged; Randy was bored witless, at least at the outset. To him it was just an obstacle standing in the way of his appointment to the vice presidency. He had been in Washington long enough to know, in his heart of hearts, that presidential commissions are for the most part things to be ignored, a vermiform appendix to the body politic. It was always the same.

Important personages are appointed to the commission, with instructions to—by all means—study the problem in all its complexity, get to the root of it, and report back to the very highest levels of government. Six, nine months go by, with occasional fifteen-second sound bites on the evening news of commissioners sternly telling witnesses that they were not coming clean with the commission; the witnesses replying that, really, they're doing their best (give us a break). In due course, the commission delivers its report. There is a day or two of news coverage. The media reports the findings, that the United States is about to run out of molybdenum, or be overcome by bacteria emanating from geese; or that filthy, disgusting Arabs have no right to own American seaports, no matter how moderate they are; or that the government has no disaster plan ready in the event an asteroid the size of Rhode Island lands in the Pacific Ocean; or that the CIA failed to detect the cold war, the Korean War, the Vietnam War, the Tehran embassy takeover, Grenada, Iran-contra, Iraq's invasion of Kuwait, Bosnia, the attack on the USS *Cole*, 9/11, Operation Iraqi Freedom, Operation Oh Shit, Now What?; or that really there was no excuse at all for launching those cruise missiles against Papua New Guinea.

These revelations are duly followed by grave *tsk-tsk*ing and chin rubbing and hand-wringing about how these vitally important issues are *still* being mishandled and even ignored by the government. The commissioners are officially thanked for their diligent efforts and given commemorative paperweights with the wrong middle initial. The president and the relevant cabinet secretaries and government officials pledge to give the commission's recommendations "the most serious consideration" (which is to say, none whatsoever), and everyone goes back to ignoring and mismanaging the vital issues.

Six months later, one of the ex-commissioners writes a pained and well-argued op-ed piece in *The New York Times*, complaining that nothing—not one single recommendation—has been acted upon. Whereupon a junior White House press secretary issues a pained, not-very-well-argued statement saying this is simply "not the case." Moreover, that as a result of the commission's "fine work," a number of things have been done, though he is not at liberty to go into the details. Moreover, further study is needed, as this is—"indeed"—an issue of vital importance not only to the nation, but to all nations. And that's the end of it.

The TATA Commission, on the other hand, was proceeding rather differently. The proceedings themselves were eminently watchable. One pundit pronounced it a new kind of reality TV show, where instead of being voted off the island, you were voting to kill the contestants.

The pros and cons of Transitioning, which had started policy life as a notional "meta-issue," were being fiercely debated on live television and beamed into millions of American homes. The names of the commissioners, most of whom had been obscure Washington lobbyists and special interest advocates, were now familiar, and none more than Randolph K. Jepperson, Cassandra Devine, and her sparring partner, the Reverend Gideon Payne. As these pugilistic spectacles wore on, the public's view of Transitioning was evolving. More senators had come over to the pro side, though the anti side was hardening. But a surprising 38 percent of the American public now favored having the option of being legally euthanized in return for huge tax breaks and subsidies. Posters were going up: UNCLE SAM WANTS TO KILL *YOU*!

*   *   *

"The chair recognizes Foggo Farquar, chairman of the President's Council of Economic Advisers," Randy said. "Mr. Farquar, good morning. You were asked by this commission to study the economic impact on the U.S. Treasury of the Transitioning proposal?"

"Yes, I was."

"And what were your findings?"

Mr. Farquar took out a large binder whose contents were projected onto a screen in the hearing room.

"The so-called Baby Boomer population cohort," he said, "numbers approximately seventy-seven million people born between 1946 and 1964. Given the rate at which they are currently retiring and withdrawing funds from Social Security, as well as the Medicare and Medicaid systems, we estimate"—the next slide showed a series of bar graphs, all the color of deep red—"that Social Security will exhaust its resources approximately two and a half months from now."

"From today?"

"As of noon. Yes."

"That's not very desirable, is it?"

"I would call it very far from desirable, Senator. But those are the numbers. They do not lie."

"Have you then run the numbers in the event that Transitioning becomes the law of the land?"

"Yes. As I was requested to, by this commission."

"And?"

The next slide showed more bar graphs, all colored black.

"According to our projections—at the direction of this commission—in the event only twenty-five percent of retiring Boomers opted to, um, Transition at age seventy—"

The commissioner representing ABBA interjected, "They would of course have the option to do so at age seventy-*five*."

Cass rolled her eyes.

"Yes," said Mr. Farquar, "though that would of course significantly decrease the savings to the Treasury. In the event, the savings to Social Security based on Transitioning at age seventy would be . . . approximately eighteen trillion dollars over seventeen years."

"Are you then saying," Randy said, "that for each one percent of Boomers who Transition, that would save the United States Treasury about one trillion dollars?"

"Approximately, yes."

"Mr. Chairman," Gideon interjected.

"I'm not finished questioning the witness, Reverend Payne. I'll yield when I am finished. Thank you for your patience." Randy returned to his witness. "That's quite a savings to the Treasury, is it not?"

"Yes. Of course, the total savings would be offset by the tax benefits the government would be offering in exchange for Transitioning—the elimination of death taxes, free medical, and the other benefits described in the bill. Those benefits," Mr. Farquar said, looking toward the various Boomer special interest commissioners, "do seem to be *increasing* as the bill progresses. At any rate, the overall impact of Transitioning would be, yes, decisive and consequential and indeed beneficial to the government in terms of revenue outlay. I mean, inlay."

"Are you saying in effect that this would save the Social Security system?"

"Oh yes. Absolutely. Social Security would become solvent. Something it has not been for a very long time. You understand, Mr. Chairman, that I take no position on the issue. I'm just a simple numbers cruncher."

A ripple of soft laughter went through the chamber.

"Thank you for crunching, Mr. Farquar. Your witness, Reverend Payne."

Gideon said, "Mr. Farquar, you have a degree in economics, do you not?"

Randy leaned forward into his microphone and said, "Reverend Payne, Mr. Farquar is one of the country's most eminent economists. He is the president's top economic adviser. I think we can take it for granted that he has a degree in economics."

"I did not mean it as an insult, Senator Jepperson. But since we as a nation are in deplorable economic shape today, I thought I would just inquire."

Another ripple of laughter.

"We're not here to harass our witnesses, Reverend Payne," said the chair. "Proceed with your questions."

"Senator, I well understand the purpose of this august body. Mr. Farquar, I apologize for my frankness. But we are here, after all, to study a most grave issue. As it were."

"I appreciate that, sir."

"So you're saying, Mr. Farquar, that this . . . Transitioning is the . . . *final solution* to the Social Security crisis?"

An awkward, embarrassed murmur went through the hearing room.

Cass had been anticipating this. A few days ago, Terry had said to her and Randy, "Sooner or later he's going to call us all Nazis."

"Reverend Payne," Foggo Farquar said, his face reddening, "I am most certainly not saying that."

"But you implied it. You did say this would finally solve the problem."

Cass broke in. "Mr. Payne"—she steadfastly refused to call him "Reverend"—"why are you comparing Mr. Farquar to Adolf Hitler?"

"I am merely trying to let some light into this miasma of moral degradation to which you have led us, Miss Devine."

"This isn't the Wannsee Conference, Mr. Payne. We're not talking about exterminating six million Jews, Gypsies, homosexuals, Catholic priests, and mentally disabled. We are talking about a voluntary program by which Americans could opt to do something altruistic, even noble, on behalf of their children, in the face of intractable irresponsibility by the federal government."

"Your nobility is showing, Miss Devine."

"Mr. Chairman, permission to question the witness."

"Proceed."

"Mr. Farquar," Cass said, "am I correct that your wife's family emigrated from Poland in the 1930s?"

"Yes, they did."

"And why was that?"

"They were fleeing Nazi persecution, on account of their being Jewish."

"Were they successful in this regard?"

"Not entirely. My wife's father was the only one to make it out alive."

"Thank you, Mr. Farquar," Cass said. "Sorry to put you through that. I'll yield the balance of my time back to Mr. Payne."

It was a good moment for the Transitioners. Gideon Payne was seen about town in the days following with red blotches on his face. The consensus was that they were from burst blood vessels. But another development prevented Cass from taking a victory lap.

Police in Budding Grove, Ohio, arrested a pudgy, soft-faced twenty-nine-year-old nursing home attendant named Arthur G. Clumm and charged him with putting to (permanent) sleep thirty-six residents over a six-month period. This might have been just another one of those self-appointed avenging angel stories, only the police found his somewhat unkempt apartment plastered with photographs and clippings of—Cassandra Devine. They impounded his computer and found that the cache of his Internet search engine was chockablock with CASSANDRA blog page views as well as sites linked to CASSANDRA.

During his interrogation by the police, Nurse Clumm showed no remorse at all over having dispatched nearly three dozen senior citizens and, according to the Ohio State Police detective sergeant who conducted the interrogation, blithely and repeatedly referred to his deceased charges as "Wrinklies" and "resource hogs."

On being apprised of this tiding, Gideon Payne lifted his eyes toward heaven and said aloud, "Lord, Thou art *truly* just and bountiful."

Terry Tucker's reaction was in a different key, consisting of a single word beginning with the letter *f,* uttered loudly.

Cass's reaction was somewhat more dignified but equally dismayed.

She and Terry reached Randy on his cell, on his way to a fundraiser in Hyannis.

"Oh, hell," Randy said. "How's this going to look?"

"We weren't calling," Terry said over the speakerphone, "to alert you to a public relations triumph."

"Well, you'll have to insulate me," Randy said.

"That's my boy," Cass muttered. "First one into the lifeboat."

"What?" Randy said.

"I was just praising your moral courage, to Terry."

"Is this ghastly person Clumm *connected* to you in any way?"

"Yes, Randy. We've been having phone sex for years."

"Please tell me you're kidding."

"Of course I'm not connected to him, you idiot."

"Well, why in heaven's name is his apartment a *shrine* to you?"

"Randy," Terry said. "John Hinckley shot Ronald Reagan to impress Jodie Foster. As I recall, Jodie Foster wasn't impressed."

There was silence on the line. Randy said, "Is that going to be our line?"

"No," Terry said. "We're going to need something better. We'll keep you posted. Go raise money." Terry hung up and said to Cass, "Do we really want him a heartbeat away from the presidency?"

"Our leader," Cass said. "He makes you want to take the bullet for him."

"Never mind him. We got some spinning to do."

Chapter 25

Gideon carried his own bully pulpit wherever he went. In the days following the arrest of Arthur Clumm, he was ubiquitous, on every TV show, fulminating and demanding that the attorney general investigate "all links between Arthur Clumm and Cassandra Devine's diabolical death factory."

Watching this explosion of spittle, Terry said to Cass, mentor to student, "You caught the operative word in there, right?"

" 'Diabolical'?"

"No. 'All.' Not just one link. All links. Subtle, in a diabolical sort of way."

Arthur Clumm's salamandrine visage was on every front page and TV show. Here was Arthur, in jailhouse orange jumpsuit and manacles, being transferred from Budding Grove jail to a more secure facility. Here was Arthur again, arriving at the Cunch County Courthouse, wearing a flak jacket and a—what's this?—blanket over his head. "What's the blanket for?" a reporter asked. "To confuse snipers," replied a sheriff's deputy.

At his arraignment, Arthur, in the best tradition of American criminality, pleaded "not guilty." It transpired that during his interrogation, he had called CASSANDRA "my personal goddess and inspiration." It was further revealed that Arthur possessed an autographed photo of Cass, with the inscription "Keep up the good work." This was not good news for the Cass camp.

This grim tiding was revealed to her by way of a phone call from a reporter for the *Columbus Dispatch*. She told the reporter the truth—

namely, that she received many requests for photos and autographs from followers of her blog.

The problem was, the reporter informed Cass, that the postmark on the envelope containing the autographed photo was dated in the middle of the six-month period during which Arthur had taken it on himself to euthanize half the population of the Budding Grove nursing home.

"Oh shit," Cass said. She immediately added, "That was off the record."

The reporter said he wouldn't be able to quote her exactly, as the *Dispatch* was a family paper, but that he would have to quote her as uttering an expletive.

She told Terry about the call.

" 'Personal goddess'?" he said. "Uch."

"I feel like Transitioning myself."

"Why so glum?" Terry said. "I thought women liked being on pedestals."

"I'm dead meat," Cass said.

"Cass, you didn't . . . know this creep?"

"Of *course* not. I get thousands of requests for autographed photos."

"Why did you write, 'Keep up the good work'?"

"I have no idea. I don't remember every autograph, for God's sake. He probably wrote that he was a nurse or—I don't know. You don't think I'd encourage a freelance mass murderer?"

"You weren't, like, urging him to put people to sleep."

"No."

"Well," Terry said, "that's a relief. Good to know that one of my senior vice presidents isn't moonlighting advising serial murderers."

"Hilarious," Cass said. "*So* hilarious."

Not long afterward, two FBI agents appeared in the reception room of Tucker Strategic Communications.

"Your friends are back," Terry alerted Cass by intercom. "It's always nice to have a couple of G-men in the waiting room. It really impresses clients. Especially the big corporate ones."

"Terry, I'm sorry about this. But—"

"Just don't tell them anything until I get Allen. It's always good to talk to Allen. He's a great guy, and he only charges seven hundred an hour. Which, under the circumstances, is going to come out of *your* next paycheck instead of mine."

Allen Snyder arrived and conducted a $700 discussion with the FBI agents over the finer points of something called Rule 41 of the Federal Rules of Criminal Procedure. Cass and Terry, listening in, gathered that it had to do with the Fourth Amendment to the U.S. Constitution and "probable cause"—in this instance for searching the hard drives of Cass's computers. Allen eloquently maintained that they had no such probable cause. The agents argued that they did, and if it came to that, they would be more than happy to return with a search warrant.

"May I have a word with my client?" he said. The FBI men assented in the laconic way of their ilk.

Allen, Cass, and Terry huddled in another office.

"Is there anything *on* the computer?" Allen asked.

"Like what?" Cass said. "Coded messages to the Death Angel of Budding Grove telling him to exterminate a whole nursing home?"

"I meant, is there anything on the computers that you wouldn't want them to see? Personal matters. . . ."

"I—I mean—I keep a *diary*."

Allen nodded gravely. "A diary."

"It's password protected. But the FBI will probably figure out a way through it."

"Is there anything in the diary that could cause you a problem?"

"You mean like sex stuff?"

Allen blushed.

"I'd just as soon not have the FBI poring over my diary," Cass said, flustered. "There are no lesbian fantasies or numbers of private banking accounts in the Cayman Islands or plots to assassinate the president or Osama bin Laden's private cell phone number. . . . But it's a diary. I tell it things. That's what you do with a diary."

Terry groaned.

"All right," Allen said in calming tones. "I'm going to insist that they have no probable cause. At the same time, I don't think we want headlines saying that we're refusing to cooperate with an FBI investigation into"—he gave Terry a weary glance—"serial murders."

When the agents and Allen had left, Terry said, "Diary?"

"So?"

"It's a company computer."

"Oh, please. If you're worried about the FBI finding incriminating material on my company computer, I'd worry more about the company-related stuff. Like your proposal to the government of North Korea about putting on that celebrity pro-am golf tournament in Pyongyang. Or our pitch to ExxonMobil for the 'Adopt a Sea Otter' plan. Or the media plan for the Mink Ranchers Association about how more people get rabies from minks than from rats. Or would you rather worry about my diary?"

Terry, color draining from his face, said. "I better call the IT people. We've got some deleting to do."

"What about damage control?"

"Delete first, control damage later."

The senator from the great state of Massachusetts called. He'd heard about the "personal goddess" comment and the "Keep up the good work." He said, "Don't worry. I've thought it all through. We're going to be fine. You and Terry could spin your way out of a hurricane. By the way, I won't be back in town for a while."

"Why not?"

"I'm going on a listening tour. If I'm going to be a national candidate, I've got to get myself out there. I'll check in from the road. Good luck!"

It had been a long day. Terry and Cass repaired that night to the Unnamed Source, a bar around the corner from the office. She told him about the call from Randy.

"A 'listening tour'?" Terry snorted into his bourbon.

Cass said, "The first listening tour in history took place in France, in 1848. It was conducted by a man named Alexandre Ledru-Rollin. One of the leaders of the revolution of 1848. One day he saw a mob going by his window. He jumped up and said, 'There go the people! I must follow them! I am their leader!' "

The TV over the bar showed Arthur Clumm, Nurse of the Year, making another fashion statement in bright orange with stainless steel wrist and ankle accessories.

Terry waved over the bartender. "Would you turn that thing to ESPN?" The bartender went to find the remote control. Cass idly watched the "crawl" at the bottom of the screen, the distracting ticker tape of generally pointless news bulletins.

. . . SHARES OF ELDERHEAVEN CORP STOCK DOWN 8% IN WAKE OF BUDDING GROVE FACILITY DEATHS . . .

In the next instant, the screen switched to a Major League Baseball player who had gained seventy-five pounds in less than a year, all of it muscle. His lawyer, sitting next to him at a table, was staunchly averring that his client had never taken steroids and was pounding his fist on the table, complaining about the "unconscionably sloppy custody chain with these urine samples."

"Merciful *Jesus*," Gideon Payne was saying over the phone. He had loosened his tie and with his free hand was waving off a minion who was approaching with a face of woe. "*How* much of it do we own? . . . Thirty *percent*?" Gideon's eyes darted back and forth like beads in an abacus. "That's minority ownership. . . . I *know* it's almost a third, Sidney, I can count . . . but it's still . . . *minority* . . . We don't . . . we don't . . . We *do*? Well, who in the name of all angels and archangels signed off on *that* dumb-ass scheme? . . . What is the Elderheaven Corporation doing administering the personnel division of a nursing home in Blooming . . . *Budding,* whatever Grove—"

"Reverend," interrupted one of Gideon's minions, "it's that reporter from *The New York Times* again. He says—"

"*Go. Away,*" Gideon mouthed. "Now you look here, Sidney. You're going to have to deal with this out of *your* office. I need space around me on this. A lot of space. *Vast* space. I want you to create a, a, *desert* around me. *You're* the chief operating officer of Elderheaven Corporation. So *assume* the mantle of chief and start operating. As far as I am concerned, I wasn't in the same *room* when this deal was signed with

Budding Grove. I was not in the *country*. I was not on the *planet*. Not in the same *solar system*."

Gideon hung up, exhausted and in a molar-grinding fury. The minion was hovering.

"What do you want, Templeton?"

The minion Templeton presented Gideon with a list of the media calls that had come in following the revelation that Arthur Clumm, Death Angel, was technically on Gideon's payroll.

The *Financial Times*... *The New York Times*... *The Washington Post*... *USA Today*... the *Los Angeles Times*... *The Wall Street Journal*... the *Jerusalem Post*... *The Jerusalem Post*? For God's sake....

Gideon wiped his brow with a handkerchief, dismissed Templeton, and looked up at the ceiling and muttered, "You're not *working* with me today, Lord."

Cass and Terry had made a $100 bet, as they rushed back to the office from the Unnamed Source with renewed spring in their step, as to how long before Senator Randolph K. Jepperson called, pretending not to have heard the news about Gideon Payne's one-third ownership of the Budding Grove—"Budding Grave" in the tabloid press—nursing facility; furthermore, to announce that he was abandoning his "listening tour" because there was no one out there really worth listening to and was ready to get back to sitting on the Transitioning commission. Cass bet that he would call in before noon the next day. Terry bet after noon. Randy's call came at twelve-fifteen p.m., so they decided to spend the $100 on a good, splurgy lunch at the Calcutta Club.

Cass said, "What would you say if I extended an olive branch to Gideon?"

Terry tore off a piece of naan and dipped it in crispy okra and yogurt. "Fine, as long as you were smacking him across the face with it."

Cass smiled and forked a piece of Manchurian cauliflower. Terry popped some chicken tikka masala into his mouth.

"Right now I would guess he's frantically building some kind of moat around himself," Terry said. "*He* didn't hire this wacko. *He* didn't know. Elderheaven's a huge company. Yada yada. Why should *he* be held responsible? *He's* just as horrified as anyone. More horrified. More horrified than you, anyway. *You* were this hairball's inspiration. His 'personal goddess.' Sending him autographed photos saying, 'Kill! Kill! Kill! Keep up the good work!'"

Cass dabbed a bit of bhindi from her lips. "What we ought to be doing is calling time-out to Gideon's and my catfight and shifting the spotlight onto Randy."

"I'm kind of enjoying the catfight. Everyone is. Why cancel the best show on TV?"

"Not canceling, entirely. But shifting the focus. Look, it's worked, in a way, the whole Transitioning thing. It's got the government focused and on the defensive. If he's really got a shot at the vice presidency."

Terry stared, a forkful of karavee bhindi suspended in midair. "You don't honestly think they're going to give it to him, do you?"

"Why take chances? You were the one always telling me you wanted to elect someone president."

"Sure. I also wanted to sleep with Grace Kelly, play with the Rolling Stones, and throw the winning touchdown in the Super Bowl. Instead I ended up running a beauty parlor on K Street for corporate criminals. Life is funny sometimes."

"So, here's your shot. This could be one of those moments of synchronicity. The stars are in alignment."

Terry looked up at the ceiling. "Those are light bulbs, not stars."

"You want to throw a winning touchdown? Put on your spikes. The game's started."

"What about Transitioning?" Terry said.

"Meta-issue. Pointless now. I was trying to get my generation out from under this Everest of debt. Randy just added more to it with his giveaways. Jumping into bed with the Boomer lobbies. Your generation. Honestly."

"Those people don't speak for me."

"Oh, come on. You know what the Boomer concept of sacrifice consists of? Three-day ground instead of overnight air delivery on your fifty-inch plasma screen high-def TV. Why did I ever think that Boomers would step up to the plate and do something altruistic? And don't tell me about Bill Gates giving away all his money. He's got tons left."

"So Miss Go Long is giving up?" Terry said.

"The FBI wants to seize my computers to see if I've been issuing kill orders to deranged male nurses. Right now I'm not in a position to go long on advocating legal suicide."

"See your point. Jesus, that reminds me—we gotta delete those files."

"But with the right handling, I think we could give the senator from the great state of Massachusetts a shove toward the Oval Office. Whatever your personal feelings for him. Speaking of which," Cass said, "he seems to have asked me to, uh, marry him."

Terry stared. "You buried the lead."

"I was going to mention it."

"What did you tell him?"

Cass said. "A Washington answer. I told him I'd get back to him."

Chapter 26

"**W**ell, what in the name of God *does* the FBI know?"

The president, in no good mood, as usual, spoke from an exercise treadmill. His physician—a four-star U.S. Navy admiral—had admonished him sternly about his blood pressure and sedentary regimen. Bucky Trumble, whose own BP and cholesterol levels were nothing to boast about, stood close by in the manner of courtier, having to raise his voice over the whirr of the rubber belt and rollers.

"They don't think this Clumm character was taking orders from her. There are no phone records to or from. Or e-mails. Still, they want to look at her computers, but—"

"If there's no e-mail on his computer, why would there be any on *her* damn computer?"

"Well, sir . . ." A gym, even one with only two people in it, not counting Secret Service, is no place for nuanced conversation, and what Bucky had to tell the president was all nuance, little black dandelions of scheming. "I was thinking that it might be interesting to see *what's* on her computer. If you see what I mean."

"Huh?"

"If you see what I mean. Sir."

The president grunted. "You don't have to shout. Yeah, yeah. Well, what's holding them up? Seize the fucking computer. They're the FBI, aren't they? You get a warrant, you say, 'Hand over the computer.' What's the big deal?"

"The Fourth Amendment?"

"Fuck the Fourth Amendment."

"That would be the FBI's view of it, sir, but her lawyer is maintaining a different interpretation."

The president pressed "Stop" and climbed off the treadmill. He was breathing heavily and glistening with sweat.

"The problem, sir," Bucky continued in a lower voice, grateful for the cessation of the machinery, "is that to the extent we—that is, the attorney general and the FBI—put her in the hot seat, it could impact on our friend the Reverend Payne."

"Prick."

"Yes, sir, but nonetheless, *our* prick. Turns out that his nursing home corporation, Elderheaven, owns a one-third stake in the Budding Grove home where the incidents took place—"

"Incidents? Place was a damn *slaughterhouse*."

"Yes. And the families of the thirty-six dearly departed are making quite a hullabaloo. . . ."

A smile came over the president's face. "Well, isn't that a damn shame."

"But let us bear in mind, sir, that his support among the pro-lifers and evangelicals is going to be critical next fall. We're going to need every single vote. So to the extent—I'm speaking hypothetically here, you understand—to the extent that Cassandra Devine were . . . somehow *linked* to this madman . . . that would certainly take the heat off of Gideon."

"Hm. Yeah. Go on."

"And to the extent that Cassandra Devine was implicated in a serial murder investigation, well . . . it would collaterally implicate Senator Jepperson. Problems solved."

The president gave Bucky an appreciative look. "Keep going."

"Jepperson and Devine are intimately linked. There's even talk that they might marry."

"Buck, is this one of those situations where I don't really want to hear the rest of what you have to say?"

"I don't see any need to drown you in details," Bucky Trumble said, smiling. "You've got a country to run."

*   *   *

"Awfully good of you to come, Frank, on such short notice," Bucky Trumble said to Frank Cohane.

"No problem," Frank Cohane said without bothering to sound sincere. He was wondering why this urgently requested interview was taking place not in the Oval Office, or at least somewhere in the West Wing of the White House, but in a decidedly downscale restaurant of indeterminate Oriental orientation called Wok'n Roll, in a decidedly downscale neighborhood of Arlington, Virginia. From the characters outside on the sidewalk, it looked more like downtown Santo Domingo or Cité-Soleil than an exurb of the capital city of the United States. The place felt—*uch*—sticky. At this stage in his life, Frank was more accustomed to starred Michelin restaurants.

Frank leaned in toward Bucky across the table. His body language said, *I don't want to be here, so why don't you get right to the point.*

"Frank, you know all about computers."

"Bucky," Frank said, "I own a software company with a market cap of fourteen billion. So, yeah, I guess I 'know all about computers.' "

"I was wondering if we might enlist your help on a somewhat sensitive matter."

Frank listened to what Bucky Trumble proposed. Bucky managed to make it sound like just an elaborate fraternity prank.

"Jesus, Bucky."

"Is it technically feasible?"

Frank stared back. "Yeah. And technically illegal."

"One day President Theodore Roosevelt was discussing a matter with Philander Knox, his attorney general. Knox said, 'Oh, Mr. President, do not let so great an achievement suffer from any taint of legality.' "

"That's a really inspiring story, Bucky. And how did it turn out?"

"Everyone lived happily ever after, prospered, and died in their sleep, old men." Bucky stood and put out his hand. "The president said to give you his very best, Frank, and to let you know how grateful he is for your continued support. He also said to tell you how much he's looking forward to showing you just how grateful he is." Bucky winked. "At the start of Peacham version two. Thanks for making the trip east."

Thus Frank Cohane, billionaire entrepreneur, was left to contemplate his stale bowl of kung pao seagull or whatever it was congealing in the bowl, in a dingy restaurant 2,500 miles from his coastal California Xanadu, where the air had the tang of salt and kelp and pine.

What a thing to ask a father to do, he thought. The nerve of these people.

Allen Snyder arrived at the office of Tucker Strategic Communications wearing an expression that did not augur good news. He told Terry and Cass that the FBI would be arriving shortly with a federal warrant authorizing seizure of Cass's desktop and laptop computers. The judge had assented to the U.S. attorney's argument that Cass's scribble on the photo—"Keep up the good work!"—constituted probable cause to investigate whether she had directly influenced the Death Angel of Budding Grove.

"Bye, bye, autographs. Jeez," Cass said.

Terry said, "At least we were able to delete some of the sensitive client-related stuff."

Allen frowned. "Terry, there are certain things I'd rather you not tell me."

"Whatever," Terry said.

"I've done some research into data storage," Allen said. "The bottom line is that there's really no such thing as delete. There's something called 'hard drive mirroring.' You think you've deleted it, but it lives on in some server in Kuala Lumpur. And it's gettable. You remember the Abramoff e-mails, the Enron e-mails. Those were all deleted, too."

Terry blanched. "Oh, my God."

"I'll do everything I can to limit the search. Under Rule 41 I can try to insist on being present during the search."

The FBI arrived. As they were unplugging Cass's desktop, Terry pulled Allen aside and whispered to him, "If you see any file names labeled 'North Korea' or 'Otters' or 'Mink Ranchers' . . ."

The FBI agents left, Allen following.

"Well, gosh willikers," Terry said, clapping his hands together, "what a great way to start the week. So, did you sign autographs for any other interesting people? Osama bin Laden? The Taliban?"

"Oh, relax, Terry. They didn't seize *your* computers. No one cares about your sea otters."

"Oh yeah? I promise you, my little senior vice president of Tucker Strategic Communications, that ExxonMobil will definitely care about our sea otter proposal—if they read about it on the front page of *The Washington Post*."

"All right," Cass said. "I'll activate Randy. What's the point of having a U.S. senator for a boyfriend if he won't intervene with the FBI for you?"

Terry snorted. "I hear the galloping hooves of cavalry."

"Honey bun," Randy groaned, "I can't meddle with an FBI investigation. For heaven's sake. I might be appointed vice president of the United States. How would it look?"

"I'm not asking you to meddle. Just to call up the director of the FBI and tell them not to leak client-related stuff to the press."

"I'll think about it. By the way, how're you coming with those volunteers—the ones who said they'd testify as willing to kill themselves at age sixty-five?"

"*Transition*. Try, please, to get used to the word. But wait a minute. *Why* can't you call him? I didn't commit any crime. There's a principle involved. Even if it's not a principle you can cash in on right away."

Randy sighed. "I . . . What if I do and they leak it that I called? You're my girlfriend. How will it *look*?"

"Like you cared about the girlfriend?"

"Awkward," Randy muttered. "Damn awkward."

"Okay." Cass shrugged. "I just hope they find the diary file where I quote you calling your mother a 'cunt.'"

"What? You wrote *that* in your diary?"

"It's a diary."

"Why would you . . . Oh, my God. Cass. What *else* did you put in there?"

"Well, let's see. Stuff about our sex life. How you like to take cherries and—"

"Cass!"

"What can I tell you, sweetheart? I'm a girl. Men look at themselves in mirrors. Girls write in their diaries."

"Jesus. I don't believe this. What were the names of these FBI agents?"

"Antrim and Jackson. They looked kind of lean and hungry. One of them kept touching his gun."

Cass hung up. Terry had been sitting next to her throughout the phone call.

"Did you really put all that in there?"

"As if. Please."

Terry nodded in the way of a pleased mentor. One of his maxims, imparted to all his protégées, was: Never tell a small lie when a big one will suffice.

"So what's with the cherries?" Terry said.

"Wouldn't you love to know."

"This meeting is called to order."

"Mr. Chairman," Gideon Payne said, "I wish to make a statement." Gideon did not look well. His jowls sagged, and he had small blue circles under his eyes. He looked awful.

"Go ahead, Reverend."

Gideon adjusted his spectacles and read. It was a lengthy and somewhat rambling excoriation of Arthur Clumm, Death Angel of Budding Grave—Grove—ending with a somewhat tedious, solemn, and verbose reaffirmation of the value of human life. Gideon normally ran on high-test; today he rattled, as if running on diesel.

"Mr. Chairman, may I say something?" Cass said.

"Yes, Ms. Devine," the chair said cautiously.

"As we proceed to investigate the feasibility of *Voluntary* Transitioning, I too think it would be appropriate to have a moment of silence—for the victims of Budding Grove, who were *involuntarily* murdered. By Mr. Payne's employee."

"Damn you!" Gideon exploded. "He's no 'employee' of mine! And you, madam, are a she-devil! A she-devil! And I *cast you out*!"

Cass raised an eyebrow and said quietly, "Mr. Chairman, I was under the impression that I was in the hearing room for a presidential commission. I seem to have wandered by mistake into the chamber reserved for exorcisms."

PAYNE CALLS DEATH DIVA DEVINE "SHE-DEVIL" AS TRANSITION HEARINGS DEGENERATE

"Geedeeon," Monsignor Montefeltro said, looking worried, "dear friend. How does it go with you?"

Monsignor Montefeltro knew very well that it was not going well for his dear friend Gideon. He, along with everyone else in the country, had been glued to the proceedings on TV, and he had seen Gideon's tantrum. The chair had had to adjourn the session. Some said that Payne's fulminations were a disguised attempt to derail the proceedings. But if it was an act, it certainly looked very convincing. Gideon looked like a man on the verge of a heart attack. To be sure, he was under terrible strain owing to the lawsuits against Elderheaven. Lawyers were circling. He'd been served with papers by the ones representing the first wave of aggrieved families.

Cassandra Devine, meanwhile, had sat there at the dais, arms crossed, coolly rolling her eyes, an almost bemused expression on her face.

The two men sat in their usual meeting place, the monsignor's house in Georgetown. The grandfather clock in the hall beat a calming metronomic tick-tock in contrast with Gideon's agitation. It was cool and air conditioned, but Gideon kept having to mop perspiration from his glistening brow with his silk handkerchief. He downed the first two glasses of chilled 2001 Gaia & Rey briskly, gulpingly, as if trying to put out a fire that was smoldering somewhere within him.

For his part, the monsignor was in a pleasant frame of mind, having that week persuaded four wealthy Catholic widows to leave practically all their earthly possessions to Mother Church. The Vatican was well pleased.

"Massimo. It's been the most *awful* time," Gideon said. "This Clumm maniac . . . I'm being sued by the families for . . . tens of millions . . . and on top of it this woman, Cassandra—she's got me all twisted *up*. Did you watch today?"

"Eh, no," the monsignor lied whitely, "I was busy. I'm sorry."

"Well, I made a fool of myself today. A terrible, pluperfect fool, and in front of the whole world."

Gideon poured himself a third glass of wine. "She knows where all my buttons are, and she presses them every time. I—I can't help myself." A look of panic crossed his face. "The truth is, Massimo . . . do you want to hear the truth of it?"

"Yes, Geedeon. Of course."

"I love her."

Monsignor Montefeltro's eyes widened. "But Geedeon. How can this be? She attacks you at every opportunity."

"I can't explain it."

"Try." The monsignor, known as one of the silkier confessors in Rome, filled Gideon's glass.

It poured from Gideon like water sluicing from an overburdened dam. He loved Cassandra Devine, loved everything about her. He loved her first name, her last name ("I know it's spelled differently"), her looks, the way she abused him just the way his mother used to. (Is Dr. Freud in?) She made Gideon "all goosey." The monsignor made a note to look up the word in his *Dictionary of Modern American Slang,* but he had a good idea what it meant. The man was a wreck.

By the time Gideon was finished, he'd gulped down several more glasses of wine. He was glassy-eyed and spent, but calmer.

"You won't . . . ," he said faintly, "tell what I've told you, will you?"

"Of course not, Geedeon," Montefeltro said, though strictly

speaking, since Gideon was not a Catholic, there was no actual confessional bond of secrecy involved.

"Geedeon, with all respect for your feelings, I don't in complete honesty think there is a future for you and this Cassandra Devine."

Gideon sighed. "No, no. I know. Oh, hell's bells, Massimo. I can't account for my feelings. It makes no sense at all." He sounded drugged. Well, the man *had* drunk six glasses of wine. "As long as I'm at it, Massimo, I got another confession for you. I've never *been* with a woman."

"Ah." Montefeltro nodded, rather hoping this was the last confession of the evening. It was one thing to listen to old Catholic biddies tell him they'd been rude to their chauffeurs, but he didn't really care to go spelunking in Gideon's soul. God knew what goblins lurked there.

"God loves you for your purity, Geedeon. You serve Him as the apostles served our blessed—"

"I would *like* to be with a woman."

"Ah. Yes, well . . ." The monsignor nodded, now in full confession-hearing mode. "We all have certain feelings. This is natural. Even I from time to time—"

"I'm not attractive to women. I know that."

"Nonsense! You are a . . ." *Well, yes, true, you look like a frog.* "A powerful man. People all over the country, the world, respect you. You are the Reverend Geedeon Payne. Friend of the president."

"Everyone thinks I killed my mother."

"No, no, no. Impossible."

"If I were a girl, I suppose *I* wouldn't want to get involved with a man who killed his mother."

Monsignor Montefeltro shifted in his seat. His facial muscles were starting to knot. No more wine for Gideon. The white wine had a high sugar content.

"Geedeon—"

"Do you want to know what happened that day at Frenchman's Bluff, Massimo?"

"Only if you desire to tell me. But if you don't—"

"*She* tried to kill *me*."

"Eh?"

"She wasn't right in the head. The doctors had diagnosed a terminal brain tumor just three weeks before. I was driving. We stopped, just like we always did, for the view. Then suddenly she reached over and shifted the car into drive and put her foot down on the gas. I said, 'Momma, what are you doing?' I tried to brake, but we were on gravel, on a downslope. The car just kept going, sliding. I said, 'Momma, what are you doing?' She said, 'I'm done living. We're gonna meet Jesus together.' I said, 'Momma, but I'm not ready to meet Jesus!' She said, 'Well, he's ready to meet you, boy!' By then we were five feet from the edge. All I could do was open the door and roll out. The car went over with her in it."

Monsignor Montefeltro stared.

"I made up that story about how the parking brake failed. I couldn't tell everyone what really happened. That my own mother tried to kill me? And it ended with everyone thinking *I* killed *her*." Gideon shook his head. "I've spent my whole life working on behalf of life. Crying over unborn babies, praying over the brain afflicted, keeping them alive. Preaching on the sanctity of every human being. And now . . ." He let out a long, plaintive sigh. "Now I'm in love with a woman who's the poster girl for legal suicide. And on top of that, I got people suing me for tens of millions of dollars 'cause of some *psycho* male nurse!"

He glared at Massimo. Behind the exhausted eyes burned a bright, furious fire. "It ain't right! It ain't fair! You're a man of God. You got a direct line to the Almighty. You got a switchboard at the Vatican, straight to heaven. Well, next time you and your cardinals are talking to the Lord, you ask Him: What did Gideon Payne do to make Him want to take a giant crap on him! You ask him that!"

Monsignor Massimo Montefeltro said to himself, *Caution. Caution. You are dealing with a wounded creature of the American swampland. Speak very softly. Keep your fingers away from his mouth.*

"Geedeon, what you tell me gives me the most enormous pain."

"Well, it should! It damn well should!"

"Remember that it is only through suffering that we come truly to know God."

"Aw, what a bunch of crap."

"Geedeon. Please. It is the entire basis for our religion!"

"Not mine. Not anymore. This boy is *done* with suffering! This boy is going to party down and howl at the moon and get *laid*! I am going to *know* women! I'm going to know them every which way from Sunday! Now, you go get us another bottle of this *fine* Italian grape juice. You and I, Massimo, we're going to get drunk tonight. We're going to get good and truly and royally drunk. And then," Gideon said, "you and I"—he belched—"we're gonna get *laid*!"

Chapter 27

Frank Cohane pondered Bucky Trumble's bizarre request on the way back to California in his jet. He was able carefully to analyze the conversation, by virtue of having recorded it.

It occurred to him as he pressed the "Play" button on his pocket digital microrecorder that he was amassing quite the audio archive of his dealings. Bucky Trumble's voice came through clear as a bell. Frank listened as the chief aide to the president of the United States asked him to plant outgoing e-mails on his daughter's computer in order to link her to a serial murderer. Frank thought, *Wow. And I thought* I *could be devious.*

He ran the scenarios through his mind. Scenario one: success, reward, a significant cabinet post in Peacham's second term. Secretary of the Treasury, a title you got to keep for the rest of your life. Scenario two: success, Peacham loses election, no reward. Scenario three: lack of success, disgrace, prosecution, prison. Scenario three lacked appeal.

Frank analyzed scenario three again and again, evaluating every node and decision marker. He concluded that Trumble's request could be accomplished at technically negligible risk. Less than . . . he calculated . . . one-tenth of a percent. Not quite zero tolerance, but—acceptable.

He thought it through one more time and decided that the risk of being disgraced and in jail was—unacceptable.

So where does that *leave us? If you don't play ball, no cabinet post.*

He played the tape again. Had he made any self-incriminating comment? The answer was: No. Nothing. He hadn't said a word. He had listened to Bucky Trumble's request; had commented on its gross illegality. After that, Bucky got up, said how grateful the president would be if Frank contrived to put his own daughter behind bars, and—left. He, Frank, had said nothing. In any court of law, and even in the higher court of public opinion, his silence could be construed to be that of a father horrified to the point of muteness on being asked to act so heinously against his own flesh and blood.

He was in the clear.

And now Frank Cohane had an epiphany. Instantly, he chided himself on how obvious it had been all along. He felt a surge of satisfaction as he looked down on the sunset-drenched clouds going by. He signaled the rather dishy stewardess—a feature on Air Frank, as it was called within the company—to bring him a Scotch on the rocks.

He leaned back in the soft teal-colored Italian leather and gazed out the window again. He was at forty-six thousand feet, alone in his own jet, flying toward the setting sun, home to a forty-thousand-square-foot, as-seen-in-*Architectural-Digest* house overlooking the Pacific; to a woman—tiresome, lately, but who still lived up to her end of the bargain, providing him with on-demand, world-class sex. He had everything he wanted or could possibly need—and now he had just figured out how to get even more, and completely risk-free. Frank Cohane felt a surge of well-being.

"So?" Cass asked Randy. They were in his Senate office building, following a long day of commission hearings. Gideon Payne hadn't shown up; probably still licking his wounds.

Randy had been evasive all day. Every time she brought it up, he said he didn't want to discuss the matter in or even *near* the commission hearing room. Senators, who spend most of their waking hours within a few feet of a microphone, sooner or later become convinced that the entire landscape is listening, even if they really have nothing worth listening to.

"Did you call the FBI?"

"Honestly?"

Cass said, "Randy, you've got to stop saying that. It sends a signal: *Normally, I lie through my teeth*. Trust me. I teach corporate executives how to lie. But the answer is, yeah, I'd like to know. Honestly."

"I got my guy Speck working on it. If anyone can find out what's going on with the FBI and your computers, he can. I still can't believe you put all that stuff in your diary. I'm not even certain I ever called my mother a cunt to you."

"Why can't you just call the FBI directly? You're a U.S. senator. You're supposed to throw your weight around."

"Because it will leak that I'm trying to protect my girlfriend."

"So? It'll get you the girlfriend vote."

"I promise you that I am every bit as anxious as you are to get your bloody computer back. My God. Mother was a pillar of Massachusetts society. And you calling her a cunt."

"No, *you* called her a cunt, darling. I just wrote it down."

"The entire board of the Society of the Cincinnati attended her funeral! The governor came."

"Well," Cass said, "let's hope your guy Speck is as good as you say he is. I wonder why Gideon didn't show today."

"He's probably under his bed in the fetal position," Randy said. "Don't worry. He'll be back. You can continue tormenting him. By the way, you given any more thought to my proposal?"

" 'By the way'?"

"Problem?"

Cass sighed. "You're asking me to marry you, and you preface it with 'by the way'? You sure know how to make a girl feel like item number eighteen on your to-do list for today. 'Haircut.' 'Ask Cass if she'll marry me.' 'Fix garage door.' 'Vote against emergency spending bill.' Are WASPs genetically incapable of being romantic?"

"You want me to get down on my one good knee?"

"Forget it. I'll get back to you."

Gideon Payne was not under a bed sucking his thumb, in the fetal position. He was upright, though barely, in the parlor of Monsignor

Montefeltro's Georgetown house, taking tiny sips of black coffee and nursing a head that felt like a blacksmith's anvil. Demons, large ones, perhaps even Beelzebub himself, were pounding on the anvil with sledgehammers, making the most terrible noise.

"Do you want more Alka-Seltzer, Geedeon?"

"*Oh* . . . ," Gideon whimpered, waving him off with a feeble motion. He put down the coffee, picked up the Ziploc bag full of crushed ice, and put it to his forehead. It felt corpse-cold and waxy. A large bruise empurpled several square inches above his left eye; a small gash in its center crusted over with blood.

Monsignor Montefeltro, fearing anew for his $15,000 antique Tabriz rug, which reeked unpleasantly of Mr. Clean bathroom cleanser and other things, nudged a wastebasket closer to Gideon.

The monsignor himself did not feel 100 percent. Out of sympathy for Gideon, who was clearly going through some kind of breakdown, he'd kept him company in drink, at least up to a point. Gideon had consumed four bottles of white wine. (Total cost: $460.) Montefeltro himself had consumed perhaps the better part of two bottles, rather more than his normal intake, even when working on a recalcitrant widow. His tongue felt furry and sticky, the inside of his head felt like the entrance to hell. He had already taken four Advils.

He relived the horror of the previous night. At some point while drinking his fourth bottle, Gideon had staggered to his feet and shouted, "Let's go get us some *pussy*!" Whereupon he had pitched forward into an eighteenth-century Venetian rosewood ebony-and-ivory-inlaid table (cost: $8,000), reducing it to splinters and opening up a gash in his forehead.

Montefeltro managed to revive Gideon, offering a sincere thanks to the Virgin Mary that the inebriated Protestant had not bled to death in his living room. The parlor now resembled an abattoir. Upon reviving, Gideon copiously voided the contents of his stomach onto the Tabriz and onto Monsignor Montefeltro.

Since the monsignor preferred not to have to explain to his house-keeper why the parlor was a lake of vomit and blood, he rummaged through the basement for something that looked as if it had to do with cleaning, eventually finding a bottle of yellow liquid with a label displaying a bald smiling eunuch with an earring. Why this should symbolize cleanliness to Americans was a question the monsignor did not pause to resolve. He got down on his hands and knees and cleaned the horrific mess himself, a very different office from symbolically washing the congregation's feet on Good Friday. By the time he finished, Gideon revived and, now feeling greatly improved, demanded more wine. At which point the nightmare began in earnest.

The monsignor had gone off to make a pot of coffee in the kitchen. He was no more used to making coffee for himself than scrubbing the floors. Finding all the ingredients took time. When he came back to the room with the coffee, he found Gideon on the phone—Montefeltro's own house phone—having what sounded suspiciously like a conversation with the dispatcher of an escort service. The true horror came when he heard Gideon giving out the monsignor's address.

Gideon hung up, smiled, belched.

"Geedeon, what have you done?"

"Lysol," Gideon said, looking at the rug. "Lysol's the thing. Make all the nasty germs go 'way. . . ."

"No—who were you talking to just now? On *my* telephone?"

Gideon contemplated the unpleasantness of his barfed-upon pants legs and shoes. "You got any extra duds? Can't entertain our lady friends looking like this. *Hic*."

"Duds? What are you talking about? Geedeon, who were you—"

"Always liked the way you looked. Cassock. *Hic*. With the little scarlet—*hic*—buttons. You must have another one up there. Can't wear the same cassock day in—*hic*—day out. *Hic*. Might have to let it out a bit in the belly. *Hic*. I'll take one of them crimson skullcaps. Just *love* the crimson skullcaps."

"Geedeon. Listen to me. Please. Please. Who were you talking with on the telephone?"

Gideon smiled a big beaming smile, broad as the Potomac River. "Donnnnnn't you worry about a thing. I ordered us up a couple of—*hic*—hotties. *Hic*. Russians. You know what they say about Russian

girls? *Hic.* Yours is named . . . Tolstoy. *Hic.* Mine's—*hic*—Dostoevsky."
Gideon began humming "The Song of the Volga Boatmen."

Montefeltro relived the agony of what followed: the ringing of his
doorbell; having to physically restrain Gideon from getting up to answer
it; more ringing; insistent ringing; angry ringing, accompanied by loud
banging on the door. Then the ultimate horror: His phone rang. Cautiously he answered and heard an angry voice, Russian accented, saying,
"Mr. Montefeltro. Your dates are outside. Please to let in."

Porca miseria! The awful-sounding woman knew his name. His
phone number.

"Excuse me," he said, "there must be a mistake. I don't know what
you are talking about."

The Russian voice said, "No mistake. We have caller ID. Are you
going to let them in, or you want I'm sending men?"

"No, no men!"

"You want girls, then?"

"*No!* Look, it's . . . I am sorry, it's all a bad mistake. Good night.
Thank you. Good night. God bless you." The monsignor hung up the
phone.

"Where's my Russian girl?" Gideon said. "Where's my little baboooo-
shka? Back in the U.S., back in the U.S., back in the *USSRRRRRR.* . . ."

"Geedeon. Please. Quiet. Shut up."

"That's no way to speak to a—*hic*—man of God. *Oh, I'm a man
of God.* . . ."

The doorbell rang. The phone rang. The besieged monsignor
answered.

The voice, now icy, said, "You owe one thousand two hundred dollars. Six hundred for each. You don't want massage, no problem. But
you owe one thousand two hundred dollars for making massage house
call. Or I am sending Ivan and Vladimir."

"Okay. Please. Wait. A moment."

In a panic, Monsignor Montefeltro ransacked his home for money.
Monsignors tend not to keep on hand large sums of cash.

Gideon had passed out again. Montefeltro rummaged through his
pockets and found his wallet. It held a bit over $300. The doorbell rang

and rang. There was a loud pounding on the door. Ivan the Terrible and the probably even more terrible Vladimir.

He saw Gideon's expensive-looking gold watch fob resting against his bulging, vomit-splattered vest. He took it and the even more expensive-looking gold watch it was attached to. He went to the door, opening it with the lock chain attached, and peered out. There he saw two Valkyrie-tall Russian-looking ladies, attractive (in a cheap sort of way), smoking cigarettes, and wearing faces of fury.

"Why you not open door?"

"Shhh. *Prego*."

"You're —*priest*?"

Agnus Dei . . . In the confusion, Montefeltro had forgotten to re-move his Roman collar.

"No, no. It's—a costume. It's costume party. We're having a party. Yes. But everyone is now asleep. Thank you for coming. Here." He handed over the cash and gold watch and fob.

"What's this?" said Tolstoy. Or Dostoevsky.

"A gift. Very valuable. Please. Go. Now. It's all a mistake. A terrible error. Please. *Dasvidanya*. God bless you. I love Russia. Wonderful country. Good night. Good night."

He shut the door, threw the bolt, and braced, sweat trickling down his neck, for another ring of the bell or the phone or Ivan's jackboot to come through the door.

Silence. The makeshift emoluments had done the trick.

Omnibus sanctiis et Tibi, Pater . . .

He heard from the parlor: "Where's my Russian girls?!"

Chapter 28

Allen Snyder, looking un-upbeat and definitely lacking spring in his step, arrived at the offices of Tucker for the meeting he had hastily called with Terry and Cass.

"I've got some good news and less good news," he said, trying to smile through resisting facial muscles. "Which would you like to have first?"

"The good news," Cass said.

"The bad news," Terry said simultaneously.

"The good news: There's nothing on the computer linking you to Arthur Clumm. Legally, for the time being, you would seem to be in the clear on that one. Though it remains a bit of a public relations . . ."

"The word you're looking for is 'nightmare,' " Terry said.

"Then what's the bad news?" Cass said.

"They found those files relating to your North Korean project. Some golf tournament?"

Terry said to Cass, "I thought you deleted those."

"I did," Cass said.

"They found them," Allen said. "I'll explain the technology later."

"Why not save it—for our arraignment?" Terry said. "Oh, great."

"It's typically the deleted files that interest them. Let me ask you— did the North Koreans approach you, or did you approach them?"

"No, no—they approached us. Absolutely," Terry said.

"Were you in direct contact with their government?"

"No way. There's this NGO here in town, the—what's it called, Cass?"

"Association of Totalitarian Asian Tyrants?"

"*Cass*. Could we be helpful, please?"

"It's called the U.S.-Korea Mutual Understanding and Promotion Society."

"Right," Terry said. "Not a big office. Just one guy who chain-smokes. Mung Park. Mr. Mung Park."

"And they wanted you to do what, exactly?"

"The way they put it was like, 'To promote harmony and understanding between North Korea and the community of world nations' by putting on a pro-am golf tournament. In North Korea. They have a golf course, apparently. A really challenging course. Over there, a bunker's really a bunker. Our job was to put it on. You know, wrangle celebrities."

"Celebrities?" Allen Snyder said.

"There wasn't exactly a groundswell of enthusiasm. But O. J. Simpson indicated some interest."

"Real A-list," Cass said to Allen.

Allen digested this information. He said, "You're aware that North Korea is on the State Department list of sponsors of international terrorism. American citizens are prohibited from doing business with North Korea."

Terry, rallying to his own defense, said, "We were more just exploring a theoretical . . . you might say, avenue of convergence. Nothing . . . specifically . . . definite?"

Allen stared.

"Terry," Cass said. "We're surrounded. Give it up."

"What has it come to," Terry said, "when your own government turns into Big Brother, knocks down your doors, seizes your computers, and comes after you with all its formidable resources for trying to contribute something—just something—a *gesture*, to . . . to . . ." He looked at Cass. "I forgot. What was it?"

"Harmony and understanding."

"Right."

"Let me deal with the FBI," Allen said. "I imagine we'll be hearing from them soon." Just then, Terry's secretary buzzed him to say that two agents from the FBI were outside wanting to speak with him and Cass.

Allen went out to run interference.

"I'm thinking we should have a separate reception area," Terry said. "One for clients and one for the FBI. We'll make it nice for them. Potted cactuses. Copies of *American Rifleman*. A TV showing *America's Most Wanted*."

"About the computer," Cass said to Randy. He was scribbling notes for a speech on a legal pad.

"Um?"

"There's good news. And other news. Which do you want to hear first?"

"Given my druthers, I'd only ever want to hear good news. I thus gather your news is something less than good."

"They didn't find anything about your mother being a c-u-next-Tuesday. Or what we do with cherries."

"Well, *what* a relief," Randy said with a miffed air, looking up from his legal pad. His glasses were perched on the end of his nose, giving him a supercilious WASPy air. "So if you Google 'Senator Randolph Jepperson' and 'cunt,' you won't get two thousand matches. *Quel joie.*"

"So, you want to hear the other news?"

"Not particularly," he said, going back to his legal pad. "But I have a feeling I'm going to anyway."

"Terry and I were sort of in discussion with . . . it was this business deal . . . really, no big deal."

"Um?"

"Probably never would have even gotten to that. Deals like that fall through all the time."

Randy continued scribbling his announcement speech.

"Tell you what, Cass," he said. "I won't look at you, and you tell me what you need to tell me. How would that be? On the count of three. Ready? What was it you said about truth telling being just like riding a bicycle? One . . . two . . . three."

"The FBI found some files on the computer that make it seem like Terry and I were"—Cass made a dismissive sound—"working with an NGO trying to facilitate one of those, you know, hands-across-the-seas type of deals where you, you know, adopt a private sector, bilateral, really more *multi*lateral . . ."

Randy looked up. "Did you just have a stroke?"

"Huh?"

"Because you're making no sense. Why don't you just tell me what it is?"

"Okay," Cass said, using her best casual, matter-of-fact tone. "They're curious about some files pertaining to a golf tournament Terry and I were discussing with a foreign government. That's it."

"What government?"

"Korea."

"Well? I don't see the problem."

"Technically speaking, North Korea. How's the speech going?"

Gideon Payne groaned and attempted, very slowly, to rise to his feet. "Merciful Jesus . . ."

Monsignor Montefeltro, looking like Torquemada about to issue a death sentence at the Inquisition, sat in the chair facing Gideon. He had moved it back in case Gideon vomited again.

"What . . . happened?" Gideon said woozily.

"Very much happened," Monsignor Montefeltro said in a clipped tone of voice. "Would you like first to hear about *my* evening? And then I will tell you about *your* evening?"

Gideon was now on two feet, listing to and fro. He patted his vest pockets, sensing even in his distress that something was amiss. He began patting all his pockets.

"My watch. My fob. They're gone." He looked at the monsignor more alertly. His brain was like a mastodon struggling to free itself of a tar pit.

"Where's my watch and fob?" he said accusingly.

"You don't remember?"

"I don't remember *anything*," Gideon said, turning his pants pockets inside out.

An old Italian proverb suddenly came to Montefeltro: *"Si non è vero, è molto ben trovato."* If it isn't true, it is a happy invention. He said, "You gave it to your friend. Miss Tolstoy."

Gideon scrunched his cheeks; his eyes peeped out through fatty slits. "What are you *talking* about? Give away my watch? That watch has been in my family since 1864!"

"Why don't you sit down, Geedeon. And now *I* will tell you *your* confession."

By the time Monsignor Montefeltro finished his recitation of the evening's events, changing one or two details, Gideon looked ready for a funeral parlor. His skin had gone the color of waxworks.

"But . . . but . . . I don't remember *any* of that," he moaned.

"Consider that a blessing. Of course you don't," Montefeltro said, not unkindly. "You were drunk. Extremely drunk. Four bottles. Very good wine. Expensive."

"But why would I give my watch, my precious watch and fob, to a—Russian who-re?"

"Two Russian who-res. Perhaps to avoid being beaten to death by two very large Russian pimps."

"Did I . . ." Gideon now looked frantic. "Did I . . . *consummate*?"

"Do you mean were you intimate with her? No—God be thanked. To think of the disease you could catch from such a woman. The bubonic plague, probably."

Gideon shuddered. "I have to get my watch back. You have no idea. It's precious. Family heirloom. They gave it to my ancestor for superlative marksmanship—"

"Geedeon, were I you, I would give thanks to God that I am still alive today. And buy *another watch*!"

"What was the name of this, this escort service, you called it?"

"How should I know?" the monsignor said heatedly. "I am not *familiar* with escort services! I am in the kitchen, making you black coffee to make you conscious, because you are vomiting all over my house and destroying my family treasures—look, the table, eight thousand dollars—and when I return, you are in here, on my telephone, making phone calls to *prostitutes*!"

"Well, I'm sorry, Massimo, if I was overserved."

"Overserved! You drank my entire cellar!"

"I'll make it up to you," Gideon said edgily. "Meanwhile, I would appreciate it if you would assist me in the matter of my watch."

"Geedeon! *Forget the fucking watch!* We are lucky to be *alive,* I tell you! The madam—the keeper of this brothel that you telephoned on *my telephone*—she called to inform that she is going to send people named Ivan and Vladimir to break the legs of us both! You should be having high mass offered in every cathedral in America to give thanks. You should get down on your knees and pray."

Gideon surveyed the carpet. It did not look suitable for kneeling. "There's a problem."

"Of course there's a problem! This brothel now has my phone number! Do you understand the *scandal* that could happen?"

"Oh . . ." Gideon put his hand to his eyes. "It's worse than you think. The watch has *my name* on it."

"*Porca miseria.*" Monsignor Montefeltro considered. "My conclusion is that it is not a wonderful situation for either of us."

"I'll report it stolen," Gideon said. "That's what. I'll call the police and say it was stolen." He reached for the phone.

"Geedeon. *Not. That. Telephone!*"

Gideon rummaged for his cell phone.

Montefeltro said, "Wait. Think a moment. If you report to the police the watch is stolen and for some reason the Russian whores are found with the watch, what then? They will tell them everything. Including that *you* gave it to her. You can deny all this to the police, but they will produce their phone records with the call from my phone. Can you *imagine* the headlines? Can you *imagine* the scandal, Geedeon? For *both* of us? You can get a new watch, you *cannot* get a new reputation!"

Gideon looked defeated. He moaned, "Pray with me, Massimo. I have sinned." He started to kneel, but then, after surveying the detritus of the lost night, said, "Is there some . . . other room where we might make our rogations?"

"That depends if you have finished with the throwing up," Montefeltro said a bit testily. "All night I am cleaning. It's not pleasant."

"I'm sorry, Massimo," Gideon said, summoning from deep within the remnants of his dignity. "I was not myself."

The phone rang. Montefeltro picked it up without saying hello. He heard:

"Is residence of Montefeltro?" said the familiar, horrid, foreign-accented voice. Montefeltro tried to formulate some response, but nothing came.

The voice said, "This is escort service from last night. You owe nine hundred dollars. You want to give me credit card number, or am I sending Ivan and Vladimir?"

Chapter 29

Frank Cohane was at the helm of his twelve-meter yacht *Expensive* off Monterey Bay in a stiff breeze, running time trials in preparation for the America's Cup, when his cell phone went off. Whenever Frank was on the boat, his cell phone was programmed to accept calls only from his secretary, who was instructed to call him only if it was a matter of apocalyptic urgency.

"Yeah, Jean, what?" he barked. *Expensive* had just rounded the upwind mark. The crew was setting the spinnaker, a delicate procedure and one requiring total concentration from the helmsman.

"I'm sorry to disturb you, Mr. Cohane, but there's a reporter from the *Yale Daily News* insisting that he speak with you."

"The *Yale* what? Who?"

"He says he needs to talk to you about a story he's writing saying—these were his words—that you, quote, bribed Yale to keep them from expelling Boyd. . . . Mr. Cohane? . . . Sir?"

"*Fuck!*" Frank Cohane threw the cell phone overboard.

"Mr. Cohane—sir! She's jibing! *Jibe-ho!*"

There was a loud rip forward, the sound of $60,000 worth of Mylar turning itself from a huge mono-bosom into something resembling a shredded party favor.

"Mr. Kane?" Jean said to the *Yale Daily News* reporter. "I'm sorry to keep you holding. Mr. Cohane and I were cut off. He's at sea, on his yacht. Let me try to reach him. I'll call you back."

Charlie Kane, Yale sophomore, staff writer for the "Oldest Col-lege Daily"—as the *Yale Daily News* proudly called itself—told Mr. Cohane's pleasant secretary that his deadline was in three hours. He hung up and went back to writing his story.

It had come to him, as many of the really good stories do, in a hand-me-down way. A girl in his philosophy class had a friend who had gone out with Boyd Baker. Boyd was one of the campus's more conspicuous party animals. He'd managed to flunk all his courses and had been asked to leave and spend a year, as Yale put it, "reassessing your priorities." And then nothing happened. He just stayed.

One dawn, after a long night of snorting Ritalin and Ecstasy with his girlfriend, Boyd confided to her that his stepfather, some humon-gously rich California tech guy, had bribed Yale to the tune of $25 *mil-lion* to keep him on. *What a great story!* Charlie thought. The election for next year's editorial board was coming up, and with a story like this under his belt, Charlie would have a good shot at editor in chief.

While he waited for the phone to ring, Charlie typed: "Attempts to reach Frank Cohane on his sailboat were unavailing." He looked at the sentence, deleted it. He Googled "Cohane" and "America's Cup," exam-ined the matches, and typed: "Attempts to reach Frank Cohane aboard his ultra-high-tech, well-named yacht *Expensive* were unavailing."

He wondered if he ought to change "attempts" to the singular.

"Who's got a phone?" Frank Cohane snapped his fingers. "Who's got a phone? Someone's got to have a fucking *phone*!"

The tactician rummaged in a carry case and handed him his.

"Take the wheel," Frank said. *Expensive* was back on an upwind tack now, having rounded another marker. Frank stormed forward, stepping on the hands of several crewmen who were leaning over the rails, hiking to windward to counterbalance the boat. They knew bet-ter than to say, "Ow!" much less, "Hey, watch where you're going, asshole!"

"Jean. It's me. Patch me through to that Yale kid."

*   *   *

"Mr. Kane? I have Mr. Cohane on the line. Go ahead, sir."

"Mr. Cohane? Hello. My name is Charles—"

"Yeah, yeah. Look, this is Frank Cohane. What the—"

The portion of Frank Cohane's brain that was not on fire with rage and fury tried to say, *Easy does it, big shot.* But when driven men board their own yachts and assume command, the inner Bligh is invariably released and does not easily relinquish the helm. Frank Cohane couldn't help himself.

"—*fuck* is this you're telling my secretary? Did you use the word *bribe*? Did you actually say *bribe*?"

Charlie Kane, all of age twenty-one, had not yet in his brief career as a reporter been bitch-slapped by a California billionaire. He had only one thought in his mind: *editor in chief.*

"Ah, well, sir, it does appear that you visited the president's office on the twenty-fourth of last month. According to the president's appointments calendar. And the development office records do show a donation made later that same day from the Cohane Charitable Trust in the amount of fifteen million"—Charlie's source had inflated the amount of the bribe, but he'd caught the error—"and your stepson, Boyd Baker, had, previous to that, been informed that he was on academic suspension. He confirmed that detail himself."

Frank winced. *Boyd! Imbecile!*

Charlie Kane continued, "And the fact is that he is still enrolled at Yale. So in connecting the dots, I—"

"Connecting the dots? Connecting the dots? Do you think this is some kind of game? Let me ask you something, Mr. Kane," Frank said. "Do you know how many lawyers I have, just on staff?"

"I wouldn't have that information, but from the way you're asking, I'd guess, quite a few, sir?"

"Twenty-five. Twenty-five lawyers. Full-time. Sharks, all of them. Great whites. They never sleep. They just keep moving forward, suing everything in their path. . . ."

"That does seem like a lot of lawyers, I agree, sir."

"You're fucking damn right it's a lot! And if they're not enough, I can afford to hire every other lawyer in the country. And I will, if you print a false and malicious story—false, malicious, libelous, *and* defamatory. I'm formally putting you on notice here that—Jesus Christ, I . . . I can't even *believe* I'm having to tell you this. Is there a crime in giving money to your college? Don't you think I *care* about Yale? Do you think I give this kind of money to, to—Harvard?"

"I don't think that's really the point here, sir."

"Mr. Kane," Frank said, trying a calmer, cooler—indeed, icier—tone of voice, "understand something. For your own well-being. Understand that I will sue you—you personally, not the *Yale Daily News*—if you print a story saying that I quote-unquote bribed Yale. I give you full warning. I will take the food from your table, from your parents' table, and from your grandparents' table. Am I making myself clear?"

"Actually, sir, my grandparents are deceased."

"Don't fuck around with me, you little zit! Look me up in *Forbes* magazine. I have resources you can't even imagine. I will grind your bones to dust and use them for fertilizer. Do you hear me? . . . *Kane?*"

Charlie Kane could hardly believe his luck. *Dude was postal!* His fingers flew over the keyboard. "Um-hum."

"What you do mean, 'Um-hum'?"

"So that is your comment? That you're going to impoverish my family and turn me into fertilizer?"

"My comment? My *comment*, Mr. Kane, is that you're a dead man. Let me spell it for you, so you get at least that much right: d-e-a-d. Got it?"

"Yes, sir. D-e-a-d. Thank you. Good luck with the race."

And with that, Frank Cohane hurled another innocent cell phone into the vast deep of the Pacific Ocean. He stormed aft to the wheel. As he did, the crew leaning over the rail withdrew their hands, one by one.

A winch grinder murmured to the man next to him, "Skipper's in a good mood today."

All Bucky Trumble got to tell the president these days was bad news, and as the axiom has it, in the long run this does the bearer no good. The high-and-mighty much prefer to hear, "Sir, your approval ratings are through the roof!" or, "Sire, the enemy has capitulated!" than the endless servings of distress and gloom that seemed to constitute Bucky's daily political briefings. Today was no exception.

"What?" the president grunted without looking up. "What?"

In the old days, he would have said, "Well, if it isn't the Buckmeister! Sit down, you sad-ass cocksucker, pour yourself a drink, and gimme all the dirt." Now all Bucky got was, "What?" short for, "What now?"

"I have the FBI report on Cassandra Devine's computer, sir."

"Go ahead."

"They didn't find anything on it that would link her directly to Arthur Clumm, the male nurse."

The president looked up at Bucky sourly. "I was under the impression that you were working on that."

"I thought I had worked on it. I don't know what to tell you. I'm certainly going to call Frank Co—"

"Don't." The president held up a hand. "Don't tell me anything I don't need to hear. Tell me something I *want* to hear. Even if you have to make it up out of whole cloth."

"As a matter of fact, there is something. Seems Devine and her PR boss, Tucker, may be involved in illegal business dealing with North Korea."

"North Korea?" the president said, brightening. "Well, goddamnit. Why didn't you tell me that first? That's good work, Buck. Fine work. Ho, ho. Oh, you're a clever cocksucker, Bucky boy." The president chortled.

Bucky thought, *He thinks I planted it.*

"Sir, I'd love to take credit for it, but, uh, this fact is in fact a fact. That is, it's real. They found it on the computers."

The president looked taken aback. "Oh. Well, fine. Okay. Even better. So can the FBI throw her ass in jail?"

"Well, sir, it's not like they were selling F-16s or missiles to North Korea or anything like that."

The president frowned. "What *were* they selling 'em?"

Bucky tried to make it sound as traitorous as he could. "Sir, these two jokers were conspiring with the government of North Korea, a government declaredly hostile to the United States, to"—he cleared his throat—"to put on a golf tournament."

"Golf? Did you say golf tournament?"

"Yes, sir. A corruption of one of the most democratic pastimes in the civilized world. A totalitarian golf tournament. In Pyongyang. Behind enemy lines. Ostensibly to promote—I'm quoting directly—peace and understanding. In actuality to provide cover, to paste a big smiley face on a ruthless regime. And God only knows what else they might be up to. It's big, sir. Big."

The president stared. "Who in hell gives a rat's ass about a golf tournament? Goddamnit, Buck, you had me thinking they were giving 'em enriched plutonium or anthrax or—"

"The FBI seems to think it's serious enough. Want the headline? JEPPERSON'S ADVISERS ON NORTH KOREAN PAYROLL."

The president considered. "Well, I *do* like that headline."

"Thought you might." *Whew.*

The president's leather chair squeaked. "Now, a headline like that, you don't want to spend it right away. You want to hold on to it for a while. Save it for just the right occasion. Like . . ."

"Before the New Hampshire primary?"

"Or even after. You'll convey this to our good friends at the Bureau?"

"I'm shakin' it, boss!" Bucky said brightly. "I'm shakin' it!"

It was a line from the movie *Cool Hand Luke*. Bucky used it in the old days, when just he and Governor Peacham were flying around in a single-engine Cessna hitting a dozen campaign stops in a day. Back then, Peacham would laugh and laugh at the line, which conveyed just the right amount of irony and servility. Now all he said to his faithful retainer was, "Okay, then," and went back to his paperwork, an impassioned personal plea to the head of the Federal Reserve not to raise the prime rate to 20 percent.

Bucky returned to his office, feeling thoroughly exhausted and a bit ungratefully used. He loosened his tie and checked his e-mail. He had three hundred, including one from his assistant slugged "Urgent— Read ASAP."

He opened the e-mail. It contained a link to a story in the online *Yale Daily News*. What on earth kind of urgency could there possibly be in a story in a college newspaper? He clicked on the link and read.

"Oh," he said to no one in particular, *"shit."*

Frank Cohane's secretary, Jean, reached him as he was driving home from the yacht basin. (He kept a spare cell phone in the glove compartment of his Ferrari Enzo.)

She read him the story in the online *Yale Daily News*. When she got to the paragraph where the hapless Boyd admitted, on record, that "yeah, I guess my stepdad sort of dealt with the situation, threw some bucks at them, whatever, made them an offer they couldn't refuse. He's pretty cool that way," Frank's fury reached such intensity that for his own safety he had to pull the Enzo over to the dirt shoulder and hyperventilate.

According to Kane's story, "Yale has no official comment, but a spokesperson in the development office notes that 'Mr. Cohane has been, and continues to be, a wonderfully generous supporter of Yale.' Dean of Undergraduates John Wilkinson did not return repeated calls asking for clarification as to Baker's academic status."

"Is that it?" Frank moaned.

"Yes, Mr. Cohane. In the meantime, you've had quite a few calls. Mr. Trumble from the White House: 'Urgent, please call right away.' Also President Reigeluth of Yale: 'Urgent, please call as soon as possible.'"

Frank hung up and deliberated which call to return first: the chief political adviser to the president of the United States or the president of Yale. Eenie-meenie . . .

"Buck. Frank."

"Frank. Jesus."

"What can I tell you? Fucking kid reporters."

Frank was about to unleash a stream of expletives on the topic of his moron son-in-law when, ex nihilo, an inspiration occurred, and with not a second to spare.

"What can I tell you," Frank said. "I love that boy. He's like my own son."

Silence. Frank waited to see if this inspired bit of spontaneous mendacity had hit its mark.

"That's very, uh, decent of you, Frank."

"Ah, well," Frank said, "the old Washington solution, right? Hurl money at the problem and see if it'll go away. They can't prove a thing. So I'm generous. Last I checked, it's not a crime."

"Frank," Bucky said, "I was actually going to call you about another matter."

Frank had forgotten to activate the recording device on his car phone. He did now. "Yeah? Shoot."

"That, uh, matter we discussed? About the FBI and those computers?"

"What computers?"

Bucky sounded uncomfortable. He could hear cars going by on the other end and assumed Frank was on his cell phone. He didn't like to speak too candidly on those. "At the Wok'n Roll? Remember?"

"Oh. Yeah. That. What about it?"

"Well, I had been kind of left with the impression that you were going to follow through on that thing we discussed."

"Follow through? How do you mean?"

Bucky's discomfort became suddenly acute. "Frank?"

"Yes, Bucky?"

"Are you . . . recording this phone call?"

"I record all my phone calls. In fact, I record all my conversations. Even the ones in crummy Chinese restaurants in Arlington."

"Frank—what are you saying?"

"Nothing. For the time being. I'll be in touch. Tell the president I'm looking forward to this campaign. In fact, I want to be closely involved. Closely."

Bucky's breath came in gasps. Frank hung up.

Frank's next call was to the head of his Internet division. He instructed him to pour a major amount of Spider Repellent™ all over the online *Yale Daily News* so anyone Googling "Cohane" and "bribe" and "Yale" would come up with zero matches.

Having blackmailed the president's top adviser and taken care of his own little scandal—not bad for ten minutes on the shoulder—Frank Cohane put the Enzo in gear, roared back onto the eucalyptus-scented Pacific Coast Highway, and gunned the engine toward home. He was actually looking forward to torturing Lisa with the latest evidence of her son's nincompoopery. Under the circumstances, he felt entitled to squeeze every drop of satisfaction from it, while at the same time congratulating himself on having outfoxed a very big bad wolf. Bucky Trumble's balls now belonged to him. As Frank reflected on it, with instincts like his, he should be quite an asset to the Peacham campaign. Yes indeed, quite an asset.

He whistled as he drove.

Chapter 30

Gideon Payne was in pain, and not just physical.

Try as he might to remember having willingly handed over to the two odious Russian prostitutes his precious watch and fob—handed down all the way from his sharpshooter ancestor—he couldn't. He had no memory of it. None. ("An alcoholic blackout, perhaps," Monsignor Montefeltro suggested.) And now those two—shudder—Muscovite jezebels not only knew what Gideon looked like, but were in possession of a watch engraved with his name. The thought of it gave him chest constrictions.

He did, vaguely, dimly, unfortunately, remember using the monsignor's phone on that dreadful night of nights . . . and asking the directory operator for the number of an escort service. "Any—*hic*—escort service." Oh, the wages of sin.

Now, every time a phone rang—any phone—Gideon trembled and broke out in cold sweat. Was it—them?

He heard a chastising voice inside him, mocking: *My, my, my, how the wicked do lie . . . in wait upon the Judgment Day.*

He kept a low profile. He must show up at the last meeting of the Transitioning commission. He had to. But what if the Russian jezebels watched C-SPAN? *Oh, Lord. . . .*

Monsignor Montefeltro, meanwhile, now found himself in a deepening hole of his own digging.

The monsignor had decided that the only thing to do was pay the wretched Russian blackmailers the $900 they were demanding. He got the cash (from his personal account), put on civilian clothes and bug-eye dark glasses of the kind once favored by Jackie Onassis and Greta Garbo, and arranged to meet the ghastly Ivan or Vladimir—he didn't ask which—at a designated street corner in Georgetown, far from his own home. Once there, he handed over the envelope to the cigarette-smoking Russian, who ripped it open, thumbed the bills, and then grunted at him, "Is not enough."

"What do you mean, 'Is not enough'?" the monsignor protested. "You asked for nine hundred dollars. *Here* is your nine hundred!"

Ivan-Vladimir shook his head. "No. One thousand two hundred dollars is price for both girls."

"Nine hundred you asked for. Nine hundred I give you. And I tell you good-bye! *Dasvidanya!*" The monsignor stormed off in a fury.

By the time he reached home, he was sweating profusely. When he walked in, his phone was ringing. He picked up and listened.

"Is priest Montefeltro? Is escort service. You owe three hundred dollars."

"I tell you before, I am *not* a priest! It was a costume party!"

"Costume party with two people?"

"You said nine hundred dollars! I gave your gorilla nine hundred dollars! Go away!"

"I make mistake about money. Just like *you* make mistake. Big mistake. Now you are owing three hundred more."

The iniquity! "All right, all right," the monsignor said. "I give you the three hundred. Then it's finished. But I want returned the watch and the chain that I gave you."

"No."

"*Sì.*"

"No. Watch with chain is tip for girls. Who is Gid-yon Pine?"

Sweat poured anew from the sacerdotal forehead. "I don't know. It's an antique watch."

"Is name on watch. Gid-yon Pine. Is he the one who called for the girls? He have a different accent from you. From south. It wasn't you who call. You are Italian. Italian priest. According to caller ID, house is belonging to Massimo Montefeltro. So that's you, yes?"

The besieged monsignor closed his eyes and summoned angels and archangels with flaming swords to smite the wicked, then opened his eyes to find himself still in the parlor where the sin had taken place, still smelling faintly of Protestant barf and Mr. Clean.

"All right, all right! Tell your Ivan or Vladmir I will meet him at the same place with three hundred dollars. Then we are finished. Finished forever."

"Is not necessary."

"*What* is not?"

"To meet at same place. He is now at this moment outside your door."

The monsignor hung up. A moment later, it rang again. Expecting the Russian, he barked into it, "Russian pimp! I am getting your money!"

He heard silence over the line and the faint static hiss of an overseas telephone call, followed by a tentative female Italian voice saying, in Italian, "This is the Vatican operator. Is this the residence of the Monsignor Massimo Montefeltro?"

Jesu Christo.

"Yes, yes," the monsignor said in Italian, in a somewhat different tone of voice. "There was another call, to a wrong number. A nuisance." He summoned his dignity. "It *is* Monsignor Montefeltro who speaks. Who is calling him?"

"Cardinal Restempopo-Bandolini is calling. One moment, please. I will connect you."

Had it been any normal Tuesday morning, Montefeltro would have been delighted and even honored to receive a phone call from the holy father's *consigliere principale*, personal confessor, and supreme director of the Congregation for the Propagation and Defense of the Faith. Each of these portfolios was impressive enough; combined, they made their possessor the second-highest-ranking cleric in the Vatican and thus the Catholic faith, consisting of over one billion adherents. Even other cardinals trembled at the approach on marble of the scarlet-slippered feet of Bonifaccio Cardinal Restempopo-Bandolini.

So for Monsignor Montefeltro, this call, coming at this exact moment, was an occasion not of pride, but of pituitary gland panic. He

stared into the infernal abyss, to the accompaniment of doorbell ringing and the concomitant banging of a meaty Slavic fist.

"Massimo," said the high-pitched voice over the phone.

"Eminence." *Thump-thump-thump. Ding-dong. Thump-THUMP-
THUMP.*

"Fraternal greetings."

Thump-thump-thump . . .

"And to you, Eminence."

"I am calling on a matter of the most grave importance."

THUMP-THUMP-THUMP.

"Massimo, there is a noise."

"I beg your indulgence, Eminence. It is—construction. They are
building a . . . chapel. May I call Your Eminence back from a more
tranquil telephone?"

"No, no, I must shortly accompany the holy father to an important
meeting. My specific instructions will arrive in writing, by courier. But
I wanted to tell you personally that there is a profound concern about
this Transitioning bill in Washington."

"Ah. Yes, I am following it closely, Eminence. Most closely."

THUMP-THUMP-THUMP.

"You are instructed personally to denounce this bill—publicly—in
the most vehement language."

"How do you mean, publicly, Eminence?"

"From every pulpit. Especially television. You are very good on the
television. You are to be our leader in America on this matter."

Monsignor Montefeltro's mouth went as dry as an empty holy
water dish.

"But, Eminence, surely," he croaked, "the *American* cardinals, the
papal nuncio, they are all much better suited than I to—"

"Massimo. Hear me. I am expressing to you the desire *of* the holy
father himself. This is the greatest honor. You have pleased him. He
reposes in you the greatest trust."

"The holy father is too generous. I, I must—"

"Now I am going to tell you a *great secret* which you must not
reveal to anyone. You are to be elevated to cardinal archbishop after

the new year. You are to become the next papal nuncio to the United States. But you are not to let the holy father know that you know this. He wants to tell you himself. For it to be a surprise. Are you not pleased, Massimo?"

THUMPTHUMPTHUMP.

"Yes, Eminence."

"You don't sound pleased."

"I am overwhelmed."

"Very well. Now, attend me closely. You are authorized to say, on behalf of the Holy See, that should this abominable bill of 'Transitioning' become the law in America, the holy father will issue a bull of excommunication—to any American Catholic who supports it. Do you understand?"

THUMP-THUMP-THUMP. DING-DONG-DING-DONG-DING-DONGTHUMPTHUMPTHUMP.

"I think they are installing the bell of your new chapel. I must go. Good-bye, Massimo. God be with you."

"Good-bye, Eminence."

Monsignor Massimo Montefeltro slowly hung up the phone, the same phone that the head of the pro-life movement in the United States had used to telephone an escort service, one of whose employees was at this moment trying to kick in the front door. And now the pope in Rome himself had just issued instructions to the monsignor, whose phone number and—better yet—face were familiar to several employees of the escort service, to appear on every television screen in the country . . . in order to express moral indignation.

THUMP-THUMP-THUMP.

Across Rock Creek and a mile down Pennsylvania Avenue, another phone was ringing just as Monsignor Montefeltro was hanging his up.

Bucky Trumble sat forlornly at his desk, contemplating the pink bottle of Pepto-Bismol. His stomach was a Vesuvius of churning gastric juices. He was certain that ulcers were forming.

"Mr. Trumble," his secretary said, "it's Mr. Cohane calling."

Bucky took another slug of pink liquid and picked up the phone. "What do you want?"

"You don't sound very happy to hear from me."

"Are you getting the right sound level for your tape recorder? Want me to count to ten? One, two, three—"

"Ah, come on, Bucky boy. Don't play the debutante with me. You White House guys *invented* taping!"

"Get to the point."

"Isn't it nice not having to do all the bullshit? Now you can be honest with me. You don't have to kiss my ass, don't have to tell me, 'Oh, Frank, I just spoke to the president and he has you in mind for a *significant* cabinet role in the next administration.' Although come to think of it, you actually *do* have to kiss my ass. And that's what I'm calling about."

"What part of your ass needs kissing today, Frank?"

"All of it! I want in."

"In what?"

"The campaign. The inner circle. No more Mickey Mouse 'Owl inner circle' bullshit and those phony 'issue briefings by top officials.' That's for amateurs. I want to be in the room with you and the Man when the big decisions are made."

"Is that all?" Bucky said mildly. "No air strikes or missile launches? Your own personal CIA daily briefer?"

"For the time being. After we win, I'll want quite a bit more. Starting with the Treasury Department."

"Why don't we just send you the money instead?"

"That's funny, Bucky. I'm really, really laughing. Do you do stand-up on the side?"

"Don't flatter yourself, Frank. You're just another billionaire. According to *Forbes*, there are 371 of you out there."

"Yeah, I saw. But this billionaire's got you by the short ones, Bucky boy. And I'm about to give a good yank. Feel that? Want another?"

"You're damaged goods, Frank. That Yale thing—bribing an Ivy League university not to flunk out your son? How do you think that would play at your Senate confirmation hearing?"

"Stepson. And who gives a shit? And who's going to prove it was a bribe? You think Yale is going to come forward and say, 'Sure we take bribes'? So I'm generous. That's a matter of record. I give away tons of money. I give *you* money. I've just in the last week made significant donations to a number of Ivy League universities. You know what they say: Money's like manure. Pile it up in one place . . . So don't you worry about my Yale problem. That story got no legs. But nice try."

Bucky said, "I can't just wave a wand and make you head of the campaign."

"Well, if I were you, Bucky boy, I'd start waving something—your dick, if it'll do the trick. Otherwise you're going to be reading a transcript of yourself telling me to hack into my daughter's laptop and plant fraudulent, incriminating e-mails linking her to a serial murderer. Now, that *would* be a story with legs."

"I'll do what I can. But I don't know if he'll go for it."

"Sure he will. Here's what you tell him. Tell him exactly what I want. Up front. Tell him I want to be his secretary of the Treasury in the second term, and to that end, I will raise so much money for him during the campaign, you'll be able to buy every minute of TV airtime between now and the election. If you can't sell that, you're in the wrong job."

"I'll do what I can. Good-bye, Frank. And Frank?"

"Yeah?"

"Fuck you. . . . You're right. It does feel good."

Bucky hung up feeling oddly liberated. It was so seldom in politics one could be so frank.

Cass was wrangling volunteers.

She'd managed to find a few dozen sixty-something Baby Boomers who were willing to volunteer for Transitioning—though not until age seventy-five. Moreover, in return for their selfless acts of economic patriotism, they were demanding not only tax benefits well beyond the parameters of Cass's original Transitioning plan, but also subsidized burial, mausoleums, full college tuition for their children, and retroactive medical payments going back to age twenty-one. Cass estimated that the aggregate economic impact of their Transitioning to the U.S. Treasury would be a *negative* $65 billion. (She would not emphasize this fact when they testified before the commission.)

"Where'd you *find* these people? Pyongyang?" Randy asked grouchily, looking over her list while plunging his chopsticks into a container of crispy shredded beef. He was generally grumpy with Cass and with Terry these days, owing to their North Korean golf tournament scheme. Oddly, the FBI, for whatever reason, hadn't come around to grill them further. And so far it hadn't leaked to the media. Allen Snyder was clearly worth well more than $700 an hour. Randy sniffed, "I imagine you'd find a *lot* of people in North Korea willing to sign up for Transitioning. At *any* age."

"Since you *ask*," Cass said, "it wasn't easy. In fact, it's quite hard finding people of *your* generation willing to do something altruistic for their country."

"Altruistic?" Terry said, nearly spewing his hot-and-sour soup. "That's a laugh. I bet half of these volunteers you found are on eBay right now, seeing how much they could get for their body parts."

"Your generation," Cass said to Terry and Randy. "Not mine."

Terry looked up from his Chiang Kai-shek chicken. "I suppose yours would do the right thing? Dream on. Every generation thinks it's the most put upon in history. You've got your panties in a twist fretting about the deficit. My generation had *real* crises."

"Oh, please," Cass said. "Here it comes. Where were you when JFK was shot? If I hear one more Baby Boomer tell me, in mind-numbing detail, I think I'll throw up."

"I was in eighth grade," Randy said. "We'd just come back from gym and—"

Cass said, "Prosecution rests."

"It was a big deal," Randy said. "What does your generation have to match it? The day Paris Hilton's Sidekick was stolen?"

"Why is your generation so obsessed with itself?" Cass said. "You don't think it was just as traumatic for all concerned when FDR died? After four years of a devastating world war?"

"Who's FDR?" Terry said, winking at Randy.

"Sorry," Cass said, not rising to the bait. "I forgot that Boomers don't care about anything that happened before 1946."

Terry said, "That's right. We were too busy dealing with one disaster after another. JFK, RFK, Martin Luther King, Vietnam—"

"Vietnam . . . remind me, was that the war that eighty percent of your generation dodged?"

"It wasn't a very good war."

"You were waiting for a better one to come along."

"Still am," Randy said.

Terry said, "Then there was Watergate—"

"Right. That would be the event that disillusioned you poor Baby Boomers. What a shock it must have been. Here you'd been brought up to believe that sort of thing had never gone on."

"Inflation, the gas crisis . . . For your information, Miss Righteous Indignation, I spent most of the 1970s siphoning gas out of neighbors' lawn mowers for my car."

"Well, let's award the Congressional Medal of Honor to Terry Tucker."

"I hate to interrupt such a splendid jeremiad," Randy said, "but Mitch Glint of ABBA called me today. He wants to make a statement at the next commission meeting."

"What does he want?" Cass said.

"He just wants to make a little, you know, statement."

"Let me guess. The Boomer Manifesto? What else do they want that you haven't already given them? Toaster ovens? wall clocks? kitchen knives? Maybe 24/7 erectile dysfunction patches?"

Randy pursed his lips. "He mentioned something about a . . . he's got this notion for a . . ."

"Just spit it out," Cass said. "I'm beyond surprise at this point. Or dismay."

"Well, it's sort of a . . . an Arlington Cemetery, for Transitioners."

Cass stared. "They want their own cemetery? And where would this field of honor go? No, wait, don't tell me—here in Washington, on the Mall. Why not? We could tear down the Lincoln Memorial and put it there. What's Lincoln done lately, anyway?"

"I don't think they particularly care where it goes. Look, if it gets the most powerful Boomer lobby to come aboard and endorse Transitioning, what's the big deal? Politics is negotiation. You have to give to get."

"Why don't you just offer to have every member of the Boomer generation cryogenically frozen—send the bill to my generation—and brought back to life once all diseases and global warming have been eliminated and there's peace in the Middle East? Haven't the Boomers suffered enough?"

"Hm," Randy said. "Not bad."

"You can make it the centerpiece of your vice presidential campaign."

"Where are you going?" Randy said.

"To find a BMW and slash its tires," Cass said.

The final session of the Presidential Commission on Transitioning and Tax Alleviation was called to order.

Gideon Payne appeared with a large bandage over his head and dark glasses. He looked like the Invisible Man. He was terrified that the Russian hookers to whom (he thought) he had given his precious watch would see him on TV and recognize him. His appearance naturally caused a stir. He explained that he'd had laser surgery for his eyes and while recuperating had fallen down the stairs.

"I assure you," he told reporters, "that my insides work just fine." They were licking their chops in anticipation of a final smackdown between him and his adversary, Joan of Dark.

They were disappointed, therefore, when Cass, entering the chamber and seeing her adversary in this condition, went over to him. They couldn't hear the exchange.

"Reverend," she said, "what happened? Are you all right?"

Gideon, taken aback by her softness and evident concern, mumbled, "Uh, yes. An accident."

"I'm sorry. Will you be all right?"

"Oh yes. Yes. Just healing."

"I haven't been very nice to you."

Gideon didn't know what to say to that. He held his breath. He could smell her perfume.

"But then," Cass said, "you haven't been very nice to me, either."

Gideon cleared his throat. She was so beautiful. He could only croak, "Ah, no, I suppose . . . not. We got off to a bad start."

She said, "For what it's worth, he and I weren't having sex in that minefield."

"And I didn't kill my mother."

"I believe you." Cass held out her hand. Photographers snapped away. Gideon hesitated, then reached out and took her hand. It felt soft. He wanted to hold it forever.

"Okay, then. . . ." She smiled and turned and went to her seat.

"What the fuck was that about?" said the *Washington Post* reporter to a *Times* columnist.

Randy looked at Cass as she took her seat next to him. He whispered, "First North Korea, now Gideon Payne?"

"I'm tired of being pissed off at everyone and everything."

"Are you forgetting that his ancestor shot my ancestor? And that he accused me of screwing you in a minefield?"

"Randy," she said, "the only time you *didn't* screw me was in that minefield."

"What's that supposed to mean?" Randy said. The chair was gaveling the meeting to order.

"Something's going on," said the *Post* reporter, who was watching the exchange between Randy and Cass and wishing he'd brought in a lip-reader.

Chapter 31

Two Months Later . . .

Few commission reports in history—except those dealing with Who Shot the President?—have been anticipated as eagerly as that of the commission on Transitioning.

The chairman of the commission was a former senator, secretary of labor, secretary of energy, and ambassador to an acronymic organization in Brussels whose actual function no one had ever quite ascertained. His very name, Bascombe P. Bledsoe, bespoke pinstripe, wood paneling, and murmured voices. He inspired confidence by virtue of his dullness. The polar ice caps might be melting, an asteroid might be hurtling toward earth, the international banking system might be in ruins, and Latin America might be in chaos; still, Bascombe P. Bledsoe would not raise his voice or break a sweat. If the moment became truly apocalyptic, he might cough softly and say, "The situation would appear not to be significantly ameliorating." He was Anodyne Man—the perfect person to head a commission convened to decide whether mass voluntary suicide was the answer to Social Security's intractable insolvency. And this was exactly why the president appointed him to chair the commission.

Having weighed the views of the various commissioners, he summed up the commission's findings with a clarity and concision all too rare in Washington: "Further study is needed."

Those hoping for Sturm und Drang were disappointed. The pronouncement contained little Sturm and virtually no Drang.

Commissioner Cassandra Devine, on the other hand, had Sturm und Drang to spare.

"This is ridiculous," she fumed. "'Further study is needed'! You could say that about anything. You could say that about . . . paleontology."

"Darling," Randy said, "don't get so worked up about it. We gave it our best shot."

"We've been sandbagged. Don't you see it?"

"Time to move on," Randy said.

"What are you talking about?" Cass said.

"There's a time for fighting and a time for not fighting," Randy said. "This is one of those times."

The White House issued a statement thanking Secretary Bledsoe and the commissioners for their "sacrifice, diligence, and hard work." Asked about the commission's report at a press conference the next day, the president said he, too, was satisfied that further study was needed and suggested that it was time to "move on."

"Funny," Cass said to Randy, "that the White House used the same language you did yesterday. 'Time to move on.'"

"Hardly unique," Randy sniffed.

"But 'moving on' is how it got to this point in the first place. It isn't the time to move on. It's time to fix it."

"The only way to eat an elephant is one spoonful at a time," Randy said.

"Is it me," Cass said, "or do you hear the sound of a pressing issue of vital national importance being swept under a giant carpet?"

Randy put down his newspaper and listened. "Nope. Must be you."

"Did you know this was going to happen?" she said accusingly. "It feels kind of scripted to me."

"You saw the report I submitted to Bledsoe. It was teeming with recommendations. Full of piss and vinegar. I was all in favor of Transitioning. Within reason."

"Oh, please. You recommended Transitioning at age eighty-five! You totally sold out to ABBA and the other Boomer lobbies."

"Darling, I can't help it if Bledsoe buried my recommendations. He's a Prussian when it comes to keeping things in check. Veins like ice water. Hell of a squash player, they say."

"You seem awfully . . . laid-back about this," Cass said. "For someone who was championing the issue."

"What can I say? I'm a WASP. I try not to let my emotions get the better of me. Inside, I'm churning."

"Aren't you going to say something?"

"Thought I might write an op-ed piece."

Cass stared.

Randy said, "What?"

"It's not quite 'The Charge of the Light Brigade,' is it?" Cass said. " 'Thought I might write an op-ed piece. Give them a whacking big piece of my mind. But first I'll have a spot of tea.' "

"Oh, stop being such a grumpuss. Meta-issue, remember? We got our day in the sun."

"I can't even discuss it. Why don't you go write your stirring *'J'accuse!'* for the op-ed page?"

"If you really want to know," Randy said coyly, "I thought I might sashay on down Pennsylvania to the White House and point out that it's time they lived up to their part of the bargain."

"Bargain?"

"The vice presidency, darling. You're not forgetting?"

"So it really *was* a deal? You'd cave on Transitioning in return for—"

"Not 'cave.' Well, all right. Cave. But in return for being tapped to be VP."

Cass sighed. "I just hadn't realized your little arrangement was so straightforward."

"Straightforwardish," Randy said. "They couldn't exactly issue a press release about it." He gave her a peck on the forehead. "Cheer up. You're going to be First Lady of the United States someday. And then"—he grinned—"you can have your own Transition commission. We'll even make Transitioning mandatory—at age fifty. How would that be?"

"Thank you. That was truly patronizing."

"Darling, I can do a lot more for your debt-ridden generation from *inside* the White House."

"Yeah, well, send me a postcard when you get there," Cass said, her heels making a clickety-click on the polished wooden floor of the Georgetown mansion as she headed for the door.

"Where are you going?" Randy called after her.

"To overthrow the government."

"*Cassandra.*"

She'd kept a relatively low profile blogwise during her stint as a commissioner. Now, sitting in front of the glowing screen, she felt like a fighter pilot strapping herself into the cockpit, firing up the engines, and doing a weapons systems check.

She posted: "Further Study Needed—*into Transition Commission Whitewash . . .*" and happily, busily blogged until dawn.

Randy's first inkling that all was not well came when he called Bucky Trumble—only to have a difficult time getting through to him.

"Can I tell him what it's about?" Bucky's assistant said.

"It's Senator Jepperson," Randy repeated. "Senator Randolph Jepperson." He wondered if he should add, "Of Massachusetts?"

The assistant said she would "pass along the message." Randy hung up and stared at the phone. After ten minutes, he began to think that there might be a more therapeutic use of his time than trying to will an inanimate object to ring and busied himself with inserting an earmark into a highway bill. Bucky called him back five and a half hours later.

"Sorry," Bucky said. "Busy day. The Middle East just blew up."

"How unusual," Randy said stiffly. "It's normally so placid."

"So what's up? Hey, listen, what's with your girlfriend?"

"What do you mean?"

"She's going after us on that blog of hers. Saying the commission was fixed."

"Well?" Randy said. "Wasn't it? That was the whole point."

"Tell her to lighten up. She called the president 'a manipulative scumbag.' That's not the sort of language a presidential commissioner ought to be using."

"I didn't know. She doesn't clear her stuff with me. And I've got better things to do than keep up with blogs."

"Maybe you ought to start. She called you a wimp."

"What?"

"She said you were part of the quote-unquote whitewash."

"I . . ." Randy made an exasperated sound. "I'll give her a good spanking. Look, meanwhile, I need to see the president."

"Okay," Bucky said, sounding unenthusiastic. "Anything special you'd like to discuss?"

Anything special? "Well, yes. In fact."

"Like?"

"Excuse me, do I have the wrong number? Is this the White House? Washington, D.C.?"

"Yes," Bucky said, sounding as though he might be doing a cross-word puzzle or sketching out ideas for a State of the Union speech.

"Is this call coming as something of a mystery to you?"

"No. No, no. Just swamped, is all. Let me take a look at his calendar." Bucky made a clicking sound with his tongue. "It's pretty chuggy-jam this week. And the next. Is it something you want to just run by me first over the phone so I can give him the gist?"

"Not especially, frankly."

"Then we're probably . . . looking at next month. . . ."

"Next month? Look here—"

"Unless you want to fly with him on Air Force One next week."

"Oh. Well, sure." *That's more like it.*

"He's doing a flyover of the drought-stricken states. The vice president's coming along. Please don't mention that to anyone, for security reasons. Normally, they don't fly together. But since the vice president is from Oklahoma . . . Ought to be a really interesting trip. The top experts on drought and irrigation will be aboard."

"Sounds riveting. You say the vice president is going to be there?"

"Yeah. Is that some kind of problem?"

"Well, Bucky," Randy said, "that's rather what I was hoping to discuss with the president."

There was silence over the line. *"Oh,"* Bucky said, "I . . . see. I see. Yes. Yes. Well, Randy, gosh, kind of awkward. But let me give it to you straight up. There've been developments on that front. The vice president indicated to the president that he wants to stay. He got a clean report from the prostate docs at Bethesda Naval. So he's still on the team. As you know, the president is nothing if not loyal. It would have been great to have *you* on the team, but as it is, the slot's filled. I realize this must be a disappointment to you. You did a hell of a job with the commission. We'd love to use you as a surrogate during the campaign. I shouldn't be saying this, but there are going to be some cabinet openings coming available after next November. But we're going to have to work our tails off. It's going to be one tough election. . . . Randy? . . . Hello?"

Terry and Cass were going over a presentation for a client who owned a nationwide string of 550 pet stores. He wanted the U.S. Fish and Wildlife Service to relax its ban on importing a species of Amazonian salamander called a motato that absorbs moonlight and glows in the dark. He foresaw a huge demand for glow-in-the-dark salamanders and, on top of the normal fees, was offering Terry a $5 million bonus if it went through.

The problem was twofold. The head of the imported salamanders division within Fish and Wildlife had to be persuaded that the motato was not, strictly speaking, endangered. The other problem was that the salamander was considered holy by a tribe of indigenous Indians, which meant that various environmental deputies in the Brazilian government would have to be persuaded, which is to say bribed—or, in the parlance of K Street, "accommodated." Terry and Cass were analyzing this particular aspect when the door burst open and in limped the senator from the great state of Massachusetts.

"I've been calling you for two days," he said grumpily to Cass. "Why haven't you returned my calls?"

"I've been dealing," Cass said airily, "with salamanders."

Terry said to Randy, "Don't ask."

Cass said, "Less slimy than certain human beings."

"If you two want to slug it out, I could leave," Terry said.

Randy threw himself into a leather chair. "It wasn't very nice of you to call me a 'wimp' on your blog."

"Actually I toned it down. Originally I had called you a backstabbing sellout."

"Thank you," Randy said. "I'm touched. You didn't help me much with the president. I was given the impression that he doesn't like being called a 'manipulative scumbag.' Really, Cass."

He described his phone call with Bucky Trumble. "So, it would appear that we've been had."

"No, darling," Cass said, "*you've* been had."

"Whatever," Randy said. The kinda spooky look came over him. "But let me assure you—they will rue the day that they tangled with Randolph K. Jepperson."

"Rue?" said Terry.

Cass said, "It's WASP for 'pluck out their eyes.' So, Senator? What's the plan now? Gearing up to write an earthshaking op-ed piece?"

"Screw that. We're running."

Cass and Terry stared.

"For president," he added.

"Darling," Cass said, not unkindly, "what on?"

"What do you mean?"

"Well, typically when someone runs for president, they have some, you know, reason. Other than, say, hating the current president. They're called 'issues.'"

"I *have* a platform."

"I must have missed that press release. And what does it consist of? If you say Transitioning, I'm going to stab you in the heart with this pen."

"As a matter of fact, Transitioning is indeed part of my platform. Fiscal responsibility. Not handing on debt to the next generation. Accountability. Leadership—"

258 / CHRISTOPHER BUCKLEY

"Don't forget global warming. Where do you stand on violent crime?"

"I'm against it," Randy said, rising out of his chair. "Look, I could use you."

"You already did."

"I know you're sore. I don't blame you. I was an ass. And maybe it sounds grandiose to say, 'I'm going to run for president.' But ever since that day I walked into the JFK Library—"

"Tripping your brains out on LSD. *That'll* make for a stirring announcement speech."

"All right, we'll leave out that part of it. Point is, I feel that this is what my life is directed toward. Fate put us together in that minefield in Bosnia."

"You wanting a gourmet meal put us in that minefield."

"I'm trying to explain why I'm running for president."

"Randy, I'm not interested. I don't care. Want to give a speech? Go do it on C-SPAN."

Randy stood up. He looked at Terry. Terry shrugged. Randy walked to the door. He said, "Your generation is being bankrupted by my generation. I want to do something about it. There's a presidential election coming up, and I'm going to be in it. I could use you—I mean, I need you. But okay. Good luck with your salamanders."

He left.

Terry said to Cass, "Say what you will, the man knows how to make an exit."

Cass hardly slept that night, and not because she was wired on Red Bull or blogging. The next morning, as she blearily read the computer screen to find out what the rest of the world had done, she saw the bulletin from the White House announcing that Franklin Cohane, the billionaire California software entrepreneur, had been appointed finance chairman of the Committee to Reelect President Peacham.

She called Randy on his cell phone. "Okay," she said. "I'm in."

"Oh, darling," Randy said, "that's wonderful. Wonderful, wonderful, wonderful."

"Whatever," she said, and hung up.

Chapter 32

Gideon Payne, too, had been having a hard time getting through to the president, and this chafed. He was even having a hard time getting through to Bucky Trumble. Just *who* did Mr. Buckminster Trumble think he *was*? The White House might be busy, but Gideon was not used to having hours go by before his phone calls were returned. The cheek of these people.

It had been a tumultuous couple of months. First the deplorable episode at Monsignor Montefeltro's involving the Russian jezebels. His watch—gone. Probably hocked by the strumpets for drug money. He still unconsciously patted his vest pockets for it. He'd hired a private investigator to scour the capital's pawnshops and antique jewelry stores, looking for it.

Then there was the commission and Cassandra Devine's surprise gesture of reconciliation. What had prompted that? Was it really just the sight of his bandaged head? Or had some deeper, inner decency prompted it? He yearned for another touch of her hand but knew— knew in his heart of hearts—that there would not be another. She and Jepperson, that ass Yankee opportunist, were going to marry, so the rumor was.

As for the work of the commission itself, Gideon had made *his* feelings plain to Chairman Bascombe P. Bledsoe. Bledsoe seemed determined to put an end to the wretched business with his "Further study is needed" ruling. Jepperson's Transitioning bill was now stalled in the Senate, going nowhere.

Meanwhile, Elderheaven's profits were up 50 percent, thanks to the new actuarial software that Sidney, his chief operating officer, had purchased—at some considerable cost—from that software company in California. The software allowed Elderheaven to be selective in deciding which old folks to admit, and so far, it had been brilliantly accurate. The recent admissions had been dropping like flies, right and left, after signing over their life savings, leaving Elderheaven awash in cash. Which was good, since Elderheaven and Gideon needed cash to settle the damn Arthur Clumm–related lawsuits. But at this rate, the company would be able to expand, rolling up more and more nursing homes. The future looked very green indeed. And there was nothing like money to pump a man up, fill him with confidence. Gideon felt like sashaying on down to the White House, banging on the door, and demanding that the president declare his support—wholehearted support, none of this no-objection-in-principle gargle—for Gideon's memorial to the 43 million. The time for equivocation was over. Had he not fought the president's battles on the commission? Gideon was *owed*.

"Gideon! I'm so sorry not to have called you until now," said Bucky. "I've been busier than a one-legged Cajun in an . . ." *No*, he told himself, *don't use the "one-legged Cajun in an ass-kicking contest" joke with a man who calls himself "Reverend."* "Well, busier than all get-out. How are you? How's everything?"

"Well, I'm fine now," Gideon said. "I'm happy finally to hear from you, Bucky."

"I know, I know. Huge apologies. Profound apologies. So, the commission seems to have worked out."

"I would have preferred a more categorical denunciation. But I suppose in an imperfect world, 'Further study is needed' amounts to a kind of victory," Gideon said.

"Off the record, we leaned on old Bascombe pretty hard. Don't be surprised if he's appointed to the Federal Reserve Board one of these days."

"My, my, my," Gideon said, "how very different are the workings of government from what we all read about in books as children. I wonder, do the Founders weep in heaven?"

"It's good to hear your voice, Gideon. We're going to need you in the coming months. We've got a tough road ahead of us."

"So it would appear. I have *seen* the latest approval ratings. Thirty-one percent. My, my, my. Would that be a historical low for someone seeking a second term of office?"

Bucky cleared his throat. "No, no. But clearly, it's not where we want to be. That's why we're counting on you so much to help get out our message."

"Which message would that be, exactly?"

"I hardly need to tell you. Our message is your message. Vigorous moral leadership for troubled times."

"Yes, well we certainly could use some of *that*. Couldn't agree more. Which brings me to the purpose of my call. . . ."

Bucky groaned inwardly. *Here it comes. Should I pretend that the president's just buzzed me—*

"The memorial."

Shit, too late. "The president has already signaled his support for that, Gideon."

"Yes. A very wispy signal. Reminded me of the smoke signals that the Indians in the cowboy movies used to send to one another. I had in mind something with a little more, shall we say, oom-pa-pah?"

"Gideon . . ."

"Bucky . . ."

"Have a heart. It's an *election* year. We're in the worst economic shape since 1929. Due to circumstances beyond the president's control, of course. The economy's flatter'n a pancake. The government's hemorrhaging money. A memorial to forty-three million fetuses—pardon the expression—is just not"—he sighed—"at the top of anyone's agenda right now. But I promise, right after the election, we will . . . make it happen . . . somehow."

"All right, then, we'll talk. Right after the election. In the meantime, I will convey to the forty-three million *non*fetuses who constitute the pro-life portion of the American electorate that they are free to shop around for a candidate who shares their commitment to the inviolable sanctity of human life."

"Gideon—"

"Good day to you, sir." Gideon reflexively reached for his gold watch. Still not there.

Bucky shuffled into the Oval Office with all the alacrity of a sedated mental patient. The president looked at him with a long face.

"For crying out loud, we created a whole commission more or less just for him, and then made sure old candy-ass Bascombe would put everyone to sleep with the conclusion . . . what the hell's he want *now*?"

"The memorial," Bucky said. "I think he wants it next to the FDR Memorial."

"Oh no. Uh-uh. No fucking way. No fetuses on the Mall. That is not how this presidency will be remembered. The pro-choicers and women's groups would chew off my dick. You tell Gideon Payne-in-the-ass . . . Hell with it." The president reached for the phone. "I'll tell that fat little Bible-thumper *myself*!"

"Mr. President," Bucky said, "please put down the phone. No good will come of yelling at a man who commands millions of voters."

"I am sick and tired of being jerked around. Gimme gimme gimme. That's all I hear. All day. Gimme gimme gimme. I'll shove forty-three million fetuses up his ass! And I'll bet there's room for them!"

Bucky let the president huff and puff awhile longer, then shuffled out of the Oval Office and telephoned Gideon.

"I discussed your proposal with the president," he said, "and he wholeheartedly agrees that we must have a memorial on the Mall."

Bucky's call, though prompt, had come just a few moments too late. After making his lovely little speech about how he would tell his followers to shop around for a candidate, Gideon had suddenly become enamored of the idea that *he* should run for president. Why not? Lesser men had—and heck, some of them had even won. He probably wouldn't, but the experience might be entertaining. And it always seemed to have a salubrious effect on one's lecture fees.

"Well," Gideon said to Bucky, "I do appreciate that. You give the president my very best regards and tell him I look forward to our debate in the fall."

"Debate?" Bucky said. "In the fall?"

Gideon said, "That is normally when they hold the presidential debates, is it not? Though I imagine we'll be bumping into each other in New Hampshire and Iowa before then. I imagine it's very *cold* in

New Hampshire in February. Not my favorite climate. No, no. I am a creature of the South. But one must make sacrifices. I suppose I will need one of those puffy *parka* things from that Yankee store—what's it called?—L. L. Bean? Good day to you again, sir."

It was Cass's idea to have Randy announce his candidacy outside the Social Security Administration in Washington. She and Terry wrote his speech.

"This building behind me, once a symbol of a compact between the people and their government, now stands as a symbol of betrayal of the people by their government, a veritable warehouse of shame and empty promises. For Americans under thirty, it might as well be the New Bastille—the prison where all their hopes of a bright future go to die."

For the climax, Randy handed to a group of twenty-somethings (chosen, frankly, for their wholesome good looks) an enormous piece of paper with huge lettering that said:

> **INVOICE**
> **TO:** AMERICANS UNDER 30
> **FROM:** BABY BOOM GENERATION
> **FOR:** OUR RETIREMENT BENEFITS
> **AMOUNT:** $77 TRILLION
> **PAYABLE ON DEMAND**
> **— U.S. Government**

Randy was very excited by it all. He had wanted to insert the line "Boomer retirement is costing your generation an arm and a leg." And then reach down, detach his prosthesis, raise it over his head, and say, "American policies cost *me* a leg, so I know how you feel!"

He, Cass, and Terry had a heated discussion about whether it was "presidential" to wave artificial limbs over one's head during speeches. Cass and Terry finally said they'd resign if he did. Randy backed down. After he left the room, Terry said to Cass, "I'm going to Super Glue that thing to his stump for the duration of this campaign."

For their campaign slogan, they'd come up with "Jepperson—No Worse Than The Others."

It was not without risk, but there was logic to it. Cass's idea was to target the under-thirty voters, to convince them that Social Security was a form of indentured servitude; that they'd been economically disenfranchised by the previous generations. All the polling showed that the under-thirties were, in the words of one pollster, "the most cynical generation in American history." Most of them got all their political information from late-night TV comics. That being the case, Cass argued, there was no point in a slogan trumpeting Randolph Jepperson as an improvement over any other candidate. She called it "the 'whatever' factor." The idea was to say, "Here's our candidate. He might make things better. He probably won't, but at least we're not claiming he will. So why not vote for him? At least we're honest." A Mobius strip of persuasion.

It was a hard sell on the candidate, who saw himself as some kind of latter-day JFK.

Randy stared at the poster with his handsome face in profile and the slogan.

"Can't you come up with something a little more positive? This makes me sound like something on a menu that you're not sure you want."

"That's the whole point," Cass said. "That's why they'll go for it. We focus-grouped it. They loved it. Anyway, we're not doing traditional TV and radio advertising."

"We're not? Who signed off on that?"

"I did. We're putting all the money into podcasts and social networks. We're making major buys on Google, Facebook, and MySpace."

Randy looked uncomfortable. "Shouldn't we be appealing to more than just . . . kids?"

Terry said, "There are twenty-five million voters under thirty. There may be as many as seven or eight candidates on the ballot in November. There may be as many as three or four new independent parties. Our old friend Gideon Payne is gathering signatures for his SPERM party. It's going to be a crowded field. If we throw everything we've got at the under-thirties, we might pull it off."

"How do we even know they'll vote?" Randy said. "They never do. They're too busy shrugging and putting out, what do you call it, attitude."

"Because we're going to scare the shit out of them. We're going to convince them that if they don't vote this time—for you, the 'No Worse Than The Others' candidate—they're not going to be able to afford iPods and Mocha Frappuccinos. They'll be too busy paying for bedpans for Boomers."

"Hm . . . ," Randy mused. "Not a bad line. But for the slogan, what about . . . 'Jepperson, Leading the Way'?"

"What, into minefields?" Cass said. "Forget it. You do demagoguery, I'll do message."

"Hold on a mo. Who's paying whom here?" Randy grumbled.

And so Randolph Jepperson became the most formally modest candidate ever to seek the office of president of the United States.

The Establishment commentators, the punditariat, were initially appalled by the slogan. They felt insulted. Pundits expect, even demand, a certain minimal level of pretension in political candidates. This gives them something to deplore in order to affirm their own superiority. Randy's shrug of a slogan denied them this moral high ground. But they recovered quickly, and they were soon going after him for other than just his shamelessly modest campaign slogan. They attacked him for his scorched-earth Senate campaign against poor old Senator Bradley Smithers; his wealth; his affair with the Tegucigalpa Tamale; his embrace of legal suicide as a means of solving the Social Security impasse; even the Bosnian incident. There had been a lot of new wink-winking about that one on the talk shows.

"Let's face it," Cass said to Randy and Terry one day after a particularly nasty press conference, "we're going to have to deal with the were-they-or-weren't-they-doing-it-in-the-minefield thing."

Terry interjected, "Before you two go rushing out to put myths to rest, I had a focus group on that."

"A focus group?" Randy said.

"Yup. Doing a lot of I-d-I's these days. All under-thirty. In this one, a majority of them didn't even *know* about the minefield. So we told them about it. Then we fed them two scenarios. One where you two were screwing—"

"Aw, Jeez, Terry," Cass said.

"Hold your horses. The other scenario we gave them, you *weren't* banging each other. Then we asked them how they felt in the event scenario number one was true and how they'd feel if number two was the case. Want to hear the results?"

"Not really," said Cass.

"They preferred scenario number one. By four to one. They thought it was quote-unquote aces, whatever that means. They actually prefer a guy who'll risk getting his leg blown off trying to get laid in a war zone to one who just bumbled into it. So—you sure you want to go issuing Shermanesque statements about how you weren't playing hide-the-salami in the minefield?"

"What manner of planet do we inhabit?" Randy said, rubbing his temples.

Chapter 33

Gideon Payne, candidate of the SPERM party, was grappling with a similar problem. His press secretary, an old Washington hand named Teeley, had raised the subject as delicately as he could: "We, uh, probably ought to figure out a position on the, uh, matter of"—*cough*—"Mrs. Payne?"

Gideon was beyond embarrassment on the point. He said, "You're saying that the voters might want to know if it's true that I killed Mother?"

Teeley shrugged. "Something . . . along those lines. Basically. Yeah."

"Well," Gideon said, making a steeple of his fingers. How he missed his watch. "How *shall* we address that dismal business?"

"Tragic accident," Teeley said. "Painful subject. These things happen. . . ."

"Yes," Gideon said. "Mothers go off cliffs all the time. Happens all the time. Well, it is tragic, certainly. Painful, no question. But there are people back in Payne County with mischievous tongues that wag, wag, wag all day in the noon sun. I'm surprised they don't burn up. And when the national press goes a-calling on them, they will cluck and say, 'Oh yes, he killed the poor old dear. Terrible affair. He left not long after, you know, head hung in shame.'" Gideon considered. "There does exist a medical record. A few weeks before the incident, her doctors had informed her that she had a tumor. A tumor of the brain. She didn't have long to live."

"So," said Teeley, "she would have died anyway."

Gideon said, "Um . . . I suppose that doesn't quite solve the question of whether or not I sent her plunging to her death, does it? An unusual problem in a presidential campaign, I should think. Or have some of your other clients been under suspicion of murdering *their* mothers?"

"There was one whose uncle turned out to have been on Hitler's staff during World War Two. Pretty high up, too. But no matricides that I can think of offhand."

"Hm . . . Well, it may just be an intractable problem. We'll just have to work around it. I have dedicated my entire career to the preservation of life. The unborn, the halt, the lame, the brain afflicted, the elderly. We'll just have to run on that. There is the unfortunate Arthur Clumm business, but we're paying off the families—I must say, most of them seem quite happy to have the money—so I shouldn't think that will trouble us. It ought to be more of a problem for the Jepperson campaign, I should think. Ms. Devine on his staff was the inspiration for Mr. Clumm's serial murdering. I do look forward to the debates." He shrugged. "Perhaps some voters might even be attracted to someone who sent his mother off a cliff, though I don't suppose we should adopt that as our platform. Now let's have a look at those television spots your people have devised."

In his office at the papal nunciature on Massachusetts Avenue, opposite the residence of the vice president, Monsignor Massimo Montefeltro was confronting his own incipient media problem.

When the Transitioning commission issued its "further study" report, the monsignor sighed with relief and offered a prayer of thanks to Our Lady of Prompt Succor. Now, with the issue losing steam, surely Rome would calm down and not demand that he go on television and denounce Transitioning, exposing him to further harassment from the Russian *putanas* and the gruesome enforcer Ivan the Terrible.

But then that idiot Jepperson leapt in and declared he was running for president, with Transitioning as its centerpiece. *Porca miseria.* Within hours, Cardinal Restempopo-Bandolini was on the phone again, demanding, "When will you unleash our attack on this abomination, Massimo? The holy father grows impatient."

"Please tell the holy father I am a . . . gathering storm. The moment is not yet."

This Vatican idea of threatening excommunication—did they really think it was the sixteenth century again? He could just imagine how well *that* would go down with Americans. Being bullied by a pope in Rome. And not even a particularly popular pope with Americans to begin with. It didn't help that he was French.

Massimo seriously considered faking a heart attack. Certainly his high blood pressure didn't need faking.

That fool Geedeon. It was all his fault. And now *he* was running for president. What a country, America. A lunatic asylum, without enough attendants or tranquilizers.

What to do? He looked up at the statue of Our Lady of Prompt Succor. She smiled back at him, as if to say, *Massimo, Massimo, Massimo, be reasonable—not even I can get you out of this.*

The phone rang. His blood pressure spiked. He had developed a morbid fear of telephones, something of a disability for the Vatican's number two man in Washington, soon to be number one. Assuming he lived.

"Monsignor, it's someone named Ivan calling. He won't give a last name. He says he knows you. Do you want to speak to him?"

Monsignor Montefeltro suppressed a groan.

"Yes, yes." He picked up. "What do you want? I *gave* you the money."

"Am calling on behalf of charity organization."

"What?"

"For orphans of war in Chechnya. Do you wish to make donation?"

"No," said Monsignor Montefeltro. "I do not wish. I wish *you* to go to Chechnya."

Silence. "Pity. It's good cause. And Catholic Church is so rich. You have big office on Massachusetts Avenue."

"How did you find me here?"

"I follow you to work!" Ivan the Terrible sounded pleased with himself.

"All right, all right. I will make a donation to this *charity*."

"How much you give?"

"Ten dollars."

Ivan made a noise not indicative of being impressed. "Ten thousand dollars, better."

"I don't *have* ten thousand dollars."

"Catholic Church not have ten thousand dollars?" Ivan said. "Pah. You can sell gold Madonna or candlesticks. You pay gold before. Gold watch of your friend Gidyon Pine. Is same person as man on television who want to be president?"

Montefeltro no longer much cared about protecting Geedeon, since this calamity had been entirely of his making. So they'd made the connection at last. Montefeltro thought, *Perhaps Our Lady of Prompt Succor* did *hear my prayer.*

"Yes," he said. "It's the same. So why don't you call *him* and ask for donation. Perhaps he will buy back the watch."

"It's good idea. You are clever priest."

Free at last. . . .

"But you should also be making donation. Poor orphans. They are so hungry."

Frank Cohane had wanted an office in the West Wing. Bucky Trumble explained that not even he could arrange that. Under the law, campaign operatives could not occupy government buildings. "Under the law" was not a concept that particularly interested Frank Cohane, but Bucky mollified him with a White House pass so he could have the illusion of working in the White House. He also made sure that Frank got lots of "face time" with the president in the Oval. That would keep the bastard happy. That and an orgiastic night with Lisa in the Lincoln Bedroom. It was all they cared about, the big donors. They wanted to go back to their friends and say, "I screwed my brains out in the Lincoln Bedroom."

In keeping with the deal that he had worked out with Frank, once Bucky had got him the finance chairman job, Frank handed over the tape of Bucky asking him to plant incriminating e-mails on Cass's computer.

"How do I know this isn't a copy?" Bucky said.

"You don't." Frank grinned.

There was media interest in Frank Cohane, in particular about him and his estranged daughter, who was working for another presidential candidate. Washington loves such polarities.

"Do you still regard her as morally repellent?" asked a reporter for the *Post*.

"I didn't come to Washington to comment on my daughter," Frank said. He now had his own team of media advisers. "I came to reelect President Peacham."

"To *help* reelect President Peacham," his media handler gently suggested to him after the interview.

"Right," Frank said.

Frank had, amazingly, agreed to Lisa's suggestion that he hire a personal anger management consultant. Frank was a smart man, smart enough to know that he could no longer indulge his temper. It's one thing to be a billionaire and call reporters "cocksuckers," another if you are the finance chairman for the reelection campaign of the president of the United States, with aspirations to become secretary of the Treasury. The triggering event was when one of the crew members on *Expensive* told a reporter how Frank stepped on someone's hand while screaming obscenities at someone else on a cell phone.

So Frank was determined to be pleasant. Each morning, his first appointment was with the anger consultant, a small intense woman named Harriet. He would tell Harriet how he anticipated the world would disappoint him that day. She would listen, reaffirm his superiority over the rest of humanity, and then encourage him to have a good loud scream, cuss a blue streak—really dirty words—then finish off with some yoga and breathing exercises. Finally, she would give him his mantra for the day, a variation on "Don't waste your energy getting mad. You're better than the rest of them put together." It worked, more or less. Frank hadn't called anyone an "incompetent cocksucker" in over a week. He was still allowed to vent on staff.

He installed Lisa in a large redbrick Georgetown mansion that had belonged to someone who had become famous largely by initiating one of America's more catastrophic wars. Since he had agreed to anger therapy,

Lisa agreed to etiquette lessons. He hired a former head of State Department protocol to—so were his instructions—"sand off the rough edges and get her set up as a Washington hostess." Lisa's résumé was buffed up. "Tennis pro" became "tennis enthusiast." She was "an avid art collector" and "active in philanthropy." She was given her own charitable foundation—always a reliable social lubricant—which Frank funded with $30 million. Boyd, now a Yale (moolah, moolah) sophomore, was kept out of sight. Frank told him he would buy him a Maserati if he actually managed to graduate. Frank's PR people had even managed to spin the Yale bribe story to his advantage. They funneled a fat cash donation to a foundation that gave out fatherhood initiative awards. The organization was more than happy to create a special "Stepfather of the Year" award for Frank, in recognition of his "devoted involvement in the life of his stepson."

With the personal details all taken care of, Frank plunged into work. Within weeks, he had raised the eye-popping sum of $40 million for the Committee to Reelect President Peacham. He was not shy about suggesting to the big corporate contributors that he would be Treasury secretary in the next term but stopped short of saying outright, "I'm sure you want to stay in business over the next five years."

Terry busied himself with coming up with "Boomsday"-themed podcasts and flash and pop-up Internet ads designed to put the fear of God into the under-thirties. Cass blogged away on CASSANDRA to rally the troops. She was finding this harder than she'd thought it would be. It was easier getting them to assault gated retirement communities and golf courses. Getting them excited about the political process . . . *bo-ring.*

She did online focus groups. She told them, "Okay, some of it may be boring and hard work, but if you want to get it done, you have to get involved."

"Why can't we just, you know, vote?"

A generation that had grown up with the Internet and text messaging was not inclined to go around banging on doors and handing out pamphlets and doing voter registration drives. They were, however, willing to blog.

And you could, Cass found, get their attention.

"What would you say if I told you that one-third to one-half of everything you earn over your lifetime will go to paying off debt incurred before you were born?"

"That totally sucks."

She thought, *Maybe we should change Randy's slogan to "Jepperson—He Won't Suck."*

One problem they did not have was fund-raising. Randy was happy to be the first president in U.S. history to pay for his own campaign out of his own pocket. This didn't sit well with Cass.

"I think we at least ought to try to raise *some* money," she said. "It'll look better."

"Au contraire," Randy said. "Lots of my colleagues in the Senate bought their seats. I think it sends a good message: He can't be bought. He already *has* all the money he needs."

Cass had noticed that Randy had started referring to himself in the third person. One night, during a rare dinner alone at the Georgetown house, he began speaking as if he were being interviewed.

"Do you want more chicken, honey?" she said.

"The chicken was delicious. The peas were delicious. Everything was scrumptious, in fact. I remember as a child, we'd have peas with every meal. Proper nutrition was a factor. Balanced meals were a factor—"

"Randy?"

"Yes, dear?"

"Who are you talking to?"

"You, dear. Why?"

"I got the impression that we were doing a live network feed."

Randy looked around. "No, I don't think so."

Chapter 34

It had been a long time since he'd been back to French-man's Bluff, overlooking the Coosoomahatchie River. Gideon Payne was attended by several campaign aides and the crew of *60 Minutes*. The producers had even found a 1955 Cadillac Eldorado convertible with red leather upholstery.

"Will you be sending the car off the cliff?" Gideon inquired. The answer, thankfully, was no.

"It is a bit eerie," Gideon told the reporter who was doing the segment. "Most eerie."

"You're a sport to do this," the reporter said.

"My pleasure." Gideon smiled faintly. "Well, perhaps that's not quite the right word."

"Okay," said a cameraman, "we're rolling."

"Mother was sitting right where you are now, in the passenger seat. We often came to this place on our Sunday drives. We'd stop right where we are now. On that day, I put it in park, just like . . . so. Set the parking brake, so. I left the motor running. We never stayed very long. Got out of the car . . ." Gideon opened the door and got out, reporter, cameraman, and sound technician following. "And walked over to this spot here. There used to be a bush. So you see, I had privacy. I was standing here, facing away from the car, taking care of what had to be taken care of, and that's when I heard this dreadful sound."

"What kind of a sound?"

"A sort of grinding, mechanical sound. Then I heard Mother shrieking and expostulating. I zipped myself up and turned and saw that the car was rolling down toward the edge of the cliff. And I ran."

"Can you show us?"

"I was more, shall we say, *fit* in those days. I ran toward the car. Mother was continuing her shrieking, and I think trying to turn the car, also doing something with the transmission. She went over before I could reach her. It was dreadful. I still remember the sound of the car. . . . It's a moment that has stayed with me all my life. As you can imagine."

"But if the transmission somehow slipped out of park, wouldn't it have gone into reverse?"

"One would think," Gideon said. "Yes."

"And yet the sheriff's report states that the transmission was in drive when the car landed."

"Yes," Gideon said, patting his vest pocket for his watch, "I can only surmise that Mother, in her panic, managed to shift into drive. She was not very adept at driving to begin with."

"The sheriff's report also indicated that the parking brake was off."

"Yes," Gideon said, "I believe that was accounted for by the impact of the landing. It's nearly four hundred feet down. Don't stand too close."

"Did you kill your mother?"

"No, ma'am," Gideon said. "But I do appreciate your candor, and I appreciate your having come all this way to put this matter to rest."

"*Is* it at rest? Some people around here we've talked to still seem to have doubts."

"Well . . ." Gideon smiled. "I would say to you, let them come forward and present their evidence. I don't think they will, for evil shunneth the light and hideth its face at noon. No, I did not kill her. In fact, this is part of the reason I find myself a candidate for the presidency. There are those who are advocating that we drive our dear old mothers and fathers off cliffs. Surely there must be some better way of resolving our Social Security and Medicare problems, critical as they may be."

Tick-tick-tick-tick-tick . . .

Gideon watched the broadcast with his campaign staff at headquarters.

When it ended, the place erupted in whoops and hollers. (Most of the staff was from the South.) His press secretary, Teeley, gave a thumbs-up, despite the bit with the aging coroner, who told the *60 Minutes* correspondent, "I don't think we're *evah* really going to get to the bottom of what happened that day at Frenchman's Bluff." Gideon was accepting congratulations and pats on the back when his aide thrust forward and said that there was a call from a Ms. Tolstoy.

"Who?" Gideon said.

"Something about a gold watch. . . . Reverend? Are you all right? Should I fetch some bicarbonate?"

Cass had watched *60 Minutes* with Terry and Randy. Randy said, "He came off rather well, I thought. I still think he did the old girl in."

"No," Cass said. "He didn't. But there's something missing to it. Whatever. He came off well. He defused it."

Randy said, "I'll bet my guy Speck could find out if he sent her off that cliff."

Cass said, "Now, now—we're not going negative, remember?"

"Not *yet*, anyway," Terry muttered.

"I thought the plan," Randy said, "was to scare the shit out of the U30s?" U30s was their shorthand for the under-thirty voters they were after. It sounded like a German submarine.

"It's not the same thing," Terry said.

"We're going negative against Boomers, not individual candidates," Cass said. "We need a symbol. I'm tired of doing photo ops in front of the Social Security building."

"We could trash a few more golf courses," Terry said.

"Been there, burned that."

Cass's cell phone rang. She took the call.

"I guess the *Today* show watches *Sixty Minutes*. They'd like the senator"—she sighed—"to return to Bosnia."

Terry said, "Must be Presidential Candidates Acting Badly in Vehicles Week. Didn't Peacham run over a deer one weekend at Camp David while he was giving the president of Latvia a tour?"

"Racoon."

Randy said, "So. Are we going back to Bosnia? You did say the U30s rather liked the idea that we were 'doing the deed.'"

"Why not," Terry said. "Cass could give you a hand job while you drive into a minefield. Very presidential."

"I don't think so," said Cass.

"Too bad," Terry said. "Could have been our PT-109 moment."

"And in Washington tonight, a stunning announcement from the Vatican. We go now to our correspondent, Wendy Wong."

"Brian, a senior Vatican official at the Holy See's embassy in Washington today issued a stern warning to Americans not to vote for any candidate who supports legalizing suicide—or, as it has come to be called, Voluntary Transitioning.

"The warning came from Monsignor Massimo Montefeltro, Rome's second-highest-ranking official in the United States, a man said by observers to be close to Pope Jean-Claude the First.

"Montefeltro today threatened the most severe sanction that the church can issue, a so-called bull of excommunication, which effectively bars a Catholic from the sacraments. He issued the warning at a press conference:

"'Legal suicide, or Transitioning, as its proponents call it, is absolutely contrary to all Catholic moral teaching. The holy father has been watching the political developments in America. Therefore he is, regretfully, compelled to issue a bull of excommunication. This would take effect against any American Catholic who votes for, or who supports, any candidate advocating legal suicide'...

"Strong words.... Brian?"

"Wendy, why is it called a 'bull'?"

"The name derives from bullae, the wax or lead seals that popes used in the old days to seal proclamations. In any language, Brian, it spells 'tough medicine.'"

"Thank you, Wendy. In the Middle East today, a spontaneous display of affection between Israelies and Palestinians...."

Monsignor Montefeltro's discomfort at the press conference was much commented upon. Some *Vaticanisti* suggested that it hinted at a theological divide between him and Rome.

Cass and Terry were at campaign headquarters going over campaign Boomer attack ads when Randy called. He sounded frantic. He was in Minnesota on his way to a fund-raiser. Cass had insisted he hold at least a few, for appearance' sake.

"What the hell's going on?" he demanded.

"What are you talking about?"

"I just got a call from some Reuters reporter. She said the pope had just attacked me?"

"What?" Cass said. "Don't talk to anyone until I call you back."

Terry was already online. "Holy shit."

Cass read over his shoulder. "You got 'holy' right. Where did this come from?"

"Sort that out later. Now what?" Terry said. "Do we denounce the pope?"

Cass thought. "At least he's French. I better stuff a sock in Randy's mouth. He's got that old-WASP thing about Catholics. Calls them 'papists.'"

"I've had four more calls," Randy said. "I'm not going to take this from some old Frog in a miter—"

"Just *stonewall*, Randy."

"I am. But they're going to pounce on me at the fund-raiser. What do I tell them? What I'd like to tell them is the pope can go jump into the Tiber. What business is it of his—"

"You have the greatest respect for the pope—"

"I do not. I'm Episcopalian. Not very practicing, but—"

"Randy. Shut up. You're looking forward to a vigorous debate . . . you—"

"I'm not here to debate the *pope,* for God's sake."

"I'm trying to formulate our position. If you'd just be quiet for a second."

"Well, formulate fast, the limo's pulling up. Oh, hell. There's a mob of them. Vultures."

"Tell Corky to drive around the block."

"Too late. Here they come."

"You'll be issuing a full statement tomorrow morning."

"Why can't I just—"

"You're going to . . . consult. You're going to consult with . . . theologians. That's it. Religious authorities."

"Which theologians?"

"I don't know! Thomas Aquinas. St. Jerome. Thomas More. Just *stonewall*."

Cass hung up. She let out a breath and said to Terry, "Do we know any theologians?"

"On K Street?"

JEPPERSON CALLS VATICAN THREAT "A LOAD OF BULL"

Cass stared at the headline. She had already seen a dozen online versions of it throughout the night. She was tired. She found herself wishing that she had lived before the age of the Internet and cable TV, when news arrived twice a day instead of *every fricking second*.

Terry walked in. He looked as if he hadn't slept much, either. He glanced at the front page of the *Post*. "I see our boy stayed on message."

Cass looked up gloomily. "I guess I'll be spending more time on the road with the candidate. Hurling myself between him and the nearest reporter."

The phone rang. Randy.

"Well, if it isn't the Antichrist," Cass said.

"I'm a god in Minneapolis!" he said. "Have you seen the papers?"

"Yeah."

"They lapped it up!"

"Randy. They're Lutherans. Before you go nailing any more theses to the front door of the cathedral, let's see how this plays in small cities like, you know, Chicago, Boston, Miami, Baltimore, Los Angeles. Other little villages where they actually *like* the pope."

"He's French."

"Randy, he's the *pope*."

"Well," Randy sniffed, "*he* fired the first shot. I know how you and Terry hate it when I actually have an independent thought, but I have a strong feeling in my gut about this."

"So do I. Like a cramp."

"Americans don't like being bossed about by foreigners."

"Let's hope for the best. Meantime, please try to avoid the subject. I really don't want to pick up *Time* magazine next week and read that you called the Virgin Mary a slut."

The phone at the papal nunciature had not stopped ringing. Every major media outlet in the country wanted to interview Monsignor Montefeltro. Even the late-night comedy shows wanted him. A New York City tabloid put him on the front page with the headline RAGING BULL!

The papal nuncio, Montefeltro's nominal boss, was a bit put out that Rome had bypassed him and asked his number two to be Vatican point man. As for Montefeltro, he wanted to crawl under his desk. He was hoping against hope that Ivan the Terrible and the jezebels Tolstoy and Dostoevsky hadn't watched TV yesterday or seen a newspaper. Or a magazine. Or the Internet. Or . . . *Dio mio*. . . . Maybe they'd all gone back to Russia. Maybe they'd all died of venereal disease or in a gun battle over drugs. Maybe—

"Monsignor? It's a Mr. Ivan for you. He says you know him. And a Ms. Katie Couric from the television called again, twice."

"What do you want?"

"Everywhere you are on television. I think *you* will be pope someday. So, am calling for donation to orphans. Donation should be more now that you are such big important man in church. I think . . . one hundred thousand dollars. Orphans will be very happy. God will be very happy."

Montefeltro wondered if the Swiss Guard had a secret assassination unit. He sighed. "I don't have one hundred thousand dollars. Why don't you call Mr. Pine. He is very rich."

"We called him. He was *very* happy to hear watch is located. There is Mercedes SL 550 parked outside your office. Is very nice car. Why you are not donating that to orphans? Humble priest should not be driving one-hundred-thousand-dollar Mercedes-Benz. Jesus did not drive in Mercedes. He drive on donkey."

Gideon was indeed very happy to hear that his gold watch and fob had been located, though that was not the sum of his reaction.

It is unpleasant to be blackmailed at any time, but especially inconvenient when you are launching a presidential campaign, and worse yet if your name carries the prefix *Reverend*. Yet for all that, Ms. Tolstoy sounded quite friendly over the phone and made no mention of money.

"You look cute on TV," she said. "I don't think that you kill your mother. You are too nice-looking. Why you not come to my apartment? We will have party, with Champagne. Watch sexy movies. I am *wery* wet for you."

Gideon shifted in his chair. He was almost fifty years old, and no woman, ever, had purred to him this way, much less asked him to come party with her. *I am wery wet for you.*

"If I," Gideon croaked, "come, you will return me my watch?"

"Oh, *yes*. But," she said, "first you must find watch. I have many hiding places. Mmmm. Hurry, Gidyon. I so wery wet for you, I am having to change my panties."

She gave him an address in Arlington.

It occurred to Gideon, poor Gideon, that it was Sunday, the Sabbath. What was it Stonewall Jackson had said after he asked the surgeons if he was dying and they told him yes? "Good. I always wanted to die on a Sunday."

No. Mustn't. Madness. Then he thought, *The watch.* He must retrieve the watch. He would retrieve the watch and leave. Maybe, just to be friendly, he'd stay for just one glass of Champagne.

Gideon slipped out of campaign headquarters unnoticed.

Chapter 35

Randy was feeling cocky, having been proved right in the matter of the bull. Polls were running overwhelmingly against the Vatican. His own tracking polls showed a gain of four points after telling Rome to butt out. Americans, it appeared, did not welcome divine intervention.

Gideon Payne was strangely silent on the matter, even absent. The media were clamoring for his comments, yet he was nowhere to be found. His press secretary said that the candidate was "down with a bad cold" and had to cancel his schedule. The truth was, Gideon had dropped off the map. He wasn't at home. He wasn't answering his cell. He had last been seen Sunday night, the night of the *60 Minutes* broadcast. And it was now Tuesday. Tuesday afternoon.

"Where the hell is he?" Teeley demanded. No one knew. "He can't just disappear! We're in the middle of a goddamn presidential campaign!"

Cass, meanwhile, had conceived the idea that Randy should use the word *fuck* at a campaign event. The genius of this strategy was not immediately apparent to the candidate. Or, for that matter, to Terry, who usually was on the same bandwidth as Cass.

"It's how this generation talks," she said to them. "If you want to get their attention, you have to sound like them. They'll get it."

Randy stared. "Ask not what the fuck your country can do for you? Four score and seven fucking years ago? For God's sake, Cass. The FCC would fine me. And the FEC."

"Fuck 'em," Cass said. "We'll make headlines."

"As long as we're at it," Terry said, "why not a wardrobe malfunction during the debates? He can go over to Peacham and rip off his shirt. Tweak his nipple."

"I'm serious about this, guys. If you just subtly slipped it in—"

"Subtly?"

"—at precisely the right moment, it would be monster. Huge. *Tectonic*. I can't even discuss it. No presidential candidate has ever said the f-word before."

"Didn't some vice president tell a senator to go fuck himself?"

"Not on live TV. That was just some corridor grab-ass in the Capitol."

"No," Randy said. "I said no. No. Fucking. Way."

"We'll spike five points with U30," Cass said. "That would put you ahead."

"Yes, and we'd lose every other voter."

"Throw long."

"I'll think about it," Randy said. "Did you have in mind any particular script for unleashing this little bon mot?"

"Yes, in fact."

Randy went off to cast a vote.

Terry said to Cass, "I wish you hadn't planted that idea in his head."

"Hey," Cass grinned. "Got to think out of the box."

Gideon Payne was a happy man.

He had not known such happiness was possible.

He was so happy, in fact, that it was only by a superhuman exertion of will that he departed Tatiana's (Ms. Tolstoy had a first name, it turned out) apartment, a perfume-candle-scented bower of bliss in Arlington improbably overlooking the Iwo Jima Memorial.

"Darrling Gidyon," she purred, twirling his hair with a finger as he nuzzled her right nipple, "don't you must be in presidential campaign? It's two days already you are here."

Two days, a case of Champagne, thousands of dollars in ATM withdrawals, God knew how many condoms. He'd lost track.

"Ummmph."

"Come. I make you coffee and you go."

"No. I'm staying. I'm never leaving. Never ever ever. Mummmmph."

"Darrling. My boozum. It hurt. You are wery hungry boy. You come back. But for now you *must* go. Come on, I make you nice hot bath with bubble."

She got him into a bubble bath. He starting singing, "Glory, glory hallelejuah . . ."

Strange boy, she thought. And she could swear that this was the first time he had ever been with a woman.

Olga Marilova (Tatiana was not her first name, nor was Tolstoy her surname) had not anticipated this. She'd had Kulchek (Ivan) standing by, concealed in the apartment, armed, in case Gidyon Pine showed up with his own security people. Presidential candidates could be expected to be a bit hostile about being blackmailed. But when she opened the door, there he was alone, and with such an expression like a child's.

He came in. They sat. She told him the watch was in a safe place. She would give it to him for a "donation to orphanage" of . . . $100,000. She braced for a furious reaction, ready to summon Kulchek. And then Gidyon Pine said, "Yes, I think that would be reasonable. And it's a good cause. I have always been partial to orphans. I will have the money for you tomorrow." She hardly knew what to say. Then he said, "Now, my dear, didn't you say something about a glass of Champagne? I would be happy to pay for *that* right now." And one thing led to another. And he wouldn't leave. *Well,* she thought, confused, *okay, it's biznis. Good biznis.*

Wery good biznis, as it turned out. The next day, Gidyon tore himself away from her lovely breasts long enough to make a phone call to someone named Sidney, and a few hours later a short man with a look of alarm knocked on her door and handed over a steel briefcase containing $100,000. This was the easiest bit of biznis Olga had ever conducted. And she was no novice at the client shakedown. Gidyon didn't even ask for the watch! He just wanted her to get back into bed. He was . . . insatiable. A little steam engine of carnality. At one point, he asked her to marry him. She had to get him out of the apartment. She had appointments, with important clients. Regulars. Two ambassadors and a deputy secretary of state. . . .

"Jesus Christ, Gideon—where have you fucking *been*?" His press secretary, Teeley, was livid.

Gideon had a grin. He murmured, "Actually, it's the other way around."

"What?"

"Nothing. I needed a rest, that's all. I am most heartily sorry. I hope y'all were not too inconvenienced."

"We've got a goddamn debate tomorrow!"

"And I *am* ready." He began humming "Oh, What a Beautiful Mornin' " and walked off.

Teeley said to the campaign manager, "Is he on drugs? If he is, I need to know now. I don't like surprises."

"Ugly fucking state," President Peacham said, looking down on the frozen landscape from Marine One, the presidential helicopter. The president was in his usual frame of mind, not helped by the latest tracking polls showing him several points behind—Senator Randolph K. Jepperson. The only good news was that with so many candidates running—there were now over a dozen in all, including the candidate of the Free Immigration Party—no one was a clear front-runner.

"Well, Mr. President," Bucky Trumble said, sounding as bright and upbeat as he could, "New Hampshire certainly loved you four years ago. And they're going to love you tonight."

President Peacham grunted. "Doesn't look one damn bit picturesque. Might as well be New Jersey, with snow." He went back to his debate preparation book. He had not wanted to come and debate his challengers, but Bucky told him he must. His plan was to take out Jepperson here with a crippling blow. If they could beat him in Iowa and New Hampshire, the two early decisive points of the campaign, they might be able to force him to run as an independent.

They were going to hit him on Bosnia. Their polling showed that was his Achilles' heel.

It was somewhat delicate, since this meant collaterally going after Cassandra Devine, whose father, Frank Cohane, was now Peacham's campaign finance chairman, sitting just a few seats away on Marine One. Frank Cohane had said he had no objection. "Do what you have to."

The candidates had separate greenrooms, in trailers parked outside the hall.

An aide with an earpiece radio scurried up to Cass and said, "Ms. Devine—Reverend Payne has asked to see you."

Cass looked over at Terry. He shrugged and said, "Know thy enemy."

Cass and the aide left the Jepperson trailer and walked across a crusty snow parking lot to the Payne trailer. The Payne aides—most of them evangelicals—regarded her coolly. To them, she was Joan of Dark. A door was opened, and there was Gideon.

"Come in, come in out of the cold," he said heartily.

They shook hands. He held hers with both of his. "You are *very* kind to have come, my dear girl, very kind."

She hadn't seen him in person in some months. He looked well. He'd lost weight, his skin had color, his hair was no longer oily.

"Good to see you, Reverend," she said. "How've you been?"

"Very well indeed. You didn't use to call me that." He smiled. "Sit, sit. Just for a moment, I know you must attend to the senator. There's something I wanted to say to you."

Cass sat.

"I wanted to say," Gideon said, "that I personally never thought you had anything to do with that lunatic Arthur Clumm. Or that anything untoward took place in that minefield in Bosnia. I know we have our disagreements. Profound ones. But we'll have a vigorous debate on the issues. I just wanted you to know that allegations will have no place in my arguments. On that you have my word, Cassandra."

She nodded. "All right. Fair enough."

"Good, then."

"Reverend—"

"Gideon. Please."

"I saw the thing on TV. I know that you didn't . . ."

"Kill my mother?"

"Yes. But I can't help thinking that something *else* happened. That it didn't happen quite the way you said it did. It's none of my business."

He looked at her. "Someday you and I will take a walk together, and I will tell you a long story. But now let me say, for myself, I don't believe for one minute you really want Americans to kill themselves just to fix a budget problem."

Cass smiled. "No, not really."

"You're just trying to make a point, aren't you?" He wagged a finger at her. "Well, I must say, young lady, that you have certainly made it. Even if you do set a mean agenda."

Cass looked at her watch. "I have to go."

They stood. He patted her hand. "Good luck to you, Cassandra Devine. Go forth"—he smiled—"and spin no more."

She was crunching on snow across the parking lot when she heard a voice call out, "Hello, Cass." She turned and saw her father. It had been many years since she'd seen him.

"Hello, Frank."

He moved forward as if to kiss her. She held back.

"Look at you. You're all grown up."

"Look at you. All rich."

"I did try."

"Try what?"

"To make it up to you. The check. The one you tore into pieces."

"Oh," Cass said, "well, we're even. I have to go. Good luck in the debate."

"Oh, fuck it," Frank said angrily, and turned on his heel.

"Nice talking with you," Cass muttered. "Dad."

"What did he want?" Terry said when she got back to the Jepperson trailer.

"Who?" Cass said, somewhat dazed.

"The second coming."

"We seem to be fanning each other with olive branches."

"There's a whole lot of love going on in this campaign. Come on, showtime."

They went into Randy's dressing room. He was standing in front of a mirror, gesturing.

"Should I limp when I walk out onstage?"

"Why don't you just hop?" Cass said. She brushed off his jacket. "You ready, Senator?"

"Alons, enfants de la pa-trie . . ."

"Fuck off."

Bucky's plan was to wait for closing statements, when it would be too late for a counterassault, for Peacham to say, "I think a man who drives a young woman into a minefield in the middle of a war zone for immoral purposes should not be allowed within a hundred yards or a hundred miles of the nuclear button." Not a bad line, but Peacham never got to say it.

It happened sixty-four minutes in. The president had just recited a string of somewhat abstruse economic indicators suggesting that the U.S. economy might actually grow its way out from under the crushing deficit.

The moderator, John Tierney of *The New York Times*, turned to Randy and said, "Senator Jepperson, you have ninety seconds to respond."

"Thank you, John, but I don't need ninety seconds to respond. I can respond to what the president just said in four words: Shut the fuck up."

Chapter 36

The incident posed a challenge to news organizations—namely, how to report, verbatim, that a candidate for president of the United States told the incumbent president to "shut the fuck up"—without incurring fines by the Federal Communications Commission. The cautious evening network news shows bleeped the word.

For a moment, everyone in the auditorium—and across the nation—watched in mute amazement. For a few seconds, it looked as though President Peacham were going to cross the stage and punch Senator Jepperson in the nose. The rest of the candidates gripped their podiums while their mouths made fish-out-of-water motions. Randy held his ground like Stonewall Jackson at the Battle of Bull Run. Tierney, the moderator, bit down on his lip. After a pause that seemed to last an eternity, President Peacham turned on his heel and stormed offstage, surrounded by scowling Secret Service agents who looked as though they might open fire on the senator. The rest of the debate was somewhat less memorable.

Spin Alley, the area outside the hall where the candidates' aides rushed to proclaim their man's or woman's ("obvious") victory, was normally a hive of chatter. This night it was uncharacteristically hushed. Declaring victory tonight would be beside the point, like standing outside Ford's Theatre after President Lincoln had been shot to proclaim the excellence of the acting.

When Cass arrived, reporters instantly abandoned whomever they had been interviewing and swarmed in on her. She was pressed up against a wall so tightly that Jepperson staffers had to form a flying wedge to save her from being asphyxiated.

"Cass, Cass—was that your idea?"

"Does this signal a new aggressiveness on the part of the Jepperson campaign?" (*Du-uh.*)

"Aren't you concerned that the Federal Election Commission will fine him?"

She let them gabble on at her for a few minutes before even trying to answer. Finally, in order to obtain an audible sound bite from her, the beast quieted.

"I think Senator Jepperson succinctly said tonight what many Americans, especially younger ones, think when they hear the president of the United States tell them that the economy is in sound shape. It's not, and perhaps it's time for some plain talk."

"But he told the president of the United States to—to shut the— to . . ." The reporter couldn't bring himself to say it.

"I heard what he said. It's an expression favored by young Americans to signify 'Really?' or 'Gosh, that's wonderful.' The senator was, I believe, using it ironically. For his generation, it has a more, shall we say, literal meaning."

"But you can't talk to a president that way. It's not—presidential."

"Is it presidential to deceive the nation over and over? Senator Jepperson feels that the young people in this country are being robbed of their future by politicians who can't see past the next election. Why should they be accorded respect? Respect is something you earn. Senator Jepperson respects the office of the presidency. And he will treat it with respect when he becomes president. Meanwhile, my guess is Americans tonight are saying, 'Give him hell, Randy.' "

Not quite. In fact, large numbers of Americans were phoning in death threats to Jepperson campaign headquarters and calling their congressmen and senators and demanding that they denounce him; others were calling the White House to say that they were appalled and writing scorching letters to the editor. But this barrage was coming from older voters. The younger ones, Cass's U30s, generation whatever—they, too, were communicating as fast as they could, texting and blogging. And they liked—quite liked—what they had seen that night.

"Senator, many, including a number of your own colleagues in the Senate, have called on you to apologize to President Peacham. There's even some movement to censure or even to impeach you. *Will* you apologize to the president?"

Randy was on *Greet the Press*.

"No, Glen. I have no plans to do that."

"Why?"

"Because I don't regret what I said. In fact, I'd say it again. In fact—"

"Please," Glen Waddowes said with a look of panic on his face, "this is a family show."

Randy smiled. "I wouldn't want to upset the sensibilities of any of your viewers, Glen. Sure it's tough talk. But these are tough times. And when a president of the United States stands at a podium and tells outright lies as the nation comes down around him in ruins, maybe it's time someone grabbed him by the lapels and said, 'Enough!'"

"Speaking of lapels, that button on yours . . . is that . . . ?"

"It says STFU, Glen."

"I won't ask you to explain what that stands for."

"I understand"—Randy smiled—"but if I may, let me explain what *I* stand for. . . ."

The buttons were Cass's idea. She had had tens of thousands of them ready to distribute the morning after the debate. It had all been hush-hush. She'd even had the campaign's lawyer make the button manufacturers sign enforceable confidentiality statements. She didn't want it to get out that the Jepperson campaign had prepared them in advance of the debate. No sense in ruining the illusion of spontaneity.

Editorials were predictably shocked—shocked: "Gutter Politics," "The Gloves Come Off," "Senator Foulmouth," "Candidate X-Rated," "No, Senator, *You* Shut the @#$% Up!"

The blogosphere, however, was delighted, wallowing, humming, aglow, streaming video, happy as a giant cyberclam. To the U30s, Randy had "dropped the f-bomb." The TV and newspaper punditariat acknowledged that it was a "hinge event" and "for better or worse— almost certainly worse—a paradigm shift." To reporters mind numbed by prepackaged, sanitized candidate statements, it was a gift from the campaign gods. Meanwhile, the Jepperson campaign was overwhelmed with U30 volunteers wanting to help. Fashion designers were rushing out lines of STFU clothing. Cass was triumphant. *Time* magazine put her on the cover—her second cover of *Time* and only thirty years old— with the headline THE UN-SHUTUPABLE CASSANDRA DEVINE.

Ten days later, Senator Randolph K. Jepperson finished second in the Iowa caucuses, behind President Riley Peacham.

Cass knew from the look on Terry's face that something was wrong. They were in Manchester, New Hampshire, two days before the primary. Randy was within three polling points of Peacham.

"What?" she said.

"I just got a call from *The Washington Post*. Wanting to know about our North Korean golf tournament."

Cass sat without taking off her parka. "Aha."

"Yeah."

"Trumble."

"Probably." Terry snorted. "Though I doubt Peacham—or even your dad—stood in his way."

Cass considered. "Did the *Post* have . . . details?"

"Enough"—Terry sighed—"for a headline on the order of JEPPERSON'S TOP AIDES ASSISTING EVIL, ROTTEN, DESPICABLE NORTH KOREAN DICTATORSHIP WITH IMPROVING IMAGE."

"Oh dear," Cass said. "Well, that's it, then. Did you explain that the North Koreans came to you, not the other way around?"

"Yeah, but I don't think *that's* going to be the lead."

Cass stood. "He's speaking to that self-esteem group. I better intercept him before the *Post* reaches him."

Randy listened to what Cass and Terry had to say with a mix of facial expressions, most of which included a furrowed brow. When there was no more to say, Cass handed him a piece of paper.

"What's this?"

"Terry's and my official resignation from your campaign. Be sure to say that you were appalled to learn about it all. And that you immediately accepted—actually, demanded—our resignations. With any luck, they'll move on."

Randy looked at Terry. Terry shrugged. "You're within spitting distance of Peacham. You don't want to get bogged down in this."

Cass said to Terry, "Could I talk to Randy for a minute?"

"I can't do this without you," Randy said.

"Sure you can. Just keep telling them to shut the fuck up."

Randy tore up the piece of paper.

"I appreciate the gesture, but I already posted it on the website."

"You stood by me. I'll stand by you. We'll tough it out."

"That's sweet but completely suicidal. If you make it, you might actually be in a position to fix this mess. I wouldn't draw a whole lot of satisfaction from thinking I stood in the way of that. Hey"—she smiled—"we're a long way from Turdje."

Randy was blinking back tears. Cass reached over and stroked his cheek. "You can't go in front of the Greater Manchester Self-Esteem League looking like that."

Two days later, Randy finished second in the New Hampshire primary, three points behind Peacham. The big surprise that night was Gideon Payne, who came in third. An impressive showing—and now it was on to South Carolina.

Chapter 37

The details of Terry Tucker's North Korea pro-am golf tournament scheme were avidly gone over in the press. One article, noting that North Korea's only golf course had been built with slave labor (as had everything else in that unhappy country), was headlined "Field of Screams." But Cass's and Terry's resignations had insulated Randy from significant collateral damage. After the initial huffing and puffing, most accepted it for what it was—another Washington PR scheme to shake a few shekels from one of the world's nuttier dictators—and moved on.

The White House, on the other hand, did its best to keep the issue alive. En route to Charleston, South Carolina, aboard Air Force One, the president invited the press forward to his cabin. Bucky had suggested a leading question to a reporter friendly to the administration.

"Sir, will your Justice Department be pursuing legal action against Mr. Tucker and Ms. Devine under the trading with the enemy statutes?"

"Difficult question," said the president, trying to look as if he were weighing a grave constitutional issue. Inwardly, he was feeling much lighter. No one had told him to shut the fuck up since New Hampshire. He had inserted a crowbar between Jepperson and that woman. Frank Cohane was urging him to unleash the attorney general on her. Strange, the relish Cohane had for going after his own daughter. The president didn't like Cohane. He was always dropping little hints about how he was looking forward to running the Treasury in the second term. Bucky seemed oddly tolerant of this forwardness. But Cohane was an animal when it came to raising money. He was putting a lot of his own dough, too, into various 527s that funneled the money to the party. If Peacham did appoint him to the Treasury, there would be talk of his having bought the job. But there was a campaign to wage in the meantime.

"I haven't consulted with the attorney general on that," he told the reporter. "It's his decision, not mine. Meanwhile, I think Senator Jepperson did the decent thing. For once." The reporters laughed.

"Do you feel threatened by Reverend Payne, Mr. President? He's showing strength in the South."

"I feel threatened by anyone who wants my job." Laughter. "But I'm going to work my heart out for every vote down there. This isn't a southern matter or a northern matter. It's an American matter."

"Do you still refuse to debate with Senator Jepperson?"

"I will *debate* only with candidates who comport themselves according to minimal standards of decorum. If I see Senator Jepperson inside that debate hall, I'm going to have the Secret Service wash his mouth out with soap." Laughter. "The kind with pumice." More laughter. Bucky Trumble sat in a corner, beaming, listening to his own lines being spoken by the most powerful man on earth.

"Sir, the chairman of the Federal Reserve has indicated that he may raise the prime rate another point, to twenty-two percent, in view of the fact that inflation is now running at thirty-five percent. . . ."

The media do not abandon their darlings, not when they provide such copy as Cassandra Devine. Within days of her departure from the campaign, *USA Today* ran a cover story with the headline JEPPERSON AFTER CASS: IF I ONLY HAD A BRAIN.

Randy was not generally amused by the media's declarations that Cass was his "brain." On the other hand, he had enough of one himself to know that she was. Since the night in New Hampshire when he accepted her resignation, he had been calling and BlackBerrying her constantly.

"We probably ought to cool it," Cass finally said. "Who knows who's listening in and reading these e-mails. I'm not sure the other shoe has dropped yet. Justice may come after us. And if it comes out that we're still talking, it could hurt you. Meanwhile, there's this thing I'm going to do, and trust me, you don't want to be an official part of it."

Cass's "thing" was a U30 protest rally in Washington, D.C., on the Mall at the foot of the Capitol building. On her website, Cass instructed everyone to bring their Social Security cards. She had gotten the idea from the Vietnam protests. Odd, she thought, that her inspiration should come from a key moment in the history of the Baby Boomers.

It was necessary to apply for permits from the National Park Service and fourteen other agencies and departments that ruled over democratic gatherings on the nation's front lawn. Word of this made its way on up to the White House.

"Goddamnit," said the president, "what do I have to do—drive a stake through this woman's heart?" He said this in the presence of Frank Cohane and was immediately embarrassed.

Frank, however, seemed unperturbed. He said, "Sir, I'm afraid she's out to make a fool of all of us."

"Deny her the permits," the president said to Bucky.

"Tricky," Bucky said. "The media are in love with her. If we get in the way of the permit process, it's bound to leak, and it'll look like we're afraid of her. I'd let it proceed. See what"—he shot the president a sly glance—"develops."

"How do you mean?"

"You get a hundred thousand or so kids together," Bucky said, "who knows what kind of hell's likely to break loose. Right?"

The president smiled. "You're a cocksucker, Trumble."

"Thank you, sir." Bucky smiled.

The Protest Against Social Security, or PASS, was held on the Mall on the Saturday before the South Carolina primary. Getting U30s to attend a political rally was like herding cats. They coalesced more readily for concerts than for political demonstrations. Still, they came, and in respectable numbers. The Park Service estimated the crowd at seventy-five thousand, a good showing. Vendors did a brisk business in tuna wraps and vitamin water. Many protesters carried STFU! signs. Emergency medical crews stood ready to treat anyone stricken with self-esteem deficit. Curious Boomers who looked on from the sidelines remarked that it was just like the Vietnam protests, only completely different. "In those days," said one old-timer riding by on a Segway, "we didn't have nearly the variety of bottled waters you have today. Man, those were crazy times."

As soon as it grew dark, Cass took to the microphone and instructed the crowd to take out their Social Security cards. Seventy-five thousand people under thirty held them in the air, lighters at the ready. Suddenly the stage was swarmed with police wearing a dozen different uniforms.

"Problem?" Cass said to the most official-looking one.

"Are you Cassandra Devine?" he said.

Cass moved closer to the microphone so that the conversation could be heard by seventy-five thousand people.

"Uh, yeah."

"I have a warrant for your arrest."

"You're going to arrest me?" she said, the words echoing out onto the Mall, stirring a rumble in the crowd. "What for?"

"Incitement to destroy government property, 18 USC 1361."

A rumble went through the crowd.

Cass said into the microphone, "And are you going to arrest all of *them*?"

"Anyone who destroys government property will be arrested."

Cass turned to the crowd. "Did you hear that?"

"*Yes!*"

"And what do you say to that?"

"*SHUT THE FUCK UP!*"

"All right, that's it," the top cop said to his undercops. "Arrest her!"

At the sight of the police closing in on their leader, seventy-five thousand members of generation whatever surged toward the stage in what the *Post* called a "Banana Republic tsunami." The police had not anticipated quite this degree of solidarity and were simply overwhelmed by the critical mass. The stage, which began to sway under the weight, became a large rugby scrum. Cass wrestled free of the arms of the law and burrowed toward the rear of the stage. At one point, she stepped on something soft that moved and heard a loud groan of complaint that on closer inspection turned out to be Terry.

"Come on," she said, grabbing him by the arm. They managed in the confusion to get off the stage and ran in the darkness toward the Robert Taft Carillon and, beyond that, Union Station.

"Did they get her?" the president asked Bucky. Bucky looked harried. They were in the presidential suite of a hotel in Charleston, South Carolina, late for a live televised debate that no one would be watching, given what was going on in Washington. The TV screen showed a helicopter's-eye view of what television anchors generally call "the unfolding drama."

"Not yet. But don't worry, chief, they'll get her," Bucky said.

The president shook his head. "It's a damn nightmare freak show. Just what we need, a goddamn thirty-year-old *blond* fugitive. Why the fuck did I let you and Cohane talk me into this?"

"Sir, she's not going to get away. There are ten thousand police and federal agents searching for her."

The president was back to watching the screen. The scroll at the bottom read, THOUSANDS OF ARRESTS IN "BOOMSDAY" MELEE ON MALL . . .

Cass and Terry made it to Union Station, where they caught the Red Line metro all the way to the end of the line, a place aptly, Cass thought, called Shady Grove.

They found a bar not far from the metro stop that had a TV.

"Well," Terry said, "this'll do wonders for business. 'I'm sorry, Mr.

Tucker is not in today. He is a fugitive from justice. May I take a message and give it to him in the event he is apprehended?' "

"Don't worry," Cass said. "We can always go to North Korea. I'm sure they'll take us in."

They sat in the corner, an eye on the TV.

Cass said, "This would be the moment when our faces pop up on the screen and the bartender reaches for the phone."

"We should call Allen."

"Good idea." Cass took out her cell phone.

Terry said, "Bad idea."

"Do you remember how to use a pay phone?"

"I think you put coins in it."

After several attempts, they reached Allen Snyder, Esquire. He told them that the FBI did not normally tap the phones of lawyers. He said he'd find out what he could and call them back on the pay phone. He called back an hour later and said that there was a warrant out for Cass's arrest but not for Terry's. "You can come in from the cold," he said, adding, "Do I even need to point out that if you assist Cass, you're aiding a fugitive?"

Cass and Terry made their arrangements. Terry headed back to the Shady Grove metro stop.

They said good-bye in the shadows by the parking lot.

"It's going to be cold tonight," Terry said. "And you'd better not try checking into a hotel."

"I was in the army, remember?" Cass smiled.

"Okay," he said, "but avoid minefields."

Randy had been barred by the Federal Election Commission from participating in the debates. But he had managed to turn this to his advantage by conducting shadow debates on the Internet, acting as if he were there onstage with the other candidates. The media were only too happy to include him. Just as the debate was getting started, he went online and denounced the president—this time avoiding four-letter words—for "criminalizing a peaceful demonstration" and demanded that he lift the fugitive warrant on Cass. Just for good measure, he called on him to resign.

Judy Woodruff of CNN, moderator of tonight's debate, had her laptop in front of her.

"Sir," she said to the president, "just a few minutes ago, Senator Jepperson, who is not allowed to be here, accused you of deliberately undermining a peaceful demonstration on the Mall. According to various legal experts, it is not clear that burning a Social Security card is a federal crime. Did you personally give the order to the police to intervene in the PASS demonstration?"

The president looked as though he himself were on the verge of deploying the f-word. "Judy, I came here tonight to this wonderful state of South Carolina to debate the issues, not to comment on an ongoing law enforcement matter. And that," he said, grinding his teeth, "is what I plan to do."

It was the consensus of those who watched the debate that the president did not acquit himself particularly well. Gideon Payne—of all people!—criticized the government's tactics at the demonstration and demanded that the president intervene personally to lift the warrant on Cassandra Devine. The president, now drawn in, called Cass a "saboteur" and even hinted that she was an agent of North Korea. This last assertion drew laughter from the debate audience, which, under the debating rules, is not supposed to express emotion. All in all, the president looked, as one observer said afterward, as though he were about to pass a kidney stone. He did not linger after the debate for the usual faux display of onstage collegiality and chitchat with the relatives of his opponents. Meanwhile, Randy, who had conducted his interview from a trailer outside the hall, waded into Spin Alley, where he was mobbed by delighted reporters.

Three days later, Gideon Payne won the South Carolina primary. Randy came in second; Peacham, third. Randy's strong showing was attributed to the state's historical predilection for rebels.

Chapter 38

Cass had her hair cut and dyed black at a salon and wrapped a scarf around her head. She bought a sleeping bag at an outdoors store, lifted a shopping cart from a supermarket, and became a bag lady, sleeping in parks and woods. A few days later, Terry dropped off, at a predesignated point, cash and a "clean" PDA of the kind used by intelligence agencies, called a "StealthBerry" (supplied by Randy's guy Mike Speck; it was difficult to trace its transmissions geographically). Now she could communicate with her followers as well as certain members of the media. Her fugitive status had greatly enhanced her celebrity.

There is no opportunist like a politician. Randy, sensing a very good thing, plunged in. He denounced the government for driving "the woman I love" into hiding. Cass, listening to this on her SB, rolled her eyes. Randy further demanded the resignations of the "little tyrants in the White House"—this was assumed to be a reference to Bucky Trumble and Frank Cohane. As a final flourish, Randy boasted that he would happily render Cass aid and assistance—"if she asks for it," which got him off the legal hook. Thumping the podium, Randy said, "If President Peacham wants to have *me* arrested, I say to him"—the audience braced for another expletive—"*you know where to find me!*" The line received tremendous applause and wide reportage. Everyone on the Jepperson campaign staff was happy to retire STFU.

The little and big tyrants in the White House now found themselves in a difficult if not downright intractable position. A warrant had been issued. If the warrant were withdrawn, it would look as if the government were caving in to popular pressure, for the second time, in the case of Cassandra Devine. A great many midnight hours were spent deliberating over this, at the very highest levels of government.

"Why don't we just pardon her?" Bucky suggested.

"I can't *pardon* her when she hasn't been convicted of a damn *crime,*" the president growled. His mood was worse than ever. Everywhere he went, he was asked, "When are you going to stop persecuting that poor young woman?"

Frank Cohane, the father of the poor young woman, was finding himself, too, beset by a hostile media.

"I'm not involved in any of that." He grinned tightly. "I'm just trying to concentrate on helping to reelect a truly great president."

Against Bucky's counsel, he had accepted an invitation to go on *Greet the Press.*

"Is it true that you pressured the president to go after your own daughter?" Waddowes asked. Frank froze. If you're trying to get yourself appointed secretary of the Treasury, this is not an ideal question. Frank tried to California-smile his way out of it but found himself confronted by a look of curdled contempt on the face of Glen Waddowes. Waddowes had good sources in the White House and was not known to ask frivolous questions.

"Uh . . . of course not," Frank said. Should he mention that he had recently received a Stepfather of the Year award? "I . . . she's . . . well, my Cass has always, ha ha, been an independent sort of person. Why, as a little girl, she used to—"

"Did you or did you not counsel the president to have her arrested?"

"Glen, the president hardly needs *my* advice on a question like that. I'm just a finance guy. Of course, I like to think that I'm a *capable* finance guy."

Frank felt the cold stare of millions of viewers. The only correct answer to Waddowes's question, really, was, *Absolutely not, Glen, and give me the name of the swine who suggested that I did, in order that I may challenge him to a duel to the death.*

A few days later, *The Washington Post* published a lengthy and rather well-sourced article entitled "The Dad from Hell?" There was a copious amount of biographical detail in it, including his having spent Cass's Yale tuition money—and the mortgage on the family home—on his start-up. Cass recognized her mother's unattributed quotes.

"That's some finance chairman you found me," the president said to Bucky the morning it came out. "Anything else I ought to know about him?"

Why, as a matter of fact, yes, Mr. President. He has a tape record-ing of me asking him to criminally implicate his innocent daughter in a serial murder scheme. Won't that make our day when it comes to light?

Bucky did not utter these words aloud, though they did form in his mind.

Gideon was riding a wave. The cover of *Newsweek* showed a picture of him looking like a younger version of Colonel Sanders of Kentucky Fried Chicken fame, beaming beneath a headline: PRESIDENT FOR LIFE? Inside, *Newsweek* asked soberly, "His beliefs on the sanctity of human life are shared by many, but is the country ready to be led by an old-fashioned moralist who may or may not have killed his own mother?" It was all very heady, yet all Gideon could think about was his little Russian honey. He was obsessed. He called her ten, twelve times a day, just to hear her say, "Darrling Gidyon, I am wery wet for you. When you bring me more money?"

Though very new to the business of romance, Gideon was not naive enough to suppose that Olga's apartment, decorated in a style that might be called "contemporary Russian prostitute," was that of a woman who earned her living teaching second grade and spent her nights volunteering for the Red Cross. He grew jealous thinking of her other "wisitors." He considered hiring a private detective to keep an eye on the comings and goings. During interviews with the media, while called upon to discuss his views on Social Security reform and stem cell research and the death penalty, he found himself daydream-ing of Olga and her perfumy thighs.

*   *   *

On Super Tuesday, the day when voters in a large number of states cast their votes in the primaries, several facts became apparent.

The most glaring of these was that President Riley Peacham was in trouble—or, as it is called by savvy political observers, "deep doo-doo." The second was that Senator Randolph K. Jepperson had taken serious chunks of flesh out of the president, and though he would not likely beat Peacham for the party's nomination in August, he clearly had enough votes to run on his own as an independent. The third was that Gideon Payne had a hammerlock on the powerful evangelical Christian vote and was poised to do pretty much whatever (the hell) he wanted.

Peacham had managed to mitigate some of the furor over his administration's handling of Cassandra Devine by having the attorney general issue a plea to Cass to turn herself in. If she did, the Justice Department promised "leniency and understanding."

Cass, however, had no intention of turning herself in. She had a bully pulpit. One magazine had named her "the New Swamp Fox." Her website postings were anticipated and reported by everyone the moment they appeared. The FBI, invoking some obscure antiterrorism statute, had shut down CASSANDRA, but Cass's followers kept starting new ones, called CASSANDRA.2, etc. The latest CASSANDRA was .54. To judge from the millions of hits on the site, her following was growing every day.

A few days after Super Tuesday, Randy declared that he was withdrawing from the remaining party primaries and would be a candidate for the Whatever Party, proudly named for the generation it represented. Columnist George Will dryly recorded his gratitude that "we will at least be spared a party named STFU." Randy's operatives swiftly went about collecting the requisite signatures; his lawyers began suing all fifty states and U.S. possessions to get him on the November ballot.

One week later, Gideon Payne announced that he too was withdrawing from further party primaries and would run as the candidate of the Life Party.

All this left President Peacham facing the unhappy prospect of having to finish off his remaining four challengers for the party's nomination—all of whom were staying in the race until the end so as to inflate their speaking and product endorsement fees—at which point, badly weakened, he would have to face Randy and Gideon in the general fall election.

"Where are you?" Randy said.

"Wouldn't you like to know," Cass said. Randy's guy Mike Speck had informed Randy that his phone lines were not tapped. (Since the early 1970s, U.S. presidents have shied away from overtly listening in to their opponents' telephone calls.) It was safe to talk. Even so, Cass kept these conversations short.

She said, "It's warmer where I am now." She had taken a series of bus rides south and was in New Orleans, where no one particularly cared who you were. Mike Speck had arranged for credit cards and an ID under an assumed name, so at least she wouldn't have to go on sleeping in parks.

"I was thinking," Randy said. "The night Peacham accepts the nomination, why don't you show up at Jepperson headquarters. We walk out together. That would take the piss out of him!"

"You get a bounce in the polls, and I go back to playing hearts with Pulitzer Nation at the Alexandria Detention Center? Thanks. Pass."

"They're probably going to lift the warrant on you." He said it with an unmistakable note of disappointment.

"I'm riding buses and eating out of Dumpsters, and you're worried that they'll lift the warrant for my arrest? Your concern for 'the woman I love' is really touching."

"Eating out of Dumpsters? Not according to your latest American Express card statement."

"Whatever. I did take the bus. Point is, you seem to be enjoying my life on the lam."

"Darling, it's for the cause."

"The me cause or the you cause?"

"The us cause. You're a symbol. Did you see *New York* magazine? They called you 'the New Patty Hearst.' How about a new photograph of you for the website. Holding a gun. . . ."

"A gun? Why don't I just go down in a hail of bullets. A photograph? Are you totally crazy? Let's make it really easy for them to find me."

"Look, darling, I know you're going through a lot. And I'm proud of you. Oops, I've got to dash. Speaking to the League of Transgendered Voters. Hey—we're up two points in the latest tracking poll. We've got the big mo! Call me soon. Love you. Don't get caught."

He sounded as though he were reminding her to bring an umbrella.

Cass looked out the window of her hotel on Bourbon Street and wished she could call Terry. But they were listening in on his phones, so she would have to wait for his scheduled call at the pay phone on Poydras.

"Hey, girlie! You wanna party?"

"Get lost."

Cass's new outfit *was* a bit on the come-hither side: wig, short skirt, boots. She wondered if she'd overdone it. She was just trying to blend. How ironic it would be—for the cause—if she ended up in the New Orleans jail in a hooker sweep. She was waiting for the pay phone to ring. Pay phones. What a concept. Who thought them up? Finally, it rang.

"Sorry," Terry said. "I'm late. But let me tell you why. . . ."

Someone had called Tucker Strategic Communications, got through to Terry. The person said he had "very interesting information that would be of great value to Cass Devine." Terry tried to blow him off, but the man persisted. He got Terry's attention when he told him that he worked for Elderheaven Corporation. He said his information involved a "business deal" between Gideon Payne and—Frank Cohane.

"He said he had it all on paper," Terry said. "And computer files. Real hush-hush sort of stuff."

Cass thought. "Did he say why he was contacting you?"

"He didn't know how to reach you. He wants to give it to you personally. Says he's your biggest fan. But you know, who isn't?"

"Do you think it's for real?"

Terry sighed. "Well, your other biggest fan at Elderheaven, Death Angel Clumm, lethally injected thirty-six Wrinklies. Bearing that in mind, I guess I would approach with caution. I don't know. He sounded real enough. I could have Randy's guy Speck check him out."

"No. That might scare him off," Cass said. "Speck scares *me*. You do realize that if the FBI is listening in on your office phone, they now know about this guy."

"He'd figured all that out. Said he was calling from a pay phone. He said he'd get me—tomorrow—a safe phone number. He didn't say how. I'm to give that number to you. Then you call him at three o'clock, the day after tomorrow. He'll be at the number. I'll call you tomorrow at the usual time with the number."

Terry called her the next day with the phone number. The guy had sent it to him via FedEx, addressed to an employee of Tucker. The envelope inside was marked "Please give to Mr. Tucker URGENT."

The next day, at three o'clock, from a pay phone on Napoleon Street, near Pascale's Manale restaurant in the Garden District, Cass called the number. Jerome picked up on the first ring.

"Oh, Miss Devine," he began, "I am *such* a fan. . . ."

Chapter 39

"**R**everend," Gideon's secretary said, "Monsignor Montefeltro."

Gideon hadn't spoken with Massimo in several months. He wanted to distance himself from him in just about every way—not only because of the deplorable (but ultimately felicitous) Russian business, but mainly because Montefeltro's papal bull was backfiring spectacularly with the voters. Gideon wanted to make his own case against legal suicide without the heavy breathing of Rome over his shoulder.

"Call back," he said.

"He says it's very important, Reverend."

Gideon hesitated, then picked up. "Massimo, my dear friend, pax vobiscum. How are you?"

Massimo did not sound well. He spoke in a harried sort of whisper. "Geedeon, I must speak to you."

"I'm right here, Massimo."

"The Russians. They are impossible!"

Oh dear, Gideon thought. Massimo knew nothing, as far as Gideon knew, of the relationship with Olga. And he preferred to keep it that way. "How do you mean, Massimo?"

"Ivan, that enforcer, or pimp, whatever he is—he keeps demanding money from me. I had to give him our Mercedes. Then he wants *another* Mercedes. It never finishes. We don't have any *cars* left at the nunciature! The nuncio is riding in taxis!"

"Well, don't give him any Mercedeses."

"Every time I tell him. And still he demands money. I cannot give him from the *Vatican* funds. And I have already given him all of my personal funds. It's a misery, Geedeon. A *dee-saster.*"

"Well, I'm sorry for your trouble, Massimo. But I don't really see what you want me to do."

"But, Geedeon, *you* started all of this!"

"I told you how remorseful I was. We are all sinners before the Lord."

"Never mind! Now I am left to deal with the gorilla! While you run for president!"

"In a very good cause, may I remind you. And by the way, I do wish His Holiness had taken my advice. This absurd bull of yours is doing nobody any good at all. Well, Massimo, our dear Lord faced terrible obstacles in his journey. So we must all cope in our way and offer it up."

There was a groan on the other end. "Geedeon. Ivan told me you are now the boyfriend of one of the girls. Is this true?"

"Well now, I think 'boyfriend' would be putting it rather . . . I have undertaken to minister to her. Poor little soul. She is young and very far from home."

"Geedeon. Are you *fucking* this *putana*?"

"What a thing to say, Massimo! And you an intimate of His Holiness! Shame on you, sir, shame! This conversation is over. Good day to you, sir!"

Gideon hung up and wiped his brow and patted his vest pocket, which once again bulged reassuringly with his gold watch, returned to him by his darling.

He considered. He must tell Olga not to discuss their relationship with others. He was planning to make "this *putana*"—as Massimo had so coarsely put it—Mrs. Gideon Payne. But he preferred that announcement come in the newspaper, in the wedding pages—or news pages—and not bruited about from the lips of that truncheon-wielding Cossack Ivan or whatever his actual name was. Dear, dear . . . and now he must depart. He was speaking this very noon to the Greater Lower Mississippi Anti–Stem Cell Research Association. Then there was the creationist dinner in Pascagoula and after that the ribbon cutting of the new casino in Biloxi. My, my, my. What a busy whirl these presidential campaigns were. They left no time at all for prayer and reflection.

The man on the other end of the line identified himself simply as "Jerome."

He sounded genuinely nervous. He also sounded genuinely smitten with Cass, and that made her nervous. He wanted to meet with her personally, and that made her especially nervous.

"I just want to shake your hand," he said. "And give you these documents personally. I know that you're in danger, Miss Devine. Believe me. But it would be such an honor. I don't lead a very interesting life, you know. Do you know what I did yesterday? I tabulated how much we have spent this quarter over last quarter on incontinence pads. I wouldn't mind just a *little* excitement in my life."

"I . . ." Cass hesitated. He sounded real, anyway. Who could have made that up?

"Please?" Jerome begged.

Cass said, "I'll call you back at this number in three hours."

"Oh, Miss Devine, it will be an honor. Such an honor."

She called Terry, breaking security. She said simply, "Call me at the other number in half an hour," and hung up. The "other number" was code for the next pay phone on their list.

"Jesus, Cass," Terry said when he called. "Careful."

She explained. He said, "I don't know. Could be a trap."

"I don't see that we have a choice," Cass said. "He's not going to hand over the documents unless it's face-to-face. He read me a few lines from them. They sound pretty authentic to me."

"Maybe we should call Speck? He scares me, too, but this is sort of his kind of thing, isn't it? Lurking in the shadows with a sniper rifle. The Clancy thing—"

"No, no, no. I don't want to involve Randy in this."

"He'd involve *you*, if it were him," Terry snorted. "Guarantee it."

"I need to think this through," Cass said. "I'll call you back."

Cass walked down Bourbon Street, past obese tourists and drunks, past barkers, street performers, and prostitutes, wondering just how to proceed. Then, crossing Toulouse Street, she saw a man with a YALE T-shirt and suddenly knew what to do. Perhaps, after all, you didn't need to attend to get the education.

"Mr. Cohane?"

"Yes?"

"This is Al Witchel."

The name didn't ring an immediate bell. But Witchel, whoever he was, had Frank's ultraprivate cell number. "Who?"

"I work for Mr. Wheary."

Wheary was head of security for Cohane Enterprises.

"Oh yes," Frank said, annoyed by the lapse of protocol. Why was a subordinate of Wheary's calling him? "What is it?"

"Can I call you back on a land line?"

"All right."

Witchel called Frank right back.

"We were doing a routine computer scan of the Elderheaven corporate telephone calling patterns, just part of the normal procedure, due diligence on the confidentiality agreement. We detected an anomalous pattern. We pursued it. It would seem, sir, that there's a leak."

Chapter **40**

She reflected, looking about her, that it was an apt venue for this rendezvous. The thought hadn't occurred to her until just now.

Cass had proposed to her curious whistleblower, Jerome, that they meet at the Franklin Delano Roosevelt Memorial in West Potomac Park, south of the Mall in Washington. Not because FDR was the president who had created Social Security, the system with which Cass was at war, but because the design of the memorial, sprawling over seven and a half acres, allowed for multiple exits in the case of an ambush.

It was late afternoon. There was still daylight, which they needed. She had instructed Jerome to meet her by the statue of FDR in his wheelchair. When she and Terry did their preliminary reconnaissance, he had taken one look at the depiction of FDR, with opaque bronze eyeglasses, upturned hat, and sitting on his almost invisible wheelchair, and said, "He looks like that Irish writer, James Joyce, sitting on a toilet."

Now she stood, waiting.

A voice said, "Miss Devine?"

Cass wheeled. She'd instructed Jerome not to call her that. But one look at him reassured her that it was, in fact, Jerome. He looked like a Jerome.

He was carrying an attaché, surprisingly sophisticated: leather, with straps; not something that looked as if it also contained a brown-bag lunch, milk carton, and banana.

"Gosh," Jerome said nervously, looking around. "This feels like a movie or something." He whispered, "Shouldn't we move off to the side, out of sight?"

"No," Cass said.

Twenty yards away, in another section of the memorial, but with telephoto-lens line of sight of Cass and Jerome, stood Terry and a Tucker technical employee, operating a tripod-mounted videocamera and parabolic microphone.

Jerome patted the attaché and said to Cass, "It's all here."

"And what are these documents, exactly?" Cass said.

Jerome seemed puzzled by the question. "What I told you over the phone."

"Tell me again," Cass said.

At that moment, a National Park Service ranger saw Terry and his cameraman. He approached, all business.

"Hey. Excuse me?"

"Hm?" Terry said.

"What are you doing?"

"What does it look like we're doing?"

"You can't film here."

"Why not?"

"You need a permit."

Jerome said to Cass, "The documents pertaining to the sale of the actuarial prediction software by the Cohane company to Elderheaven Corporation."

"I see," Cass said, nodding like some TV reporter doing an on-camera interview. "And what exactly does it do?"

Jerome seemed nonplussed. "Do? It, well, predicts with great accuracy how long someone is going to live. Elderheaven uses it to decide whom to admit to their nursing homes. This way, they can only admit people who aren't going to live very long. But they still have to basically hand over their life savings in order to be admitted. And under the terms of the sale, ten percent of Elderheaven's increased profits get kicked back to Cohane."

"Fascinating," said Cass, nodding away. "Fascinating. . . ."

"You need a *permit* to film on these premises, sir."

"It's a documentary," Terry said, leading the Park Service ranger away from the microphone. "About how people react to the memorial. In particular to that statue."

"That's not the issue, sir."

"Some people think he looks like that Irish writer James Joyce? They say he looks like he's taking a dump."

"Sir, you're going to have to stop filming. *Now.*"

As the befuddled Jerome continued with his explanation of the contents of the attaché, two men approached. One of them Cass recognized as—her father.

"Hello, Cass."

"Hello, Frank."

Frank Cohane stared at Jerome, who reflexively clutched the attaché to his chest. He said to Jerome, "You're in a world of shit, pal. That's stolen property." Jerome blanched. Frank turned his attention back to Cass. "As for you, you're in a universe of trouble, young lady."

Cass said, "What are you going to do? Ground me?"

Frank said to Jerome, "Hand it over."

"Sir, if you don't stop filming *right now,* I'm going to have to call the park police."

"I was just kidding you," Terry said. "We have a permit."

"Let me see it," said the park ranger suspiciously.

Terry patted his pockets. "It's in the car. C'mon, I'll show you."

"Sir, tell your person there to turn that camera off. *Now.* Or I am calling the police."

"It's in the car, right over there. I'll show you."

*　　*　　*

The stricken Jerome began to hand the attaché to Frank. Cass intercepted it.

"Frank," she said in an oddly declamatory sort of voice, "what would people say if they knew that the president's own campaign finance chairman had sold software to someone running against the president? Software that allows him to get rich by only admitting people into his nursing homes who are about to die? What would you call such an arrangement?"

Frank, alerted by Cass's peculiar tone, swiveled. He saw the camera twenty yards away, aimed right at him.

"*Shit!*" he said. He barked at his companion, a Cohane security man, "Get the goddamn case!"

The man stepped forward and grabbed it out of Cass's grip. She wasn't about to get in a wrestling match with him. She let it go. The man and Frank turned to leave.

"Frank," she said. Her father turned. "Would you call such an arrangement . . . morally repellent?"

"Okay, okay," Terry said to the ranger, "if you're going to make a federal *case* out of it." He signaled his assistant to stop. They had what they needed. As they walked off, Terry said to the ranger, "You know, he *does* look like James Joyce on a toilet. You ought to get the sculptor down here and do something about it. It's embarrassing. He was a great president, and look what you've done to him."

The resignation of Frank Cohane as finance chairman of the Committee to Reelect President Peacham was a surprise, coming as it did on the eve of the general election.

The terse announcement said only that he had "fulfilled his mission," that he was confident that the president would be reelected "in a landslide," and was eager to get back to skippering his yacht *Expensive* in the upcoming America's Cup race.

The next night, Mrs. Cohane was observed screaming at Frank furiously at the tony Georgetown restaurant Café Milano and then abruptly getting up from the table and storming out. This fact was duly reported in the *Post*'s "Reliable Source" column the next day. The Cohanes put their house up for sale and departed for California a few days later. Mrs. Cohane was still apparently out of sorts, as several people witnessed her in the waiting room of the private aviation terminal at Dulles International Airport barking at her billionaire husband.

The president lost another top aide a few days later when Bucky Trumble, his longtime political counselor, was rushed to George Washington Hospital with a bleeding ulcer. The doctors advised him not to return to the rigors of the campaign.

In a speech in Bangor, Maine, President Peacham announced that he was personally instructing the attorney general to vacate the federal fugitive warrant on Cassandra Devine. Normally, the White House affected a posture of not interfering with supposedly independent actions of cabinet agencies. In this case, the president seemed, if anything, eager to point out that this was his decision and not the AG's.

At a press conference the next day, he said, "If young people want to go burning their damn"—it was the first instance of a president saying "damn" in public—"Social Security cards, that's their business. The whole system is so screwed up as it is, that's not going to make it any worse." He then announced to an already stunned press corps that if he was reelected, he would appoint Cassandra Devine commissioner of Social Security. "And good luck to the lady if she accepts. And good luck to me if I win. There are times, I have to say, when I almost hope the voters don't return me to office in November."

This was fresh, honest talk of a kind rarely if ever heard, and the people responded.

President Riley Peacham won reelection by a narrow margin. When he took the podium to declare victory, it was not altogether clear that he was happy to have won.

Senator Randolph K. Jepperson made a strong showing in the popular vote, less so in the electoral college, the system devised by the Founders in their infinite wisdom occasionally to prevent the right person from winning the presidency. Randy, with Cass and Terry at his side on election night, limped out onto the stage and congratulated President Peacham. He refrained from holding his prosthesis over his head and spent the rest of his speech describing his agenda for the future and why he would make an ideal candidate for president in four years, or eight, or whenever. Whatever.

Frank Cohane's yacht competed fiercely in the America's Cup that fall. On the final race, *Expensive* suddenly lost steering power on the downwind leg and rammed and sank the French yacht *Formidable*. The bureau of inquiry found no evidence of damage to *Expensive*'s steering prior to the accident. The case is proceeding in the French and U.S. courts and the international court at The Hague. Mrs. Cohane subsequently left Frank for the skipper of the Italian yacht *Scuzzi*— the dashing billionaire industrialist Dino Filipacci, of Milan. No mention of this or the ramming incident can be found on Google.

Gideon Payne's attempts to portray Elderheaven's purchase of actuarial software as "a means of ensuring the very best level of care for our beloved senior residents" did not meet with success with the electorate. He came in seventh in the popular vote. Yet he took his fall from grace in stride. Some thought he appeared almost jubilant conceding the election to President Peacham. A month later, he announced that he was stepping down from the leadership of SPERM in order to marry a Russian national, Olga Marilova, a self-described "hospitality worker." They would retire, he said, to the country and raise a family, "a large family."

In January, President Peacham nominated Cassandra Devine to be the youngest commissioner of Social Security in U.S. history. ABBA and other Baby Boomer lobbies fiercely opposed the nomination on the grounds that she would "sabotage" Social Security payments to retired Boomers. Her nomination is being championed in the Senate by Senator Randolph K. Jepperson of Massachusetts, in conjunction with a vigorous public relations effort mounted by her former employer and mentor, Terry Tucker.

Massimo Cardinal Montefeltro is currently rector of the Cathedral of Our Lady of Prompt Succor in Rome. Among the *Vaticanisti* who handicap papal elections, he is rumored to be on the short list of possible future pontiffs after the reign of Jean-Claude I.

Acknowledgments

Thank you, Jonathan Karp, for brilliant editing and splendid collaboration, our sixth; Binky Urban of ICM; Nate Gray at Twelve; Harvey-Jane Kowal at Hachette Book Group USA; Sona Vogel, once again, for superb copyediting; Greg Zorthian for Spider Repellent™; John Tierney, LF; Allen Snyder, Esq., worth every penny; Steve "Dutch" Umin; Jean Twenge, PhD, author of *Generation Me*; William Butler Yeats; Jolie Hunt (STFU!); Lucy, always; Cat and Conor; and the faithful hound Jake, who never left the author's side and the tin of Milk-Bone biscuits.

—*Washington, D.C.*
July 13, 2006

About the Author

Christopher Buckley was born in New York City in 1952, which means he will be eligible for Social Security benefits in the year 2017. If, however, millions of people buy this, his twelfth book, he will consider going away sooner and leaving everyone alone. He is editor of *ForbesLife* magazine and contributes to *The New Yorker*. His best-selling novel *Thank You for Smoking* was adapted for the screen and directed by Jason Reitman.

About TWELVE

TWELVE was established in August 2005 with the objective of publishing no more than one book per month. We strive to publish the singular book, by authors who have a unique perspective and compelling authority. Works that explain our culture; that illuminate, inspire, provoke, and entertain. We seek to establish communities of conversation surrounding our books. Talented authors deserve attention not only from publishers, but from readers as well. To sell the book is only the beginning of our mission. To build avid audiences of readers who are enriched by these works—that is our ultimate purpose. But mostly we are about publishing Christopher Buckley.

For more information about forthcoming TWELVE books, please go to www.twelvebooks.com.